a novel

Lucy Ferriss

Simon & Schuster

New York   London   Toronto

Sydney   Tokyo   Singapore

AGAINST

GRAVITY

SIMON & SCHUSTER
Rockefeller Center

1230 Avenue of the Americas
New York, NY 10020

SIMON AND SCHUSTER and colophon are registered trademarks
of Simon & Schuster Inc.

Designed by Karolina Harris

Manufactured in the United States of America

1   3   5   7   9   10   8   6   4   2

Library of Congress Cataloging-in-Publication Data

Ferriss, Lucy
Against gravity: a novel / Lucy Ferriss.
p.   cm.
I. Title
PS3556.E754A73   1996
813'.54—dc20   95-36136

ISBN 0-684-80091-8

Acknowledgments

Support from the National Endowment for the Arts, the Faulkner Society, Yaddo, the MacDowell Colony, and the Virginia Center for the Creative Arts made the writing of this book possible. To its early readers—Mark Couzens, Cat Reinke, Tad Hogan, Oliver Remme, Carole Abel, Kit Ward, Donna Faye Burchfield, Elizabeth Dewberry, Kip Kotzen, and Ned Leavitt—I owe my heartfelt thanks. Thanks also to my editor, Bob Asahina, for his sound judgment and good faith, and to my two sons for their patience.

A portion of this book appeared in different form in the *Southern Review*.

To my parents, Ann and Franklin

The body, she says, is subject to the forces of gravity. But the soul is ruled by levity, pure.
—Saul Bellow, *"Him with His Foot in His Mouth"*

Obviously a major malfunction. We have no downlink.
—Stephen A. Nesbitt, NASA Public Affairs Officer

EXPLOSION

book one

chapter 1

People don't remember the Challenger much, now. When you bring it up they think at first it's an old movie; they might get it mixed up with *The Verdict*. Paul Newman, right? they try. No, Christa McAuliffe, you answer, and watch their faces broaden and their eyebrows go up. As they say, You mean, the teacher? they sound just like Reagan when the staff member gave him the bad news.

And you nod and answer the way you figure the Roman soldiers must have answered when talk turned to Calvary: *I was there*.

Only I don't bring it up, much. My life is too full, too pointed toward whatever must happen next, to waste fifteen minutes jawing over a forgotten tragedy that didn't kill anyone I knew, really. It's just that now and then it'll catch me—when I'm scraping ice from the windshield in the morning to get to work, for instance, and it breaks off in a big clear sheet, and I see those pictures, again, of the rocket launchers coated in ice. Like some kind of frozen phlegm stuck onto them, and all they needed was to cough it off. Or when I was leaning way back at the fireworks show that Lenny Dugliss put on, two summers past, and one of the Roman candles shot off toward the pine trees in a crazy arc that you knew would end in a sad little pop. "No bang," said my new little brother. The next candle was good, and the one after that launched a blue shower all over the golf course. But neither of them quite redeemed that fizzle.

It caught me that way the day my father fell off an icy ladder from the same tower where old Meyenhold's daughter had thrown herself down, long ago. As I ran to catch his body, he was suddenly plummeting from a hundred miles up, burning through the air, and I couldn't get there in time.

Or when I was dancing in New York, thinking I was gone from here forever. As if the rocket boosters had been fired, and all I had to do was orbit. I thought I'd left this world with its lousy gravity. Sure, I knew, just the way NASA knew, about the ice casings and the thin solder. But I hoped just as they hoped, big stakes built into the hoping. Until I saw a street dancer, not so different from me, jerking about like R2D2 on speed, and it came to me at once that I was in space and I was on fire. Wile E. Coyote time—look down, empty space, drop.

It happened the day JoAnn Harlett gave birth. A flash of blood and the baby falling, falling from her. Everything to which we'd turned a blind eye burst forth, the ice off the O-rings, the cord cut.

Or even this, even the spring after we got back from witnessing the explosion. I woke one morning to see five million tons of steel, more or less, pass over a man and a boy. When it was gone they rose and watched the train roll away down the tracks. If they'd lain an inch to the left or right, curtains. Sometimes, what's meant to hold breaks; sometimes what's meant to break holds. The trick is to be ready.

It's history, that's all. The shuttle went down, the gas we breathe turned to a torch. Still, each time a capsule in my life spins out, in the thin air, I find myself repeating that line Reagan used—it wasn't his, but it sounded good, and you can just picture his speechwriter rubbing her hands together when she dug it up: "They slipped the surly bonds of earth, to touch the face of God." I say it out loud, like I'm repeating my own personal creation myth, and then I go on about my business.

• • •

Right now they're shooting a long-delayed movie at the Meyenhold mansion, which is this gigantic ugly structure above the woods. Everywhere you look, extras prowl the paths, stack up the line at the P.O., run the store out of coffee and beer. "Must be a thrill for you people, all of us coming up here," one of them said to me, standing on the bridge overlooking the train tracks that run alongside our hamlet. He was a little drunk—a key grip, he'd told me he was, one of the guys who cart around the big movie cameras. "I mean, I figure this place is pretty inbred."

"You mean like my mom knows I'm having my period because my brother tastes funny," I said. I watched it dawn on him, then I left him on the bridge, frozen like a statue. Though you couldn't blame him, it was probably in the movie script, a hamlet full of immigrant families mating like bunnies while the Meyenholds played bridge with the Vanderbilts and chewed over the future of the railroads. There's a hot new actress playing the Meyenhold daughter, one of the P.O. ladies told me. "Though," she said, leaning over the counter like it was a secret, "from the old pictures, you sure wouldn't call the original a beauty! Her daddy loved her, maybe. He built that tower for her, and she used to go up there and sing. Then one night she sets the thing on fire—no one knows how—and she jumps. Well, you can smell the Hollywood in it."

Rumor has it they'll make the actress pregnant in the movie, probably by one of the immigrant help, maybe a dashing Irish boy, and since she can't bear to tell her father she throws herself off. Except they won't show her hitting the ground, smashing—only leaping up from the balcony, leaping slow motion, free of the fire and the mess of things, slipping those surly bonds.

I was there. I saw the thing spit off from the main rocket, and I knew. I was never able to explain, later, how I knew—we didn't see anything, we didn't have zoom lenses. There was just this stillness in the air right at that moment, like when the cat's caught a bird

but hasn't shaken it yet, to break its neck, and they're both looking at you, and you can't move.

Before long we'd all seen the thing a million times on TV—the
capsule like a lightning bug going *fft-fft-fft* into the sky, and then
this puff of it curving off to the right. For at least a couple of years
it was like we'd grown up with that picture, or run into it on
geometry quizzes ("If the direction taken by the rocket boosters is
the hypotenuse, and the cabin goes off at 45 degrees, what angle
is formed by an imaginary line connecting the two parts of the
capsule?")—that was how stamped it was in our heads, from TV.
Not from being there, in Florida.

To this day I don't even know who gave the money to send us.
JoAnn Harlett thought it was Gray, trying to get the town on his
good side. Give us a break, I said. I'd heard him once bitching
about the space program, he said leave Mars to the Commies,
don't they call it the Red Planet? Someone gave it, anyway, for the
freshman and junior astronomy classes. I'd chosen astro because I
kept fainting in biology class. One eyeful of a fetal pig and I was
down on the linoleum; I guess I got tired of the view from there.
And the rumor had been circulating that there might be a bus trip
to Florida thrown in. "Take McGruder's class!" That's what I remember one gum-chomping girl saying on the homebound
school bus, stuck on an unplowed road above Route 12 the winter
before. "Take McGruder's class, and you can enjoy three days on
one of these here luxury cruises!"

"Gag me," said another girl.

"Hey, it'll be heading south," said Matt McPeck. "To palm
trees."

"Can you take it one-way?" I asked, but they all thought I was
joking. "Really," I said. "I want out." I remember how the rear of
the bus lurched and jolted backward each time the driver revved
the engine in the snow. We finally had to get out and push, twelve
of us on the back bumper, gray slush splatting on our jeans when
the wheels finally jerked free.

"Hey, I'm signing on for that class," Matt McPeck said, wiping his hands on the doors as we piled back into the warm bus. "What the hell number is that?"

"Astro Two," said a boy. "Stands for Ass Froze, two days to Florida."

If I had to guess, I'd say Seth Dugliss's dad gave the money, to remember his oldest son who won a science prize the year before and then died. Mr. Dugliss gave enough—if he was the one who gave it—for two heated coaches and a motel stop in Albemarle, Virginia. That took care of thirty sophomores and twice that many juniors, plus teachers and a couple of wives. Some seventh-graders from Roosevelt Middle tagged along too, because they were the same age as Christa McAuliffe's class in New Hampshire. That made JoAnn's twin brother happy, since he was making it with a seventh grader and the trip gave them an extra chance. For the rest of us, you had to admit the trip itself was a drag—sharing the bus and the motel rooms, always having to wait for the seventh-graders to get in line or whatever they did to organize. We tended to forget where we were heading, in the end.

I was fourteen. Publicly, there was nothing I could admit to caring about. I lived where I live now—in a hamlet tucked between Route 9 and the river, the kind of place that gets listed once every five years as One of New York's Best-Kept Secrets. People here aren't inbred; mostly they're just poor. They drink a lot and they trade used stuff around. *They*'re not the best-kept secret—or if they are, the magazines that mention the hamlet don't give that one away. The secret's the woods, which loop around us like a green hammock, and the monstrous old mansions in them, and the bluffs hanging over the river when you hike through to the other side. To the people who live here, that kind of gorgeous stuff is invisible; to the people who take the train up to see that stuff, we're the invisible ones.

It's got a name, this hamlet, but no one uses it. When the film crew makes calls from the general store, they tell people they're shooting outside Windhaven. Windhaven's a name they know, but it's not a place, at least not since before I was born. There's

nowhere you can walk to in Windhaven, nowhere to call the center—just Route 9, with mini-malls popping up on either side and
historic landmarks buried in the trees toward the river or the hills
to the east. Old people in the hamlet, like Miss Flanagan next
door, tell me that Windhaven used to be a real town. The train
from New York stopped there just like it did here, to let off all the
summer people who came to stay with the Meyenholds and the
Van Slykes. Our hamlet went by its own name, then, and everyone
who lived here worked for Meyenhold—the same way they
worked for Hotung Digital, when I was growing up, before it
started laying off.

One year the Meyenholds just left; they deeded the property
over to the state. And as far back as I remember, Windhaven's
been a strip, little clusters of chain stores and fast-food places and
antique shops until you hit the broad curved part of Route 9 that
goes past the state mental hospital and lands in Castleton. Living
here is like living outside of nowhere, which in a weird way puts
us on the inside. When I used to talk about wanting out, at fourteen, it was as if once I'd reached some refugee-filled galaxy, I'd be
able to name the place I'd been marooned, all the long time up to
then.

I turned twenty-two last week. I haven't been to college, and
I'm not going. I work for a living. Already, by the time I came
back here from the city, the shuttle explosion belonged to this
quaint and distant past called the Reagan era, as if the people remembering had started to confuse things just like the Gipper had,
and they couldn't judge the distance between yesterday and the
Roaring Twenties. Not for me, though. I hadn't been back in the
hamlet twenty-four hours before I was repeating that line about
the face of God, chanting it over my bleeding father.

You know those dreams where you're pushing your legs to
move as fast as they can, but each step might as well be through
quicksand? It was like that running to my father, the day he fell.

He landed on a fence, one of those wrought-iron things with spikes designed for severed heads. By the time I got there the ground was slippery with blood, and something thick and purplish had started curling down the rusted baluster. He was screaming, I was screaming. Then only I was screaming, and his eyes had gone up in his face; and I was lifting, one hand slung over to his hips, the other below his chest, and I pushed up, not breathing, feeling my knees give way like rubber bands, until I'd popped him off.

And when I'd covered him with the tarp, and called the rescue squad, and nothing to do but wait and wait, I tried to find a way to stop up the holes. But there wasn't any way, while the blood poured out, even if my hands hadn't been shaking like a spastic. *They slipped the surly bonds of earth*, I whispered to myself, *to touch the face. To touch the face of God. They slipped the surly bonds. The face.*

And finally there was the rescue squad, pouring out of the ambulance, and they took him from me.

chapter

Or there was this. On the first day of astronomy, five months before we left for Florida, our teacher Mrs. McGruder demonstrated a Möbius strip. She took a length of paper, twisted it once, and then taped the ends so that inside and outside got reversed. "Some people say," she said, passing the strip around the room, "that the universe is like a Möbius strip." McGruder's eyes kind of bugged out when she said that—she was supposed to teach general science, but you could tell, moments like this, that astro just lit her wick. "Like a huge Möbius strip," she repeated, "only in three dimensions."

Maybe not the universe, I thought, turning the strip around when I got a turn to hold it, but at least Windhaven and the hamlet.

She made us all twist and tape strips of paper after that. Then we each cut our strip lengthwise down the middle, and it didn't separate but made a bigger, thinner flip. When we cut it again, two strips intersected. Try it yourself. No matter how far you travel or where you split off, you never shake free of that first flip that changed inside to outside. Me, I lived down in Manhattan for two years, after JoAnn had her baby, and it wasn't until I took the train north for the last time that I realized I'd just been traveling on the outside, for a while, on a path that had slid back to shadow.

One of the first things I did, when I came back from New York City, was to clean up the barn behind our house. For as long as I could remember, my father had had plans for that barn. Before he was laid off from Hotung Digital, he was going to turn it into a carpenter's workshop. He'd bought all the organizing stuff and mounted it along one wall. Hooks and clamps for hammers and wrenches; drill bits of every size, out and visible; electric-saw mount; screwdrivers like a Catholic family, from toddler up to quarterback; color-coded boxes of nails and screws and staples; the industrial stapler, gleaming on its shelf. He was going to build a deck off our house, he kept promising, one that would look out over the woods. Later, working for Dugliss Contracting, he'd bring the heavy equipment to our barn if it was a late shift and an early start the next day—he'd invested in a steel door, Kryptonite lock.

Along the side wall, hazy with dust, I found the countertop TV he'd bought to keep him company while he puttered. Or just to keep him company period, away from my mom with her late-night work and the halo she couldn't help wearing. The rest of the place was pretty junked up, by the time I got to it. I couldn't think when the last time was that I'd stepped inside the barn—sometime that same year maybe, the year the Challenger blew up.

I started hauling junk out through the overhead door—old boxes of hand-me-down tools from Dugliss, two-by-fours, carved ends of wood from the dresser he'd once promised to build me. Finally I got to where you could see the dimensions of the room. Sure, I thought when my eyes lit on the far corner. That year.

There lay the rope and torn black plastic, from the night when Seth Dugliss and his buddies tried to teach me not to poke my nose in other people's business. I'd got away from them, finally, and stepped in here to get the evidence off me, and I'd dumped the stuff there for my father to make what he would of it. He'd already stopped paying attention, by then, to his dream of a place free of cobwebs and flooded with light, filled with tools and the low chatter of the TV, where he'd have learned to make anything a person could want. So I'd never got to know what he figured from what I'd left there, because he'd never noticed that one more piece of mess. But there it was, untouched, just as if I'd left it there on purpose, for myself.

I swept, my first day back, once I'd got the big things out of the way; I got rid not just of the rope and the plastic but of the mud crusted around them on the concrete. With the main floor half cleared, I climbed to the loft. My father never went up here, so this time it didn't surprise me to find what I found: my old cross—two fat birch twigs lashed together—and a heap of stumpy candles.

Crouching, I held the candles in my hand—dull red, most of them, probably left over from Christmas, I couldn't remember. I did remember burning my fingers, the first time I lit them—arranged in a half-circle around the cross, which I would prop up on a pair of books against the wall. This was way back when I had my own little religion. Long before I left for New York, even long before the Challenger blew up, I'd chosen the barn loft for my personal church. I was maybe nine years old; the matches had been forbidden, stolen. But I'd learned to light them, after a couple of tries, without singeing flesh, and when they were all lit I used to hold imaginary conversations with Jesus. He wasn't my friend or anything. He was just this adult who didn't fuck up.

One day—I crouched, remembering this—the Duglisses trashed it. I heard the noise and went running back, and there was Seth with his older brother Nate and Lenny too, lighting all the candles and catching mice to burn. The place smelled like fried hair and the mice were whipping around on their tails, trying to bite these tongs the boys held them by. Seth was in the corner. He'd just peed on my cross.

"Hey!" Nate said, "it's Sister Stick!"

"Sister Stick! Sister Stick!" Seth and Nate began to chant. When Lenny started picking up pieces from this stained glass they'd broken, a hanging thing my mom had bought me at a craft sale, Seth waved a half-burned mouse in his face and he dropped it all. Then Nate lifted his mouse and started after me. I made it over to Gray's store and just hung out there for the rest of the afternoon, till my mom got home. I didn't tell anybody what happened, not even Gray. Either they'd have done something to the Duglisses or they'd have zeroed in on the religion thing. Either way I'd get it in the teeth. Next day at school, when Seth started in with "Sister Stick!" I rolled my eyes and said I didn't know what planet he came from, and that ended it.

I don't have a religion now. I'm not sure anyone does, really. Some survey last month said eighty percent of Americans think the Second Coming is due by the year 2000—but that's science fiction, it's like believing in *Star Trek*. Back then, when I was nine, my secret faith was a leap across a gully. On the other side were the kids at school—Dutch Reformed, most of them, a few Baptists—and right behind me stood my mother and her Friends. I thought my sanctuary in the barn could take me to the same place as the others were, like taking vitamins if you skip breakfast. After the Dugliss boys visited I packed it away—the cross, the candles, the prayers I'd made up and written down. I tucked it in a corner of the loft, where I knew my dad never went. The weekend I came back from the city, after I'd rubbed the candles clean with my thumb, I found an empty cardboard box among the junk downstairs and scuttled it all again. It's there now, as far as I know. No point destroying certain things.

Mostly I remember myself waiting, back when I was nine and for years to come: waiting for a new way to leap the gap. I signed up for McGruder's astronomy class with reverence. I meditated on black holes. I was lousy at science, but for Christmas, I got those glossy Voyager photos, my new bible. Boarding the coach to Florida a month later, I had the book tucked tight under my arm.

We were sixty high school kids and a handful from seventh grade—a lot, when you think about it, to haul a thousand miles for a shuttle disaster. After we left Albemarle the snow changed over to rain, and my head got to feeling the way it still feels in coaches, like it's been soaked in urine and hung out to dry. When we finally got to the hotel in Cape Canaveral it was like that was the point—to race up and down salmon-colored hallways, to ride the elevators and use the black bedside phones in the rooms next to the deep double beds. To get breakfast in this mauve-colored coffee shop, where they kept filling your cup so we all got wired and had to pee. Then came the delays. McGruder had warned us about delays. Still it was vastly boring, with air that was supposed to be balmy turned suddenly raw, to hang around those bleachers all day with what seemed like a billion other kids from Waco Texas or Nowhere Montana, waving little felt flags and singing dirty songs, only to have the clown in charge say they'd try again tomorrow.

That night JoAnn went off with Seth Dugliss and no birth control. The other people I knew were sitting in one of the hotel rooms watching *Reckless* on HBO. I climbed up the fire escape to the hotel roof and looked for constellations. I never can find them, even now; hills and valleys I see up there, waterfalls and tunnels. That night I just managed to spot Orion's belt, three stars like a connect-the-dots drawing. I tried to curve them into a three-dimensional Möbius strip, but I couldn't wrap my mind around the idea. Finally the morning came, and another string of delays, and then they started a countdown for real.

By this time we were pretty sick of the whole thing—it was for Girl Scouts, I'd decided already, that ten-nine-eight stuff and the whole trip about sending up a teacher. But we shut up and watched the little trucks leaving from the launching pad and the flame starting to push the thing off the ground. Before you knew it the smoke had cleared and all the rah-rah had stopped and we were just watching it, flying off, the way you watch a kite that's burst its string. And then it blew up.

"It's blown up," I said to JoAnn.

"Get real," said Seth Dugliss, in front of us. "You read too much sci fi, Stick."

"No, she's right," said Lenny Dugliss. He was a seventh-grader then and about as popular as rabies. "Listen."

Over the PA system they were starting to talk about downlink. There was a lot of static. Someone said to stand by. Around me, people were starting to sit down, suddenly real tired and a little cold. Looking up, you couldn't see much—a thread of smoke, two threads—but then we hadn't been able to see much before, just a little orange blot on the sky, getting swallowed up in the blue. On the next set of bleachers over, a teacher with a high warbly voice started to sing "You'll Never Walk Alone." And I thought, She must know the score.

That was what happened, what made for car headlights switching on in daylight across America the next day, what brewed all the mess at NASA. "We will always remember them," the President said. He didn't catch the truth any better than Lincoln did in the Gettysburg Address. *The world will little note nor long remember what we say here, but it can never forget what they did here*—we all memorized that one, the same year as the Challenger. But we don't remember *them*, the soldiers and the astronauts. We don't have any idea who won the battle, or who strapped in and then burst into pieces. We remember a sort of sweet, oozy feeling, like you get when you think back on the nitrous oxide they hit you with to take out your molars. We remember *seven*, because it's a magic number. We remember what itches at us, that's all. Me, I'm itchy way down, where I can't quite reach.

I don't want to make too big a deal of this. JoAnn's the only one I can point to who was affected directly, from that trip to see the Challenger. I mean, pregnancy. And maybe even then, it's not the Challenger to blame. You can go all the way back to what my neighbor, old Miss Flanagan, said about what rushed in after the Meyenholds and their sort abandoned the mansions. *Democracy, my foot.* Right about the time the rich people left, she would point out, Hotung Digital took over. And though people here probably didn't see a difference—just trading one warlord for another— these days Hotung's thinking of leaving as well, with seventy percent laid off, and they won't even leave mansions behind.

No. It's not even that—not, I mean, that the Meyenholds didn't lay off their staff, just put them in cold storage like vegetables while they took the steamer south and then the *Queen Mary* to some warm island, somewhere, until May. It's human nature: you see a window, you try to jump from it. If the Meyenholds were the protective wall, I'd want to tell Miss Flanagan, windows opened when they left. End result: JoAnn grows the thing inside her belly. I dream I can orbit in New York. My father takes a stab at flying— pun intended—and survives to pick up the loose scraps of faith the rest of us have left in the toilet bowl. I go to seek the mysteries back of the Meyenhold mansion—this is the end of the story, now—and I discover I've been trying, all this time, to close the window, stop things from tumbling out, when in truth the window was simply a mirror, a glass begging to be gazed into. What do I see, there? Seven astronauts: Me. My mother and father.

JoAnn. Lenny Dugliss. Gray and his son, Benjy—how he flew! All of us out of control. Looking and looking and *looking* for the face of God.

chapter 3

Certain places I don't go back to, now that I'm slated to live here awhile. My old high school, for one. The Main Mall in Castleton. The north woods—that stretch of woods north of the Meyenhold mansion, the part they never cut paths through. The Reach Out for Christ Sanctuary. The county summer camp, down that road which fronts the sign DOMINICAN BOYS, in white on faded green. The Free Zone.

The Free Zone.

It's as good a place to begin as any. Because if you don't start with the Challenger, you don't really have a starting place, and what I've come to think is that the Challenger was never the beginning but just a spot on the loopy strip—you keep coming back to it, first inside, then out.

The Free Zone was this trailer some rich screwed-up boy had bought with cash before he ended up in rehab. It sat in the trailer park across 9G from school, and kids went there to smoke or drink or cut each other's hair. Before JoAnn, I'd had a true best friend, Barbie, who'd introduced me to Free Zone. The day before she left, I remember she asked me to cut her hair there. It was a hot windy day, the little trailer windows open, and she made me cut it real short from real long, so that there were coils of dark silk left around the Free Zone for weeks after that, to remember her by. Another time, a boy from the tenth grade pierced my ears there—I never knew why he was into it, with his chunks of ice and his alcohol-soaked needle, but he was good and I lined up behind three other girls to get it done. Once a month, you had to shovel ten bucks into the kitty, which Matt McPeck and some others kept in a locked cupboard, or you'd get tagged as not participating in Free Zone.

It's not there anymore, though the trailer park is. And I did go into the park, two years ago, not long after I moved back here. I found an old couple settled in that spot, in a big white fake-colonial trailer with plastic flowering plants hanging all around the pretend porch. They asked me if I was lost, and I said no, I used to live there. Inviting me in, they gave me stale jelly cookies and a glass of Kool-Aid. They told me the earth was warming up, and from now on people who retired were better off in the North than in Florida, which would be under water by the millennium. News to me, I said.

I'd always gotten news, at Free Zone. That was where I first learned Lenny Dugliss had diabetes, and how gay people get AIDS from each other. That was where word came down about Gray being in Dutch. So of course it was where I listened to JoAnn telling me she was knocked up: that was news. A couple of guys had been in there with us—potheads, trying to draw a map of the Soviet Union and just punching each other in the arm—but they'd left their shelf paper behind and gone to catch a ride to the mall, and JoAnn and I were alone.

What we were talking about was her brother, a three-year-old nicknamed Whoopsy for all the accidents he'd had. The latest would've killed him, I said, if it hadn't been for my mom. Your mom had nothing to do with it, JoAnn said, it was the engineer. It wasn't a real argument we were having—just a way of coping with a miracle, bringing it down to size. What had happened, two weeks before, was that Whoopsy'd wandered off from their house and gone down to play on the train tracks. This was real early in the morning, when my mom and her dog, Trixie, were about the only creatures awake in the whole hamlet. She liked to walk Trixie

up over the footbridge in the quiet dawn and watch the first passenger train to New York shoot down through the woods. I figure
it was just about the moment she saw its headlight that Trixie
barked and she looked down at Whoopsy, crouched there. By the
time she'd scrambled down the embankment from the bridge, the
train was blowing its long horn, and the kid had turned around
from where he was sifting pebbles and just made his mouth into
an O, like the headlight was freezing him that way, right in its
path. My mom ran to push him off the tracks, but right as she
stepped onto the ties she got butted in the back by what turned
out to be a train engineer's elbow, throwing her clear. When she'd
got her wind and stood up again, she couldn't see anything, not
Whoopsy or the trainman, just the bright metal cars clacking past
like amplified knitting needles.

"The main thing," I tried pointing out to JoAnn, "is that my
mom could of killed herself, saving him. At least she might of lost
her arm, or maybe her leg."

"The main thing," she retorted, "is that the engineer knew how
to save him. Your mom just fucked things up, can't you see that?"

"I knew there was a spot with enough room," the engineer was
quoted as saying in the papers. "I'd studied on it. If there ever
wasn't any time to lift someone clear, I always told myself, there
was that spot."

I'd seen it too, though I didn't know what I was seeing. I didn't
even know what woke me—my mom's screaming or Trixie barking her head off, or maybe the screech of the brakes. I jumped to
the window in my T-shirt and watched as the train ground to a
halt fifty yards from our house. Only when the last car came
slowly clear of that spot did I see the the man in the blue uniform,
lying low over the ties right between the rails. Under him, practically crushed, was JoAnn's brother.

"Well anyhow," I said, "I should think your mom could show a
little gratitude. I mean at least for her being willing to risk. And
maybe the engineer wouldn't have seen a little kid without an
adult being there too."

"She don't like the attention," JoAnn said.

"She'd of got attention all right, if he'd been run over."

"Yeah, but it's like people don't think she watches close enough. Like Whoopsy could just wander off and her not know."

"Well," I said, "he could."

"Nah. She watches too close, you ask me. She's gonna notice soon how I don't get my cycle. I been flushing clean Tampax just so she'll see the wrappers!"

"Whaddayou mean," I asked, an icy feeling pricking the back of my neck, "you don't get your cycle?" I had my math homework spread out on a low table; with my pencil I'd been digging around in this filthy ashtray they kept there, trying to see if anyone'd left a roach.

"*You* know. It ain't come. I got something in the oven. A pea in my pod, goddamnit. I think that fuckhead Seth Dugliss put it there too."

"You mean in Florida?"

"No, I mean in outer space. Of course Florida."

I drew the pencil out, wiped the tip on the carpet. It was the day after spring break, I remember. School had been like calisthenics, hurting all the way; you can't believe you'll go through it again the next morning. "Are you positive?" I asked JoAnn. "Maybe you just missed, this once."

"Twice," she said. "I've put on ten pounds, and this morning I threw up. I wasn't even drinking last night."

"Maybe you're sick," I said. "I miss my period all the time."

"Me, never."

I figured she was right, JoAnn weighing what she did. The doctor had told me my periods had stopped because I was too skinny. He'd made me promise to try two slices of toast every morning and to eat lunch. Which I still used to skip except down in Florida, where lunch had been this big occasion, speeches and songs on the stage at the restaurant where they took us, so there hadn't been anything to do but pick at your stuffed tomato and crumble saltines.

But JoAnn was fat; her periods came like meals, regular. Right now she was crunching chips. "What'll you do?" I asked.

"Get an abortion, stupid," she said. JoAnn liked calling me stupid. She was the one supposed to be in tenth. I couldn't believe, even back then, that JoAnn Harlett was the best friend I had. But we were both from the hamlet, and Barbie had moved to Florida with her family the year JoAnn got put back a grade. I hadn't heard from Barbie since, not even when I'd written to tell her our class was coming down there. And when I thought how that left me with just JoAnn, I got pissed at anyone who came near me.

"I'm not sure it's that simple," I said.

"Sure it is. They just suck it out of you. Like sticking up a vacuum cleaner. Except if you do it too early, there might be something left. Like a toe or a fanny, multiplying itself in there. Then they have to do it again."

I stoppered my ears. "You ought to wait then," I said to her. Reaching across the coffee table, I took one of the markers those boys had left, and made a face on my hand, between thumb and back of palm. "It could go away by itself."

"But if you wait too long," JoAnn answered, twirling a lock of hair between her boobs and looking down at it, "then they have to shoot you with something that makes you miscarry. It's real messy and it hurts like shit. I had a cousin once got shot with the stuff in her sixth month, she was gonna have a girl. When you think how it must of looked—"

"Shut *up* about it," I said.

I couldn't stand to listen to JoAnn sometimes. The Harletts were all like that, and still are: the biggest mouths in the hamlet. They lived next to Gray's store, then; you could go by on a Saturday and hear them. I was down there a lot that spring, listening to them tell Challenger jokes. "Yeah, y'know Christa McAuliffe told the press she was gonna take the money they gave her for being a space monkey and get a little time off for a change," JoAnn's dad would say. "So now she's cashed in. She's vacationing all over Florida!" And he'd tip back in his chair and give this laugh like a sump pump sucking in water. He carried his fat in rolls; the sweat collected in his neck.

JoAnn couldn't be absolutely sure it was Seth who got her pregnant. She said she had this instinct, but then it could have been Matt McPeck, too, she'd slept with him Presidents' Day weekend. Still, she was going to Seth for the money because he had it. "His daddy's loaded," she told me as she stood up to get some chips from the cupboard. "He pulls all kinds of deals, doing construction. Seth got a brand-new Chevy truck for his birthday, the big prick."

"What if he won't give it to you?"

"What, the truck? Who wants the truck, stupid?"

"No, smartie, the money." I made the face I'd drawn open its mouth. *The money*, it said.

"I'll tell the whole world he knocked me up, that's what."

"Your folks, too?"

"Jesus, Stick," she said, her mouth full of Dorito, "you think of the depressing stuff all at once on purpose, or does it just come to you like that?"

My name's really Stickley. I'm trying to go by my first name, now—Gwyneth—but no one picks up on it. Stick's cute, they say. Fits you. But already, at fourteen, I wasn't totally happy with the fit. I had thought about changing to Ashley or Jennifer when I left home, but it seemed Stick was going to follow me around like a smelly dog the rest of my life. I could just see myself at fifty, working the customer-service counter at Jamesway with one of those *May I Help You?* tags on my pocket and *Stick* printed below it so people would know who to complain to. "Very well, *Stick*," they'd say, their nostrils pulling up like they'd smelled something bad, "I'll be writing to your supervisor." And they'd leave with the microwave they'd bought six months ago and busted and wanted to return for credit—and sure enough, the supervisor would ream me out and call me Gwyneth when she fired me.

I don't work at Jamesway now, though the fantasy clings. Kids use the nickname like it's a title—*Stick, can I have a Three Muske-*

teers? Stick, will you teach me to tap-dance? It works the way you call
a senator Senator, even when he's been voted out. I tell myself it
gives me somewhere to start from.

"Well, I'll come with you when you get it done," I said to
JoAnn, trying not to think the word *abortion* for fear it might lay
me out on the floor of the Free Zone trailer, "so long as you don't
tell me anything about how it feels. I already know it's gross."

"Shit!" she said. "My old lady's picking me up early from
school, I forgot! Put this crap away, Stick, I gotta go."

JoAnn had a new habit since we'd gotten back from Florida of
calling her mom her old lady. She tried to get me to call mine that
way, but I wouldn't. I said if I ever called her anything but Mom it
would be Wanda—that was her name, I said, and she hated it like
I hated mine.

I stashed the bong in the cupboard under the bar and followed
JoAnn out of the trailer. The sun over the fallow field was that
kind of yellow you only get in April, when light seems to bounce
off the ground and hit your eyes. The school and Route 9G stood
out crisp as drawings. Ahead of me, JoAnn was going as fast as she
could. She still walked like a little kid—on account of being fat, I
figured. Her legs chugged and she pumped her arms like she was
going uphill. Her hair was long and curly white-blond—I
thought, back then, that she peroxided it—and it bounced against
the back of her purple T-shirt. She kept stumbling over cans and
old plywood planks and the little furrows that rain had made in
the field. I wondered sometimes how she managed to get anywhere or do anything at all, there was so much of her and she did-
n't seem to take in what was just under her nose.

"Don't be in such a panic, JoAnn," I said.

"Shut up, Stick. You don't know my old lady."

"I know you're going to tell her I made you late."

"What do you care? Shit! Fucking rocks in this field!"

"She practically pisses on my mom when she sees her in the
store, for one thing."

"That's because your old lady grabbed Whoopsy! Jesus, didn't we talk about this? Plus your mom's an atheist. There's my old lady. Listen to her lay on the horn."

Mrs. Harlett had wheeled into the parking lot in her Plymouth Charger, this brown tank with bumper stickers front and back: HONK IF YOU LOVE JESUS, THE CHOICE SHOULD BE THE BABY'S, SAVE OUR SUNDAYS, PRAYER WORKS. She'd seen JoAnn and was just resting her elbow on the car horn, so this long nasal blast filled the air. They were going to one of their special religious services. I hadn't asked what for. The Harletts all belong to this sect, Reach Out for Christ, that was started in Windhaven of all places by some Australian guy who says he used to be a boxer and a convict. Back then he was just gaining ground; now he has his own show on local cable. JoAnn didn't like the Australian or going to church, but she figured she was better off than me. My mother's a Quaker, or was back then. Every Sunday Mom used to drive to this lady's house way down in Castleton and sit in the living room with a dozen other people, and they all looked at the floor until somebody said something. I'd gone once or twice and hated it, so Mom said I didn't have to go, my dad didn't go, it was just her little hobby. But people like JoAnn's mother didn't see what you did on Sunday morning as being your hobby.

"What the hell you doing out in them fields!" Mrs. Harlett yelled as we got close enough. "They just let you wander off from this school?"

"We were doing a science project, Mrs. Harlett," I said. "Pollen."

"Pollen's in the fall," she said. "I do know a couple things, it makes me sneeze." By then JoAnn had climbed in, her eye makeup smeary and her breath short, and sat next to Whoopsy's toddler seat in the back.

"I wish I had Christa McAuliffe for my old lady," she managed to say.

"Why?" said her twin brother from the front. His name was Bobby and he was even fatter than JoAnn.

"Because then she'd be dead," JoAnn said. Or I think she said that—I'd heard it before. But I didn't actually hear her that time, because her mother backed the tank up and blasted out of the lot, dust rising up behind her, sparkling in the light.

chapter 4

Two years ago, recovering from his fall, his impaling, my father got religion. It started in the hospital, with the pastor from Reach Out for Christ coming daily through the wards, checking for converts. He left pamphlets, tapes; once I found a weird sort of slide gizmo by my dad's bed, a plastic thing you could look into for a 3-D picture of the Crucifixion and then click the button to see this pastor baptizing a big blond woman. I didn't think much of it all—you're in the hospital, you let people visit and leave stuff—till we brought my dad home and set him up with a hospital bed in the library. Suddenly the old Clint Eastwood movies he used to watch had switched to Bible shows. On Sundays he tuned in to Reach Out for Christ on local cable, and on Wednesdays the guy came by to read the New Testament with him. My dad got me to fish an old cross out of the basement that I never knew was there, and he lay in the hospital bed polishing it up. Then he had me hang it on the wall, where he could look right at it.

"I've been there, Daddy," I said the once or twice he tried to talk me into a session with his picture-book Bible. "It doesn't work. Look here." I reached over to turn the page to a full-color spread. "God like Santa Claus," I said. "White beard and fat cheeks. Everything but the red suit."

"That's just meant to help you," said my dad. He laid his hand on the picture. "You don't have to see him that way."

"I don't want to see him at all. I want to touch him. And if I can't touch him, then I say the hell with it."

It wasn't a nice thing to say, to your dad. But I'd gotten jealous of him, of the way he still had all that believing in front of him, while I was so much younger and didn't have any of it left, not since the year the Challenger went up. When the days started to hint of spring, he wheeled the chair they'd given him out to the deck off the library, the deck he'd finally built before his accident, while I was living in New York. He'd sit out there, watching the woods where the mud sluiced between the pines, just the way I'd watched from my room so long before; and though the accident had turned his hair gray, it was me who felt old.

The face of God. If my dad could have understood, I would have told him how I once liked to think about Christa McAuliffe getting blasted out of the capsule into the face of God, and that was what killed her. People have forgotten now. But there was a time when they harped on that explosion, all through the spring that followed it. They went on about the astronauts and Christa—everybody called her Christa, like some character on *As the World Turns*—about the O-rings, about them blowing up. There were the jokes, like JoAnn's dad told—but then came the news about finding bits and pieces of them in the ocean, and kids started talking about what it must have been like. Whether they knew what was happening, if they ever said anything after the squawk box went off, if they died from getting ripped apart or from suffocating, if their eardrums burst, if they watched each other burn.

If you were to ask my dad about God's face, now, he'd surely say it was death. Ever since surviving his fall, my dad has come to believe—among other weird things—that there's a time in each person's life when you're meant to brush up against the Grim Reaper—say hello, kind of, so when you meet for real you're not totally strangers. He points to my mom's brush, that spring after we got back from Florida. She shakes her head, claims it's a blank for her. But then I find her staring down the train tracks, even going out and walking the ties, up as far as the bridge. I'm not so sure but she's back having a conversation with her old friend the G.R., reminding him how much she has yet to do before they can really get together.

My Voyager book wore dust for mourning, that spring; but I'd found this little manual in the sale bin at our library, the tiny arched building that used to be the famous Meyenhold family's private church, right here in the hamlet. *Sentence Diagrams*, it was called—navy-blue cover, gold stamp, a smell like baked onions. I started drawing pictures of the sentences I liked. The one about the face of God read "They slipped bonds" up on the main line, with the adverbial infinitive dropping out of the middle, sloping gently downward toward God. I lay awake rearranging the structure in 3-D, so that God's face shot away into the far distance, like the Starship *Enterprise*, and my heart rocketing after it.

Meantime Seth Dugliss turned JoAnn down on the abortion money. The day she had it out with him was the only time I ever saw her cry. We were having lunch at the mall in Windhaven, across Route 9 and the For Sale lot from school. You weren't supposed to eat off the grounds, but everyone did who could afford it. JoAnn had told her dad there was a field trip and got five bucks, enough for her cheeseburger deluxe and my diet Coke. "He says," she told me while she cried, "that I got no proof it was him, and anyhow I told him I was fixed."

"Did you?" I said.

"Sure I did!" Her voice went up just like her mom's.

"Ssh," I said. I looked around. The place opened right onto the mall, and there were kids parading up and down—kids not just from Windhaven but the hamlet, too. That was what used to burn me about being from the hamlet—we were like these country cousins who had to hang together because nobody from Windhaven ever came down to the river or to Gray's and those things were all we'd known till we came to school. "Well, he can't say he didn't do it with you," I said. "So it'd have to be a little bit his fault. They say even when you *are* fixed you can get pregnant. So he could give you a little, and Matt could give you a little, and—"

"Whaddayou think I am, some church charity?" JoAnn cried out. "Nobody wants to admit they've *touched* me, you've gotta have at least two hundred *bucks* for an abortion, whaddayou think I do, turn *tricks*?"

"Shut *up*," I said. "We'll work something out. Just don't yell about it like you were something in the papers, JoAnn. Jesus."

There was a time, back then, I admired the way JoAnn Harlett had sex. She could sleep with a guy and not care except about how tight his rear end was, and she might have done a different guy every week without even considering STDs. "I made sure it didn't hurt the first time," she told me early in our friendship. This wasn't long after Barbie left, when I was still getting used to swimming in a sea of faces at the high school. JoAnn started inviting me over for Cokes, which my mom wouldn't even stock, and I was so amazed she could get away with smoking cigarettes in her room that I stayed for hours. "I went and got a broom handle and smeared it with Vaseline and stuck it up me," she said. "So by the time I let old Nate Dugliss in I hardly felt it at all."

"How long does it take them?" I'd asked. I was looking close at her hips, trying to see if they'd got wider. I had this impression that you had to spread yourself out somehow to fit a boy in, and you could never quite close up again. But JoAnn was so fat I couldn't tell a difference. Now me, I thought my hips might break.

"Only a few minutes, usually. But Spike Saunders—you know him, he got held back last year—he kept it up for something like half an hour. I was sore, I tell you. *That* was not fun."

It was only because JoAnn was so fat that she didn't have a reputation. I'd never even really noticed her before—she didn't exist as far as Barbie's old crowd was concerned—and now that we hung out together no one passed any dirt on to me. But what I finally figured was, the boys she slept with didn't want to admit they'd done her. That was why she'd thought Seth would give her the money. "But he says," she went on over her cheeseburger, "number one, everyone knows I'm a liar, and number two, everyone knows I'm just a piece of ass. So how come, if everyone knows those things, I had six guys ask me to Spring Fling this year?"

I wasn't going to ask her to name the six guys; I was JoAnn's friend, now. We'd ended up going to Spring Fling together, which was no big surprise, and JoAnn had disappeared halfway through the evening with Matt McPeck, which wasn't a surprise either. What might have surprised her, if she'd known about it, was how a bunch of kids had got me kind of loaded and talked me into dancing. This was long before I'd taken any lessons, long before I thought I was any kind of dancer. But scared as I was of some boy breaking my hips, the thrum of the music got under my skin, and there were these girls from Barbie's old crowd who wanted to sort of play around with their boyfriends' heads—so they'd ducked me into the bathroom and made me up with black eyeliner and a ton of mascara. "God," I remember one of them saying, "your lips are really full, Stickley, you look like one of those models that gets silicone shot in them."

"I hate my lips," I said, but I let them get painted anyhow, and then these girls pulled me out onto the dance floor. The band was bad, but they were doing a number from Second Coming which was pretty hot, and after a couple of hits of whatever we were all drinking, I'd started to move. Not that there was any room to move, just bodies pressing all around you—that was what the girls wanted, me revving their boyfriends up before they moved in—but I only danced harder in the thick space, like between the music and my body we could make the whole room move, that charge from body to body. Pretty soon there was a little space around me, and the music not stopping, and my legs like lightning bolts.

"Hot *lady*," said one of the boyfriends, when the whole thing was finally over. His girlfriend had slipped under his arm, tucked her hand into his jeans pocket.

"That way you dance," said another girl, who'd had too much to drink, "it's such a turn-on. I think it must be as good as sex."

"Better," I said.

But then I'd gone skinny and scared, and I ran to the bathroom to wipe the makeup off. When I came back, head pounding, that whole crowd had vanished.

None of it mattered; that was why I hadn't told JoAnn. Plus

now she had troubles. I finished my diet Coke, crunched the ice. "I still think you oughta blackmail Seth Dugliss," I said. "But okay, so you won't. *I'll* find you the money. Now give me your tomato and finish your fries, act normal."

We went from the hamburger place to this audio shop at the mall where they used to line up a batch of CDs every day. The store's still there—but now they have security devices, and you only get to listen to what blasts out of the speakers. Back then, when the whole thing was new and unripped-off, you could pick a label out and listen to it on headphones. CD ads had been so hot, talking about a revolution and a new bend for our minds, that we thought of those shiny discs like the next thing in drugs. The only one I knew with a player was Seth Dugliss. Checking the audio place this time, I found what I wanted, a new release by Second Coming. They'd written the song that had made me dance, like that, at the Fling. "Bitch Gone in the Teeth" they called this one. On the front was a lady vampire and on the back a picture of the group. I listened to the Challenger number, where their lead singer, Jason Sweetwood, mouthed "O-rings" up close to the mike so the sound reverbed—*O-whoah-whoah-whoah-ringngng-sssss*. The audio shop wasn't the best place for listening (they figured that, otherwise no one would ever buy), but I crouched on the floor by the speaker and shut my eyes.

"You look like a freaking groupie," JoAnn said.

"This is important," I said. And I thought about passing her the headphones, but it would be like handing her ammunition. "Pretend you don't know me," I said, and pressed the play button again.

JoAnn said something about me needing sex. For a while she listened to folk-rock at another counter, but pretty soon she started to whine about leaving. "One more hit," I said, but then the manager came over and asked did I want prices on that release or was I just zoning. So I stopped moving the molecules that were dancing in me to the music, and I picked myself up. Handing him back the lady vampire, I followed JoAnn's thick walk out of the store. On the way across Route 9 I saw Seth Dugliss, a hundred yards or so down on the double yellow line, flapping his arms at the cars like some kind of demented crow.

"Look at that," I said to JoAnn, cheering her up. "Fucking suicide case."

He glanced our way and I flipped him the bird. He yelled something—it might have been "Sister Stick!" again, or maybe just "Suck me." Either way, we were out of there. I practically pushed JoAnn through a gap in the rushing traffic, and we dodged the trucks across all four lanes.

chapter 5

I started looking for the money. My mom never carried more than twenty-five in her wallet because she was working in the war zone, in the middle of Castleton at this clinic that catered to penniless people. Scum, I'd heard JoAnn's father call them. She didn't even have nursing experience, just Quakerism and energy. My dad practically slept with his money. Back then he was a HotDig, which is what they used to call Hotung Digital people when Hotung was the biggest concern in the county. Because he ran checks on the programs for the heavy equipment, his shift ran two to ten—so he was asleep when I left for school and gone when I got home and not back until I was asleep. Pretty fast footwork, I thought; he'd arranged things so he only had to see his daughter on weekends, when he mostly caught up on Z's and watched basketball and puttered in the barn. If I'd had a brother or sister I would have stolen from them—I didn't have scruples about this— but my mom thought there were too many people on the planet; she'd cut her guilt in half by stopping with me. That had something to do, too, with why I didn't get an allowance. There was too much of everything, and for every one item I bought, the manufacturers would make two more.

Anyway, my family was a dry well.

Late in April I tried selling my clothes. There was this girl Daphne who had sold every item she owned except a black knit dress, and had proceeded to wear it every single day until it got bleach on it, and then she found some jeans and a tie-dye shirt and did the same thing with them. For three days I sat outside the cafeteria with my stuff on a portable rack, and people fingered it. "Shit," one girl finally told me, "no one can wear your clothes anyway, Stick. You're too frigging skinny." A few minutes later another girl stuck her nose into a blouse and checked the size and muttered, "*Show-off*." I felt pretty out of it after that, hanging around outside the cafeteria with no one buying my clothes and the sun shining outside, so I packed it all up. I'd sold one crop-top for a dollar fifty.

The only thing left was robbing a store. Shoplifting, I mean, for stuff I could sell in Free Zone. I checked out the stores I knew in Windhaven. Video King and Jay's Wholesale were high on my list since there didn't seem to be anything too morally great about them, followed by Radio Shack and the audio place at the mall. For a while I took this possibility seriously, but everywhere I looked they had those signs about closed-circuit TV and prosecution. Then I thought of Gray's, which everyone would have been pretty happy to see robbed right from the cash drawer. Gray had been okay to me, though, so I couldn't plot that one; I didn't have scruples, but I possessed a degree of loyalty.

There wasn't much money in Gray's store that spring, anyhow. Everybody in the hamlet was boycotting him. My mom kept saying innocent till proven guilty, but I noticed she didn't seem to need quarts of milk so often, and she got this chalky look whenever she heard I'd been in the store. The first week the news was out, someone sprayed Gray's sign so it read CUNTY STORE instead of COUNTRY STORE, but he got a guy to strip it clean the next day, and after that no one did anything to him, directly. The deal was he'd done something awful to this foster kid he and his wife had, years ago. Something like rape but more complicated; I never got the story entirely straight. Once I heard my dad say there were charges against Benjy, too. Benjy was Gray's adopted son. But I got what was probably the most exciting picture from JoAnn's father.

"You had to wonder," he kept saying, that winter, tapping his cigarette ash into the little metal dish he kept on the windowsill and staring out at Gray's store. "You had to wonder." Finally someone would ask what it was you had to wonder, and he'd go on, like an unstuck record. "All them kids they used to take in. First it was Benjy, then two or three other boys from that welfare place in Castleton. Then the girls. You had to wonder. Shit, foster brats." Here he'd pull on the cigarette, and you'd watch the ash creep down the paper. "Paid fifty a month in them days, and Arlene and me was desperate enough to think about doing it once or twice. But that Gray, hell, he already had that appliance place in Windhaven, and the store here, and he'd taken over his uncle's apartments down back of the old granary. He wasn't hurting. He used to say the missus loved kids, more the merrier, and she couldn't have none."

"And you believe that! You do!" JoAnn's mom called out from the kitchen.

"Didn't say so," he answered, but not loud enough for her to hear. They never had a conversation, JoAnn's parents, just these lines they threw around the house at each other, like spitballs. "Said you had to wonder. Benjy's the only one they adopted, and he ain't right in the head. Those others come and go, no one asks where to or how come. Must of had a hundred of them, over the years. Someone else, you'd say they did it for the charity of it. You ever seen a charitable man like Gray?" Here he'd laugh, not loud, but for a long time, like the joke gave him an idea for another joke in his head, and that one gave way to another one, but he wasn't going to tell us those. "He's so charitable, why's he fleece his customers? Why's he gouge his tenants?" He'd stub out his cigarette. "He ain't got a friend in this town, that's how charitable he is."

"So what did he *do*, Dad?" JoAnn's brother Bobby would ask.

I actually thought Gray was pretty charitable. Not moneywise. But before all this mess had started he was everybody's second daddy. He'd come out on a warm day with a football and all those foster kids tailing behind, and there would be a game of touch in front of the store, where the street opens out. He'd have his butcher apron on, and he'd stand there with his legs spread open, those long arms out, trying to block our lousy passes. People would circle around us, making their way into the store, and he'd tell them just to leave the money on the counter. Maybe he gouged them, but he trusted them.

Then, too, Gray and I had a special relationship. Take the year before, the year Gray adopted Benjy, when my dad had been renovating the barn out back. I could tell my mom was pissed off about that barn, and my dad wouldn't give way. I didn't know what lay behind the bad vibes, what an invisible net we were caught in. I was missing Barbie then, after all, hugging that grief to my chest. So when they started going at it, late at night after my dad got home, I tuned out the voices rising and falling from the other room until they said my name. My name was all that mattered to me, the rest was no more than adult moods and restlessness. Avoidance, my mother would say. Waste. Hiding failure behind cardboard and nails. You want Paris, you want Egypt? my father flung back at her. You want to save the world? Go ahead. Hobby, my hobby. Not yours. Cold fish, my mother went. Bitch, went my dad. Then suddenly one night my mom said, sharp and loud, Do you want a divorce? And my dad answered, Ssh! Ssh! You'll wake up Stick!

There it was, my name. I sat up to hear my mom go, Let her wake up. Let her hear!

But my mom's question never got answered, even though I lay awake straining my ears until their voices died and I could hear my mom pecking at her typewriter, my father in the bathroom. Next morning I got up as soon as it was pale out and slipped over to the store. Gray and Benjy were bringing in the newspapers, but

Gray let me park my behind on a barstool by the window and just swing around. After a time he came over with two steaming cups of coffee; setting them on the ledge, he took the other stool.

"Who's that for?" I asked.

"You."

"I'm only thirteen. I don't drink coffee."

"One cup won't stunt your growth," he said. "And you ain't slept, and you got school today."

"How do you know I didn't sleep?"

He crinkled up his eyes and blew on his coffee. "I know," he said, "you got things to keep you awake, over at your place."

"What, you sneak around at night?" I leaned down to smell the coffee—he'd put in milk and sugar, which made the steam a little caramelly. But I didn't drink. Benjy was still moving in and out the door, lugging papers; when he glanced over he looked mean, to me.

"No," said Gray. "I don't."

He stayed close. I wanted to tell him, wanted to say those words: *divorce; let her hear.* Just to hear how they sounded, in the light of day. Outside, the first train to the city suddenly raced by— the same one that would almost kill JoAnn's baby brother, the next year. An express, it screeched around the bend by the mansion and shook the walls of the store. Years ago, I thought, when the train stopped here, a person could get on and leave forever.

"We ain't none of us responsible for what other people do to each other," Gray was saying. He was looking away from me now, out the window at his first customer, the night guard from the mansion who always brought his dog around before going home. "Just last year we had a foster boy—Kenny—you remember him, he was here a couple months. His dad stuck a knife in his mother and then went crazy. I shouldn't be telling you that."

"You know what I think," I said. I was drinking the coffee now: tiny sips. "I think my mom's doing something bad."

"Bad? How could she?" He shifted his eyes to me, then motioned Benjy to take the customer. The bell over the door tinkled.

"You know."

"I don't."

"Something . . . with someone else." I hadn't even thought it till then; I couldn't have said how the idea got in my head, it had nothing to do with people sticking knives in people. *Cold fish* had put it there, maybe. Suddenly I felt ashamed, like I'd given out a snapshot of my mom stark naked. I sucked up the coffee and started down from the stool.

"Hey. Hey, Stick."

"Never mind. I take it back."

But he was blocking my way already. "People got all sorts of reasons, Stick," he said. "And then the reasons pass, and sometimes the trouble just vanishes with them."

"I know," I said. Of course I didn't have a clue. But Gray let me go and moved back to the sales counter where Benjy and the old night guard were sharing a joke. The old man's dog gave a big snuffle at my crotch, then wagged its tail. As I went out Gray reached over the counter and squeezed my shoulder. It wasn't until later I took note that he hadn't stood up for my mom, hadn't declared I was guessing wrong.

Gray still had the foster kids with him then, and they did all the little things around the store—stock the shelves, fetch hardware from where it was tacked high up, fold the Sunday papers. A couple times I offered to help, being as I was around so much. "Thanks, Stick," Gray said, "but we're a team, and you got to keep that team spirit." Whichever of the fosters was around to hear this would grin and act shy. Sometimes I wished we lived farther away, so I could run away from home and get caught, and end up with Gray for a foster father while the court decided what to do with me.

They never stayed with him long. I didn't know the one who ended up bringing charges against him—the papers wouldn't give her name—but JoAnn said it was Kristin Lyons and she was four years older than us and had buck teeth. She lived a year with Gray and his wife, when she was thirteen. That was pretty old for Gray, actually. The only one I ever made friends with was nine when I was ten. Her name was Angelina, and she was real small. I mean tiny, like she could pass for six and get in free at the Giant Slide in Windhaven. She was with Gray because her parents had been sent to rehab and nobody in the family was in shape to take her. She didn't mind talking about her parents, she said they were always nuts, her mom was always faking being sick, and her dad popped pills that wired him up. But she didn't seem really interested in them. She wanted to be a gymnast, and Gray paid for her to take extra classes in Castleton after school. Sometimes I drove down with Gray's wife to pick her up, and she'd do cartwheels all the way from the studio door out to the car, sometimes ten cartwheels without a stop.

Now that I was a little older, with this Kristin Lyons bringing charges, and people like JoAnn's dad talking about years of this and that, I began to wonder about Angelina. I mean, if Gray was going to do anybody he'd have done her. She was adorable. She didn't cuddle up to Gray the way some of the others did, but she wasn't the cuddly type—she was always moving, trying to keep ahead of us others who were so much bigger. She stayed almost two years, then some cousin of hers got married and his wife came to have a look at Angelina, and she was gone.

She'd never talked about Gray. Well, we were too young for that kind of talk. But once we came tearing into the store after we'd beat the others through the woods—this was some kind of hide-and-seek—and we were all scratched up and dying of thirst and giggling. Gray was snoring behind the counter, tipped back in his chair, his glasses practically perched on the end of his nose. "Ain't he a lazy skunk," I said, and Angelina said, "At least he knows how to shut his eyes." Then she slipped behind the counter and took his glasses off, and rearranged his hands so they rested over his belly, on his apron. She stood on tiptoe—she was that tiny—and I think she kissed him on the cheek. He kept on snoring. We stole a couple root beers and headed out the door.

There was this, too, which I wouldn't ever admit to anyone from the hamlet: you wanted him to touch you. I did anyhow. I would come into the store after one of those football games, the leathery ball tucked under my arm, and head straight for where his apron spread across his big thighs, and his big hands would come down on my shoulders and he'd spin me around. He had big hands but short fingers, which was different from my father or JoAnn's for that matter. They had these small white palms and long fingers that seemed to kind of pluck at you; close up, JoAnn's father smelled like beer and tobacco, and my father's teeth were brown near the gums. But I liked the way Gray smelled, of hard candies and cheese and stacked newspapers. If I had trouble sleeping at night all I had to do was pretend I was wrapped up in Mr. Gray's big arms, my hips pushing into his belly, and I'd drift right off.

You didn't tell people like JoAnn's father this stuff. They'd say you were sick: a nympho. "His type's always so saintly," Mr. Harlett would go on, sitting on their porch. "I had him pegged, even before that girl blew the whistle, what with all those kids fawning on him."

"So what'd he *do*?" Bobby'd ask again.

"Both them," said JoAnn's dad. "Him and the wife. Fact I'd say she's the criminal, but they never get the woman."

"So what—"

"Them unfortunate kids." JoAnn's dad fixed on each of us now, one by one, like we were personally responsible for what had happened to Gray's foster children. "Them unfortunate kids are just toys, to people like that. Little toys y'fondle, little geegaws y'break. Nothing like a wiggly little live body to play with, for sickos like that."

We all turned red. We'd all played too rough with our toys; we knew how much fun it could be to bend something till it snapped. Gray was guilty, we were guilty. So we didn't shop there either, and the place just sat empty, things gathering dust on the shelves. A couple afternoons a week the *Closed* sign went up on the door, and you knew he was down in Windhaven with his lawyer or in court farther down, in Castleton. People started getting their milk and eggs at the Minimart up on Route 12; it was open twenty-four hours a day and had the lottery. No candy under fifty cents, and you needed a good bike to get up there, but kids can find ways to change their habits too. So Gray's wasn't the store to rob.

chapter **6**

JoAnn's youngest brother, little Whoopsy, kept wandering down to the train tracks after that first time, until Mrs. Harlett had to start keeping him on one of those halter leashes. She glared at my mom each time they passed each other, like my mom had put this train idea in his head; and every time my mom tried to engage her in conversation, she'd give the leash a little tug. A couple times we found him off his halter, standing no more than a foot from the ties, his mouth hung open like he was staring down a deep well. He let my mom take him back home, but he chewed the back of his hand the whole way. In May, Mrs. Harlett fell through a rotted plank on her back porch and popped a disk in her back. She couldn't move for a week, so JoAnn stayed home and watched Whoopsy. She was in her fourth month by then, so I guess she was glad to be out of school. She'd take her brother up onto the bridge, and they'd watch the trains shoot by under them. Only one time she lay down on the warm wood and dozed off, and Whoopsy leaned too far between the metal balusters of the railing. She felt the yank on her wrist, she told me later. I guess if she hadn't been so heavy, or her wrists so thick, he might have gone down, even dragged her right down through the rusted balusters. As it was, she took a major splinter in her forearm, and little Whoopsy ended up suspended over the silvery river of passenger cars, the halter pushing his arms across his face to stifle his yelps, his stumpy legs kicking the air away.

Of course it was Gray who heard them, got them up. Not just because he was sure to be around during store hours, but because he tended to head off trouble that way. At least, he had before his own started—by that spring he got no credit for what he did. He checked the boy's shoulders in case they'd got dislocated. He pulled the splinter from JoAnn's arm and bathed it in the Betadine he kept in his truck; he drove them home through the woods. What neither he nor JoAnn ever noticed through the whole thing was the engineer, whose head must have stuck out from the window of the rear car, whose shouts must have mingled with JoAnn's while the kid dangled there. We know the engineer saw them— the very same one who'd cocooned the boy's body, just weeks before, while tons of black metal brushed over his back—because he wrote my mom a letter announcing his transfer to the Midwestern branch of Amtrak. He knew my mom's last name, they'd been in the newspaper together. I guess he felt he had to explain himself to somebody.

For a long while I have been a Trinitarian, he wrote. *I know the world runs in threes according to God's will, and now I know myself to be an agent of that Will.* "*Thou shalt go up to appear before the Lord thy God thrice in the year,*" *Exodus 24. But I cannot be an agent of a child's death. God has sent me a warning by two—*"*Twice have I heard that power belongeth unto God,*" *Psalms 62—and it is in my power to ward off fate. My family does not want to make this move. I have been doing the Albany run for seventeen years. I like "my" passengers. Good people, hardworking people. But my Lord has spoken to me.*

"What sad rubbish," my mother said, and wouldn't show it to Mrs. Harlett even after she was on her feet and JoAnn back in school—not even years later, just before I moved back here, when Whoopsy had finally become Woody who at seven lost an arm because the car he was riding in tried to race the train. You can see him now, down at the arcade in Windhaven with the other angry kids. He pushes quarters into the machines and slams the joystick around with his one hand. He's probably got a rep, the one-armed video wizard. If I knew where to reach that engineer I'd send him a fax: *You can come back now, it's over.* But I picture him settled down after seven years, somewhere in Illinois, his kids grown and his wife reconciled to her new garden. He wouldn't want to change his luck.

JoAnn got the business for what Mrs. Harlett called dropping her little brother over the side. "That girl's got to learn the difference between a human life and a load of laundry," she said to the post office ladies when she hobbled in, one hand to her lower back, to collect her mail. If the post office ladies thought this was funny, they didn't show it. JoAnn's father laid a strap across her face that night and then grounded her for two weeks. "Bring me some fucking cigarettes," she whispered to me on the phone. "Or else a coat hook. I'm barfing my guts out. My mom thinks it's because I'm bad, I'm barfing the devil out of me."

"I'm working on the money," I told her. "Eat saltines, it'll pass."

I was fixed on this money thing. While JoAnn was grounded I couldn't think, except to count each day going by and picture how the baby was getting bigger inside her, building a heart and arms and legs, running us out of time. At school I had to see the shrink they'd sent in, to keep tabs on us since we'd got back from the Challenger. My schoolwork was suffering, he wrote on my evaluation, and I had trouble discussing what had happened in Florida. I'd gotten my first C in April, on the history midterm.

My dad surprised me; he'd nodded when he saw the grade, like he'd always known. "Now the boys'll start looking your way, Stick," he said. "Just you wait, you'll be seeing more of these, and you won't mind a bit. And don't you push her," he said to my mom. "Certain things are in nature. You made C's."

"I don't want Gwyn living my life," my mother said. Her voice was sharp, her eyebrows lowered as she turned away from us. But I liked this idea: dumb and sexy. Ever since that coffee with Gray, I'd begun to pick up little signals, all of which had made me think about my mom a certain way. They were signals I liked, which was saying a lot when it came to me and her. Signals like a new bra I caught her wearing while she combed her hair in the bathroom, after her shower. A royal-blue canister of talc with a pink streak across it, reading *Opium*. She lived two lives, my mom. In one she had a big serious proposal going, where she was going to head a new project with money from the state. Her fingers flew over the typewriter late at night, and in the morning I found a half-dozen cigarette butts in the library wastebasket. In the other life she made C's and had lacy cleavage.

I'd never have cleavage. That night I chucked my homework. I put on my Second Coming tape and set my dark *Sentence Diagrams* book side by side with the lyrics. *Surely the second coming is at hand,* went the first song, *with the beating and the shouting of the band, while the hour is come too late and the saints are gorged with hate, can you feel my lightning flashing in your thighs?* That sentence started to make a nice diagram, but the last question just hung there—I couldn't tell if it belonged to the dependent clause or if it was a run-on. Plus it didn't rhyme. I was ruining my favorite song. I tore up the paper and flicked off the light. Finding my dark reflection in the mirror I studied that, as I ground my hips to the music.

But I did work on the money, while JoAnn was out of the way. For a couple of days I hung around at lunch with the only crowd that had money, this small group from Windhaven Hills Estates that Seth Dugliss was always trying to impress with his new truck and the boutique drugs he knew how to get hold of. Some of them were from Barbie's old crowd and had seen me dance, earlier that spring. Others were new, their families brought in when Hotung bought out some other company the year before. If I'd remotely wanted anything they had going for them, that might have gotten in my way—they sense these things, newly rich people; what they want is people sucking up to them without sucking on. As it was, I didn't smell like social poison, I could admire someone's ankle bracelet without sounding like an ultimate bitch, I kept my ears open, and pretty soon a couple of them decided I could be made useful. "Listen, Stickley," one of them started, sort of curling herself around my path as I headed in to the lunchroom. "You got a sec?"

"Sure," I said. I let her lead me around to the lockers in the hall. Her name was Stephanie. She'd moved up to Windhaven from Long Island a year ago, her father was a big HotDig. When she'd first arrived she'd worn her brown hair long and straight; now it was cropped to a spiky helmet, very black, but underneath she had the same white-corn face—thin nose, rabbity eyes, weak chin. Boys found her pretty.

"This here is Charlotte," Stephanie said.

"I know," I said, nodding at Charlotte. She was part of Barbie's old crowd, dumb as dirt but beautiful, tall and large-breasted, with a waist and hips like warm wax that someone had squeezed and tapered. Her lips were pouty, lined in red lipstick.

"I liked how you danced, at Spring Fling," Charlotte said. "I'd like to dance like that."

"Charlotte," Stephanie explained, "has got a major appointment. With a guy who—get this—wants her to try for the Ford *Modeling* Agency!"

I knew not to ask what this agency was; modeling was all I needed to hear. "Like, when?" I said.

"In half an hour," said Charlotte. Her voice was breathy, like she couldn't use anything below her neck to talk. "It's just five minutes from here, he's passing through Windhaven. He said it didn't matter what I wear, but I don't know."

"He'll bring stuff," Stephanie reassured her. "They do that. But Charlotte's parents," she said to me, "will kill her if they find out she's doing something like this."

"They will," said Charlotte. "You don't know."

"So don't tell them," I said.

"That's just it," said Stephanie. She glanced around the lockers, at the hallway, checking. "Pomerantz in history," she said. "He makes people sit in assigned seats," she said. "He takes roll."

"*And* there's a quiz today," Charlotte put in. "Which I will just *flunk*," she added bitterly.

"So cut the class," I said. I knew where this was heading, now, but they felt better when I played along.

"If you cut four classes, you flunk then, too," Stephanie said. "Charlotte's cut three, counting once when she had strep. He doesn't *excuse* that."

"Prick," said Charlotte.

"Now look, Stick, you are a good kid. Everybody knows that. Even Seth says you're all right, and he says that hamlet you guys live in is just chock with goofballs."

"Plus that pervert's there, huh?" said Charlotte. "That store guy?" I lifted my shoulders, shrugged them down.

"I've got to go with Charlotte in case she has trouble parking or something," Stephanie went on.

"How'd you hear about this modeling guy?"

It was the wrong question; Stephanie gave Charlotte a what-did-I-tell-you look, and Charlotte tossed her clean hair. "Look, Stickley, this is a *com*plicated business—"

"Okay, okay," I said. "What do you want me to do?"

"Sit in my seat," said Charlotte. "Third row, second over from the windows. Take the quiz, sign my name. That's it."

"I can't take your quiz!" I said. I'd missed that part, somehow. "What the hell subject is this?"

"U.S. history up to the Civil War," said Stephanie.

"I don't know jack shit about it!" I said.

"Neither do I," said Charlotte. She started to bite her index nail, then thought better of it. Her breath was coming more rapidly. "But it's only a tenth of the grade. I won't flunk the whole course by flunking it. Anyhow, you can't do worse than me."

"He'll know I'm not you, anyhow."

"Uh-uh," said Stephanie. "Forty people in the class, he doesn't even look at faces, just the blackboard and his freaking index cards. You could be a nigger in cowboy boots, he wouldn't notice."

"Why don't *you* do it, then?" I said. "I'll go with Charlotte to the modeling thing."

"Because I'm in the class already, only I've only cut twice," said Stephanie. "Because it won't work that way. Because—"

"I get you," I said, holding up a hand. It was time to name my price. "Twenty-five," I said, and they didn't even blink. Thirty seconds later they'd paid up and disappeared.

It meant skipping McGruder's class—biology this term, who knew if they'd ever let her teach astro again? And she *would* notice who wasn't there. But I had my first big chunk of change. I found the history classroom in the north corridor, slipped into Charlotte's seat. There was only one person I knew in the class—Matt McPeck down at the other end—and he didn't give a sign. The guy behind me kicked the back of my seat and winked when I swung around, but it was approval he was handing me, he lifted one thick eyebrow and for half a second I think he thought I was cute. *The Age of Jackson*, the quiz read at the top. *Which of the following was NOT a priority for our country in 1830?*

I solved things by the way they sounded, mostly—when you had to complete the sentence *Jackson created a harsh . . .* then *Indian policy* just had a nicer beat to it than *set of gold standards, ways for the common man to get credit*, or *easing of States' obligations*. When sound didn't do it, I looked for pattern—a, b, b, b, c, a, d. They always used at least one letter choice three times in a row, to throw you off. I finished early, and almost signed my name instead of Charlotte's, and then I realized I didn't even know her last name, and had to scan the desk for where I was sure she'd scratched it in. Charlotte Petersen, that had to be it—she'd turned the *o* into a heart. Proud, I stepped to the desk to hand the thing in, and that was where the teacher stopped me.

"Step outside in the hall a moment," he said. He'd been just propped against the desk, meditating on the blackboard; now he leaned over to whisper, like a conspirator, in my ear.

I followed his plaid jacket out the door—he walked with a slight limp, like his left shoe hurt. He had one of those perfect bald spots, a big coin of pink flesh on the back of his head. Out in the dim hallway, he leaned one shoulder against the cool wall and squinted at me. "Charlotte Petersen," he said. A lopsided grin spread under his mustache.

"Yessir," I said. My head felt like nails were being pounded into it from all sides. I stuck one finger down the back pocket of my jeans and felt the two bills, tucked there. He couldn't take those away.

"At last," he said. "We meet."

"Sir?" I said. I tried to make my face as bland as I remembered Charlotte's being. This was no time for mistakes.

"Come on, girl! How many people have you had sitting in that desk of yours, in there? You kids think I don't notice, that one warm adolescent body is the same as another to old Pomerantz! Well, I'm telling you, I keep track. And that's just why, in the end, your grade's coming out of the quizzes and the exam. You remember I told you that, the first day."

"The first day?"

"You were *there*, Charlotte. Don't play the ditzy girl with me! How else d'you suppose I know you're you and not another one of your little clones? I memorize faces"—he put an index finger up to the corner of his eye, under the glasses—"that very first hour. Keep the seating chart and memorize the faces, that's my dirty little secret. You, I remember"—he reached the finger out, now, and would have touched my face if I hadn't flinched away— "because of your cheekbones. Fine bone structure, you don't see it in young girls much anymore. You'll grow up to look like Katharine Hepburn," he said, "but you won't be as smart as she is if you don't make it to class more."

"What about the attendance requirement?" I said. "Why'd you make that, if you're just counting the quizzes?"

"More people I educate, the better," he said. "This way the room is full, there are ears and perhaps even brains taking in knowledge. Who they belong to's not my concern. But you—" He shook his head, pushed off the wall. "You top 'em in nerve," he said as he pulled open the door to the classroom. "And I just hope you managed to ace that quiz."

The door shut on his chuckle. I stuck my tongue out at it and swung on down the hall. There were fifteen minutes left to the period, I could be late for McGruder and not get in too much Dutch. I pushed open the exit doors; I could cut across the back lot.

Outside the sun was brilliant, bouncing off the chrome of the cars. There, coming out of Charlotte's cherry-red Lynx, were Charlotte and Stephanie. Stephanie had her arm around Charlotte's shoulders, like she was helping her after a bad fall. And in fact Charlotte looked a wreck—her hair frizzed and mashed, her lipstick smeared, one of her leggings riding up her calf. "Hey," I said, swinging over to them. "I did it!"

Charlotte turned her head in my direction, but her eyes didn't register; the lower pout of her lip hung open. Stephanie, though, let go of her a second and marched a few paces my way. "Get out of here, you little freak!" she yelled. "Just stay the fuck away from her, you hear me?" Her voice shook. I turned and jogged toward the next wing of the building. When I was almost there, I risked a glance back. They were making their way across the field toward the trailer park, the Free Zone. Halfway there they stopped; Charlotte sort of crumpled down, and Stephanie squatted beside her, talking and gesturing with her arms. Before she could turn and spot me, I'd skipped on inside.

Once, in New York, I found myself wondering what happened to Charlotte. Who the man was, what he put her through, where Stephanie had been. I can't say it doesn't matter just because it was Charlotte Petersen, who didn't have much of a soul to start with. It did matter, it does matter. But she wasn't real to me, there in the parking lot. She was a doll who'd got messed. What was real was the twenty-five bucks in my pocket, my first big down payment on JoAnn's abortion.

In the end, of course, that wasn't real either. Not because JoAnn wouldn't have gone through with it. But by the next week, like a pure idiot, I'd thrown the twenty-five bucks away.

chapter 7

I make five hundred dollars a week now. Barring other expenses, I could pay for two and a half abortions each week. Other people can afford ten, fifteen, a hundred abortions a week.

Or you don't even need the money. That is, you do now, with the way the government's cracked down, but it used to be if you walked into a clinic without a cent there'd be some way to get you fixed up. There were probably liberal women who were married to lawyers and who sat in the foyers of the clinics from ten to two, and if you arrived during those hours without any money, they'd simply write you a personal check.

What I'm saying is, I myself can hardly believe we didn't know how to either lay hold of cash or get the thing done without it, but there's the fact. When Seth Dugliss announced that Second Coming was going to be at the River Festival over Memorial Day, and his dad could get a block of seats under the tent at twenty-five bucks a head, Charlotte's two bills floated out of my back pocket and into his hand. I heard him saying, while they floated, that if you hung around long enough afterwards, Sweetwood and the rest would try to slip out some back way and you could get them to sign something; he'd done it at another concert, he said.

I felt bad about the money for about a week, until I learned JoAnn was signed on too. She was back in circulation, a crusted welt across her forehead and right cheek, and now that she was free of Whoopsy she spent most of her spare time drinking. As for me, I was done with the Windhaven Hills crowd—Charlotte disappeared for almost two weeks after that day, and Stephanie just

shoved past me in the halls. I didn't care. After school I'd go with
JoAnn to Free Zone, where she'd get fried and I'd act fried, and
pretty soon she'd pluck my shoulder and pull me outside, where
she'd throw up whatever was in her stomach, a bagful of pretzels
or a cheese sandwich, plus some of the beer. "Pretty gross," I said
the first time she did it. I tried to kick loose dirt over the mess but
you could tell.

"That's what it looks like in your stomach," she said. "Get used
to it."

"I don't like to think about my stomach," I said. "I don't like to
think about any kind of stomach."

"Ooh. Touchy."

"They cut open a rat's one in McGruder's bio lab today, okay?
And I had to go to the nurse, okay? So don't start on me." I sat on
the stoop of the trailer, my knees weak with just thinking about it.
It wasn't just the blood, I'd kept telling the nurse, it was the whole
idea. Insides. Veins and acids, organs. The week before we'd
learned the word *subcutaneous*. I spent half my next class on the
john in the girls' room, just thinking that word. Subcutaneous. It
meant a needle stuck under the skin that was supposed to protect
you; things slipping in underneath, finding their way into your
body. Every time I stood up I started to faint. It took the hall proc-
tor to talk me out of the stall.

"Just don't eat when you drink, JoAnn," I said.

She shook her head. "Got to eat," she said, "if I'm going to have
this baby."

"Now wait a sec," I said, feeling my back pocket as if I could
still find the twenty and the five there. "I've got this camp job in
the summer, they're paying me fifty a week."

JoAnn shook her head and started back into the trailer. "Too
late by then," she said. "Five months, they start charging a bunch
more."

"But if you don't—"

She shrugged, like we were talking about this unimportant subject. "I'd just as soon have it as get sucked out, anyhow," she said.

"But your mom," I said. JoAnn's older sister hadn't been allowed on a date until she was sixteen, and then her mom had gone along, weighing down the back seat while JoAnn's sister and the date tried to do a drive-in. JoAnn's sister had run off and got married around the same time JoAnn discovered she was pregnant. JoAnn used to say she didn't intend ever to go on a date, she'd just keep slipping out her window and meeting boys in the woods.

"She don't have to know," said JoAnn.

"What do you mean? You'll show!"

"No, I won't. Fat people don't so much, and if I just keep gaining weight all over they won't know the difference. I thought about it, while I was grounded. We were all teeny babies, my mom said. No more than six pounds, any of us. I figure six pounds won't amount to a hill of beans by the time I'm through."

I looked her up and down. She had a point. I was still hoping for the money, though, especially now that I'd blown a chunk of it. As if it was this rabbit I could pull out of a hat, and I'd have JoAnn Harlett with her hand clapped on her cheek crying, Magic! As if I'd been picked for this task, like the astronauts for the shuttle, and nobody could say I wasn't doing good in the end.

"Maybe I could make some money at the concert," I said. "Get hold of some weed, or something."

"Oh sure, Stick. You really look like a drug dealer." Her hand on the back door to the trailer, she tossed her hair behind her shoulder. JoAnn was growing her bangs out, and they kept slipping down over her forehead. She had terrific hair, though, shiny thick curls like whipped margarine. "Seth'll never take you in his truck if you're gonna try a stunt like that," she said.

"What do you care? You're not going."

"I might."

"JoAnn! You haven't got twenty-five bucks!"

"Fifteen for my birthday last February, and Bobby's paying me ten to wash his gym clothes all this spring."

"But then—" It was fifty dollars we'd spent, between the two of us. One fourth of what we needed. "God, we are morons," I said.

"Look, Seth's dad got an incredible deal on the tickets. What are we supposed to do, walk away?"

"You are not *talking* to Seth Dugliss!" I said.

"Oh, yes I am." She started inside; there were three or four kids in there, one guy getting a buzz-cut from a sophomore. "I am talking to him," she said, leaning close to me, "about the false alarm I had." Curling her pink lips, she looked for a second like her mom. Her breath was sour.

"But JoAnn, what he did—"

"What he did," she said in her airy voice, "was fuck JoAnn Harlett and run. He's just a guy, Stick. And I don't trust his mouth."

And sure enough there she was, on the corner by Gray's store with the rest who were going in Seth's truck. Seth had been held back too; he should have been graduating, but he said he was going to quit after this year and drive his truck, probably for his dad. He had his own stash with him and a few six-packs, and the crowd he was working to impress were all talking about what a freaking time they were going to have. Like the sixties had arrived in Windhaven, saying: Oops, sorry, missed ya the first time through, this is the repeat tour.

"You don't have to go," my mom had said the night before.

"Shows what you know."

"Your curfew's eleven o'clock. Tell them it's past your curfew."

"Then they just won't take me, and no one'll give a shit."

"So? Do you give a shit?"

Some parenting book had taught my mom to talk that way; it was a clever ploy. But she'd been up late with the computer again the night before that, her head full of proposals and case studies and Quaker ideas. It wasn't me keeping her awake—I just had to take the heat her tired self threw off. It was like when we got back from Florida and she had come in my room and talked about NASA and guns in space. Like that was the issue and not Christa who'd touched the face of God. Now I was dreaming myself into a romance comic with Jason Sweetwood at the wheel of an XKE, the hamlet a zillion miles away, and she was talking peer pressure.

"I give a shit," I'd said.

As I climbed into the back of Seth's truck I could see her watching from our porch. "Find a pay phone when you get sick of it," she'd said on my way out, "and call me. You can tell them you met some boy and he's giving you a lift home."

I could tell she thought this was a really bright idea. "Sure, Mom, good move," I said, and I wiggled my fingers at her until she went inside.

We were thirteen crammed into the back of the truck. Charlotte was at the far end, looking like a model again, her head tucked into some football player's elbow and her mouth curled mysteriously. I got jammed up against Lenny Dugliss, the little mouse-burner. He kept mumbling lyrics under his breath, something about thighs and knives. All Duglisses were trash in those days; Lenny was spooky trash. JoAnn once said he looked like his mom, who'd died young; I said his mom must have been a vampire. White white skin and black hair, and long fingers like E.T. Around his wrist he wore this little chain with a metal plaque, like an ID bracelet, only his had a picture of a snake instead of his name on it. The year before, the troopers had picked him to help train their rookies; Gray's son, Benjy, went with him while he took off into the woods, pretending to be a lost dog or a wanted criminal. For eight hours he led the troopers on a chase, until finally they sounded an all-clear from one of their cars, and he came out of the woods with Benjy, grinning. "He hides like a wild varmint," Benjy'd said. "The places we squirreled away—I couldn't find 'em again if my life depended on it."

Seth drove fast, but still it was a half-hour to Castleton. I finally leaned my head back and watched the stars whizz. How many astronauts can you fit in a Volkswagen? Seth had asked when he closed the tailgate. Two in the front, two in the back, and seven in the ashtray. Christa McAuliffe lay in the dark ashtray flat and stiff, like a Barbie doll. Some little girl had put her there to hide her but now the driver pulled out the tray, dropped a burning ash, and whoosh!—Barbie-melt.

"Yuck," I heard myself say.

"Wake up, Stick," JoAnn was saying. "Take a toke, we're in Castleton."

I sucked it in and held it. The truck was starting down the hill. "Let's just keep going," I croaked.

"Where to?" shouted Matt McPeck from the other side.

"End of the world," I said.

"Same thing," said spooky Lenny Dugliss. "Castleton is the end of the world." They all giggled at that, but it was the dope. We dropped down off the highway into the amber lights, and I finished the roach.

We found a place to park about half a mile from the concert, over by the train yard. It was cold, for May, and already dark. There were all these people walking up the road, some of them carrying coolers. Seth chased his rich friends into the darkness; his brother tagged behind. I started out walking with JoAnn, but we sort of merged with this other truckload of kids from Windhaven and there was this guy Darryl that JoAnn lit onto. She was looking good, for JoAnn: she had on her black crochet top that showed the little daisy tattoo on her left shoulder, and she'd done her hair up in a high ponytail. Darryl was kind of overweight too, but he had a nice jacket and long hair, like pictures I'd seen of Jim Morrison. He kept laughing and sort of tweaking her upper arm. So I dropped behind.

You could say I got lost.

For a while I was on course with these people, and you could hear the warm-up band over the hill to the river. They weren't too bad, kind of funky metal. And I would swear to this day that I could have been a groupie, I was so fixated on Jason Sweetwood. But then it seemed I'd come down to Castleton for some other reason—not to hear Second Coming at all but to walk and walk. I found my feet going over the railroad tracks, then across a parking lot, and next thing I knew, I was by myself on the street where all the Italian bakeries are, the other side of the train station. The streets there wind around, with narrow sidewalks and old street-car tracks coming up through the asphalt. Somehow, no matter which of them you follow, you go past the same crumbling brick buildings with their same potted plants over the storefronts. Back in those days, just as the streets unwound, you ended up in the flat space of the Main Mall.

The Main Mall was built before anyone had figured out what a mall should be. It's been torn down since, to make way for a sort of tinselly convention center. It was never covered, for one thing—just this street with curbs and trees planted at either end, so cars wouldn't drive down it anymore. And already by that spring, half the stores in it had been boarded up. Down at the end there was a pizza place with a lit sign, and overhead there were these really dim streetlamps. Stepping over the curb onto the walkway, I smelled beer and an ashy dampness, like someone had had a fire going in the middle of the open space a while back and snuffed it out.

The Main Mall was a place you weren't supposed to go, but nobody I knew did anyhow because there wasn't any action. Whoever had built it had fucked up, that was all. But now while my friends were listening to songs about thighs and knives and JoAnn and Darryl were figuring a soft quiet place to get laid, I just wanted something old and seedy. I wove in and out of the black lampposts, slapping them with my palms—right, left, me and the posts like Maypole dancers. Their hollow insides rang out. Almost no other sound invaded the Mall, just traffic from Van Dyke Boulevard a few blocks away and a jukebox, probably at the pizza place. No voices. A couple of black guys went shuffling by, sticking close to the buildings like beetles. At one point I passed an alley, and when I glanced in—the gray light barely shining that way from the lamppost—there was this woman glaring at me. At first I thought she was one of those store mannequins, thrown out, but she was smoking a cigarette and I could see the smoke. I started weaving a little faster, and then the troll came out of the shadows.

I picked him for a troll right away. There I was, still slapping the lampposts, when he comes strolling down the middle of the mall as cool as you please and stops to whistle at me. Then he turns my way and sidles over. He had this very flat head that came up to about my neck, and he'd combed his hair far over the way men do when they think they can fake not being bald. He was wearing a madras suit, and I remember thinking he must be sweating inside it; I could smell those dyes, the way they stink. "Girlie," he says to me. "Girlie, slow down."

Now I wasn't completely street-stupid; I never would have agreed to meet some guy from a modeling agency in a motel. Plus I'd been around that part of Castleton before, waiting for my mom to get off work. But I could have knocked this guy down with my pinky finger, and whatever I smell in the air it's not rape. So I go, "Whatcha want?" and I let my hand glide over the next lamppost.

"Yustle?" he says. I don't get it, so I stare. "Yustle?" he says again, and wrinkles gather in the center of his troll forehead, like he's trying to talk to a foreigner. "C'mon," he says. "Do me for fifty. Quick, like five minutes. I got a rubber."

So it dawns on me he's asking if I *hustle*, that he wants me to fuck him for money. Hey! says molasses brain. This is prostitution! Sure enough he's pulling out two greasy twenties and a ten, like I wouldn't believe him. The next lamppost I don't go past, just swing and swing around, slow.

"Like, where?" I say, and I could have kicked myself for saying that. If I'd been a real prostitute I'd have had a place to go.

"Verona," he says, and his anvil of a head jerks in the direction of the pizza place. "I got a room there," he says, so I figure he doesn't mean the pizza place but a hotel somewhere, the other side. This little whistle-sound kept coming out of his mouth, like there was a blowhole in there.

"That's not enough," I say, looking down at his bills. It was his hands that really reminded me of a troll. One of them was missing the pinky, and they were both gnarled up and blotchy.

"Whatcha want?" he says, and his blowhole wheezes. "Hunderd?" He sticks the other paw in his back pocket and comes out with a billfold.

And I'm thinking about JoAnn's pregnancy, how we can wipe it away. Also about my dad: *Certain things are in nature* had been sticking in my craw, I was sick of being a virgin. I didn't see this troll as a hip-breaker. And he'd said he had a rubber. I'm thinking, Maybe he'll do it and then not pay; but then I figured I could get the money up front. He's wheezing, waiting.

"Hundred fifty," I say. That plus the first week or two of day camp ought to do it.

"Aw, girlie." He looks sad, but I hang tough.

"You get what you pay for."

"C'mon. Hunderd and dinner. You could do with a square meal, hunh?" In and out went the air. If I have to eat with him, I thought, I'll puke.

"Hundred fifty." I turn my head. A sort of warbly echo fills the air: the concert, upping the decibels. When I turn back he's in front of me. He reaches his little troll arm up, then he pulls at my neck. Then he kisses me on the lips. It's wet, it's licoricey, it's rancid, I hate it. His tongue pushes at my teeth.

"Ya got no mouth," he wheezed when he let me go. "That kinda dough, ya gotta work your tongue." He looked up at me, giving advice. In the gray light his skin looked like fish scales. Then he turned and shuffled away. I'm fourteen! I almost yelled at him. I'm a virgin! But I didn't know if I wanted him to meet my price or if I wanted to get him arrested. Anyhow he was gone, and someone was giggling. I whipped around and saw this couple holed up in the entranceway of a jewelry store, passing a paper bag back and forth. They were into each other, but they might have heard. I looked down at my sweatshirt, my slashed jeans hanging on me: maybe the whole thing was a joke. Whores wear makeup, like the woman in the alley; she was a whore. What a crock of an idea.

The streetlights dimmed as I looked up at them. Power black-out, I thought. And the amps'll go down on Second Coming, and there'll be a riot, just what this town needs. I started walking fast away from the Main Mall, in the direction of the music, but the streets all dead-ended into parking garages or fenced-off con-struction. One of my sandals had a loose sole, so I wasn't walking right—it gave this soft little flap with each step—and my feet started to hurt. I sank down in a corner once and cried, and when no one came I got up and banged my fists on the brick wall there, hurting myself on purpose. I started thinking I should have let him do it to me and taken the money, I couldn't feel grubbier and lonelier than this.

By the time I got back to the truck the sole had come off my shoe and I was thirsty. There was a swallow of flat Coke in a bot-tle in the front, and also a blanket, which I laid down in back. It was there I curled up until Lenny Dugliss found me.

"I got an idea," he said, climbing in, "about the stars." This was his way of saying hello.

"How come you're not at the concert?"

"Somebody threw up on me," he said, and showed me his leg.

"God. Get them off."

"I ain't got underpants on."

"You're only twelve, Lenny. What'm I going to do, goose you?"

So he took them off and flopped on his back. "You can't see most of them from here," he said. "My dad says it's the city lights."

"Your dad's right."

"The strong ones make it through, though."

"Yeah, well, they're probably closer to us. So they're brighter."

"Not all of them. Some are real far away. Like Spica—see, up there?—it's almost three hundred light-years. But it's strong, it's first magnitude. Only the countryside's too busy, there're too many of them to pick out the real strong ones, the ones that got something to say."

"Yeah, too busy," I said. "Make me laugh." I sat up and tried to laugh, but it came out *huh, huh*. "So what've they got to tell us here in Castleton?" I asked him.

"They're trying to get us to come out."

"Where?"

"*There,*" he said, like it was something I ought to know by my age. I sprawled on my side and looked at him. His little wang lay between his legs like a slug in the tight spot between two leaves. You wanted to flick it off. I pulled my eyes away and up his shirt to his arm and then his index finger, still pointed at the sky. His thin neck shone white in the dark truck; his face was a shadow with pockets of deeper shadow, like the dark inside of a plaster mask. "I'm going sometime," he said, like he was telling me he was going camping in Maine that summer.

"Yeah?" I said. "Well, take me with you."

When JoAnn got back she looked pretty smeary. Darryl wasn't with her. He was riding home with his friends, praying nobody asked him questions, this wasn't one to brag on. "Where'd you take off to?" she asked me, her breath thick with rum and Coke.

I shot her this little smile, for all the world like we'd been doing the same thing at the same time, me with the troll and her with Darryl, only I'd got paid for it. "Had a ron-day-voo," I said. Behind her swarmed the rest of them, trashed and silly. Lenny and I sat up to make room for them as they clambered into the truck. Charlotte Petersen stepped on my ankle as she made her way over. She gasped, "I'm sorry!" and for a second our eyes locked; I got this sudden sinking sensation way deep in my gut, like it was the troll himself who'd met her from the modeling agency—but before I could do what I wanted, which was just to touch her hand or something, she was down in the dark corner at the far end again, fitted safely into her football player.

Matt McPeck was miming one of the songs; pretending his thighs were congo drums, he was wagging his head and beating on them. Seth had started the engine. Lurching over potholes and train tracks, we moved into the caravan heading north on Route 9. The cold metal of the truck's side banged against the back of my head. Someone had scored a fifth of tequila and was passing it around, but I didn't drink; I'd seen a movie once where this guy had drunk from one of those bottles with a live worm in the bottom, only he'd drunk the worm, too, and the thought of that worm in his mouth and throat had made me so sick I hadn't put the stuff to my lips since.

"What the fuck is that?" said JoAnn after we'd got going.

"Is what?" I said, passing on the bottle.

"What you said."

"Rendezvous," I kind of mumbled, watching little Lenny Dugliss take way too big a swig. It was a nice word, but it wasn't what I'd had. Plus I'd spent twenty-five dollars on the ticket. That was a hundred twenty-five dollars, gonesville.

"Awesome," she said.

This slow, deep wave of regret washed over me as we climbed the hill past the mental hospital and on through the gauntlet that was Windhaven. I needed a joint, but no one was smoking. Glad that it was too dark for anyone to see my face, I let the tears wash over it and into my mouth. So many things could have happened and hadn't. There had to be a way to change the course of things, to make a difference. I tipped my head back the way Lenny had, and let my heart expand into the dark, impenetrable air. Then I felt a slight pressure at my side and looked down. He'd fallen asleep against my rib cage, the little starwatcher—his mouth just open, his face pure as a little kid's. I tucked my arm between his head and the sharp metal, and I felt his weight settle against me.

chapter

The summer camp was named Tortuga, some Indian word, but the six of us who helped out there called it Torture. I'd pulled the ten-year-olds, the Chameleons. Their main counselor was Anne-Marie, who worked the rest of the year with my mom; she had charge not just of them but of the whole camp. Pound-the-counselor was their favorite group sport, with me as substitute for Anne-Marie. When I took off my clothes I looked like an assault victim, unripe plums starting up on my shoulders and thighs. Back at the hamlet JoAnn cracked jokes. "What is it, one o'clock archery, two o'clock S and M, three o'clock first aid?" she said.

"Four o'clock birth control," I shot back.

"Five o'clock missionary position!" she howled. She thought everything was funny, even this baby she wasn't going to have out.

I have to admit, I admired how she kept getting fatter—beyond the baby, I mean. Her mom was so mad at her she'd made JoAnn let out all her own clothes. Seth Dugliss must have figured he made a narrow escape. He was sitting splay-legged outside Gray's store the first time I decided to go back in there, the week Camp Torture started. I had to step around him to reach the door. "Hey Stick," he said.

"Hey, asshole," I said.

"Doing the big no-no, huh?"

"It's a free country." I looked down at his leg, which was still stuck out, making it hard to get the door open. I was already nervous. The idea was to get inside the place, where no one would see me from the other side of the checked window curtains. Not to freeze the frame here, on my way in.

"I hear you're up at that camp, where my kid brother's at."

"Could you move your foot?"

"Ain't you a a little young to be a counselor?"

"I dunno," I said. I looked down at the foot again; his jeans were muddy toward the bottom, his leather high-tops cracked where the toes bent. He didn't need to know what I did. "Ain't you a little old to be a high school junior?" I retorted.

"You little bitch," he said, moving the foot. "I was trying to be friendly."

"Yeah, well, get friendly with your own type," I said, stepping around him. "Plenty in that bait shop up on 9G."

His mouth dropped open just a little, and for that second he looked like a gangly country boy, all ears and badly cut hair and sunburn. But in the next second I was past him, through the door into the store, and words he flung at me from the other side were like some bad TV show going on in the next room. No matter what he said, I reminded myself, he'd screwed JoAnn and run.

And I was inside that dark cool place, that place I'd already started packing away with my childhood. Behind me the bell had tinkled. Then the door shut, and you could hear the latch click. There wasn't any sound in there, no voices. Now, I knew already a few people had been shopping there. People like old Miss Flanagan, who didn't have a car; people like Seth Dugliss who didn't give a shit. But they went in one at a time, not in a bunch the way we used to, with all the grown-ups catching up on the dirt and the kids cadging each other for candy money. I didn't see Gray, so I just went to the dairy case for a pint of milk—it was fresh, and there were some quarts and half-gallons there too, all that week's date—and then up to the register to wait for my cigs.

I was into Virginia Slims since camp had started, and I could see them there, in a special case left of the register. But I'd already decided Gray's was not the place to rip off, and you don't just grab for cigs; you wait. So I stood there feeling stupider by the second.

"Aw, forget it," I finally said out loud. Then there was the sound of wood creaking, and the trapdoor that led to the cellar opened, and Gray's son, Benjy, appeared, hauling up a sack of potatoes.

"Hey, Gwyn Stickley," he said slowly, which was already weird because he'd always called me Stick. "What can I do you for? Hang on a sec."

"Where's your dad, Benjy?" I said.

"Had to go downtown." He set the sack down and dusted off his hands. It was hard to watch Benjy do anything. Not that he was clumsy or spastic or anything; but nothing about him seemed completely formed. Like he was made of clay, with lumpy parts here and there, still soft. He took off his baseball cap, scratched his head, and replaced it. His hair underneath was sand color, like mine, only curly, a little too long on top, matted by the cap. The cap seemed part of his uniform, along with the gray sweatshirt and the red handkerchief that hung out of his back jeans pocket. His lower lip stuck out just a little, like he was pouting; he'd suck it in when he started to talk, though, and you could tell his mind was divided as to whether he should concentrate on controlling his mouth or on getting out the words he needed. Today we have a dozen words for what had held Benjy back; in those days, *re-tarded* pretty much covered it. "What can I do you for?" he said again, sucking in the lip.

"Just some Slims regular, Benjy," I said. "They're the ones in the brown stripe pack, behind the counter here."

"I know that," he said. But he went on down the aisle, straightening cans.

"And this milk here, too."

"Gotcha," he said from down by the beer case.

I was getting nervous; someone could see in through those curtains, if they cared to. "I can come back later," I said.

"Naw, naw. I just had to find these olives, here." He reappeared, and finally came round back of the counter. He was smiling at the jar in his hand. "Got a call from Miss Flanagan, she said save the extra-large pitted for her."

His eyes were a light blue and almost perfectly round, like my mother's, only veiled by heavy, sleepy lids. My dad had said they kept him on medication.

"Virginia Slims," I reminded him.

"Yup," he said, reaching up; then he must have caught the look in my eye because he added, "They ain't stale, Gwyn," as he put them down.

"You charging one fifty?" I said. "Minimart's up to that."

"Nah, my pop says one forty. Your mama get that job she was after?"

"Yeah, she heard last week."

"Well. You oughta be proud," he said. And he grinned like I'd shown him a prize I'd won. "My pop says to con—con—"

"Gratulate her," I said. "I sure will." I took my change, and it wasn't until I was out the door that I wondered how Benjy knew about the new job, or anything outside those walls. He'd been out of school for years—there wasn't much they could do with him, there. He'd spent his time either at the store or volunteering with the fire department, until the guys there voted him out because of the charges against him and Gray. For a while he'd been a kind of pal to Lenny Dugliss—Lenny was too smart for his age, I guess, and Benjy too stupid, so they met in the middle. Other than that, he just shadowed Gray. Only I recalled, thinking it through as I stepped out into the warm air, that Gray had a talent for knowing other people's business just out of breathing the same air they did. All he had to do was pass the news on to Benjy.

Seth Dugliss lifted himself off the stoop and went in for his turn. Watching him, I figured I might as well come back. Nothing terrible had happened. A few packs of cigs plus the occasional root beer could hardly be called supporting the store. So I went on my way, and next day I did pretty much the same thing.

"I'm not saying he's gonna rape her in broad daylight," my dad said to my mom when they got wind of it. This was after two weeks of camp counseling. My mom had started her new job, which came out of the grant money she'd been after for so long;

she was running a shelter for homeless and beat-up people, in a new building just south of Windhaven. "Just, it makes it look like we're taking some stand on this thing. I got no stand on this thing. Either Gray abused 'em or he didn't abuse 'em, and the court's gonna decide, and meantime there's plenty places to shop."

"What do you want me to do?" my mom said. "Make the place off limits? Tell her we're judge and jury?"

"I never liked that guy," said my dad, which was his way of answering her no. "Too nice to everybody. How come he couldn't have no natural children?"

"His wife—"

"She's not that little. She could of done it. Naw, Harlett's put his finger on it. They wanted something from the world, those two."

They were talking late at night, of course; those days my mom didn't get home until just before my dad did. I'd had frozen pizza on my own for supper, and now I was supposed to be in dreamland. There weren't so many fighting words in their talk as there used to be; I hadn't heard *divorce* for months. Now they just harped on Gray. Harping on Gray helped them get along; and the reason they and everybody were after Gray was he'd wanted something from the world. Well okay, so did I.

The next day, Tuesday of the third camp week, dawned hazy and heavy: thunderstorm weather. JoAnn had given me five bucks to buy beer at the end of the day. She'd been hitting her father's case in the basement pretty hard, I guess; anyhow she wanted to try a more legit source. I tucked the bill into the back pocket of my jeans before I set out. We'd talked about doing this a bunch of times before Gray ran into trouble, but we always figured we needed to wait till we were driving age. But now, who knew how much longer Gray'd be around?

I rode my bike to the camp, the only part of the day I liked, pulling out of the hamlet on Old Post Road and then ducking

onto the new road into the state park they'd built by the river, all
the low areas still blanketed with fog early in the morning so you
had to trust the bike like a horse to take the bends the right way.
The new marina had just been built, for the weekenders who put-
ter their boats up and down the river, and I usually came out of the
fog the same time I passed above the jetty. I heard the sailboats
like ghost ships down there, metal clips clanking against the
masts, as I scooted out of the park onto Route 9.

It was three miles to Windhaven this way, thirteen to Castleton.
The other side of Castleton was the college my mom had started
to go to, before she met my dad. My idea was I'd get into the college and live down there; and when I finished, some invisible door
the other side of Castleton would swing open and I would step
through it. It wasn't bad, for a fantasy; it even had a chance of happening, back then. At the sign with the Dominican cross I
swerved off Route 9 onto the dirt road and stopped the bike for a
second, catching my balance, before I went on. The sign stayed
because the county was cheap; the Dominicans didn't run the
camp anymore. Everything was county by then, which meant a
couple of potbellied guys who came by once a week or so to check
how Anne-Marie was running things. Anne-Marie was about
thirty—real strong, sort of horsey, except she limped a little on
her left leg and that side of her face was messed up from an accident she'd been in. The skin on it sagged like a week-old balloon;
when I talked to her I didn't look straight at it, but sort of up to
her forehead or her hair, which was thick and cut almost like a
boy's, just coming a little over her ears. But she was getting her
nursing degree and you could tell the door was opening for her,
she'd be out of here before long. The day before, she'd told me
she was getting married in the fall, and I decided that if she could
get a guy to marry her with a face like that, she could do anything,
even if she was a Quaker. So the bike ride and Anne-Marie, those
were the pluses of my job.

The Chameleons were waiting for me on the benches by the
softball field. "Hey Stick, we took a vote," said the worst one—a

button-nosed girl named Tania, who'd already started to sprout breasts. "We forfeit the softball game and head down to Dino's."

"Yeah!" they all yelled.

"Number one, we're not allowed off the grounds," I said, parking the bike. "Number two, I can't drive. Number three, none of you's got any money."

"You dickhead," said Tania.

"You got money, dickhead," chimed in one of her buddies. "You get paid to do this."

"And you're third base," I told her.

"Not me! You seen who's over there?"

I looked over to the pine trees that edged the field. Lenny Dugliss was sitting under the biggest one, a few feet from third base, with a couple of other Rattlesnakes, which is what we called the oldest boys. They were smoking cigarettes, probably stolen from the counselors' tent. He'd been pulling stuff like that since the first day of camp, when he set free the pair of white rats they kept in the nature tent. Tania had said the snake bracelet he wore meant he had fits, and the Chameleons had labeled him Rattle-creep.

"So stand on the other side of the base," I said. "It's not like anyone makes it that far, anyhow."

They groaned; there was some whispering about how they were going to get me later. But I'd smartened up, in two weeks. "Play one more inning and win," I promised Tania at the bottom of the fourth—we were up against the ten-year-old boys, the Dragonflies, who were pretty easy to beat—"and we can go hang in the Ping-Pong tent."

"All *right*," she said, and whispered to the others. Ten minutes later we were perched on the Ping-Pong tables, drinking lemonade and talking about boys.

Basically, I told them lies. I felt bad, letting them think that even a twerp like me could have sex—but it was one way to keep from getting beat up, and they drank in every word I said. Plus Anne-Marie usually walked by while we were sitting there. She'd see them all quiet and focused on me, and she wouldn't rope us into some asinine project like making piñatas.

I just told them stuff JoAnn had told me. I didn't tell them about the troll on the Main Mall or anything like that. Once, I said there was a tall, dark junior who took me for a ride in his car after Spring Fling, but I only let him get to third base; another time I told them about a couple of guys who practically raped me at the Second Coming concert. That day, in the Ping-Pong tent, I got going on Florida, confessed I'd lost my virginity to a gentle boy from California up on the hotel roof, the night before the Challenger went off. It sounded pretty romantic, to me.

"Yeah, well, you know Christa finally had an orgasm that day," said one pudgy girl from the other Ping-Pong table. "It was that final rocket booster that did it." She paused here, for effect. "As she came she went," she finally said, and the whole circle of them burst out laughing.

"Jesus," I said. "You're fucking ten years old. Where'd you learn the word *orgasm*?"

"MTV," said Tania.

"I just think that's so cool," said another, "that video where Madonna tells her dad she's keeping her baby?"

"Ah'm keepin' mah bay-bee," they started to sing.

But I'd put a damper on the day, reminding them how young they were. The rest of the morning they acted out, threw around the potatoes from the little kids' potato race, punched me on the arm, that kind of thing. But what kind of joke was that? What the hell did they know about the face of God?

I rode home under a hot sun, in sixth gear, pedaling furiously down the slope toward the marina. Tania's mother, seven months pregnant and fit to be tied, had stopped in that afternoon; I was in a foul mood. A couple cars passed me, towing huge clumsy motorboats, and I had to swerve onto the gravel. "Getcherself a helmet!" one fat guy barked at me. I only paused once, at the grassy knoll near the woods, above the railroad crossing, where I threw the bike down and lay on my back, panting. My shut eyelids were bright red, facing the sun; the sweat from my back trickled along my skin and then down into the grass. I could feel myself turning into a plant, into a rock. Then the bugs smelled my sweat and started buzzing around me. I got back on the bike and coasted down into the hamlet.

I almost forgot to stop at Gray's; it was only seeing Benjy, emptying a box into the Dumpster, that reminded me. As I went in the heavy door I fingered the five in my back pocket. It felt crisp in there, almost phony, like a folded ticket. I hadn't asked JoAnn how she'd got it, or why—I figured her dad had started counting the beer cans in the basement fridge finally, and come up short. And I already knew why she'd dumped this job on me; it was because Gray'd never sell to her, but I had a fighting chance. So I got some Slims and two bags of Skittles, then I let my hand slide around to pull out the five.

"Oh," I said, like I'd almost forgotten, "and my dad asked could I get him a six-pack of Miller. He gets off so late, you know."

Gray gave me that don't-con-me look that people in business put on. Then he saw I had crumply money for the cigs and a crisp bill for the beer; or maybe the town had beat up on him, so he didn't give a shit. For whatever reason he just pulled the pack out of the cooler, no questions. While he was at it I pulled a container of milk from the dairy case and tucked it in my backpack. I made myself look straight in his eyes while I paid for the beer. Then I settled the six-pack into the bike basket and pedaled across the tracks into the woods like a wildcat.

Here's where I was headed. Since school was out and we didn't have any way to get to the Free Zone, JoAnn and I had sort of set up in the abandoned tower at the north side of the Meyenhold mansion. The place was closed that summer for renovations— Seth Dugliss's dad was in charge of fixing it up, but his crew knocked off around two, and the couple of rangers who prowled the woods and the marina never went up that way. There were two huge stones missing at the base of the tower, for a crawl-through, and inside you could look all the way up to where they'd boarded over the burned turret. Light chinked in, white lines down the walls. There were bats, but high up. Otherwise it was perfect.

JoAnn wasn't working that summer. She was supposed to be volunteering for some Gospel theater at the Reach Out for Christ church. Only they didn't call it a church, they called it the Sanctuary, and she'd get driven up there every morning and then either hitch back down here if her mom was working or take the bus to Castleton and do the mall. Once she'd had sex with the guy who was giving her a ride down here. "He couldn't believe I didn't care," she said when she told me about it. "His pecker shrank right up when he saw he didn't have a fight on his hands."

"Was he cute, anyway?"

"Shit, no. He smelled like Listerine, and he had this big droopy mole under his eye, I wanted to bite it off! But Christ, what's one prick, to get where you're going safely? I read about those girls who got theirselves cut up in pieces, across the river a few years back. I ain't some virgin idiot."

At the end of the day she was supposed to take the bus home, so she'd always come walking from that direction. I couldn't believe she got away with this. It just proved again how thick JoAnn's mom was, lucky for JoAnn.

I parked the bike behind the ruined stone wall, way below the mansion, and took the weedier trail up the hill. Usually I liked coming here after camp. I liked walking by old stone walls and ruined gazebos that used to be part of a fancy estate and were getting soaked up by the gnarly trees and the splotchy, moving light and shifting breeze. It was a place to disappear into. But today my own lies and that Challenger joke and Tania's mom had thrown me off. I couldn't disappear, and I wished I'd gone to the mall or something.

Around the bend I saw a couple deer, young ones, and we all froze for a minute. Shafting down between the pines, the light turned them a coppery color; their ears twitched at the bugs, and their nostrils flared, sniffing me. Otherwise they didn't move. I could feel the six-pack, weighing down my left arm, and the candy melting in my pocket. I sniffed at them, too: they smelled like pee and pinecones. Flies were landing on their eyelids, their eyes like huge drops of chocolate, melting. I clucked my tongue, to be friendly, and they bobbed their heads. Then there came another sound—JoAnn, coughing, from just outside the tower. Glaring like I'd double-crossed them, the deer sprang away. It took only a few seconds for them to disappear in the trees. Birds rushed from tree to tree over my head, making little sounds in their throats, and I went on up to where the path gave onto the open hill.

"I could eat a cow," JoAnn said, when I'd scooted the six-pack in and followed after. "It's amazing. The more I eat the more I can eat. You wonder if it ever stops."

"I just got Skittles," I said. I was blinking; my eyes had to adjust, from the bright sunlight.

"And beer."

"Yeah, but I don't want to do that again, he's creepy about it. Oh, and I fingered some milk."

"For you," she said.

"Uh-uh. And no Skittles till you drink it."

"Who's having this kid, you or me?"

"You don't feed it, it'll suck the calcium outta your bones," I said. I handed her the carton. "Good girl. Now here's the Skits."

"Gimme a brew first, I gotta wash the taste of this shit out."

"You're in a great mood."

"Yeah, well." JoAnn tipped the bottle back. "Pastor Gwilliam says he's gonna tell my mom I never make rehearsal. It's not like he needs me—Christ! I play a frigging junkie, I lie around till I see the light, then I jump up and dance to this Jesus Christ music with all the others. The asshole just wants me there to paint sets."

"So what're you gonna do?"

She poured some Skittles and held them out. I shook my head. "He doesn't want to go to bed with me," she said.

"It can't get you everything," I said.

"So I told him I'd come for a week solid and paint the set, and

I didn't care about really being in the thing. And he's got plenty of pretend junkies." She popped open another beer. "He says he'll think about it, but I may be screwed."

I lit a cigarette and opened a beer. Inside the tower the air was cooler, moist. We'd done some decorating. JoAnn's sister's old bedspread, wedged between stones in four spots, made a sort of bat-free ceiling, and scattered all over the round dirt floor of the tower were a dozen beanbag chairs we'd found in the dumping ground where the train station used to be. They were all colors— pink, purple, one striped lime green and black; they looked like beat-up Christmas packages. I'd brought my cassette deck and tapes—Second Coming, plus a series I'd ordered from a catalog on tap dancing.

Who can tap? the ad had read. *Anyone who can walk*. Ever since the Spring Fling, I'd felt this new sort of jumpiness in my legs. I'd never been real coordinated, like for sports, but there had been another big dance at the end of the school year, and another group had sort of pushed me onto the floor by myself, and my legs had gone at it, again. So what the hell, I'd thought. The series was only thirteen bucks, they mostly wanted you on their mailing list for other junk. And the big yellow book that came with the tap dance tapes had great pictures of Tommy Tune in a tux, looking like he was made of India rubber and always grinning. I'd found a big piece of plywood near the tower, and when JoAnn wasn't around I'd put on the tapes and practice—*step, step, rattle, rattle, brush, ball, change!* In the fall I was going to take lessons, which I hadn't told JoAnn about.

"Tania's mom came to the camp today," I said.

"How come?"

"To pull her out. She said it wasn't a healthy atmosphere, that Tania was coming home singing dirty songs."

"Hey, Goody Two-Shoes, whatcha been teaching them?" JoAnn grinned like she'd just opened a box of chocolate, all caramels and no creams.

"Teach? Christ! What do you teach ten-year-olds who start the day singing, 'Boom, boom, ain't it great to be bum-fucked'?"

"So—don't tell me—Anne-Marie fired you, and now you can come to play rehearsals with me!"

"Naw, she didn't fire me. But I had to apologize to this lady's face."

"I'd of spit in it."

"Naw. I said, 'Yes ma'am, I agree that "Roll Me Over in the Clover" is not appropriate for camp singing.' I said we'd learned it in Florida before the Challenger blew up."

"Bet that set her back a notch." JoAnn grinned, proud of me.

"Yeah, but you know, JoAnn." I blew out smoke, rolled the ash of the cigarette against the edge of an empty tuna can. "It really freaked me out, to look at this lady."

"Why? She was swinging a hatchet, or what?"

"No, no." With my free hand I hugged my knees. "It's just—I was apologizing to her belly, it felt like, JoAnn. I mean, she was way, way pregnant. I couldn't even believe she was walking around in that heat," I said, "much less letting herself get so pissed off. I think I saw her baby kick under her dress." JoAnn had rolled away, on the beanbags; she was putting in a new tape. "JoAnn, can we talk about this baby?"

"Who, hers?"

"No, yours."

"No."

There was a rustling outside, and then the low opening where the stones were gone went dark. We looked at each other but sat still. Gray, I thought. He's followed me, checking on the beer. And the weird thing was I hoped he'd heard us, heard the word *baby*.

"C'mon, you guys," came a voice—warbly, about to crack: Lenny Dugliss.

"Look," I said as he stuck his head in, "we're talking here."

"Naw, really? I thought it was rats." He bent his lean body down, scooched through. His hair hung over his eyes, which blinked in the dim light. There was something wrong-looking about his face.

"This is the place that girl set on fire," he said, looking up at the bedspread. "I wouldn't build it again, if I was them."

"Whaddayou want, Lenny?" I said.

"Gotta sit down," he said. Dropping his backpack, he sank onto a purple-flowered beanbag.

"What the fuck happened to your face?" asked JoAnn.

"Ran into a door," he said, trying to sound eighteen and sounding about eight. "Are you pregnant?"

"Have been," said JoAnn.

"Jesus," I said. "What're you blowing it to him for?"

JoAnn opened the second bag of Skittles. "He ain't got a mouth," she said. "Do you, honey?"

"My brother do it?" Lenny asked.

"Well now, that's a matter of opinion."

"I can just leave right now," I said.

" 'Cause he says"—Lenny flicked the hair from his eyes, and I made out the plum-colored welt on his cheekbone; I was getting familiar with that color, myself—"if you ain't gonna use that money he give you to take it out, he'd like it back. The money, I mean."

"He never gave me no money," JoAnn said. "And I had it out yesterday. I'm resting up."

"I thought you told him it was a false alarm," I said.

"Looks like he didn't believe me," said JoAnn.

"Well, I gotta—" Lenny's eyes flitted about the tower, like he was looking for an answer somewhere in the chinks of the granite. His fingernails were long as ever, but clean today: you could tell he'd taken care, used an orange stick. "You got any proof?" he said.

"You gonna do something about that bruise?" JoAnn answered back.

"Wasn't Seth who give it to me," Lenny said, shaking his hair down over his face. He tipped his head back onto the beanbag. For a minute there he looked so little, with his ears too big for his head and his T-shirt hanging off his shoulders, I forgot how he once burned a mouse in my church or how I'd thought he looked like a witch. He made me think again of Angelina, and how Gray had maybe hurt her and I'd never know. There were two beers left in the six-pack. I took one and went over to Lenny, and pushed his black hair aside and set it against his cheek. He tried to pull away, but I held his head. "It's cold," I said. "It'll keep the swelling down."

"What'm I gonna do now?" he said, looking up at me like I'd given him a set of instructions to start with.

"My mom," I started. "My mom's got this place, this shelter south of Windhaven—"

"My old man never hits me," JoAnn interrupted. She'd opened a comic book, *Amazon Woman*, and spread it on the ground. "I won't let him."

"Give us a break," I said under my breath.

Lenny jerked his head away, to size up JoAnn. "Seth said I could get money from you," he said.

"Well he never gave it," she repeated. Three candy wrappers and three beer cans lay in front of her, plus the milk. She was looking a little green. "You can just remind him of that for me," she said.

"I ain't no messenger," said Lenny, and leaned into the cold can I held to his cheek. "Got my own messages," he said, and his good eye winked. Then he shut both of them. Before I knew what to think, his breathing went even and shallow.

"He's asleep," I said to JoAnn.

"So? Let him." She sucked on her beer and turned a comic book page. "His brother never give me a dime, the cheap shit."

"What if he's had a concussion?"

"A what?"

"You know. When you get hit on the head. And the blood—" I had to bite my lips, I got this image of what happened, inside. "The blood sort of floods your brain, and it's okay if you keep going, but if you fall asleep you're screwed."

"Who told you this? Counselor training?"

"No. Gray. He says a washing machine clocked him on the head once when he was unloading it for his dad's store, and he felt so clumsy he didn't tell anybody, but he went to bed that night and fell into a coma for five weeks."

"And you believe that," said JoAnn, sounding like her mother, "you do."

"No," I said. I felt like I was talking underwater, the tower was so cool and the day outside so heavy, the insects droning beyond the stone walls. I just kept holding the beer can against Lenny Dugliss's sleeping cheek. "Shouldn't we shake him, or something?"

"In a while," said JoAnn, turning the next page. "He's a wasted little bugger, though, ain't he?"

I pressed the can closer, and when I shut my eyes I seemed to see blood back of the lids, bursting out of the veins, washing through.

We left him there, finally. I shook him a few times but he wouldn't wake, and when we'd finished the six-pack JoAnn was sick.

"Gross," I said.

She'd heaved the Skittles and some other stuff onto some loose dirt against the wall, and she was kicking it covered, like a cat. "C'mon," she said. She led the way, hands and knees, out the opening.

In the woods, the crickets had started up; the whole world was thick and green, so many things growing so close together. There was no sign of the deer. "I gotta come from the right direction," JoAnn was saying. "They already know I'm jerking them around."

She moved off down the path. "I'm gonna get my mom," I said, following her, "for Lenny." But JoAnn didn't hear me. Her mind was on other things, on the lies she had to tell.

chapter 9

It was almost a year exactly since the accident had happened to Lenny's big brother. Not Seth but the oldest one, Nate—by all accounts the best of them, if you had to rate a Dugliss. He was usually in charge, which is why I blamed him most for trashing my barn loft. But he could turn things around, too. It was Nate who taught me how to ride ice on the golf course, that same summer when I was nine and he was going on fourteen, and he took me up to the top of the hill just like he owned the place. It was Nate (or at least I'd heard it was Nate) who had finally started kicking Seth's ass for screwing up at school. It was Nate they followed that Fourth of July, while we were all on the lawn by the church finishing up hot dogs and waiting for it to get dark enough for Gray's fireworks. In fact it seemed like it was for Nate that the siren had gone off suddenly and the fire truck had come careening out of the firehouse and down Old Post Road. He took off the second we heard it, with Seth and Lenny streaming behind. And no matter how many times anyone tries to replay what happened, to change the ending, you can't put Nate in a place where he isn't out front, in charge of his own short future.

That was before so many things. Before the weekend people gave up on cobblestoning Old Post Road and let it go back to the cracked-up asphalt they like to criticize so much. Before the charges came down on Gray and all the foster kids left. Before anybody had heard of Christa McAuliffe. And of course before JoAnn had gotten knocked up. I'd sat next to her and watched them hop the back of the fire engine—first Nate, then Seth;

Lenny didn't run fast enough to make it on. I saw old man Dugliss tear after them, calling them punk brats. It was all like a dream, moving slow, with nothing to be afraid of. On the church driveway, I remember, the asphalt shimmered; the air smelled of hot dogs and stale beer. Gray was over by the golf course, setting up his annual fireworks show. He was the head of the rescue squad then, and everyone trusted him; we'd each chipped in two bucks for the fireworks. When the Dugliss boys went by I guess he yelled at them to get the hell off that truck. By then they'd gone past the crowd anyway, and the fun part was over, so they did it. They did what he said, they jumped.

The road was all torn up then, for the cobblestones. Wherever they landed was bound to be rough. Seth just rolled and rolled and ended up in a hedge. But Nate hardly rolled at all. He landed in a dusty patch, flat on his back, and by the time we got there, Gray was at his side and ripping Nate's shirt off. He balled up a fist on Nate's chest, then wham! hit that fist with his other fist, so hard that Nate's arms and legs flopped up and down just like a rag doll's. Then he did it again, wham! and again, wham!

"Stop it!" yelled old man Dugliss. We'd all run over by then; only the fire truck had gone on with business. "Stop it, you sonofabitch! You're killing him!"

But Gray didn't stop hitting Nate. He yelled a couple times for the rescue squad ambulance, but other than that he just kept slamming Nate and leaning on him until his own face was red and there were three men keeping Dugliss off him.

And that was how Nate died. They said it was something to do with his heart, something weird like it missed a beat when he went down from the fire truck. It was like one chance out of a zillion. For a long time after that day, I went to sleep with my hand in that spot under my jaw where you can feel your pulse, trying to feel if it would miss. But even though everyone said the trouble had been waiting there, in Nate's heart, you got this feeling they blamed Gray. And maybe he did fuck up. Maybe that was why, when I first came out of the woods and saw him standing there on the porch steps, just watching for me, I didn't rush to tell him Lenny Dugliss might be in a coma, up at the Meyenhold tower. I should have; but I just waved at him from my bike and swung over to my empty house. I parked and went into our kitchen, where the phone was.

Ben, my mom's assistant, answered the phone. "Haven House," he said. Haven House was its name, this shelter my mom had got money to set up in a defunct elementary school just past the last strip of stores in Windhaven. Ben was Anne-Marie's boyfriend; he'd done a double major in prelaw and social work and was so smart and good that he made me nervous. I asked for my mom and he said she wasn't there, she'd driven down to Castleton to file some papers. "She said she'd be back by six," he went on. "Which I hope, because I've been here since eight this morning. You want me to give her a message?"

"Yeah," I said. "Well, no, not exactly. It's pretty complicated. Maybe just tell her to call me."

"You okay, Stick?"

"I'm fine. Just tell her to call, okay?" There didn't seem much more to do, when I hung up. I didn't want to go back to the tower, to find Lenny still unconscious there. I took a shower. I got out *Sentence Diagrams* and diagramed the lyrics of "Tea for Two." At six-thirty I called Haven House again, and Anne-Marie answered.

"I'm keeping Ben company," she said, laughing. "We ordered a pizza."

"You heard from my mom?"

"Are you kidding? She's probably found some councilman to keep late, haranguing him for funds. I could drive up there, if you need something, Stick."

"No, no. Just didn't know what she wants me to cook for supper."

"I'll bring you some pizza."

"No, that's okay."

I went outside. The street was baked dry in the long summer sun. If the store had been open, it would have been just closing, now: suppertime. I had never paid too much attention to what kept my mom at Haven House until late in the evening. I was old enough to stay home by myself, that was all that mattered. But now she wasn't at Haven House, she was out with a fat councilman in Castleton when I needed her—*her*, not anyone else. I paced around the house; I looked out the front window toward the woods that blocked our view of the mansion, hoping to see Lenny Dugliss walk out from there. My mom was out with a councilman, and Christ only knew what she was doing with him. The lingerie I'd noticed last year, the perfumed talc, all came back to mind, tied neatly together. I paced faster. My eyes kept flicking to the phone; I was ready to hit it, the way Brer Rabbit hits the tar baby because it won't speak. Finally I picked up a little crystal bird my mom kept on the bookshelf behind the TV.

It was a dove, its body fat and round. She used to keep it on the coffee table, until one day she came home to find the table smoking: the light passing through the crystal was setting the wood on fire. She moved it to the bookshelf, out of the sun; it had been there ever since. Just a few months before, she'd told me it came from an old boyfriend, long before my dad, the one who turned her to Quakerism. I held the dove in my hand; it was heavy and smooth. I paced around like that for a while. Lenny was in a coma in the Meyenholds' charred tower, and my mom was nowhere, worse than nowhere.

I stopped at the door, facing the windows, where the dying light filtered in orange. I felt the anger rise in me, like fire catching onto paper. Then I flung the crystal dove at the standing globe in the corner, and bolted out the door, running toward Gray's.

After I'd leaned on the bell for a good minute and a half, Gray's wife came downstairs from the apartment they kept over the store. When she opened the door her eyes blinked in the sunshine; her face was pinched and pale.

"I got to talk to Mr. Gray, ma'am," I said. I tried to sound like a Bible salesman, but my breath came short and fast.

"He's sleeping," she said. "Something you need at the store?"

"No, I just— Please, Mrs. Gray, I didn't come to bother him. It's important."

"Well, I'll see," she said, and climbed back upstairs on her little bird-legs in their beige panty hose. Slowly the door swung shut in my face. I stood there waiting for Gray while the sun disappeared suddenly behind a mass of dark clouds, a thunderstorm brewing behind my back. It had been thunderstorm weather since morning.

"Hey Stick," Gray said, stepping out. "Need something else for your dad?" He winked at me, I think, but I couldn't appreciate the joke.

"There's not time, Mr. Gray. It's about Lenny Dugliss," I said. "I guess his dad or someone beat him up."

He closed the door behind him and was moving already to the gravel drive. "Where is he?"

"Up the hill," I said to his back. "At the Meyenhold place."

"We'll take the jeep then." He started it up, and I climbed in the passenger side. I didn't think you could take a car along the shortcut, through the woods. Dust blew up all around us. He hammered questions at me over the motor, and I answered. But he never asked why I'd come to him, and it wasn't until we'd parked the jeep by the iron fence at the mansion that he asked me how long it'd been since I saw Lenny fall asleep.

"Around three, sir," I said. "JoAnn was due home. Don't tell her folks, though, because—"

"Three! Shit, Stick!" He spun round and caught me by the upper arm. It was the first time I'd heard Gray swear. His hand on my arm was trembling. "Your brain shrunk up in that skinny body of yours? That's almost four goddamn hours!"

"I know, I was trying to call my mom at Haven House, and they said she'd be back—"

"One year since Nate, and now this." He was cutting up toward the tower.

"But this ain't your fault, Mr. Gray. It's my fault, I knew he was here—"

He stopped. The sky had gone almost black already, but I could still see his face flashing light. It was concentrated in his forehead, just over that straight nose of his, and his skin pulled back over his cheekbones.

"Christ!" I said. "Don't stop now! I mean, it's just around the corner—"

"That was not *my fault*," he said. I'd have thought he was mad at me, but he wasn't even talking in my direction, he was talking at the great gray building, like he was reciting. "I took CPR, and I did CPR on that boy, and I did it by the book, and nobody else did a damn thing, and that boy died. Now this whole town full of sapsuckers can just get off my back. I did it right, can't anybody get that clear?"

His voice had cracked. When he turned to me he wasn't mad—just freaked, just not ready for this one. "I can," I said. "Can we just have a look at Lenny now, please?"

But Lenny wasn't there.

"I guess he's okay, then," I said. I picked up the flashlight we always left and flicked it around. Above the cotton bedspread, you could hear the soft bats, fluttering upward. "I guess he went along home."

"Would you let up on the guessing a little bit, girl?" Gray said. He'd never called me girl; only the quaver in his voice took the sting out of it. He'd come through the opening on his belly. Now he took the light from me and shone it like a detective: at the comic books and the candles stuck in old bottles of Ripple wine, at my portable tape player and JoAnn's poster that she'd sent away for to *Playgirl*, at the rolling papers and beer cans—his beer cans—on a milk crate between beanbags. No Lenny. "C'mon to Dugliss's with me, I am not facing that maniac alone."

"I gotta get home," I said, but he didn't hear me. "Look," I said. Now that Lenny wasn't lying dead in the tower, I wasn't worried about him anymore. I was afraid of Lenny's dad. Mr. Dugliss always walked with his head thrust forward, like a dog, and he drove his fancy new van like the weekenders, too fast down Old Post

Road. "Either Lenny's home and catching it," I told Gray, "or he's hiding. You don't want to get in more trouble than you're in around here, do you?"

Gray whipped around, huge. He might have had his palm lifted; I know something made me flinch, realizing I couldn't just run out of there. But then that arm dropped, and he shone the flashlight at the low opening. "Let's go," he said. When I caught up to him on the grass he said quietly, "I don't suppose you know that boy's condition, do you, Stick?"

"I told you," I said. "He's beat up."

"He is also diabetic. You know what that means?"

"Means something's wrong with—with your blood," I mumbled. I could feel it on the insides of my elbows: the skipped heartbeat, the blood gone bad.

"If he don't get his insulin on time he'll faint. He might even go in a coma. I been watching him on sweets since he was eight years old, and he's sly, too. Now you're not an adult so no one else will, but if that boy dies I am holding, holding you"—he bit his lip, I had come to him and he didn't want to draw a bead on me—"holding you personally responsible. I am not taking the rap on this one. Now get your skinny butt in the car."

As we pulled into Dugliss's driveway the storm started up—lightning cutting over the golf course, and that metallic taste in the air, and fat raindrops slicking down our hair. Lenny wasn't home. As soon as I saw old Dugliss light into Gray, though, I knew Lenny wasn't the half of it. He started right away on Nate, on how Gray'd killed Nate and now he was after letting Lenny die in the tower. We kept telling him we'd searched, the kid wasn't there, but you could tell what he was thinking—the girl, ghosts, curses. When he quieted down Gray made me tell my bit, and I said how I'd been hanging in the tower and he'd crawled in with that swollen cheekbone—Dugliss didn't wince at that—and I put a cold Coke to it and then he fell asleep. I left out JoAnn, the beer, the cigs, all the stuff that didn't matter and spelled trouble. Dugliss believed me about as much as you'd be-

lieve NASA. Meantime Seth was on the phone, getting out the
rescue squad.

That night still comes back to me, now, in dreams where the air
is charged with the storm passing through, the wind coming from
the north down the river to sweep the rain, at first across our faces
and finally out of the valley. I'm always heading out with the rest
of them, people from the hamlet in hooded raincoats, without
faces, their shapes backlit by the lightning receding over the low
hills to the southeast. There's always this low mist around all the
bushes and weedy forest bottom. And I wake up unsure what it is
we've all been searching for—until I go back over days and weeks
and finally years, and remember.

One of the searchers had Lenny's insulin, from his dad. He
didn't need a hit until morning, they said, but just in case he'd
had a sugar reaction, or something. Another one carried orange
juice. The fire department came, hoisted a ladder, shone
torches everywhere around the upper part of the tower—he
couldn't have climbed, no footholds. Meantime the rest of the
mansion blazed with light. The park rangers who'd arrived
checked it for broken windows, forced doors; they beat around
the thick bushes that hugged the foundation. The old place was
tight as a drum, was what they reported. He had to be in the
woods.

By the time it was pitch-black out, there were maybe thirty of
us, all these fuzzy arcs of light flitting like Tinkerbell through the
trees, freaking the deer and shutting up the owls. My mom had
gotten home and followed the crowd up to the mansion. Too late
to help, I told her, and she just pinched her lips together and ran
her eyes over the crowd, trying to pick out old Dugliss. And Gray
was out there too, with Benjy tailing him and no one complaining
about it. People just called one thing, Lenny, so after a while it
wasn't a name or even a word, just this new sound the forest was
making: *Leh-eh-nnee, Leh-eh-nnee.*

•   •   •

My mom made me come home around midnight. She went ahead of me, though, to see if my dad was back, while I picked my way across the railroad tracks and down the hamlet's one street. It was then I spotted Seth Dugliss, with a circle of guys from Windhaven, guys I didn't recognize as part of his rich crowd—these ones had already graduated, I figured, or quit school. They were slouched against Gray's store on the side by the big green Dumpster, passing a bottle around. Which normally I wouldn't have cared about—but I heard Seth laugh, just as I drew near, and it was the kind of stupid, sloppy laugh you get when you aren't thinking about anything but the drinking. Suddenly all the mess, not just of Lenny but of everything that got left to chance and ended by being fucked up, hit me somewhere below my stomach, and I marched over their way. Not thinking, just tired and mad and coming at them.

"Real funny," I said, stopping right in front of Seth. "Him being out there and all because of you."

"What the fuck are you talking about, Skinny Stick?" His head lolled, trying to get a fix on me.

"About your brother, asshole. You're the one sent him to JoAnn and me. And you never even gave her that money, you know you never did. You'd crucify your own brother. God, what a stinking family."

"Hoo, hoo! Who's the girlfriend, Seth man? You've got a live one here!" said one of the other guys. Seth kept looking at me, squinting his eyes like he wanted to make out if I was real.

"You don't want your buddies to know, do you?" I kept on. "Don't want 'em to know you slept with JoAnn, just because she's overweight! Don't want 'em to know you slipped up and got her *pregnant*, do you, Seth Dugliss?" I could hear my own voice, shrill and bratty. I had my hands on my hips, leaning forward.

"I'm a stud," said Seth, and hiccuped. They all laughed.

"Looks like this one's hot for you, man," said another of the guys. They were all in shadow, just a lineup of black jackets and jeans.

"You didn't give the money to *her*, and you didn't give it to *him*, and you're gonna pay the consequences." I couldn't stop, little fool that I was—I had to make an impact.

"Am I." He turned to his friends, and a slow grin spread over his face. It was a big, square face, handsome except for cheeks and lips that were too thick and waxy. "I could think of a few consequences for girls with mouths like this one, hey guys?"

"Hey," said the tallest one, over next to the Dumpster. He started moving my way; the feeling below my stomach turned into a hard knot. Then I heard my mom's voice, calling me from down the road. Just as I turned, a hand gripped my elbow, holding me back.

"I'm wasted, now," came Seth's voice, suddenly near my ear. "But you wanted damage, you got damage. You fucking mention my brother's name, and you'll find out consequences, *Stick*."

"Lenny," I hissed back at him. "Lenny Dugliss. Your brother, your brother, your brother." I tore myself loose, and ran all the way to my house.

If I had known where Lenny was, I wouldn't have set such things in motion. But I was young, and thought I knew right from wrong.

chapter **10**

All the next day it rained. Watching my mom pull away for work, the wipers blinking across the windshield's forehead, I remembered how she used to shoot home early on exactly this kind of rainy, lonely day, how in the late afternoons she used to fix us both a glass of sherry. And it used to be I liked holing up with her like we were roommates, hearing how she'd pierced her ears twelve times before her mother finally let her keep the holes, and then only because there was so much scar tissue building up; about how she'd slipped out from her college dorm to marry my dad and live in this crummy apartment in Windhaven where rats sometimes swam up into the bathtub from the flooded drain. But since she'd gotten the grant and made Haven House happen, she'd been home early exactly twice, and then she'd gone straight to the computer.

Now, with camp cancelled due to rain, my dad upstairs snoring, I sat alone by the picture window watching the troopers' cars enter and leave the woods, hearing the roar of the helicopter they finally sent over to scope out the area looking for Lenny. Late in the morning a car drew up to our house, and the trooper who got out opened his trunk and pulled out a box which he brought up to the door.

"I understand these things here belong to you," he said, setting it down in the front hall. Inside were my tapes and player, plus JoAnn's comic books and a couple of badly rolled-up posters.

"Are we in trouble for using that place?" I asked.

"It'll be bricked up now," he said. "If you think you're missing anything else, you can call the station."

"What about Lenny?" I asked as he turned to leave. He pivoted real slowly on his heels. "Haven't you found anything?"

"I don't have to answer your questions," he said. His voice was even, not mean-sounding. "You're missing something, you call the station. That's it." And he turned again and hurried through the rain to his car.

My head throbbed, tears aching to spill out. Carefully I lifted the tape player out of the box and plugged it in. Trixie came and sniffed at the woods smell on the machine. She had a German shepherd's nose, the kind that won't quit; I finally pushed her away. Putting on the first side of *Anyone Can Tap*, I shuffled badly around the dark room for almost an hour. *Back shuffle shuffle back kick pause tap*, I whispered to myself, *tap slide double click kick heel toe!* while the voice on the tape crooned, *Ev-ery-thing's com-in' up roses.* . . . When it finished I put it on again, wiped the sweat from my neck, and shuffled more, anything to eat up time.

"Aren't you bored?" my mom asked, when she finally got home and shucked off her raincoat, "alone all day like this?"

"Dad was around for a while," I said. "And I've been watching the troopers."

I'd flicked off the tape player when my father came down for his breakfast at lunchtime. Give your old man a little show, he'd said, but I told him I was no good, and pretty soon he'd finished the paper and gone out to the Minimart for what he called decent coffee. It was what he used to say when he went over to Gray's to catch up with the other men who worked splits or nights.

"Your father mention the lawn?"

"Only that it was too wet to mow. Those troopers didn't come back after lunch, either."

"Why don't you call one of the other kids who help out at camp? They've got to be stuck home too." She was gone in the kitchen already, getting iced tea. I followed her.

"D'you think they've given up?" I asked. "On Lenny, I mean."

"Oh, no. No, I'm sure they haven't." Her voice was light, absentminded; she dipped a finger into a jar of peanut butter and licked it. I could tell something was brewing. "But listen, Gwyn honey, we've got to talk about that tower."

I followed her through the kitchen to the library. Any other family would call it the den, but to us it was the library because that was the way my mom talked. "God, it's humid," she said, sinking into the deep red chair she always read in. "I bet this storm won't even clear the air." She picked a piece of ice out of her tea glass and rubbed it over the back of her neck. "I swear I'm going to break down," she said, "and spend the office reserve on air-conditioning."

The ice water glowed like a slug's trail all around her neck. You could see where the skin was just starting to sag, under her chin, and it was a real surprise to see age creeping up like that on my mom. She was a beautiful lady—always had been, and still is, even now. I mean beautiful like a model, like one of those people they photograph wearing Gap jeans. She has this very straight tawny hair, which she cuts short these days but wore, back then, just above her shoulders, making a perfect oval frame around her face. Her lips aren't too full, the way mine are; but they're wide, always a little apart, and in those days she didn't have to do much to make you think she was smiling. Her nose has got a little bump in it, same as mine; we both got it from her father, my Grandpa Benjamin, whose posed photo was the only family album she kept, smiling down at us from her old piano. I used to think her bumpy nose didn't matter, though, because her eyes got you from either side of it. My dad was crazy about her eyes. He said they calmed him down, like two pools he could float through. I on the other hand thought her best feature was her breasts, which dipped and nestled in the cups of her bra like happy seals. I used to watch her pat them dry after a shower and I'd think how mine would never be like that.

And the truth is she never had any idea she was a knockout. People told her—but there was always this little furrow in her forehead, like she was working on a problem. She met my dad when he was taking the train to work construction in the city. He told me once he found her at the station down there, trying to wake the bums up to give them a bowl of soup. She wouldn't give him any—he'd laugh when he came to this part—because she said he looked too well fed. Next week he skipped a shave, took the early train in, and sacked out on a bench, and he let her wake him up with split pea.

I think about her taking care of him, even though she didn't have to. About what her life had been before he came into it, and what she forced it to be after. About how her instinct was to save Whoopsy at the cost of her own limbs. She'd have saved me, too, if I'd been a toddler she didn't know, on the tracks. She'd have knocked me clear of danger and then—if she survived—she'd have taken me in her arms and soothed all the fear out of me. The wrinkle in her forehead would have smoothed out for a minute, and I'd have thought I must be dead, because this angel was holding me.

I believe she wishes to this day that she could have saved me like that. If only I'd come into her life a stranger, and not tainted by being flesh of her flesh. If only the world hadn't needed her more than I did, if only I hadn't seemed to require the world's cold air against her warm breath.

"It's not the tower we oughta be talking about," I said, picking one of her reports off her desk and riffling it. "It's where you were when I tried to call you. If you'd of been there I might've done something right instead of wrong. But no, you're such a do-gooder that you're out having drinks with some *councilman*. And the troopers'll find Lenny and make him go live home with his dad, and as soon as they're gone—"

"Gwyn, you're not being fair," she said. She dropped the ice cube back into the glass and took a drink; I imagined it tasting of the salt she'd rubbed from her neck. "You said yourself he didn't tell you it was his dad, and there's no record on Gus Dugliss. You can't go throwing a child into foster care just because another child says—"

"It's not what I said. It's what I saw. And I'm not a child."

"It's too hot to quarrel," my mom said.

"It's because he's a Dugliss you don't care," I said.

"Don't be stupid, Gwyn!"

"It's because he's too rich and trashy," I said. I put the report back down. "It's just like with Mr. Gray. If Lenny was one of them nigger babies from down in Castleton you'd be at the judge with an order yesterday."

"Don't you use that word, Gwyn," my mom said.

"Nigger baby," I said.

"You want to talk, Gwyneth? You want to tell me what you were doing in an abandoned structure filled with cigarettes and beer? You want to tell me what happened to my crystal—"

The phone rang. While my mom went to answer it I shuffled

my feet on the floor, the routine from "My Heart Belongs to Daddy." My own heart was doing double time in my chest.

"That was Mrs. Harlett," my mom said when she got back. She was rubbing her phone ear, like it had been socked. "She wants you away from JoAnn, JoAnn away from you. Quits, finito. She thinks you're a bad influence." There was just the ghost of a smile at the corner of my mom's lips.

"It was my telling Gray that done it, wasn't it?" I said, stopping my feet. "Just because people blame him for Nate—"

"She says JoAnn told it out in church this morning. That she'd been there with you, and you'd been drinking, and that's why you left Lenny."

"Well, that ain't true," I said.

"Not," my mom said. "That's not true."

"It's a lie either way. I don't know what anybody does going to church on Wednesday, anyhow. And it's nothing compared to what I could rat on her."

"Gwyn." My mom took my hands and pulled me onto the arm of her big red chair. The furrow in her forehead deepened. "You're so worried about whether the boy'll be found—well, let's worry about what'll happen once he *is* found. Let's worry about *you*. You're not *helping* me, Gwyn."

I pulled my hands away. I had called her, twice. She'd been out diddling a fat politician. I got up and walked to the other end of the library with my eyes squeezed shut, hard enough to see red flickers in the black. It was only when I turned and unlocked my eyelids that I caught a jagged refraction from the lamplight over her head: the crystal dove, broken cleanly in two pieces, back up on the bookshelf. Her peace dove, her old boyfriend. She had been going to ask. "Look, I like Lenny Dugliss," I heard myself saying. "I'd stash him in my bedroom if I could, but he ain't there."

"Not," said my mom.

"And it wasn't Lenny who was drinking. Just JoAnn and me. Her more than me. Jesus, what a bitch in heat," I said. For just a second I remembered the baby in her, but I pushed that out of my mind.

"You want to tell me about the drinking?" my mom said. "You want to tell me who sold it to you? You want to tell me about the grass?"

"No," I said. "No, I want to get out of here. I'm sorry about your—your glass bird, there. You can tell the Harletts to go fuck themselves, excuse my French."

She didn't stop me. I crossed the library to the front hall, went to the closet and got out my black slicker with the hood, and headed out the door into the steady rain. I took the muddy path into the woods, where everything was so trampled you couldn't tell what direction anyone'd gone in. I climbed all the way up the hill, to where the land opens up for the Meyenhold mansion. The tower was all bricked up, little white flags around the place where the opening had been; you could see the mortar was still wet.

So I stumbled around the muddy path by the rusty iron fence, out to the sloping meadow that ran to the river. Then down the grass and back into the thick tangle of trees, along the paths no one knew about, past the old granary into the knobs and hollows above the river. Dark branches pulled at my socks, my bare legs. Finally squatting, soaking wet, in the deep leaves and pine needles that had drifted into one of the hollows, I clutched my knees and tried to listen. Nothing came beyond the steady rain and the far-off, hollow sounds of the marina. But I was sure Lenny Dugliss was out there, somewhere; and in my foolish arrogance I handed myself the job of finding him.

"Gonesville," I told my kids at camp the next day. "He's probably somewhere outside Atlantic City by now."

"He's sick or something, ain't he?" one girl asked.

"Diabetic," I said, real cool. "He needs insulin. But there're clinics, down in the city. He'll be okay."

"My sister's diabetic," another girl said. She was one of the worst, a tubby little Baptist with triple-pierced ears. "She's only eight. She's learned to give herself shots already."

"Eeuw," said a couple others. We were sitting on the sunny slope by the badminton court, waiting for Anne-Marie to find the racquets.

"How come that Gray was lookin' for him, that's what my mom wants to know," said the first—Tania, the one who'd sung those songs to her mother. "She says they oughta look in Gray's cellar, that's what she says."

There was this minute of quiet, while they all wondered what that meant, Lenny in Gray's cellar. I could have spoken up then, could have set a bunch of ten-year-olds straight. But I felt the way I'd felt as a kid, sledding the slope back of the mansion, Suicide Hill we called it. Like I knew I was out of control, and the angle was all wrong, but it was too late to roll off the sled.

I saw JoAnn twice that afternoon. The first time was outside the Minimart on Route 12. Some guy had let her off there, after her play rehearsal; she was getting cigarettes and waiting for her dad to pick her up. "I hear you're not supposed to be talking to me," I said.

"Oh, they'll get over that," she said. She was sitting on the bright orange bench outside the store, her buttery hair blowing in the hot breeze. "But we gotta find a new place. I can't stand being home all the time. They freaking *watch* me."

"You heard anything about Lenny Dugliss?"

"That little creep," she said. "I hope the bugs eat him alive."

"You didn't have to tell your mom I bought the beer and stuff," I said.

"You didn't have to take the whole business to that pervert at the store," she snapped back; and I put a lid on all I might have said about how one of us could have stayed with him while the other went for help. Instead I took a deep breath and then told her I was going out to the woods that night, to find the kid myself.

"Now don't blab it to your mom," I said.

"Are you kidding? It's such a stupid thing to do, I wouldn't embarrass myself."

"It is not stupid. You remember how Lenny kept the troopers guessing last year. He knows those woods better than anyone. He just didn't want to face the music with his dad. I bet he's not far from the mansion, even. There's probably a basement window they forgot to check. I'm just gonna wait around there awhile, see what I see. I'll bring some food and stuff. You don't got anyone with diabetes in your family, do you?"

"Christ, Stick."

"Well, he needs medicine. But I'll find him, first."

Her dad pulled in, then, and I got back on my bike. The next time I saw JoAnn was down in the hamlet, not long after, standing by the P.O. arguing with Seth Dugliss—over the money, I figured. I coasted past them, and just saw JoAnn curl her lip as I went by.

Even as the evening light faded, the side of the tower that faced west was still hot. I'd fixed myself a stack of cheese and crackers for supper and left a note on the kitchen counter saying I'd gone over to JoAnn's. My mom would freak at the idea of me crossing the Harletts' threshold, but she wouldn't have the nerve to call over there and face Mrs. Harlett. I had a couple of hours, at least, to myself. I'd covered my face and arms with bug spray and my hair with a baseball cap; mosquitoes whined around me but didn't attack. Hanging from my belt was my dad's high-intensity flashlight, and parked against the stone of the tower was the bag of fruit and no-salt corn chips I'd got at the Minimart. I'd seen the deer again, both of them, and they'd nuzzled around in the blackberry bushes while I sat still and watched. By now they'd loped away and were folded into the thick brown of the forest. In their place had come crickets, just starting to whine, and the quick scurryings of squirrels as the sky darkened. Nothing frightened me. I was a magnet, I thought, and sooner or later Lenny would be drawn to me. If he didn't show up here in an hour, I'd move deeper. And again the next night, and the next. I sat still as a rock, waiting.

Then there was a black plastic bag over my head, and someone yanking it tight at the hips. I suppose I yelled; I don't remember any sound. Just the dry slickness of the plastic on my face and the push of bodies, it seemed like lots of them, strapping my legs below the cinched-up bag. A knife, I thought at first, they'll stab me with a knife through this plastic. I scrunched up my chest. But they just hoisted me, like a sack of garbage. I beat at the inside of the bag with my fists, but there were strong hands clamping me down, and the inside of the bag got hot and airless almost right away. So I just stiffened and let them take me.

I knew these woods, even then; but when you're getting carried over a bunch of shoulders, head hanging down, it's hard to keep track. Crazy as it sounds, I thought at first Lenny was behind all this. He'd been off raking together a gang of runaways, like the Lost Boys gone rotten, and now they'd picked me as their first victim, just to see how wicked they could be. We went down, then up; a couple of times someone stumbled over a root and I heard them shout *Fuck!* and then the rest going *Ssh*, and by the range of their voices I knew they were older than Lenny. There were five of them, maybe six. I tried to take shallow breaths. I knew there was air coming in at the legs, but that wasn't much. I thought of little Whoopsy, pinned under the engineer on the tracks, sucking air from the gravel bed. My face had rubbed against the inside of the plastic, and every time I parted my lips I tasted insect repellent. A couple of times I tried to kick, or jerk out of their hands, but they just gripped me harder. I'd have landed on my head, anyhow. Finally they lowered me down, and then a belt or something went around my rib cage, trussing my arms.

I wasn't talking, by then. I'd gone somewhere deep inside myself, the way you might if you'd hurt yourself terribly badly and had nothing to make the pain go away. But they didn't hurt me. They whispered. They said, *Ooh, ohh, Lenny*, and *Sugar Stick, Candy Stick, Stick it to me*. Their voices never got above that raspy whisper. I tried to listen if I knew them; they were all guys, I could tell that. They were moving real close to me, their lips near my ears through the plastic. *Fuck me, Lenny, you little hot rod*, one of the voices whispered. After a while of this I knew it was all a joke,

the idea of a joke that people got in this godforsaken place, which
was to tar and feather a person and then laugh your head off while
they died of skin suffocation.

Then they got tired of it. I could hear one voice I recognized,
Matt McPeck's, somewhere in back of me, saying, "So what do we
do with her? We just leave her here?"

I don't know, man, another voice said, whispering. *I ain't in
charge.*

"How 'bout we dunk her?" said Matt's voice, and then their
footsteps came up to me, and their whispers: *Want to take a bath,
Stick? PCBs and gasoline, set you on fire. Lenny'll love ya, baby.*

They had me on their shoulders again, and we sort of jounced
downhill, until I could hear the planks of the old mansion dock
under their feet, that hollow wooden sound over the water. Then
I got flipped over, and the hands were at my shoulders and feet.
Inside the black plastic I saw it, got myself ready for it: water,
maybe six feet deep, over my head anyhow, with those thick weeds
tangling around my feet. I'd be able to kick and I'd have some air
in the bag, holding me up, and if I could just get to the shallows—

"Heave HO!" They were shouting now, all together, so I still
couldn't tell the voices. They rocked me back, forth. "Heave HO!
Heave— Hey!" Matt's voice again. Someone had let go one of my
shoulders, and I dropped like a log until the others caught me and
lowered me to the dock. "Whatsa big idea?"

"I ain't goin' in to fish her out," said a deep voice, and I knew
this one now too. I should've known it even at a whisper: Seth
Dugliss. Seth Dugliss making me pay. And all because that retard
JoAnn had blurted it out that afternoon when they were fighting,
back at the P.O. She'd used it as a weapon, shouting at him that
her crazy friend was going out alone tonight to save his brother,
and it was all his fault. So he'd caught the hint and come with his
chums to teach me one.

Ssh. Matt again, whispering. *Whaddaya want, then?*

Take the bitch in to Gray's. Some other voice.

Or we could do her ourselves, man. Here.

"Not worth it. Not fucking worth it. I'm outta here," said Seth, loud and sure, knowing I'd recognize him, wanting me to. I could feel his foot on the board by my face, then a dozen feet treading the dock, the wood shaking. Then they were all gone. I think I cried a little, but the taste of the insect spray was like metal, and my eyes stung already. My baseball cap had come off, floating somewhere in the black bag. I wanted to ask if anyone was still there. Then I thought, whoever's left'll be the one to toss me in. Or use the knife, after all, as a big fat joke. So I just lay there, like the log they'd made me, listening to the night sounds.

I bit my way out, finally. It was a full moon, plus the spotlight from the mansion sort of drifted down the slope. Once I could see, it wasn't too hard to work my fingers down and untie the rope around my knees. Then for a long while I didn't move, just sat there on the half-rotted dock with the bag around my neck and arms, cinched to my waist like a monk's robe.

The last thing I wanted was to go back to the hamlet. Under the dock, the weed-filled water lapped at the old pilings. People used to bring boats up here, steamboats up the Hudson with all their trunks and their servants aboard. That was when the dock was five times longer, and they'd disembark and stand on the planks twirling their parasols, trading news of who was here and who'd gone, and where to. You could get out of this place, back then.

Cutting a path through the weeds, a handful of ducks came toward me, quacking hopefully in the dark. They thought I was some wacked-out tourist, out of season in the dead of night, come to toss stale bread crusts at them. "Fuck off," I said when they got within earshot. They circled around, the ripples behind them making oily patterns on the water. Then they glided away.

Those guys. They'd done the same thing to Lenny. The black garbage bag and the ropes. Only they'd tossed him in, they'd really done it, and the tide had pushed him downstream and finally sucked him down to the river bottom.

Now that was crazy, more than crazy with Seth being Lenny's brother and no more of a monster than anyone else in the hamlet.

Crazy, and I had to get up from the dock and clear my head before
I totally lost it. But still I didn't get up. I was tired, bone tired. I
felt like I could lie down on the dock and shut my eyes, and in a
minute I'd be asleep. And when I woke up the whole thing would
be a dream—not just Seth's revenge, but Lenny disappearing and
JoAnn getting pregnant, and everything since the Challenger had
gone up and then busted apart in the blue sky. I'd wake up and be
back on the bleachers in Florida and someone would be shouting
over the loudspeaker, "We have downlink!" Or else I'd be dead
and wouldn't have to wake ever again and think about going back
to the hamlet.

An owl hooted. The moon went behind a dark cloud. A cold
wind stirred the river, and the little laps of water seemed to hurry
against the pilings, making quick swallowing sounds. At some
point I got up—balancing on my knees, then tipping back to a
crouch, and when I had that stabilized, uncoiling to stand up. My
left arm had gone to sleep. My legs took me along the woods and
came out at the railroad trestle. I ended up by the old station, back
at the hamlet.

When I reached my house, I ducked into the barn where my
dad kept his tools. With a rug blade I cut the rope binding my
arms, and shrugged the whole thing into a corner. Let him find it
there, I thought—as if what had happened was his fault, for being
a guy, like the others. Let him wonder. But of course he never
would find it, or at least never pick it out of the general mess in
there. Next I tried tiptoeing into my house from the front door,
through the hallway that led straight upstairs. But my mother was
rounding the corner from the kitchen to the library, and her eyes
followed Trixie as the dog came out wagging to have a lick of me.
"Oh, darling," she said as she flicked the hall light on. "What have
they done to you?"

And even though it wasn't much that I told her, wrapped in my
bathrobe after I'd showered and drinking sherry on her bed up-

stairs, it was almost enough to make me glad the whole thing had happened, just to get those eyes centered on me. It wasn't stupid of me, she kept repeating, it wasn't stupid but good-hearted and brave and maybe just a little foolish. And I was being brave now, not telling her who'd played such a sick, violent joke. Even though she wished I would tell, and soon, before they did it again.

"But anyway," she said, brightening, lifting her tawny hair off her shoulder with her hand, "you don't have to worry about Lenny."

"What d'you mean?"

"I should've told you, I suppose I should've told you yesterday. Only there were reasons—and I didn't trust that JoAnn, Gwyn, you can see why now—"

"Told me what?" It was hot, still, in the middle of the night, but my neck shivered right at the base of my spine.

"Well, honey, his brother found him and hid him a few hours, and then drove him down. Anne-Marie admitted him before dawn yesterday morning. Lenny Dugliss is absolutely safe and healthy, staying with us at Haven House."

I knew it was late, but I knew JoAnn's parents stayed up late too; they liked the old movies on cable, she'd said. So I stood there in my bathrobe, banging on the back door, until her mother came and opened it to scowl at me.

"Don't look like that, Mrs. Harlett," I said as I came into the light and the screen slammed behind me. "Please don't look like that. I've come here—I've come here because I want, you know." I swallowed; the yellow of the kitchen stung my swollen eyes. "To convert."

chapter **11**

I like rituals. I don't think it's a bad thing, either. To know that the
weekend before Halloween you take all the summer clothes out of
the closet and drawers, separate out the ones you've trashed, pack
the rest up in the suitcases you've just spilled the winter woolens
out of. In April to do the process backward, adding a stop at Buck-
a-Pound Dry-cleaning and dropping mothballs into the suitcases.
Or little daily rituals: washing my face in the morning, checking
the bird feeder on my way to the P.O., waving to the 8:12 south-
bound train as it sails by before I tuck myself into my car.

These are not routines. You do routines without thinking about
them. When I wash my face, I press the hot washcloth to my skin,
dip it back in the water, then rub real slow up from my chin to my
hairline, with a stop to press my palms against my closed eyelids.
I dip the cloth again, squeeze it dry, then hold its warmth against
the back of my neck while I curl my head down toward the basin.
I'm aware of all these little motions. I don't know how clean they
get me; I doubt a face needs to get clean, in the morning. But
there's something holy in them, just like there's something holy in
feasting your eyes on the slice of sun that cuts down the red brick
of the post office wall. If holy means a feeling that sets you free to
love the angry world we live in, which is what I think it means.
But I'm kind of alone in that belief. Even now, we don't talk about
holiness in my family. And Mrs. Harlett sure wouldn't approve of
my idea of what's holy. Holy, to her, was where all the rituals were
leading, in the end—an entirely different place, full of good
smells and visual excitement, where nothing weighed on her and
everyone approved.

Her kitchen, that night: I can't get the smell of it out of my nose. Bacon grease and pot roast, with cheap cleaner on the gritty linoleum and cigarette butts in the ashtray. She'd been standing by the counter when I came in, dressed in her bathrobe and curlers, smoking and clipping coupons. "I've been looking for Jesus all my life," I told her. She let go the coupons and plopped herself down at the kitchen table and started to cry. *Bah-oog, bah-oog*, like a foghorn. "Hey, Mrs. Harlett," I said. "Don't take it so hard. I'll be a good Christian. You'll be proud of me." And I believed it almost as soon as the words were out, even though I had run over there to get revenge on my mom, to hurt her in some deep and terrible way.

She waved me over to a box of Kleenex on the kitchen counter, so I pulled out four and brought them to her. She blew her nose loudly on three of them, then took up the fourth and wiped her eyes carefully, not smearing the night cream. "I de*nounced* you," she said when she could talk. "In front of the *Assembly*."

"That's okay," I said. "You're entitled, Mrs. Harlett. We'll work it out."

And we did, right then and there, even though I had to swallow some pretty syrupy crap about JoAnn, how she'd been pure as milk until I came along and introduced her to alcohol and "other things." How Mrs. Harlett had made JoAnn promise to stay away from me before, but then I'd gone and sucked her into meeting me in that tower where we could do the Devil's work if we wanted, meet boys and talk blasphemy. I swallowed it; I was tired, and the Harletts' kitchen was warm, and the sherry working in me. I kept my eyes on Mrs. Harlett's arms, which she gestured with while she talked. They were puffy under her sheer pink robe, dimpled at the joints; some carnival guy might have twisted her out of a balloon. She leaned on one elbow and shook a forearm at me. "I know where your mother goes on Sundays," she said. "And don't tell me it's some accident kept your daddy out of Vietnam."

That woke me out of my drowse, for a second. I hadn't thought about my dad and religion, ever. He'd had asthma, he always told people. "Nobody ever taught me right," I said to Mrs. Harlett, my

tongue thick in my mouth, and she smiled. I'd have to be bap-
tized, she said. I'd have to be set straight on the path. I'd have to
stop going to those Meetings.

"Oh, those," I said, feeling victory flow slowly in my bones. "I
never had any truck with that."

"Well, child," she said, beaming now, her cigarette smoldering
unnoticed in the tray. "What our creed says is forgive, you might
as well learn that now. Come over here to Mama."

And I had to do it. I had to get in that marble-fatted, pot roast
lap and be hugged. I thought I might faint. But I was tasting the
bitter triumph I wanted, I was showing my mother what betrayal
meant. And there was God, still, waiting to be found, waiting at
the Reach Out for Christ Sanctuary for all I knew.

When I crept back home again, I was more careful than before,
and managed to get upstairs and into my bed while my mother
still paced the kitchen, watching pointlessly out the window that
gave back her reflection. And even later, when she stepped into
my room and drew her breath in with surprise, and then reached
to pull the sheet over my shoulder, I did not stir.

I didn't see Lenny Dugliss for weeks after that. I saw his
brother, and the rest of them; I stared them down when I went
into Gray's store, which I still did. I shook inside my skin but I
stared them down, and when one of them tried to smirk at me I
smirked back. After a time they got tired of howling with laughter
as soon as I'd gone by. Once I saw just Seth, not at Gray's but in
the parking lot of Camp Torture, where Lenny had never come
back. He was talking to Anne-Marie, holding a few of Lenny's
things he'd picked up: swim trunks, towel. He didn't smirk or
howl then, he just looked at me. And I waited, pretending to tie
my shoe, until Anne-Marie'd gone back to our group, and then I
stood up and said in a high thin voice, "I didn't know you'd taken
care of him. How was I supposed to know?"

"You wasn't," he said. And he got back into his new truck,

which was already looking not so new, and started the engine. I took a step closer; I wanted to ask about the money, what was the truth of the money he was supposed to have given JoAnn. He didn't look so waxy, sitting in that truck. His dark thick hair was disheveled, and there were sweat stains under his arms—he looked like a full-grown man, the freshness rubbed out of him. Staring straight ahead, he said, "You didn't deserve that, what we done to you," and then he put the truck in reverse and pulled out. So I never had the chance to ask.

The Reach Out for Christ Sanctuary was this huge white stucco building in the shape of an upside-down V, but kind of loopy on one side, like a cliff-hung ski slope. The members had built it all themselves, and it seemed it had been in construction for- ever. Even that summer, whenever Mrs. Harlett parked out back, I got out of their car into an area filled with old scaffolding and hunks of plasterboard piled up under a tarp. Inside, a huge metal cross hung at the front, where the sun shafting through the long skylight lit on it so fierce you had to squint, looking that way. In front of the cross was a little stage, and on either side there were filmy curtains, closing something off from view. The ladies of the church had embroidered three big hangings that came down from the ceiling. *REPENTANCE*, they read. *OBEDIENCE*. *BLESSING*.

"I am telling you he never gave me the money, and I don't want to hear no more about it," JoAnn said when I asked, the first time her family took me with them. I hadn't told her about the tower, about the garbage bag. She wouldn't have felt bad for practically sending Seth out to get me; she would have thought it was funny, like they did. Even if they'd done it to her, it would have been funny; JoAnn Harlett was a good sport. "I am just glad you thought of doing this," she said while we waited for her brother Bobby to stop talking to his seventh-grade girlfriend in the park- ing lot. "I can hardly believe you had it in you."

"A person has to do something for a best friend," I said. Not really meaning it, just not wanting to talk about my mother and Lenny Dugliss and the woods—but when I saw her blush and bite her lower lip I was almost glad I had. I never could figure out my feelings about JoAnn. But then her brother caught up and we all got funneled into the Sanctuary.

We sat in folding chairs. JoAnn explained they were still raising the money for real pews; they'd only finished the indoor space that spring. It was impressive, I could give it that—high ceilings up to the top of the ski jump, all fresh pine, with that big skylight and a picture window at the back looking over the river. First the choir sang—they'd come out from behind one of the curtains— and then this tanned, heavyset man with a broad broken nose stood up in front of the microphone. Right away he raised his arms and started preaching, shouting really, the way they do on those TV shows, only with a peculiar twist to his words, like he had gum stuck in one side of his mouth. "Pastor Gwilliam," JoAnn whispered, and then I remembered he was from Australia, the ex-convict.

He started with Lenny Dugliss, who'd been in the papers at last. The headlines had ragged a little on Haven House for harboring him—they called him a *fugitive*, straight out of a Western—but they hadn't mentioned Gray or how Lenny's dad had beat on him. Now Pastor Gwilliam raised his arms and sort of whooped. *A boy is found!* he shouted. *And had we not sought him, even as Jesus said, "I will seek the lost lamb, and bring him into the fold"? A boy is found, and I read to you today, from the scripture of Luke, where another son returns, prodigal and penniless, to his father's house. . . .*

I didn't get to hear much more because JoAnn started whispering in my ear.

"Y'know what I always think about, here at church?" she whispered. I shook my head. "Sex," she said. "My head just empties out, and all these nasty thoughts come pouring in. You ever do that?"

"No," I said. "I don't have sex either. But if I did I'd use protection. I'd make sure—"

"Ssh!" Her mother worried her eyebrows at us, and I bowed my head. But JoAnn barely stopped for breath. She tossed her long bangs back and leaned closer. "Here's one," she whispered. "You ever think what it's like for a guy to put his tongue down there?"

"Where?" I whispered.

"*There.*"

"No, JoAnn, I never do. It's gross."

"No, really. Not one of those assholes who tries to kiss you and then sticks his tongue in your mouth and doesn't know what to do with it, just leaves it there like you oughta bite it off. I mean some really sexy guy, who knows how to slide it around."

"You mean like Jason Sweetwater, in that new video," I said.

"No, I mean like Mel Gibson."

"He's a twit," I said. "He's five foot six."

"He's got a tongue, that's all we're talking about here. You know what your mound of Venus is?"

"Course I do," I said. I saw Mrs. Harlett squirm in her seat, like she wanted to reach over and smack us. JoAnn flicked her hair back.

"Okay, say he started there. With his little tongue, just the tip of it, darting around like a fish in a net, looking for the way out. He'd clear away all your pubes, find his way to your crack, then slither in and out, quick, a few times. Then he'd tilt your hips up, you know, with his hands, so you'd be positioned just right. Maybe he'd tuck a pillow under your bum. He'd start in with real long strokes, reaching his tongue *way* back and just sliding it forward, in between the folds, first on one side, then on the other side. He'd stop right at the top, and you'd be dying. But then he'd go do it again. There'd be that one spot, there, that he hasn't touched, and that's where you want him to put his tongue, only you don't even think about it like a tongue anymore, it's just this thing, this *it*, that is pulling you along, and the ride's getting faster, and faster—"

I tried to move my head, but there wasn't any getting away from her. She had her lips right up next to my ear, so she could speak incredibly softly. And the less I squirmed the less JoAnn's mom noticed us. On the stage, Pastor Gwilliam was shouting. I wanted to hear him, but JoAnn's words kept filling my head. "Then," she was saying, slowing down, "finally, he gets hold of your clit. You didn't even know your clit was there until he got hold of it, but he's got it, and he's pulling it out of its little old hiding place, his lips are like velvet, you know, tugging on it and lapping it up. And he's got your hips in his hands, he's squeezing them. His tongue is going a mile a minute, then suddenly it stops and he gives one last, incredible suck. And then you just explode. Right into pieces."

She sat back with a real satisfied look on her face. I was feeling the blood drain out of mine, and between my legs was wet. I forgot how we'd been best friends, outside; it made me furious that JoAnn's stupid talking would make me cream my pants. I crossed my legs and listened as hard as I could to the Australian at the front of the room.

He was into the feast part. *"Hurry!" cried the father. "Get the prize calf, and kill it, and let us celebrate! For this son of mine was dead, but now he is alive." And so should we all come to life, brothers and sisters, I tell you. Today it is not just that boy who was found, it is all of us who have been wandering, our spiritual bellies empty, in the desert—* He stopped here to wipe his forehead. Talking was like boxing for him, you could tell he was feeling beat up. The microphone whined in the pause. Next to me JoAnn was picking at a scab on her knee, probably thinking about Mel Gibson's tongue on her clit. I was getting pissed at this pastor. I mean, it was one thing to get your spiritual belly filled, like the prodigal son, and another to be Lenny Dugliss and get tossed back at your psychotic father.

Only the Lord, my friends, only the Lord can make the feast to feed us! And we have to come to the table ourselves! We have to return to the fold!

"Yeah, but if the prodigal son's father had hit him on the head—"

I started whispering to JoAnn, but I didn't have her technique; Mrs. Harlett was on me in a second, frowning and *ssh*ing. I sat back and let the strange-accented words wash over me. The organ took up where Pastor Gwilliam left off, and the choir did another number. I let Lenny Dugliss go, and I let go the way his brother had looked, straight ahead, fighting to remain an asshole even as he apologized. I shut my eyes and tried to see God. When I opened them again, a large gray-haired lady had taken the mike, and Mrs. Harlett was straightening herself.

"Now is our sharing time," the gray-haired lady said. She had on this flowing blue dress, and makeup that made her skin glow like a wet peach. "Let us bring the power of the Lord with us here. And as we also wrestle with the Devil—for he exists—let us bring that struggle into this Sanctuary, that we may battle him together and with the great help of our Savior Jesus Christ."

Mrs. Harlett stood up right away. A skinny guy in a dark suit— I recognized him from the hardware store in Windhaven— brought a mike on a long cord over to her. JoAnn's brother grinned at me; JoAnn kept her hair like a wavy curtain over her face. Her mom cleared her throat of what sounded like a lot of phlegm. "I've brought a sinner in with me today," she said. "Like the savage in the wilderness, she didn't ever know God, and so she'd gone wrong at every turn, and tried to bring my daughter wrong with her. I told you about her before." There was a general murmur; I stared down. Mrs. Harlett went on a bit about me being a lost sheep, and the fold, and at the end she asked me to rise, only I didn't hear; I was scraping away at the paint on my folding chair by then, at a spot where a U shape had already been chipped away. Then JoAnn poked me and I stood, and they all drummed their feet for me. The skinny guy shoved the mike under my chin.

"Thank you," I said, and sat down. And the shuffling stopped so I could look up toward the stage like everyone else. Except for one woman. She was sitting about three rows ahead of us, and you could tell she'd been waiting for me to peel my eyes off the floor. She was shooting dagger looks at me, and with her fat elbows propped on the back of her folding chair she had her index fingers crossed in an X.

After that first visit I went back every week, all summer, with the Harletts. My mother stopped saying anything about it; we had a silent war going, and I was winning. Pastor Gwilliam asked me to join the cast of the play, and I made rehearsals on Saturdays and Wednesday afternoons, when I didn't have camp. At the end of summer they opened one of the filmy curtains and dunked me in a tub of tepid water there during the service. And all that time I couldn't see anything, when I thought of Reach Out for Christ, but that woman with her fingers crossed. Because part of me wanted to prove her wrong, prove I was just as idiotic and pious as the rest of them. And part of me knew she had me nailed.

"How come you told me that stuff?" I asked JoAnn that first time, as we filed out of the Sanctuary into the hot day. "How come you talked that way, in there?"

"What, you got something better to talk about?" She pulled me ahead of her family. "I read somewhere," she said, "you can put a Junior Mint down there, to get them started. Sort of like training a dog."

"JoAnn!" her mother barked. She came huffing up to us. "You stop that chattering in church, hear me? People hear every word you say."

"Do they, Mama? What'd I say, huh? Tell me." JoAnn nudged me with her elbow. Her mother didn't answer. I dropped behind a little—to where, watching them walk along together, I could study the way JoAnn moved. I'd seen pregnant women, when they were starting to feel their babies. They walked like they were balancing eggs on their navel. But JoAnn wasn't carrying herself like that. She just swung her hips in that wide, smooth way fat people do. Since winter she'd put on maybe twenty-five pounds—mostly around the middle, but her arms were thick too, filling out the wide sleeves of her T-shirt.

I thought how you couldn't walk that free and easy if you were pregnant. You couldn't talk that way, about wanting a boy to lick you. I felt a little thrill across my shoulders, a hope that JoAnn was wrong, that her periods had just stopped for no reason. But I didn't dare speak the hope for fear it would break the spell—for fear she'd start, that instant, to walk like a pregnant person, to sway her back in and reach behind, now and then, resting her hand for a second on the back of her hip.

"Hurry *up*, Stick," she said, and I gave a little prayer before I hustled to catch up. *Dear God, let JoAnn just be fat.* But she was more than fat, in the end, and nothing God or any ritual could do about it, I was her only help.

chapter **12**

Camp finished up that summer without Lenny ever coming back to it. I did see him around the hamlet, usually in the truck with his brother. Once he surprised me, coming by the house to look for my mom. I told him she wouldn't be home until dark. "Something wrong," I asked, "up at your place?"

"No, it ain't that." He stood squinting on our doorstep, his black hair falling into his eyes. He was all healed up, where he'd been hurt.

"I *tried* to get hold of her, you know," I said through the screen door. "The other night. I didn't just go off and leave you."

"I know that." He shoved his hands in his pockets and looked around, like my mother might come in the driveway right then. "I just wanted to ask her about this other dude who was there when I was," he said, still turned away from me. "Wanted to find out what happened to him."

"What's his name?"

"I don't know. He was an old guy," he said. "He was crazy, I think. He said he was thirsty, all the time. I kept giving him apple juice. He said I was the only one who knew how to keep his thirst down. I could go back if she wants, give him juice." He moved a stick around on the porch, with his foot.

"You know," I said, "the people she works with, they come and go."

"Yeah," he said. "They come and go." And then he went, off on what looked like a new bike, a black racer with a mess of gears. I shrugged and went back in the house, thinking how his father had money to spend on him, at least.

I was a hundred and fifty dollars richer, from Camp Torture, but there wasn't much use for the money as far as JoAnn was concerned, anymore. I saw her every day, those last few weeks of summer. I don't actually remember much about the Reach Out for Christ play; it was supposed to be *contemporary*, that was what the blurb in the local paper said, *a Fable for our generation*. What I remember of Pastor Gwilliam is how much rehearsal time he spent telling us his personal history. He'd come all the way here from *Oh-stry-liah* to bring us the Word, he said. He'd been a boxer, a thief, and a drug pusher before he found Jesus; but he didn't look like any of those things now. He looked like he worked out, and he wore Reeboks and nice, new-smelling polo shirts. He said I was playing the most wasted junkie he'd ever seen. He said it with this dimple denting his tanned cheek, like I had a career in it.

He would tell my dad the same stuff about himself years later, after my dad's accident. "Now, that is an amazing man," my father said once when I came into the hospital room just after Pastor Gwilliam had left. "To overcome what he had to face—you know his brother died in a street fight, in Melbourne? His only relation by then, it's incredible. To overcome that and then be here, so far from his birthplace, and give himself to the rest of us. You never told me, Stick."

"Told you what?"

"What a remarkable human being you met, through that JoAnn. I tell you, if Gwilliam can't sell a person on a life in Christ, nobody can. I'll stick by that."

"Dad," I said. "It's hooey."

"Don't talk about a place you haven't been to, daughter," said my dad. "You were too young to grasp what that man has to say, is all."

My mom never stopped thinking Pastor Gwilliam was a thug. If she hadn't been so worried about my dad even surviving, she'd have picked a fight over the whole business. As it was, she just gave me fast hugs outside the hospital room and said she was glad I'd kept my sanity. She reminded me of the first thing she'd said when I'd told her I was going to be in Gwilliam's play, which was that she couldn't wait to see the IRS catch up with him. "And now it's happened," she said. "In the paper today, indicted on three counts."

"So tell Dad."

She shook her head. We were standing in the hospital corridor, changing places by Dad's bedside—me on my way out, her coming in from Haven House. "I'll leave him alone, just the way I left you alone," she said.

"But you didn't leave me alone," I said. "You made me stop after that summer."

"You wanted to stop, really."

I considered arguing this one with her. But she was looking real haggard, sleeping every night in the pull-out bed at the hospital. She wanted to remember herself as a saint, so fine. I had a lot else on my mind, by then.

But she hadn't been a saint. "That man is a phony and a humbug and he wastes young people's precious time," she'd said when the performance date for the play drew near. She had a new voice by then, all authority. "So you cannot be in this 'Christian' play past September, Gwyn. Especially not if you want to take those dance lessons."

"Sure I can," I said. "Dad wants me making C's in school, anyhow." I nodded at him, over in the La-Z-Boy. He'd been around a lot, that summer; something was wrong, at Hotung. He'd started going over there in the daytime, being home in the evenings, then sometimes not going in at all. He kept to himself, while this was going on; when we ate dinner together he talked about tools he needed in order to fix up the barn, in back, and he hardly took account of me. "You remember Dad," I said to my mother; pushing the situation. "Your husband?"

My mom hadn't flinched. "Ginger Rogers on a religious crusade," she said sarcastically. "There's your future."

"JoAnn's my friend, Mom," I said.

Her upper lip showed white, the way I'd seen it do with my dad when he didn't give in to her. "Then you need," she said tightly, "to help your friend. Help her slim down, or she'll die young. Help her use her brain or she'll get brainwashed. She'll end up following some phony Messiah down to a church in Venezuela. She'll end up drinking poisoned Kool-Aid."

"Or maybe she'll end up happy," I countered. We'd been through this kind of thing before. "Maybe she'll end up singing 'We Are the World' every summer and it'll make her feel good."

"She'll end up believing in faith healing and hating black people. She'll end up anti-Semitic."

"She already is," I said.

"Jasper, do something about this." My mother pulled herself up from the couch and tapped him on the shoulder. Her tap was a small neat one, like a clerk punching a cash register key.

"Why shouldn't Stick pray?" my dad said from his chair. He hadn't slept; loose gray bags hung under his eyes. "It's a good habit. I grew up praying," he said.

"Really?" I said. This was news. "What church?"

"Oh, not a serious church like your friends go to. Just Catholic. Smells and bells." He turned his newspaper inside out, the sheets rustling. "Now I never have to take a sleeping pill. I just start the litany and I'm out."

"Sometimes," my mother said, "you burn me up. You have no idea what direction your daughter's headed in."

"Hail Mary, Mother of God," my dad said, and he dropped the paper to the floor. Tipping his head back, he started to snore.

So already back then the religion thing had become, like Lenny Dugliss at Haven House, an off-limits subject. Maybe my mom thought that at least I'd quit drinking. Neither of them had any idea how important it was for me to keep an eye on JoAnn; they just figured I was unpopular, they figured girls needed friends the way little kids need stuffed bears.

And they had no idea what there was to admire in JoAnn. Like how she'd still sleep with guys, all through that summer. She found guys everywhere—not just church play rehearsals but the Windhaven mall on Saturdays, even the county fair back in June. It was like she sent out sex bleeps.

"What the hell, at least I'm safe, now," she said.

"You better watch yourself, JoAnn. You can *hurt* it, doing that stuff."

"It's not like falling down a flight of stairs, Stick. Some people say the kid likes it, even. Stimulation."

We'd gone like that, from talking about getting rid of it to taking care of it, like we'd adopted a secret pet. "Maybe you *wanted* to get pregnant," I said. "Maybe that's why you forgot about protection."

"When this is over, I want to get *spayed*. You know, like they do to dogs?"

"Jesus, JoAnn. I wish we would of gotten it out of you, you wouldn't talk this way."

Still, practically every time I went into Gray's store, I stole a carton of milk and made JoAnn drink it so the baby's bones wouldn't rot. Since we'd been cleared out of the tower I'd stopped doing beer with her, but she wouldn't quit. She said she needed the calories.

"Milk's got calories," I said. This was in her basement on a Saturday, after play rehearsal. JoAnn was toasted, I was on my tenth cigarette. I'd discovered you could get a nice high from nicotine if you did it all at once, dragging deep and lighting one cigarette with the butt of the other. I wasn't getting into a habit; I'd space out the sessions. For three days or so I'd go cold turkey, then all at once I'd pull a whole pack into my lungs.

"You drink the milk, little mama," JoAnn said. "Maybe you can have the kid too."

"Gross me out," I said.

But JoAnn was the one having the kid, if there was going to be a kid. And we still hadn't talked about how it was going to be born, or where, or what we were going to do with it then.

I began to harbor the idea of telling Gray. People had left him pretty well alone, since that night he'd led the search for Lenny. Plus he'd put up a sign announcing that the store would close after Labor Day—the tourists would be gone by then, no one but locals to shop there and they wouldn't—so I guess they'd got what they wanted, the ones who thought he'd done awful things. When he saw me in the street he didn't go on by, the way he'd started to since the county took his kids away. He stopped and asked what I was up to, now my job was finished. It was funny to see his face change, when he looked up and saw me coming. He'd become just a little smaller, a little weaker since all his trouble started, as I've said. His mouth seemed pinched at the corners, his eyes nervous; he'd taken to wearing a Yankees baseball cap, that summer, to hide where he'd started to bald. But he'd spot me and crack out a fat grin. You couldn't tell if it was a mask he kept handy or if it was his real self, with all that joy, just hiding away from what he'd done or what'd been done to him. Sometimes Benjy'd be with him; Gray would have taken him up to do some work on the apartments by Route 9, maybe. And Gray would make Benjy tell me about something he'd seen or done the day before, like a fish he'd caught from Gray's boat or the crazy drunk he'd watched the other guys pick off a roof the night before with the fire truck. Gray'd stand to one side, his hand stroking his chin, and watch Benjy and me talk together, like what he saw and heard just then was making him overflow with happiness.

So I knew he still liked me, whatever he'd said to me—*Girl,* he'd said, *I'll hold you personally responsible*—in the woods that night. And he was a pretty safe bank for personal deposits, was what my heart told me, no matter what the papers and the people in the hamlet had to say.

It was a peculiar sort of crush I had on Gray, that summer. I guess I'd always had a crush on him—on his long, muscled arms, his sloping shoulders, the way his broad chin tucked in toward his neck while he stroked it. He was a big, handsome man who liked me and who wasn't my father. Natural enough. But then, by that summer, he had got just a little bit dangerous, too. Who knew what things he could do, in the secret dark, to make a girl feel that way? Nothing like the stuff JoAnn talked about, I was sure, and nothing like what she did, either, with boys—nothing that pushed inside and tore at you.

The first day I decided to tell him about JoAnn, I found him holed up in the air-conditioning, doing the crossword. He did his usual quick change when he looked up, erasing the sour, pinched look and putting on the sunny grin. Rumor had it he was about to be indicted; crucifying would've been quicker, my dad had said that morning. I got a diet Coke and took a stool by the window, and when Gray stood up I noticed his store apron hung loose on him. He reached under the counter and held out a red Twizzler. "Seems to me, Stick, you're down to where your body's eating off its memory banks," he said. "Have some brain food, here."

"No, thank you," I said. "I'm not allowed snacks after three o'clock."

"C'mon. I've seen you in here after three."

"That was for JoAnn," I said.

"She's getting to be quite a porker, that girl."

"People are just different," I said. I took a nervous sip of my Coke. "It runs in her family, my mom says."

Gray spun the Twizzler with his thumb and forefinger. The grin was still there, but lopsided. "I used to see her," he said, "climbing out her window at night. You do that too, Stick?"

"You know I don't, Mr. Gray."

"Haven't seen her at it, this summer. Maybe she's gotten too big to get through. Shame for a young girl to let herself go, like that."

"JoAnn ain't let herself go," I said, not very loud.

"Hasn't she? Girls gain weight, like that, early in life, and they can have trouble later. Having babies, and such."

He dropped it, at that. My nerve, all my intentions went running down the counter and onto the dusty floor, like I'd spilled my diet Coke. But I hadn't spilled it; I chugged the drink, and scurried home to where my dad was out in his workshop, banging around, threatening to build us a deck.

He'd been laid off, by then. Which wouldn't seem to have much to do with Gray or with JoAnn Harlett, and it didn't except for how one thing leads to another. My dad got laid off along with eighty-five others, the first time Hotung had let people go in its history. First it had been shorter hours—as I've said, he was around the house more. Then they cut back the whole night shift, and offered him a daytime desk job, handling orders, four days a week. Only just as he was about to cave in and take it, they cut that, too, and handed him severance instead.

I'm not proud of how I took this change. I didn't want to be around it. I didn't want to hear my parents talking about money, and I didn't want to hear my dad's voice crack like that. So every morning, as soon as I could after my mom had driven off to her noble office at Haven House, I took off to JoAnn's place or to the woods.

The woods were buggy, but if there was a breeze I could make it out to the bluffs over the river and practice diagraming sentences or work out tricky tap routines, singing to myself, until the mosquitoes found me. A whole page of *The Hobbit* I managed to diagram that August, and I learned the Brazil double twist before I'd had even a single lesson. JoAnn's house, on the other hand, was noisy and smelly, but they loved me there, now I'd converted. Plus they were always running down to the mall or out for pizza, and bringing me along. One thing I'd never figured out was how people like JoAnn's parents could be home all the time and be always spending money—while, up to then, both my parents had been working full shifts but we'd never had any spare cash. It was like some trick we'd never managed to figure out.

Anyway, I'd spend the afternoon on JoAnn's front porch, staying away from my gloomy father, and I'd listen to her uncle go on about things like this crazy lady who'd laid herself across the railroad tracks and covered herself with brush so the train wouldn't know, and got her head chopped off. "Found it down by Winston's stockyard," said JoAnn's uncle, who was as fat as JoAnn, only bigger, "a good thousand feet from the rest of her. And you want to know what happened to her legs?"

"No," I said from a corner of their porch. This was a week after Camp Torture had ended. I was putting pink lotion on mosquito bites.

"Well, why not? The lady's dead, she don't care. Let me tell you just where her legs got tangled up."

"It is *gross*," I said.

"Hoo!" called out JoAnn's mother from the dark inside. "I should think it would be. God's got his ways with women like that. I hear she took a cleaver to her child when it was five, got one of his fingers. Her people are all nuts, I hear. Mormons."

"Her legs"—JoAnn's uncle leaned into her brother, but the rest of us could hear—"got drug by a pair of dogs into a lot where there used to be a gas station, and they would've been chewed past recognition if a third dog hadn't wanted in and started a fight, see. The one took off with the lady's leg so fast he got it trapped on the struts of that old billboard by the trestle, down there, and the next engineer spotted it as he went by."

On and on went their mouths. I couldn't stand it anymore, that day. I capped the bottle of bug lotion and waved at JoAnn, who was scooping up onion dip with nachos, throwing in her two cents with her mouth full of sour cream. The crickets were whining, black clouds looking over the river; the air had gone sickish with too much sun and dust and the smell of gasoline. As I stepped off the Harletts' porch a few fat drops of rain pelted down.

I left in the direction of Gray's store. I still had a yen to tell him. Telling him—it would have been an intimate thing, a way of sealing the specialness between us without getting near all that other mess, that mystery of what he'd done to the foster girls. The idea of telling him was a kind of honey on my tongue; I could almost taste the words I'd use.

I didn't actually think any of these things, then; I didn't know how to think them. I thought only, Maybe it will happen. And so headed over there from JoAnn's noisy porch, in the coming rain. But just as I set foot on the stoop I spotted the car. Blue Honda, my mom's car. Parked beside the store, on the other side, by the Dumpster. And on this side—I whipped my head around—Gray's Plymouth was gone from the lot, his wife was gone.

Carefully I peered over the checked curtains that ran halfway up the windows. I could just make out the top of my mom's head, on the other side of the counter, next to Gray. The sign on the door was turned to *Closed.* I stepped off the stoop and sped around to the back of the building. My breath was tight in my chest. Behind me, a carload of tourists from the park pulled up, saw the sign, wheeled away. I stopped at the back entrance to the store, the wide door for deliveries. When I was sure no one could see me I went up the three rickety steps and slowly turned the handle. It clicked open, and then I was inside, in the dark storage area behind Gray's store. The air smelled of rancid onions, of kerosene and old beer bottles. I stood still, breathing, until my eyes had adjusted. There were some chinks in the walls, for light, but the day was getting darker by the second. When I could make out the boxes and piled sacks, I stepped quietly around them, my sneakers silent on the cement, and into the back of the store. Gray hadn't turned the lights on, and the rows of food hid me from the front counter. I got down on my knees and scooted forward, past the dog food section and the houseware items. Then I heard Gray clear his throat, and I froze. This was far enough.

I don't know what I expected to hear pass between Gray and my mother. I was all ears, but what I was listening for—that can't be answered. I was just listening, holding my breath.

"You oughta leave," I heard Gray telling my mother. He was talking softly, leaning close to her probably. "Encourage him to look down South. Get out of here, Winnie. This thing isn't gonna turn around, and you'll wind up hating each other."

"I wonder." My mom's voice was breathy, not much more than a whisper, she'd been crying. "Maybe we already do. Hate each other."

"No, Winnie. No."

"All right, not hate. Resent. He *knows*, Henry. Five years ago he got an offer down in Pennsylvania, and I wasn't even working then, and I wouldn't. God, I was a bitch to him."

"No. Not a bitch. Christ, you've carried it off, all this time, and you've been fine to him—"

"I've *loved* him."

"Yes, yeah, of course loved him. I should've said loved him. He can't blame you for things before. This came before!" His voice had a fierce edge to it, and there was silence for half a minute, or rather no words—just slight sounds, they were touching each other. "I've hoped you'd come to *me*. With your troubles."

"*You're* the one who's had troubles. We haven't even talked about that."

"Let's not talk about that."

"I've been awful." Her voice was rising, clear and measured. "I've been as awful as the rest of the town. I've told Gwyneth not to shop here."

"A shrewd move. Or maybe you think I'm guilty too?"

"I hope you don't sell her cigarettes, is all."

"She's a good girl, Winnie."

"I know." Silence again; she blew her nose. "She'd love to leave. To live somewhere more—sophisticated, maybe."

"And he could find work."

"Yes, yes, but I can't. Not now, not with this hanging over your heads."

"But you can't do anything by staying here. Except torture yourself. Now kiss me, Winnie, and let's get you out of here. Emma'll be back any minute."

"Okay." My mom pushed back her stool. "I guess it wouldn't look good for you, huh? To be caught with the neighbor's wife, just now?"

"I'd tell them we were history. They could look us up in the history books."

My mom didn't answer. When I heard another stool scrape against the floor, I stretched my neck out—very carefully, keeping in the shadow of the aisle. The store was dark now, rain had started pelting the windows. Gray and my mom were standing behind the counter, kissing. Only it wasn't a passionate kiss, like you see in movies; it was more like a peck and a hug, then a slightly longer peck and another hug, their bodies rocking gently back and forth. Like they'd got used to kissing each other a long time ago. Gray was a lot taller than my mom, so her face got kind of buried in his chest, and he had to lean down to kiss her. Finally they stopped, and Gray turned away from her to part the checked curtains hiding them from the street. "Pouring," he said.

"It's okay," said my mom. "I've got the car."

And then they didn't say another word, at least not one I heard, before she'd tinkled the door and run out into the wet afternoon. I heard the Honda's engine. Gray stood there a long while—I leaned out a couple times, and saw just his back and head, looking out over the curtains. If I moved now, I knew he'd hear me. So I just held my breath when he cleared his throat and walked down the middle aisle, passing me just six feet away. He went up the back stairs, over by the dairy case; I heard the door to their apartment shut, above me. Then I ducked down the aisle and out the back.

At that very moment, right when I took a breath of the rain-drenched air outside, the crush I'd had on Gray began to slide away. As if it had been a crush on me, not him, I could feel the air filling my chest again. Only I didn't much like it—I didn't like the sensation of moving my muscles with nothing to constrain them, of blood circulating aimlessly through my body. The rain hammered my clothes as I walked a roundabout way home. I wasn't particularly jealous of my mother. She couldn't feel the things I felt. What I'd witnessed was something complicated and a little sad. That honeyed rush I'd felt, meaning to tell Gray—the *fatefulness* of it—had all spilled into the adult sadness. Now, whether I liked it or not, I had other things on my plate.

I never asked my mom about Gray. Instead, that night, I reported to her about Lenny Dugliss coming by, about him asking after the old guy who'd been thirsty all the time. She was rinsing chicken in the sink. "Oh, he's in the hospital," she said, "on an IV. He's got cancer, they think. When did you see Lenny, Gwyn?"

"I dunno," I said. "A while back. Where's Dad?"

"Out in the barn." She said this not angrily but sort of dismissively, like he was to be found in the barn from now until further notice. Dropping the chicken on a paper towel, she turned to dry her hands. "Why?"

"I want to find out what he knows about Mr. Gray," I said. I was watching her face. "Whether he and Benjy have been indicted. JoAnn's dad says once they're indicted they ain't got a prayer."

"Not," said my mother, automatically; but her face was white. A big stew of feelings, the crush still fighting for life, hit my chest. I hurried out to the barn before it got the better of me.

chapter **13**

By the time school started that year, I knew I wasn't interested in what it could do for me, anymore. There were classes and there was life, and a thin enough bridge between them. I made sure I didn't flunk; I steered clear of Pomerantz in history. I still thought, then, that I had three years to go, which turned out not to be so. But anyhow it was the next two months that had me hanging off a cliff.

JoAnn was cool and sweet as a cucumber, even though her face by then had broken out from all the candy she'd stuffed herself with and she'd had to stick gussets in the clothes she'd let out already. If this pregnancy was for real—I had to tell myself *if*, ever since that first day at the Sanctuary, willing myself to doubt—it was getting pretty late on. Finally I worked up my nerve one morning to ask her where she planned to have the kid.

She just stared me down.

"You know," I said. "What hospital. Don't you have to do it in a hospital?"

"You think," she said, "after making myself into this gigantic pillow, I'm gonna waltz into some hospital and let the whole *world* know?"

"You could do it real quiet," I said. "We could take the bus down to Castleton and find some place there. You could give a phony name. Nobody'll care so long as you're white. I heard Mr. Dugliss tell my dad people're paying ten thousand dollars for white babies these days, they're not going to ask questions."

"Boy, are you stupid," JoAnn said. It was creepy, by then, to watch her face when she talked to me. Her cheeks had gotten so big that her mouth just seemed like a little red hole in between them, and when her lips moved they always acted like they were sucking something. We were sitting on the outside steps at school, waiting on the bell. "First of all," she said, holding out her thumb to count, "you have to pay money just to walk into a hospital."

"That's not true. There's the emergency room. They can't turn you out if you're unconscious."

"But having a baby ain't an *emergency*. You have to have medical insurance, and you have to have your own doctor. You can't just walk in. So that's second, your own doctor, which I don't got." Out shot her index finger: two.

"I got a doctor," I said. "My mother takes me to him because I don't get my periods. He wants me to get fat. He'd love *you*."

JoAnn made a noise with her lips. "Sure, a guy who knows the whole hamlet, that's just what we need. Thirdly"—she held up her fuck finger—"you can't just take a bus to the hospital to have your baby, like you were going to the dentist. You can't decide to have your baby at all! Your *baby* decides when you're going to have it, and then you go into labor whether you like it or not, and it's all over."

You'd think I was incredibly dense, not to know these things. I wasn't too young to know; JoAnn had it all down, and she was a washout at school. But I had no siblings to clue me in, and I stopped listening whenever McGruder or whoever was teaching biology started talking about insides. I sat there on the steps, feeling sick. I hated for JoAnn to make me look dumb. It was like the first time we'd gotten stoned together, in eighth grade. She'd told me to open my mouth after I'd dragged on the joint, and when I did, all the smoke just poured out because I hadn't inhaled. She'd laughed and laughed, and I'd hated her.

"Fourthly," JoAnn was starting now, but I grabbed her puffy hand and pulled it down to the cement step. I was steaming.

"Just exactly how," I asked her, my hand wrapped around her wrist, "do you plan on having the thing, then? Or are you still gonna tear it out of there?"

"Oh, I'll have it," she said, her little hole of a mouth working. "All by myself. Except you'll help me. Y'know how the Indian women dropped their papooses? Right in the field, and they kept on hoeing? Well, I figure if they can do it so can I."

"JoAnn, I can't," I said. I could feel my face go white. I wasn't mad anymore.

"Whaddayou mean, you *can't*? All you have to do is hold hot towels and cut the umbilical cord when it pops out."

"Don't talk about it. Please." I'd let go her wrist. I bent my head to my knees.

"Look, I've got this book about it. It's got real photographs, it shows you how your cervix dilates, and the amniwhatever fluid—"

"Don't." My head was getting light. The bell had rung. I hadn't eaten anything that morning, and I could hear all these shoes clopping by me. "Insides make me faint," I said. "Jesus, JoAnn, I always figured you'd have a *doctor* there. I'd be lousy at it. I mean, what if you had some kind of *problem*—"

"I am not gonna have any problems," said JoAnn. "My mother never had any problems, and I am very young. Anyhow, I'd rather die than go anywhere where I had to tell them who I was."

"Lots of girls have babies, JoAnn."

"Yeah, but they all do it to get their boyfriends. They aren't ugly to start with, like me."

I'd never thought till then that JoAnn knew she was ugly. I reached over, squeezed the hand she'd been counting with. The second bell rang, and together we lumbered up the steps into the building.

The Miracle, JoAnn's book was called. I started looking at it in the middle of the night, when I'd woken from a dream and couldn't get back to sleep. It had all the usual drawings of the fetus pushing the mother's belly into a hill, plus real photographs. It was the same woman in all of them, heaving and sweating and getting wired up to different machines. As soon as I saw the diagram of amniocentesis—that needle pulling fluid, *sucking fluid*—I knew I was in for it. I put the book down and shut off the light. But the next night and the next I tried again, turning on the light in the bathroom and sitting on the john in case I got sick, and I managed to read a couple of pages at a time before the pictures got to me. I'd seen pictures like them in science class, but I'd never had to *look*, before. At its little fish-shape, in the early weeks, with those huge shut eyes in its head and those little veins. At all the other things that come pouring out of you when it's born, water and mucus and blood, and at how they cut you to make room for the head. Cut you there—and I'd cup my hand between my legs, like a knife was after me already. *There.*

Then I tried again to think that JoAnn had to be wrong about this thing. She'd fucked up her system, taking birth control pills off and on like they were aspirin. Or else she was just fat, and lying to me. She'd had her periods, right on time, only she wanted to put on all that weight and she was embarrassed because I was her best friend and I was skinny. I repeated these ideas to myself, like they were good-luck charms. *JoAnn's no more pregnant than I am. Look how smooth she walked, that day going out of the Sanctuary. Look how still her belly is. She can't have those things going on inside her, and be so still.* Somebody would have known by now, I assured myself. There were supposed to be all these signs.

When the indictment finally did come down on Gray, not long after school started, he closed the store. Practically no one noticed by then except me and Miss Flanagan—and my mom, I figured, though I never saw her car parked there again. The last time I went in, there was nothing but cans left on the shelves, and the cigarette display was empty. Gray was handing out candy, a big pile of it on the counter, mostly Snickers and Bit-o-Honeys. "Guess you noticed we're closing shop," he said, holding out a Mounds. I took it but just dropped it in my jacket pocket. "But you want anything, Stick, you know I'll send it your way. Emma wants to cart this stuff down to the food pantry in Castleton," he said, like this was an idea I'd disagree with.

"Nobody'll shop with you at all now, huh?" I said. In my pocket, my thumb ran over the smooth wrapper, the little waves of chocolate underneath.

"Aah," he said. "Nobody wants a local store, anymore. It's all the mall and the Minimart. They'll spend two bucks on gas to save two bits on a gallon of milk. We're a country gone loco. Man needs a break from it."

I looked at him sidelong. Why was he acting like I didn't know the score? "Y'oughta just leave this place," I said.

His mouth pulled to one side. "They don't let you," he said. "The state don't."

"Oh," I said.

I thanked him for the candy and stepped out of the store. I'd come there for cigs, and he didn't have any. To my surprise he followed me out. Standing on the concrete step, he lifted his baseball cap, scratched his head underneath, and replaced it. From deep in the thinning woods you could hear the sound of a jackhammer: Dugliss's work crew, my dad among them, setting up to do repairs on the Meyenhold mansion. My dad had taken to working for Dugliss three or four days a week—he claimed he liked being outside, using his hands for something besides filling out inspection forms, but I wasn't sure I believed him. Gray said something about the day, about Indian summer. But we were both just staring at the woods. Finally I blurted out, "Y'know Lenny Dugliss is back living with his dad."

"I know that."

"My mom says they don't even get a social worker. She says it's an isolated incident, you don't get a social worker for that."

"He's a good boy, that Lenny," said Gray. He produced a Bit-o-Honey and handed it to me on the step; I pocketed it. "Only good one of the lot. He'll be okay."

"You think."

"Did you know, when he was four, I saved that boy's life?" Gray leaned back against the doorframe. I waited him out. Eyeing a bottle cap on the second step, I reached down with my foot and tried to flip it over. "Goddamn older brothers thought they'd break into West House, that one deep in the woods," Gray said. "Use Lenny to squeeze through a broken attic window. Only of course the guard pulls up on the old logging road while they're watching him shinny up the drainpipe, and they take off without a glance backward. Lenny didn't squeal, I guess, just kept climbing. They ran down here, of course. I ask where the little guy is, and when I get there he's just hanging, his sweater caught on a metal snag. Couldn't wait for a ladder—I just hoisted myself up the two stories, pulled him down. He was blubbering all right, by then."

I can't say how it was I knew Gray to be lying. Maybe it was just not having a crush on him anymore, it cleared my head. The cap flipped over, and I bent to pick it up. *Give a dollar to Jerry's kids today*, the underside read. Jerry's kids, Gray's kids, they were all the same to me. Then I got this quick picture in my mind, like a flash card, of Gray coming on to Lenny, the way a guy would to a girl. Who had I thought Gray was, that he could have saved Lenny from his own dad? "That was real brave of you, Mr. Gray," I managed to say, swallowing half the words.

"You still think I'm guilty," he said then. It was the reason he'd followed me out: to ask. He was on the lower step; when I looked up, our eyes were even. He squinted against the reflection of the sun from the glass door of his store; the blue of his iris was just a glint, a bright chip squeezed between his lids. "Don't you, Stick?"

"You ain't given me any reason to think otherwise, Mr. Gray," I said. Which I know was not kind. But I guess I thought Gray was asking for my help, and I had enough on my plate with JoAnn Harlett. And to go the other way, to protest, *No, I know you didn't do those things*, amounted to confessing the thing that scared me most, which was that it didn't matter to me, because I had loved him, once, before I'd come to know what I thought I knew.

After that day, the store was shut and locked, dark inside. Late at night I'd step out of our house and go by the big windows and peek in. The cans were all still there, plus a couple of loaves of bread getting moldy on the shelf. As far as I know, Gray never took anything to the food pantry. Maybe the people there turned him down, thinking the stuff would be poisoned.

"He could still be innocent," I said to my mom one Saturday. Testing her. "Innocent until proven guilty, you said yourself, it's in the Constitution."

"I don't want that man's name mentioned in my house," she answered, but her voice was shaky.

"Don't you?" I said. "I thought it gave you pleasure." She glared at me, then, but I didn't go on. If I had I would have ended by telling her I knew and I condemned her. But I didn't condemn her. The problem was simply that she would hide what she could from me, the way she had with Lenny Dugliss. When really, the only thing that would bring me back to her was to get a grip on what she had going with Gray. And then, just as my mom opened her mouth with a retort, my dad banged into the house to get his keys.

"Sure miss that store," he said. "Now I've got to drive twelve miles just to pick up a ratchet."

"I'm sure Mr. Gray'd reopen it," I said, "if any of you people would shop there."

"Oh no," said my father. "I don't sacrifice principle for a piece of hardware." He went into the kitchen and grabbed an apple out of the fridge. "They're at trial now," he said, meaning Gray and Benjy.

"Trial?" I said. It was hard to believe Gray was waiting for anything more—it seemed like indictment ought to be the end of it, like he'd paid his debt already, with his store gone and his name fouled. "You mean like a courtroom?" I said, following him into the kitchen. "Lawyers, a jury?"

"Just a matter of time, now," he said, biting into the apple.

"What'll they do to him?" I glanced over at my mom, who'd fallen silent through all this. She had retreated to the library and flicked on the computer; she stood staring at the screen, not

touching the keyboard. Through the doorway, in the light re-
flected from the monitor, her profile looked pale, bluish.

"Not enough," said my father, starting out the front. "In the old
days, you know what they did to people like them."

"Nope," I said. "What did they do?"

He tossed on a jacket on his way out, and threw me a sharp
look. "Nothing you need to put under your cap, Miss Nosey."

"Jesus," I said. "Why'd you bring it up, then?"

He came close to me, put a hand on my shoulder. I could smell
the sawdust on him. Collecting unemployment, he could work
under the table for Dugliss, and now he was getting to do carpentry. "You just keep away from that Gray character, Stick," he said.
"I been hearing from Gus Dugliss how you hung around that
store this summer. It's girls acting like that cause this kind of trouble, in the first place. Hey." He put his long finger under my chin
and tipped it up. "You're the brainy one, that's what your mom
keeps telling me. So use your noodle, huh?" And he pinched my
chin, just hard enough to hurt.

People like my dad just wouldn't give on this issue. Meantime I
stuck my nose to the windows of the store and tried to make out
if Gray was in there, alone or with Benjy maybe, skulking behind
the pickle barrel. But all most people including me ever got of
Gray from then on was a glimpse as he went out and came back in
his vanagon, the same one that used to hold all the foster kids.
Parking in the gravel lot by the store, he'd unbend himself from
the car and stretch before he hauled his files from the back and
headed upstairs; he might have been a traveling salesman back
from the road.

We saw Gray's wife even less than Gray. One day, though, coming home from school, I caught her taking down the checked curtains. She was so tiny she had to stand on a ladder to lift the rods
off. Then she shucked the cloth and draped it over her shoulder
while she hung the empty rod back. She wasn't keeping her balance too well. I was watching through the side window, and
caught my breath a couple times. But she got them down—ten,

counting the little frills on the tops of the double doors—and proceeded to lay them out carefully on the counter. She folded them
with the corners matching, pressing them out with her hands, till
she had them stacked in a neat, soft square pile by the deli cooler.
She lifted them up the way the page in "Cinderella" lifts the royal
pillow with the glass slipper on it. She carried them out the front
door and around the side. Then she opened the lid of the Dumpster, and tucked them in.

JoAnn's mom thought she was the guilty one. I sat where I was,
on the stack of tar-drenched ties by the railroad tracks, and while
she climbed the back stairs to their apartment I tried to see her the
way Mrs. Harlett did. *Rich* was the first thing I thought. Not that
she dressed rich. She wore the same black poly pants all the time,
with one of those drippy short-sleeved sweaters, in aqua green or
pink, puckered at the neck and sleeves. But there was that smug
tuck to her chipmunky cheeks, like she'd just known there was going to be all this money, someday, and no one to look down on
her. There was her jewelry, too—plain but solid gold, people said.
She'd had it on just then, as she took the curtains down: a thick
chain around her neck, drop earrings, a couple bangle bracelets
on her left arm. Being rich like that was really what Mrs. Harlett
blamed her for. Being rich enough to boss people around—to
stand there, little and scrunched over, her arms folded across her
rib cage, and tell other people what to do.

Only what was the thing Gray's wife had told the foster kids to
do? Touch themselves? Touch her? Lie there and let Gray touch
them?

"God, you'd think he'd suffocate her when they fuck," JoAnn
said when I told her what I'd seen.

"Maybe they don't," I said.

"Maybe that's why she went after those boys," said JoAnn. "So
she could screw and still breathe."

"Who says?" I said. "She's not indicted for anything! Christ,
this town! Like you're all a bunch of saints!"

"Maybe," JoAnn went on, popping in a Twinkie, "her thing's

really with Benjy. He's scrawny, too, they'd be like a couple of chickens on a bed."

I felt bad and sick about it all. Gradually even my picture of my mom and Gray, kissing behind the counter, faded away, so that I wasn't sure what I'd seen and what I'd invented. When my dad first started doing contracting work for Dugliss, he and my mom started having late-night arguments again. I sat up listening, as if I could tell she was giving her love to someone else, to Gray, from the way she baited her husband. *You going to take kickbacks from the county, like him? Bleed the coffers so there's nothing left for my program? You can't work for Gus if you don't.*

I thought I was over my crush on Gray, by then. But I would dream of him holding me down, pressing me onto a bed with the thick comfort of his body. I woke restless, my pulse racing.

The play we'd been rehearsing with Pastor Gwilliam didn't come off until the third week of school. It was like the last ritual of fading summer—the crickets whined in the bushes by the dirt parking lot, leaves had begun to scatter the wide walk to the Sanctuary. My mom had said she wouldn't come, and I told my dad I didn't want him there. "Look, I don't mind saying that Australian looks like a big phony," my dad said. "But he's not the one I'm coming to see. I won't poke fun."

"Well, you ought to," I said.

"Then why are you going to that place, honey?" He tipped back his glass of orange juice and chugged it. We were both up, Sunday morning, while my mom slept—he was meeting Gus Dugliss at a new job site, and I had to finish sewing costumes at JoAnn's house before church. My dad didn't try to get me to eat breakfast anymore. He was beginning to understand the way our house worked, that I wasn't going to linger after supper or watch the TV news with him. He'd have to catch me on the fly. It wasn't that I didn't like him. It was just that whatever spot a person like him might have filled in my life had closed up. When I was eight, maybe, or nine—those same years when Gray had had all those foster children, and I wanted to be one of them—then my dad might have taken me, I don't know, fishing, and talked to me about boys. Maybe he'd have thought I was pretty, and maybe it would have mattered, then and ever after, even today.

"JoAnn's my friend," I said.

He shook his head. He's never been a stupid man, my father. He was a company man, until Hotung laid him off—he believed in company picnics, the softball team, the corporate United Way drive that he headed one year. He's got a bland, company face—broad sniffly nose, receding hair that was still brown, then. But the pain of having to work with Gus Dugliss had burned off some of the company fog that had stuck to him. He seemed sharper, to me.

"Okay," I said when he didn't answer, "I'm doing it to drive Mom crazy."

"Hardly seems worthwhile," he said evenly.

"Say I believe in God then," I said. "I don't care. Just do me one favor, Dad, and don't come to this play."

Pastor Gwilliam tried to comfort me. The Reach Out for Christ people were my family, he said. This was after the performance, after he'd laid his manicured hand on my shoulder and offered to baptize me. I wasn't sure Pastor Gwilliam was a real person and not some kind of android, fine-tuned to be smooth and genial until he had to rev up a sermon. He had the palest green eyes I've ever seen, the iris like cracked sea glass. The next week, when he'd dunked me in the baptismal tub, he gave me a red rose and a prayer book. I thanked him, and someone got a Polaroid of me in my dripping T-shirt with a huge dorky grin on my face.

I still have that picture, somewhere. When I look at it I can almost taste the punch Gwilliam spiked for me after the service, and the weird damp kiss he planted on my neck. Years later, following the indictment that made my mom so smug, Pastor Gwilliam would plead guilty to mail fraud and tax evasion; they convicted him along with one of the slightly older, excited girls who'd hung on him, that day. When I saw his picture in the paper, I searched the clean, strong lines of his forehead and the strained tilt of his jaw up from his neck. I was looking for the price he must have paid, in the end, but I couldn't add it all up.

That day, I took his rose home and put it in a bathroom glass by my bed, where it would quickly wilt. Then, lying back, I let the tears wash over my temples, spilling into my ears, the way I had when I was little and the Duglisses wrecked my make-believe chapel. My mom poked her head in my door and said why didn't I come to her Meeting, just today. But I told her I'd looked at plenty of living room carpets in my life, and God wasn't in any of them. My mom said they weren't looking for God, they were looking for the center of things. I told her I didn't believe in centers.

Which is the absolute truth, even today. I ride on the stream of my life, pulling my past along with me in pieces, jagged and half formed. If I stopped to look for the center of it all, I would surely drown; as it is I ride fast, take the rapids, keep my head up. Pastor Gwilliam does the same, for all I know.

chapter **14**

Packing my feelings about Gray away in a sealed chest, I pulled out tap dance as if it could take their place—one hunger standing in for another. My teacher's name was Philomena. "Like the bird," she told us at the first class. The brochure she'd sent out said she'd danced in *Me and My Girl* on Broadway and for ten years in Radio City. It quoted Bunny Briggs saying, "Philomena's not just a dancer. She's a *hoofer*." My mom was paying for the lessons, but I'd bought the shoes through the mail, a strapped patent-leather pair that pinched my toes. You had to buy the taps separately—heel and toe, light and heavy, full or spot.

"Good shoes," Philomena said. "You'll wear 'em to death. A girl can always use a talent."

Her studio was called Hot to Trot and stood in what passes for downtown Windhaven, the place on the strip where the stoplights stand maybe a hundred yards apart and aren't timed. Her hair was bright yellow, pulled high in a ponytail out of the fifties. Her skin made me think of those close-up pictures of dry, cracked mud in some African country. She went to the tanning salon every day. The salon was next to her studio, and on the other side was Chunky Chicken; you could smell the deep-fat fryers through the mirrored wall. The only girl I knew in the class was Charlotte Petersen—Charlotte, who'd cut class for her modeling appointment and come back looking like she'd been laid out by a steamroller. On weekends, I learned, Charlotte went with her mother to do Broadway auditions—Philomena was a *godsend*, Mrs. Petersen said the first day. Besides her, there were these two Catholic girls from across the river and a tall black girl from Castleton who stood off from the rest of us and looked superior. We started with one-step buck routines and worked our way up to "Tea for Two" with tricks like wiggle-sticks and over-the-top, which Philomena could still do so well you thought she'd stolen her legs from someone else's body.

I didn't tell JoAnn I was taking tap. The bus dropped me two afternoons a week at Haven House, where I checked in with my mom and then walked along 9G a ways and across at the second set of lights to the little shopping strip where the studio was. I was usually a few minutes early. Philomena would be sitting on the floor in the studio, smoking a cigarette and listening to jazz. I'd change and start doing the stretches she'd shown us—heel to buttocks, heel to pelvis, knee to ribs, head to knee. Philomena thought I had nice long muscles. While she finished her cigarette she told me the places to go in New York for studio work and for auditions. She told me stories of the tappers she'd seen come in from Idaho, from Kansas; how they would hit the city for Macy's Tap-O-Mania and then just stay. She described them the way you'd describe a doll: *sweet turned-up nose; platinum hair done in a flip; a waist you could put your hand around.* She was crazy about them. And she looked at me, at all five of us, not like we lived outside Windhaven and had screwed-up families, but like material. We'd either go places or we wouldn't.

"I started in Miami," Philomena said. "When it was hot, before all those Cubans came over. White or black, hoofers like me had their pick of work. That's where I met Fred Astaire. He was already old by then, but you couldn't tell it when he hit the boards. God, what stems! He said to me once, he said, 'Phil'—that's what they all called me, then—'Phil, you look me up when you get to Radio City. I'll buy you a Rusty Nail at Fat Tuesday's.' Only of course by the time I got there he was gone to the other side."

Back in Miami, she'd lived with a gangster who took all her money. That's what she called him, a gangster. "Oh, and the stuff he was hooked on, girls—I tell you, Mrs. Reagan is dead on, you gotta say no to that stuff. You gotta find boyfriends who'll say no. I didn't understand that, at the time. So I'd go out and hoof it, and he'd slam me against the wall and take the boodle."

We got all this from her while we were warming up, stretching and shuffling. The Catholic girls' eyes got wider as she talked, and they never said anything. Charlotte, her toes still turned out from the ballet class she took down in Castleton before she came to Hot to Trot, asked plenty of questions about Radio City and Fred Astaire. I wanted to know about the gangster. When class was over and I had to wait for my mom to pick me up, Philomena pulled a bottle of gin out of her small brown cupboard and lit up a cigarette. "Don't think I'm offering you any," she always said. "I can see you've got the wild eye."

Her voice made me think of Rocky Road—dark and hard, with these soft marshmallowy spots. Someday I was going to tell her everything—about JoAnn, about Seth and his gang in the woods, about how it all seemed to start with the Challenger, the face of God. Meanwhile I was beginning to make my feet precise and fast, to hear all the clickety-clicks, the doo-be-do-be-do-yaas in the tapes she put on. "You're boiling, darling," she said to me once, after I'd whipped a thirty-two-measure combination. "You're on fire. You gotta cool down those skinny legs of yours. Just give me a cramp roll now, take it slow on the brush. Ah-one two three four . . ."

If I told her all that had gone on, I said to myself that night while my legs fidgeted on my bed, she wouldn't have to have it explained, the way other people did. She'd just take it in, with that sort of half-grin that pulled across her face, the lipstick smearing on her upper teeth. She'd mull things over while we girls double-clicked around the studio in our leotards. I'd think this way for an hour or more, and finally crash into sleep with it all decided. Only I'd wake the next morning clearheaded, with my secrets snug in my own safekeeping, and decide not to tell her a thing, just to listen and listen.

I got Philomena to fill out the form so I wouldn't have to take gym in school, and I spent most of my gym periods practicing tap routines in the bathroom—bathrooms have a great echo—or reading the New York papers they got five days late in the library. It was going to be a lousy year, gradewise. We were supposed to study "The Raven" in English class, but I got so sick of it, one day during gym in the library, that I drew out a blank sheet of paper, laid it horizontal, and penciled a line across the middle to start a diagram. From there it went onto another sheet and another, the sentences stacking up like Legos. When the librarian came around I would tuck the sheets under the *Times* and focus on who'd got fired from NASA that particular week. Your folks want to hear how you spend your time? the librarian asked me once while I flipped through Arts & Leisure. My dad'll love it, I told her. He lives for C's.

What kept me going with tap was that no one doing it had to be coordinated or strong, or even graceful. We just had to count the beats and move our feet real fast. "Honi Coles calls this the math of dance!" Philomena would shout. "Your feet are percussive instruments, girls, snare drums and tom-toms. Shake it *out*."

We had a recital almost right away, Columbus Day weekend. Philomena said she had to get more students or she'd have to close the studio, and the only way to get students was to show us off. Charlotte and I were doing the airplane number from *My One and Only*. The Catholics were trying to act like black street dancers from *The Tap Dance Kid*, which had just come out, and the black girl was imitating Gregory Hines's solo in *White Nights*. Philomena herself did a number from an old Ginger Rogers movie, which the adults went wild for, and she brought in a couple of her friends who weren't all that great to do this medley of sixties tunes that everyone laughed at. Plus we demonstrated our stretches and step routines. The whole thing only lasted about forty-five minutes, and at first I thought the only people who'd come to watch me were my mom and Gray, who made me nervous because they sat in the back with just one empty chair between them. I was wearing this aviator outfit—Charlotte was bustier, so she got to be the girl—with a gray hood and goggles, and gray stretch pants and then my regular tap shoes. "I don't look like a flier," I'd said to Philomena when she first tried it on me. "I look like a big gray bug that lost its feelers."

"Yeah, well, you'll dance like a flier, that's what matters," she said.

"Fliers don't dance," Charlotte put in. She didn't mean to be funny. She was just literal. She had all the steps perfect—her mom probably made her rehearse before breakfast—but she never got any pleasure from tapping, as far as I could tell. Her arms moved where Philomena told them to; otherwise they hung at her sides. Going by her face, she might as well have been working a treadmill. I figured she looked that way in her ballet class, too, and in the modern dance she took at the community college, even at the voice lessons her mom had started her on that year. She treated me like a friend at Philomena's, though I was careful never to ask about Pomerantz the history teacher. She had a boyfriend in community college now, she told me once after class, who wanted to marry her as soon as she was out of high school. Her mom didn't think he was classy enough, but Charlotte didn't care, she'd leave all the money behind; her eyes shone, planning the future, like three kids and a part-time bookkeeping job was a world she could only yearn after. Anyhow, I wasn't sorry to be paired with her. I even loved my tiny solo, showing off for my "girl" after I'd supposedly done some trick flying; I got to do wiggle-sticks at the end. At the start of the recital, though, when I peeked through the makeshift curtains and spotted my mom and Gray, my heart plugged up my throat. I ran backstage for water. "I'm gonna screw it up," I said to Philomena, who was standing by the light console. She gripped my upper arm—not rough, but enough to stop me dead.

"You're my best girl," she said, "and you're playing Tommy Tune. This is easy for Tommy Tune. You're going to save my school, darling." And she tweaked my nose. When it came to Charlotte's and my turn I couldn't help glancing toward the back row, checking that the seat between them was still empty. But the lights blinded me, and the next thing I knew, I was dancing, and then the thing was over.

Afterwards, while the Catholic girls giggled and Charlotte's mom dropped names with Philomena's friends, I slipped back of the studio. I was glad Gray had come to the recital, I decided; I'd done okay, it was good to have an audience. And they hadn't really sat together. I had it so worked out, as I pulled off my tight patent-leather shoes, that when someone I was sure was Gray tapped my shoulder, I didn't even jump. I just looked up, calm and then surprised. "JoAnn!" I said. "I didn't see you out there!"

"Hey, that's good. Maybe I'm not such a whale as I think." She gave me a fat mischievous grin. "You were fucking good, Stick."

"Oh, it's stupid," I said. "I know that."

"Sure, it's stupid," she said. "But what's *really* stupid's how you never fucking told me."

"I dunno, JoAnn. It's not like—"

"I thought you got sick of looking at me after school. Not that I blame you."

"No, no." I looked around for my mom; she was out there in the studio, talking to Gray. "It was cool of you to come, JoAnn," I said, and for the first time ever I felt like I really liked her.

"At least it was free," she said, "and my dad dropped me."

"We'll give you a ride home," I said.

She glanced out at my mom and considered. "Okay, I guess. Listen." She leaned in to me; I could smell spearmint on her breath. "You started reading that book yet?"

"Sure, I have."

"You cool with all this?"

"You got a couple weeks at least, don't you?"

"Week after Halloween, it's due."

"I still think you oughta talk to my doctor."

"So that's what I get." She'd stepped away, still whispering. "I come to your crappy little show, and you won't do a freaking thing for me."

"Well, Christ, JoAnn, the farthest you think ahead with this is how do we get it out of you. What about when it's out? It'll be a *person*. I can't stop thinking about that."

"Well, I can."

"How?"

"By having enough else to worry about. Look, maybe my sister'll want it. Or maybe I'll get lucky and it'll come out dead."

"Don't talk that way!" I looked down, away from her, into my tap shoes; they were still warm inside, ripe with sweat.

"Why not? I'd of had it out last spring if I could. Three months or nine months, dead is dead. Meantime I gotta make sure my mom doesn't come in the bathroom when I'm there. I gotta make sure you'll keep your mouth shut and your ears open for when I call you. I gotta hope *I* won't die. I gotta—"

"Ssh," I said. I'd just noticed the black girl from Castleton, who was sitting at the makeup table, running cotton swabs over her face; she turned to glare at us. "I said I'll be there for you," I went on, "so I'll be there. You're not gonna die."

JoAnn stepped in, then, and gave me a squeeze like I'd handed her a present. I tossed my clothes on and led her out to break up the talk between my mom and Gray, and Benjy, who as it turned out had taken that empty seat, had joined the space between them while the recital went on.

Maybe I had to prove something to JoAnn; maybe I wanted to imagine myself as both real generous and real clever. Maybe I didn't want to think about that chance of the baby being born dead, didn't want death to be the happy ending. At any rate, I did something the day after the recital. Trying to break the habit of being poor that my parents had got into, I'd banked almost all the money from Camp Torture. By the time I'd earned it, that past summer, it was already too late to get JoAnn an abortion, but I'd had her in mind as I socked it away anyhow. Now, of course, it seems plumb crazy that we let the time slip by, like sand through our fingers. Not just missing out on abortion clinics but on prenatal adoption centers, private arrangements, *anything*. We just leaned on Destiny, the way people did in the Middle Ages. But with the time come and gone, I owed something to JoAnn, since I'd have spent the money to get her baby out if I'd had cash in my hands, back in spring. That was how I felt, that was all I knew.

So I counted up the number of days from that night in the motel in Florida, when JoAnn said she'd done it with Seth Dugliss. She was off by a week, going by her book; it had to be due the Tuesday before Halloween. I added a day before and a day after, though—in case she went early or late, was my idea, which shows again just how much I knew. Then I called the Outer Haven motel, which is only about two miles from the hamlet, and I made a reservation for three nights. I gave the guy a phony name, Katie McAuliffe. "Any relation?" the guy asked. "You know, to the . . . to the teacher?"

"Everyone asks that," I said. "No."

"Well, you'll have to send us a deposit, Miss McAuliffe, or give me your MasterCard or Visa number," he said.

"How much for?" I said.

"One night in advance," he said, as if I should have known.

"What if we don't get there by that night? What if we get there on the second night? Can we use up the advance then?"

"If you fail to appear by one a.m. on the first night of your reservation, you forfeit the deposit and the reservation is cancelled," he said.

"So," I said. It was like a math problem, one of those abstract problems they gave us on standardized tests. I just had to circle the right letter. "If I want to be sure to get the room all three nights, I got to pay you up front for all three nights."

"I guess that's accurate, Miss McAuliffe," he said. He sounded like a message machine.

"Well, how much *is* that?"

"For three nights—single occupancy or double?"

I had to think a second. "Single," I said finally. Only JoAnn was going to use the bed.

"That comes to one hundred and twenty-three dollars, Miss McAuliffe, with the tax."

"Okay," I said. I had a hundred fifty left from summer, mostly because I hadn't told JoAnn I had it. And to think I almost could have got that much from the troll at the Main Mall, five months back! I asked the guy if I could send him a money order; he didn't like that, but I guess they needed business.

So then I had to go through it all at the P.O. I picked the one at the mall, where they didn't know me, but still the woman kept going, "Outer Haven *Motel?* Did you say motel, dearie?" and I was positive someone from our class was going to walk in any second. The lights in the mall make everything too bright and flat, even the P.O. Just like shopping's turned into a social activity, so the P.O. is kind of recreational. People mail off packages at the mall P.O.; they buy crazy postcards at the concession just outside and send them right away. I could hardly count out the wad of bills I'd brought, I was so nervous, and I signed the thing on the wrong line so the woman had to do it over.

But I finally got it off. And I felt so good after I'd finished and made my way home that I actually asked my mom for a glass of sherry. Then we tucked ourselves into chairs in the library and talked about my tap recital. She wanted the dirt on Philomena, and I told her about Fred Astaire but not about the gangster or the drugs. We talked and drank the way we would have if I'd never had JoAnn in my life to worry about, or if I'd never seen Gray with his hands like that, on my mom, in his store. Just as if.

chapter **15**

But I *had* seen his hands on her, on my mom—and now it was my mom I couldn't get out of my head. My mom as a person, I mean. As Wanda Stickley—Wanda Connors, before she met my dad. *Winnie*: that was for Gray, and for some of her older friends in the hamlet. She grew up here, which always surprises people from outside. They figure it was my dad who came from the area, and my mom who gave up something better to come back here with him. But she'd lived seventeen years in a frame house the other side of the golf course with her father, my Grandpa Benjamin. Her mother had died when she was tiny; her dad ran the old quarry we used to play in, before it closed down.

So she'd known Gray way back, from when he was driving his father's appliance truck and she was doing no-hands on her bike. Once he had to take her to a 4-H Club lamb show—she told me this when I was growing up, before the name Gray went off limits. "My dad and his traded favors," was the way she put it, and taking her and her lamb Mistletoe to the show was considered a favor. He sat up front with some new girlfriend, maybe one of the city girls he knew from runs down to Castleton, and my mom sat in back with the lamb. She was tall for her age, too tall she thought, and she didn't much like 4-H. But Gray'd helped her bring the lamb into the shed, where he talked to it, chucked and whistled to it, until it settled on the straw and he ran his hands through its nubbly wool. "He told me she was a 'beaut,'" my mom said. "He said I'd 'done her perfect.' Of course I didn't win a prize, but I was just so grateful to him for saying that, I waited till the next year to quit Four-H."

Then Gray had gone off to fight in Korea, and when he came home from the service he had his Emma, his little bird-wife Emma, with him. Not long after, my mom started commuting down to college in Castleton, where the Quakers found her out. There was that boy, then, the one who gave her the crystal dove, nameless and sweet in her memory. During the early sixties she packed thermoses of soup for the bums at Grand Central Station, taking the train down there. And so on. That was all I knew, for the longest time. It all made sense—all except her and Gray, that day at the store—and so I didn't ask more. I only wished she'd gotten out, gotten really out, so that I'd have been out too.

But my mom was a plant, sucking up the groundwater. Even with my dad laid off—*because* my dad was laid off, I'd say if it made sense—she started going around that fall with a kind of *zing*. By the time my dad had finished his first contracting job with Dugliss and was nursing a pulled tendon, I could tell he was bending over backward not to hate her for being psyched. "Breakfast!" he'd say, easing himself into a chair in the kitchen. "D'you know how long it's been since we had breakfast together in the morning, Wanda? In the *morning*?"

My mom would smile, like they were on a Folgers commercial. "Twelve years, Jasper," she'd say. Then they'd start on the muffins or oatmeal or sausage, like my mom had been cooking that sort of thing every morning for twelve years and my dad had just missed out. He kept patting the seat next to his and saying, "Breakfast, Stick," whenever I came through the room, but I never stopped. I told him the smell of eggs made me nauseous.

"Sorry to hear about your tendon, Mr. Stickley," JoAnn said when she came by in the afternoon.

"Oh, hey, JoAnn, I'm not sure I'm cut out for this contracting work anyhow. I'm more a company man, y'know. Like some cider? I got this out at the orchard, Dickerson's. Hadn't gotten over there in *years*."

"Sure, Mr. Stickley, thanks." JoAnn took everything anybody offered. Me, I always started with *No*. "But you got laid off from the company, my daddy told me," she called while he was getting her a glass.

I cringed, but he called back like all this was perfectly normal. "I'm just the first wave, y'know, JoAnn! That company was past due for a shake-up! Your father, now—you're lucky he's in maintenance." He came out with the rust-colored cider.

"Toilets," JoAnn said. "He cleans toilets."

"It's steady work, anyhow. Always be a need."

"Let's go," I said to JoAnn. I didn't want her starting on my dad, with her fat-girl tricks.

"Wait a sec." He wasn't used to this. "Where you girls headed? Stick? Your mother—"

"We'll just be at JoAnn's church," I told him. "There's a sing-along."

"But supper—"

"Prayers and pizza," I told him. He looked from me to JoAnn and then back to me. It was beginning to dawn on him that I was spending a lot of time at JoAnn's church, and that the whole thing might be mixed up with God, in some way, and that he'd done nothing but joke about it. Then he looked at JoAnn again, a long look, and to this day I've wondered if he could tell. I mean, my father was never terrifically aware, but he hadn't seen JoAnn in a while. Day by day there wasn't that much change, but after a month you had to notice a difference. She was popping some of her gussets by then, and her bangs had got long, past her eyebrows, so you couldn't really get a fix on her face.

"It's okay, Mr. Stickley," she said. "My mom and brother are coming too. Y'oughta try it yourself sometime, now you got time on your hands. Just singing, you know. Guitar." And she touched me in the small of the back, to steer me to the door.

"Thanks, JoAnn," said my dad, nodding and nodding. "I'm still a busy guy, one thing and another. You need a donation, though? Here. Here, Stick, take this along for the collection," he said, and fished in his wallet for a dollar. Then he stood in the door as we walked off, tall and sort of hunch-shouldered, like he was apologizing for himself.

"Now there's a good dad," JoAnn said when we were out of earshot.

I shrugged. "He doesn't beat me or anything."

"Good," she said. "Because I can't have you hiding out down at your old lady's shelter like that Lenny Dugliss. I need you around awhile yet."

Later JoAnn fed the dollar to the Coke machine in the basement of the Sanctuary. It was enough for two cans, and mine tasted especially good, like it was the last diet Coke I'd ever swirl around my mouth, like my dad had bought it for me.

I never knew, either, if my dad was truly clueless about my mom and Gray. He liked to put a good face on things, to pull the curtain closed on them until they'd passed by. The only reason he wanted Gray put away was that he believed what he read in the newspaper, and "alleged" was good enough for him. He wouldn't hear a word against Dugliss, no matter what Dugliss had done to Lenny; he worked for Dugliss now, and that was the end of it. The only one in town he really disliked was Benjy, Gray's adopted son. "They shouldn't let witless perverts like that post bail!" he fumed, when the charges had first been brought. "When they don't even know right from wrong! I knew it was coming, I knew it from the moment that storekeeper brought that idiot in. I knew it, Wanda!"

I expected my mom to argue him down on that one—innocent till proven guilty—but she just shrugged and went on with what she was doing—gardening, I think. "Raving doesn't help, Jasper," she said when he started in again. "You better watch it, or someone'll come lock you up. For disturbing the peace." And she got the weirdest smile on her face, like it was a look she'd paid for and had to use. This was before I ever saw her with Gray, before I saw the sexy underwear. And for my money, whenever I saw Benjy coming down the road or unloading the van with Gray, I couldn't imagine him doing more than trying to kiss a girl. There was something soft in Benjy's center, something you could hurt easily as a baby rabbit. But I didn't argue it with my dad either. I had bigger things on my mind, already, by then.

Just one other time, I saw my mother and Gray together—and it didn't prove a thing. This was on a day when my mom couldn't pick me up at Philomena's so I'd said I would walk back to her office and hang with Anne-Marie. My mom was supposed to be at a meeting in Castleton. Home with his pulled tendon, my dad was reading *MacWorld*; he was going to learn hardware engineering, he'd started saying, and shift to another company. I walked back along 9G in a cool October wind, the cars just flicking on their headlights as the sky deepened. Bits of gravel stung my calves as the car tires spat them out; there wasn't any sidewalk anywhere in Windhaven, except the block by the library. The shoulder of the road was thick with yellow maple leaves. On the other side of the little mall where Philomena had her studio stood a tall stand of trees, spiking upward now against the sky, their fluttering leaves like distress signals. Cars crowded past me. I turned my jacket collar up and hunched my shoulders into the wind as I walked. I might have been trudging through a postnuclear wasteland. None of this felt real—the gravel, the mall, the column of cars blinking on like massed fireflies; none of it made any sense. I wasn't walking through a city or a neighborhood or a town or the woods, but through nowhere, and the wind felt filthy as it slapped my face.

Then as I approached the first light I saw Gray's vanagon, second in the row. He'd just switched on his lights. My first thought was he could give me a ride, even though with the way they timed the lights he couldn't move any faster than I walked. But being in a car would civilize things; I wouldn't hate the wind, or the road it swept through. Just as I came alongside the passenger door, though, the van started slowly to move, and I saw my mother was in the seat there, with someone else in back. They drove on through the intersection and then had to wait in line as the next light went from green to red. I hurried to catch up to them, and when I did I saw the person in the back was Benjy, and he was leaning forward between the front bucket seats, looking from Gray to my mom and back again.

I just stood there, on the gravel shoulder, my feet deep in blown leaves, clutching my canvas bag with tap shoes and warm-up gear. My hands were cold, but I let them hang down. I thought the three of them in the van would notice me—and my part was easy, I could say I spotted them and naturally I wanted a ride. So I kept standing there, but my mom didn't turn her head, and Gray and Benjy both seemed focused on her. I couldn't make out their faces very well—as I said, it was just on the edge of nightfall, and darker inside the cars than out—but Gray kept nodding his head, and now and then raising his hand palm outward, like he wanted to interrupt my mom and say something. And at one point, just after the light finally changed back and the cars in front of them started to crawl forward, my mom reached out and took that hand, and held it, and then I think Benjy started to talk. But I couldn't make out more, because they began to move as Gray released my mom's hand, and even though I ran to catch up with them at the light, they barely squeaked through as it changed to amber.

"You want to know?" I finally burst out when Anne-Marie kept asking me what kind of bug I had up my behind, after I'd walked to Haven House and my mom wasn't there. "She's got something going. She ain't at any meeting, like she tells you. She's got something going with—with—" I couldn't get myself to say his name. "She's committing adultery," I announced, and took a stool by the stove. Anne-Marie was portioning out sweet potatoes; it was suppertime, with at least twenty people staying the night at the shelter.

"That's ridiculous," she said. "You read about that kind of thing in a book. Your mom's crazy about your dad."

I was looking at the bad side of her face, the expressionless side, which didn't give me a clue how much she meant what she said. I slipped off the stool and walked around to the other side of the stove. "I know what I know," I said. "You people think— All you Quakers think she's such a good person, setting up this shelter and getting the money and all. But she just does what she wants!"

"We all do what we want," said Anne-Marie.

"Yeah, well she cares more about setting the world up her way than about my dad or me."

"Maybe she needs the world set up a certain way in order to care about you." Anne-Marie had filled her tray with little Styrofoam bowls of steaming orange goop. She hoisted it and stepped out to the dining room, where people sat hunched in folding chairs, up and down two long tables. Ben was out there, working the room. She came back and started on a sheet cake that sat on the counter, cutting it into neat squares.

"You *knew*," I said, watching her. "You've always known about this."

"I have not. I don't even believe what you're telling me, necessarily." Anne-Marie's knife slipped; bright blood started from her thumb. "Oh!"

"I'll get a Band-Aid," I said. When I got back she'd taken the stool to sit on, and was gripping her hurt thumb. Together we wiped it with a tissue and stuck the Band-Aid on.

"Look," she said, moving the thumb carefully, as if it had been broken and not just cut. "All I'm saying is that your mom is something special to me." She had her serving spoon in the sweet potatoes but was just moving it back and forth. "And if anything can make her happy I want it to. And quite honestly, Stick, I want that more than I want you and your dad to have a cozy time of things."

"Tell me," I said. "Please, tell me what you know."

But just then Ben poked his head in the door. "You gotta get out here, Annie M. Billy's talking beer again. Says he'll come in the kitchen and find where we hid it at if we don't bring out a bottle."

Anne-Marie gave me a look that said, *Later*, and then pushed through the swinging doors to the dining room. I considered a minute, then followed her.

The room was what used to be the school cafeteria; the tables were all a little low for the grown people sitting at them, and there were others stacked up against the far wall. Overhead, a strip of dying fluorescent lights flickered unevenly and gave off a low hum. At the end of the second table, a big dark-skinned man was holding up his empty glass, waving it around. He had a black knit cap on, and beard stubble on his face. "I tell you I got a fuckin' *thirst!*" he was saying to Ben. "I tell you my *food* won't go down. Ya sonsabitches give us this poison and then tell us we got no rights. I been twenty-one for twenty-one years, man! I got a *right!*"

"Not to what we don't have in the kitchen, Billy," said Ben, trying to get the glass from him. Their arms went in circles, one chasing the other. Next to me, two little girls, their brown hair hanging around their shoulders and their sweatshirt sleeves rolled into deep cuffs, slid off their chairs onto the gray linoleum below the table. The woman next to them leaned down and scolded in Spanish, but they giggled and crawled away. The other eaters tended to their food or else watched Billy; a couple of them laughed, and one shouted out, "Lock 'im up! Hey, Billy, you wanna drink, go downtown!" while another thumped the table with the flat of her palm, *slap, slap, slap*. I went around the table to the other side and squatted down to where I was face-to-face with one of the little girls. "Boo," I said. Her eyes were drops of chocolate; a scar cut across her lip.

"How dry I am," Billy was starting to sing, above and behind me, "nobody knows. Nobody knows, how dry I am."

"Aah shaddup," said a man next to where I crouched, and he kicked out his leg. It just missed the little girl's nose, and caught my hand. I stood up and backed away, and that was when I saw my mother come into the room.

The mumbling, which had grown louder since Billy started singing, quieted down. She shrugged off her coat and dropped her briefcase, and then she went straight up to the big man. "Billy, you old goat," she said, and without a second's pause she reached up and put her arms around his thick dirty neck. "You're getting better, Billy, you're getting stronger," she said. "That's a fine singing voice you got there."

She pulled away; he was grinning, two front teeth missing. And then—this was the biggest surprise—she sang. Just like him, only in a light alto. "How dry I am, nobody knows. Nobody knows, how dry I am."

And the next thing, they were all singing it—all except the kids, the little girls I'd seen and a couple others who'd slipped under the tables as well and were picking up crumbs, like dogs—and my mom had gone over to Ben and whispered something in his ear. He ducked out to the kitchen and came back with an armload of cherry cola and a stack of paper cups. They kept singing it, *How dry I am*, while he filled cups, and then my mom came over and tweaked my shoulder, to signal me out of the room.

"It's a fun old place, sometimes," she said, when the kitchen door had swung shut behind us.

"You betcha," said Anne-Marie.

They traded a look, and laughed. And I couldn't help it, I felt swelled up and proud. No matter what it was I'd seen, out on the road; no matter what Anne-Marie wasn't going to get to tell me, now.

So that was my mom, or what I could piece together of her. I know more now, but it's still in pieces. Dr. Stangel, the guy she took me to because I didn't get my periods, said she was an A-type personality. I thought of her sometimes in terms of letters, like that—like this was Mom being A, this was Mom being K, and so on. Something I didn't share with Dr. Stangel.

I didn't share much with him, in fact. He was this Nazi type, who kept tipping back in his swivel chair and pinching his thin nose between his two index fingers. If I'd given him anything to go on he'd have tipped forward suddenly and let go his nose; he'd have exploded with a sound like *ah-ha!* as if the sound was a string of phlegm, and he'd have looked deeply satisfied.

Dr. Stangel thought I was anorexic, except I wasn't quite skinny enough. He'd done tests on my thyroid and my hormones, and none of those was enough to throw me off the charts. I just didn't get my periods anymore; they'd started when I was twelve, and stopped a year later, about the time my friend Barbie moved away.

"You don't want to menstruate," Dr. Stangel said.

"Sure I do," I said.

"It frightens you—the idea that you could have children."

"It's not top on my list of concerns," I said.

"How do you feel when you think of boys? Of sex?"

"I don't have a boyfriend, if that's what you mean," I said. I wasn't going to talk to him about how it felt to be dancing; that was probably a sure sign of a crazy person.

"What about your teachers? What about this minister, at the"—he checked his notes—"Reach Out for Christ group? Do you . . . *feel* anything? Do they frighten you?"

"Look, Dr. Stangel," I said, "you're barking up the wrong alley. When I really want to get my period, I'll get it. Nothing to do with my weight. Nothing to do with boys."

"I want ten pounds on you," he said. He tipped forward in his swivel chair and scribbled out a list of weight-gaining drinks. "On the other hand," he said when he handed it to me, "if you'd *lose* ten pounds we'd have a diagnosis." Which is what I think he secretly wanted. I decided to hold steady.

I hadn't mentioned JoAnn to him either. Though I came close once, that fall, after I'd made the motel reservation and finished reading *The Miracle* and started popping awake in the middle of the night, sweating, believing at last that this birth was really going to happen. "Listen, Dr. Stangel," I said, after he'd given me his October lecture ("*Two* slices of toast for breakfast, and *butter* on them. Not just jam!"), "I've got this friend."

"I'm listening," he said. Putting my file down on his desk, he swiveled his chair to face me.

"Well, this friend, she's not like me at all. I mean, she's *fat*, and—" I stopped; I giggled nervously. He smiled, nodded, encouraging me to go on. And if I'd known what I wanted Dr. Stangel to do I might have gone on; but what I really wanted was for JoAnn to shed the baby the way fat people lose weight, so I could call the motel and get my money back and be done with it. "And I don't know," I said. He didn't move; his hands rested on his knees. He was waiting, hoping; I had to give him something. "Do you ever think about the Challenger?" I asked.

"You mean the space shuttle?"

"Yeah. Do you ever think about how they died?"

His hands relaxed; he crossed them over his white coat. "I guess everyone does."

"Well, d'you think they knew? Going down? Or do you think they were in this kind of denial, hoping somehow it wouldn't—you know—that God would save them, or . . . "

Dr. Stangel was cool, this one time. He didn't push me, he didn't ask what this had to do with the fat girl. He moved one hand over to my knee, which had started to shake just a little. "If they got a chance to pray," he said, "it was probably for it not to hurt too much."

Which was something of the sort of answer I was looking for, in terms of JoAnn. A way to control the consequences I was beginning to name to myself, one after the other, as we hurtled through time as fast and inevitable as gravity, toward what only looked like the end of things.

chapter **16**

Now that Gray's was closed, our neighbor Miss Flanagan had started coming around with little shopping lists. She made the rounds of people who were out of the hamlet on a regular basis. Usually she paid five dollars for you to fetch and deliver her groceries, but one day she brought by a book for me instead.

Tap Your Way to Stardom, the cover read, and she made it clear she'd given me a treasure that was worth a lot more than five bucks. She stood there on my doorstep while I flipped through the book, her skin like cracked china and her hair in little amber waves pinned to her head. Miss Flanagan was an old gossip. I didn't trust her, didn't trust the special interest she had in our family. But if anyone asked me, even now, how I felt about Miss Flanagan, I'd say I'd have done anything for her, right up to the minute she died from leukemia, a month after I came back here to the hamlet to live.

I used to think Miss Flanagan would never die. She was like West House and the other grand guest houses in the woods, crumbling so slowly that they'd begun to join with the woods. Standing on our porch in the crisp fall, she smelled of ripe pears and dried berries. The book had this cartoon of a thin clownish man who I think was supposed to be Fred Astaire; the color had faded from gold to a dull mustard.

"Let's see a routine," she said in her reedy voice. "C'mon out here on the porch and show us. You learned to do a buffalo?"

I told her I hadn't, but I gave her four measures from "My One and Only." I had sneakers on, which just whispered against the wood of the porch, so it hardly sounded like tap.

"They had a show, don't you know, up at the house when I was a wee thing," said Miss Flanagan. When she said the house she meant the mansion. "Brought a group up from New York on the steamer, and we little ones watched 'em get off at the dock. I thought I'd never seen such pretty girls! All skinny, like you, and dressed to the height of fashion. Had their own little combo, and they performed in the Greek amphitheater, you know, the place that's all grown over with weeds now. Back then they laid these enormous boards down over the stones, and they just tapped their hearts out right in the middle of the woods. When they were almost done they brought Mrs. M. down on stage. Would you believe it! Seems she'd kept her talent in reserve all those years, just in case she didn't marry somebody rich, or maybe he lost it all and she had to fend."

"A girl can always use a talent," I said.

"Can she? I never got one. I'll catch myself a man instead, I thought, and then he got killed. Electrical accident, you know, one of his own appliances got him. A clothes dryer it was, gone haywire. I hadn't banked on that, you see."

"Who was he?" I asked. I'd been riffling the pages of the tap dance book. It had these black-and-white photos of famous hoofers, mostly black, all on that shiny paper they used to print pictures on. The pages in between were yellow, now and then with line drawings of featureless people, showing you how to move your arms and legs. But now I set it down. I'd never known Miss Flanagan had been married. Everyone called her Miss.

"My husband managed the estate," she said. She pulled herself up a little straighter, and a muscle jumped in her neck. "*Plus* he set up that appliance store, which was a new thing then. Only thirty-five years old, but he had a beautiful head for business. Believe me, it's people like him who keep people like the Meyenholds rich! Oh, but you know who he was," she said. She gave me a wink. Miss Flanagan's eyes were watery; she still used makeup on them, which made them look smudged, like she'd been crying.

"I sure don't," I said, looking up from the book.

"Why, Gray's daddy," she said. "Didn't you know he came to this town a widower with his boy?"

My hand found the porch rail. "No," I said. "I didn't know that."

"Oh well, we were only married a year. His name never got far enough into my head for me to keep it after he died; I was Flanagan again within a month. Just think what a pickle I'd be in now if I had to claim his poor devil of a son!"

"You think Mr. Gray did it?" I asked her. Picking up the book, I started thumbing again, but the drawings blurred.

"Of course not," she said. She clucked her tongue.

"Why not? Everyone else does."

"Everyone else is sick with jealousy. That girl, you know, she wanted him to adopt her, and he wouldn't! There was a cleaning girl, up at the mansion, tried the same thing long ago with his daddy. Only there was Mr. Meyenhold then to set the record straight. Now it's all the mob. Democracy, my foot." She shook her head sadly, turning to look out at the road as if she could see the change there.

I'm twenty-two now, and Miss Flanagan is dead. I never got it straight from her what had happened to the Meyenholds. She'd been around in their heyday—when the train stopped at our hamlet just for them, and in the summer all their rich friends came and stayed for weeks on end. It was because of them there were all the paths through the woods, all the outbuildings and guest houses, the extra stables and the gardens. Then I don't know what happened. I don't think they lost the money. They just got bored with taking the train up here, it wasn't fashionable anymore, maybe they wanted to be where the shopping was better and you could see this year's movies once in a while. When they quit the place they left their paintings and their rugs and furniture in the houses and told the state to do what it wanted.

The way I see it, the Meyenholds never accomplished anything but getting rich. They owned the land twenty years tops; they barely had time to build all the houses and grade all the roads and then they got bored. Even the big dark portraits on the wall in the main house aren't of their family—they bought them at auction in Europe. It's handy for the movie, handy for people like Dugliss who charge top dollar to the Renovation Committee, which is this weekend thing headed by blue-haired ladies out of the city. Last time I went by, his crew was replastering columns that had been made of fake marble in the first place. They finished the tower, and the movie people have promised to burn a model and not the real thing, so it'll stand there for tourists to ooh and aah at when the movie's done. The guest houses rot away in the woods. Every now and then some gang of boys gets a bee in their ass and goes out to trash one of them. Miss Flanagan used to wring her hands over that. If the old boss were here, she'd say, he'd have them sent to reform school, parents or no parents.

Gray's father and Miss Flanagan—it made me laugh a little, after she'd left. Like *Upstairs, Downstairs*. It must have been just about the time Gray took my mom to the 4-H show that his dad died. Miss Flanagan hadn't raised him, after that. There had been that uncle, the one who took over the appliance store and rented out apartments; or maybe he'd had an old grandfather, another servant helping to close up the big estate. Then the Meyenholds went away and Uncle Sam whisked him off to Asia, and he came back and was a grown man.

While Miss Flanagan's view of things didn't exactly hold a lot of weight, I felt a little better for Gray that he had her vote. When she'd gone I went upstairs and slid *Tap Your Way to Stardom* under my bed, next to *The Miracle*. It was the week before Halloween, the afternoon light already low. I imagined being my mom, her heart a little soft for this older boy whose father'd died, who was tossing his life into the army. Democracy, her foot. I went for a long walk, out to the old granary in the hollow below the bluffs that overlook the river. For an hour or more I pitched rocks through the highest empty window, hearing them land with an echo on the floor I imagined to be inside, strewn with glass shards and bird droppings, empty of wheat.

Meantime the Outer Haven Motel was waiting for JoAnn and me like a bright, strange planet. When I woke up, the morning of our reservation, it took me a second to name the bubble of anticipation that had filled my chest while I was sleeping. The first day! I'd finally made it all the way through *The Miracle*, through the part about the milk letting down in the mother's breasts and the umbilical cord falling off. The words had swum in front of my eyes, sometimes, but I'd never put the book down, never let nausea get to me. Plus for three Sundays straight I'd sat in the Sanctuary at Reach Out for Christ and prayed to Pastor Gwilliam's God not to let me fuck up. Now the main thing giving me the jumps, as I sprang out of bed and checked the weather, was that JoAnn shouldn't find out about the motel too soon. The way I saw it, you had to catch people like JoAnn on the upswing, just when they needed the thing you had waiting for them.

Everything in me buzzed and tingled. I chattered so much at breakfast I was almost through a second piece of toast before I remembered I'd sworn never to do what Dr. Stangel ordered. It was cinnamon raisin, the kind my dad had started to buy, with whorls that the butter dripped through. He was upstairs shaving, trying to keep his good habits. My mom was sorting out piles of paper on the kitchen table for some report she had due to the city council. She'd been up most of the night on the computer in the library. I knew because I'd got up to use the bathroom twice—I must have been excited already, in my sleep—and heard her clicking away on the keys, like a telegraph operator in one of those old movies, trying to get the news through about the Pony Express. I could have tap-danced to those keys, *tap-a-dee, tap-a-dee, bom-bom*.

Now she looked awful—at least, as awful as she could look—with her hair yanked up and her dress wrinkled, and a spot at the hem I wasn't going to mention. But she turned around when she'd stacked the papers and asked why I was so chipper.

"Why not?" I said.

"You're humming, Gwyn. You're not the humming type." And she looked like she was making a joke, but also like the sound hurt her ears, a little.

"New habit," I said, washing the toast down with coffee. I hadn't even known I was humming. "Feelin' Groovy" it was— from that awful sixties medley Philomena's friends had put on.

"And look at you eat! Have you got a project or something at school today? Did they start the astronomy class up again? Honey?"

Now she was turned all the way to me, like I'd just told her some big news. I put my coffee on the table and leaned toward her. "I have diagramed 'The Raven,' " I said in what I thought was a sepulchral tone. " 'Deep into that darkness peering, long I stood there wondering, fearing.' "

"All right, Gwyn."

" '. . . dreaming dreams no mortal ever dared to dream before,' " I finished. "That's four participial adverbs and one participial adjective with an adverb and an adverbial prepositional phrase. Slopes and slopes. I even worked in the dashes and repeats."

This was true. I'd switched, finally, from regular sheets out of my notebook to a roll of shelf paper I'd found in the barn. Diagraming "The Raven" had nothing to do with why I was excited, but I felt like spilling secrets, and I couldn't spill JoAnn's. Later I would hand that diagram in instead of an English paper; it would net a C+, with no comment.

"I didn't think you kids had to do that anymore," my mom said, pulling back a little ways. "I thought that kind of teaching went out with creationism."

"What's creationism?" I asked.

She sighed and began stuffing the papers into her briefcase. "Nothing you can diagram," she said. Before she left she gave me a peck on the cheek. "Don't lose the mood," she said. I smiled, a

little crazily. I wouldn't lose the mood—or the baby, either. That
was how my thoughts ran, toward Mission Successful.

JoAnn and I went to the mall at lunch. I thought she looked
paler than normal. "How do you feel?" I asked her. "You gonna
have it?"

"Shit, I don't know," she said. "I sure wish it'd drop soon. I feel
like some kinda whale."

"Well, you don't look like you're gonna have a baby," I said.
The morning had sobered me up; I was still testing her, a little.
"You just look fat."

"Tell the baby that," she said. "When this whole thing's over
my first move is a diet. Weight Watchers, my sister did it. A hundred fifty by Easter or bust." She scooped ketchup with her fries.

"It'll be five months old by then," I said. I looked to see if that
registered, but JoAnn's face had gone twisted, like one of those re-
flections you get in a fun house mirror. My heart jumped. "Hey,"
I said. "Is this it?"

She didn't answer at once. She put her Coke down and crossed
her hands over her belly. I was all set to tell her about the motel—
I just had Consumer Economics and Spanish that afternoon,
nothing to miss. Then she looked up; her face straightened out.
"Gas," she said. "It's awful. Got nowhere to go, I guess, and it
feels like a knife in me."

"Are you sure?" I said. "Gas and a baby, I mean, they could feel
the same."

"Please." She rolled her eyes. "I'll tell you when, okay? I want
this thing over as much as you. Man, these fries shit. You think
they got rat parts in them?"

We walked back over Route 9. I didn't see her anymore at school
that day, and when we walked up the golf course to get her a candy
bar at the machine by the caddie shop, she wouldn't talk about it.
That night my mom said she thought I'd lost the mood; I didn't answer, just sat on the floor in front of the TV, surfing channels.

Later I stayed up as late as I could, finishing the "Raven" diagram—the *nevermores* were giving me trouble, they kept popping up as predicates—and waiting for JoAnn to ping my window with a rock. I started thinking I should have told her about the motel, instead of planning to whisk her away like some fairy godmother. The whole night went by, I dozed and dreamed, and she didn't come get me.

The next day Lenny Dugliss had an insulin fit. I guess it happened on his way to school—Seth used to drive him in the new truck and drop him at the junior high, but the high school was closer, so when it happened they stopped there. When our school bus pulled in, the parking lot was already jammed with paramedics and rubberneckers. I saw Lenny get wheeled onto the ambulance. They had him on a stretcher, dead white and biting on what looked like a washrag. His jacket was off, his sleeve rolled up, and a cotton ball taped where they must have just given him a shot. Seth trailed after him, looking scared.

"Is he dead?" asked the kid next to me.

"No, he's just a weirdo," said the one next to him. "He's the one run away last summer."

"He oughta be in an institution," said another as I backed away. "That's what my mom says."

My knees went weak. I made it over to a low wall and sat down, my head between my legs. Blood, I started thinking. Lenny's blood. The feeling of it gnawed on me—the needle that had gone into him, the insulin rushing through his veins. When I finally looked up, the parking lot had emptied and Matt McPeck was standing there, staring at me.

"Worried about your boyfriend, Stick?" he asked.

"Up yours," I said.

"He ain't gonna live long. Not with that disease," he said. He held out a cigarette and I took it; smoking on school grounds was illegal, but the proctors had taken care of the Lenny crisis and gone back inside. The smoke felt good in my lungs, it steadied me.

"I just don't . . . I can't explain it," I said. "Medical stuff, stuff to do with blood—it weirds me out."

"Better not have any babies when you grow up then, huh?" he said, and crinkled his eyes. It half occurred to me that Matt McPeck liked me, and then I remembered how he'd been the second candidate, after Seth Dugliss, for knocking JoAnn up.

"You're a guy," I said, taking a deep drag. "You don't have to think about that stuff."

"We think," he said. "We think, sometimes."

He dropped his cigarette, crushed it under his heel, and walked off. I stayed and finished mine, thinking. By the time I'd caught JoAnn in the hallway between periods, I'd decided to tell her about the motel—in case I got run over by a truck in the next twenty-four hours, I told myself, so she'd have a place to go anyway. But as soon as I started with, "Y'know, when you get the first contraction," she said, "Oh, can't you shut up about it! I gave you the book to read, just read it and know your stuff and don't ask me!"

I shut up and went on to my next class. Before school was done for the day we'd learned Lenny Dugliss was out of danger and back home, and so shutting up seemed like the right thing to have done. And there went the second day.

I called the motel just once, on Halloween, to ask if there was any way I could get a refund. There was a lady on the other end, real brassy and in a hurry. I wondered if the message machine guy had been fired; the way I missed hearing his voice, you'd think he'd been in on my secret.

"If you'd like to cancel your reservation right now, for tonight," the lady said, when she could tell I was stalling, "I think I could persuade the manager to let you have one night's charges back. McAuliffe, is that right? Any relation?"

I figured it out quick: seventy-seven dollars. Then I figured that if I canceled, with my luck, JoAnn would go into labor right after dinner. All Hallows' Eve. "That's all right," I said, trying to sound older and rich, like seventy-seven bucks didn't matter, "we might make it tonight after all. No relation."

chapter 17

JoAnn finally came and got me two weekends later. I could not believe it even when it was happening. I kept whispering to myself, "This is real, this is real," so that I wouldn't think it was some dream and I didn't have to do anything. It was a bright, warm Saturday: I remember the way the sun aimed in my window from the gap it had reached between the low hills northeast of us. November here is usually a lineup of damp, gray days; my dad used to wear his sunglasses, not because anything shone, but just so he could believe it was the glasses and not the day that made the world look so dull. I'd gotten over the motel thing. I'd stopped thinking about JoAnn's pregnancy, to tell the truth. Not that I didn't believe in it—I believed, by then—but that it had gotten to be a sort of permanent condition, or one that would just reverse itself one day, and we'd look back and laugh about the months when she was pregnant. Or maybe I'd just started to get used to things being out of my control.

Anyway, this bright day burst forth, and before anyone woke up I was heading out on my bike to get grapefruit juice at the Mini-mart. Just as I took the corner JoAnn came stumbling across the street and grabbed my handlebars. Her forehead shone with sweat and her pimples were bright red, like red ants stuck on her face.

"You gotta come with me," she said.

"Okay," I said, though it was like someone else saying it. I got off real slowly. "I had a motel reservation," I said as I leaned the bike against Miss Flanagan's hedge, "but it's canceled out now."

She acted like she didn't hear me. "We gotta go to the tower," she said. "Listen. Can you go stand outside my window and I'll push my blankets out to you?"

"We can't go to the tower, JoAnn! They bricked it up, remember?"

"Shit. *Shit.*"

"It's all right," I said. "I'll think of somewhere. There's other places, it's all right."

"We gotta just go to the woods, I can't get far."

"Sure," I said. "What does it feel like, JoAnn? You sure this is *it?*" She still didn't hear. She was looking around the street like she expected someone to walk down it and shoot her. "What about hot water?" I said.

"I filled up this enormous thermos my mom takes to auxiliary," she said. "It's—ouch, *shit*—it's on the back porch. While I go upstairs you go grab it."

"Was that a contraction, JoAnn?" I asked. But she'd gone off already, toward her house. I was just some kind of tool to her now. My legs danced around a little, wanting to dart over to Gray's dark apartment, or up the road to Dr. Stangel's little white frame office. But I'd never make it there and back before she freaked. If I'd told one of them, I thought, if only I'd told *somebody*. Instead I went to get the thermos and washrag, and then I waited under the window to catch the blankets when they tumbled down. For all I knew, Gray was actually watching us—it wasn't that early, maybe seven-thirty; I'd caught sight of JoAnn's mom fixing coffee in their mustard-colored kitchen, a cigarette dangling from her lips, oblivious. JoAnn tossed the blankets and a flowered sheet and then came down the back way, right by the kitchen door. "C'mon," she said, handing me a couple more washcloths and a bottle of peroxide.

"Where to?"

"I don't know. The woods somewhere. Least it ain't raining."

We went the roundabout way, over the tracks by the water tower and through the dry brush where the train depot used to be. With the sun still low the air was amazingly warm for November, and we both started to sweat. I had to look where I was going, with all the blankets piled into my arms and some rough patches to pick my way over, but I could hear JoAnn behind me all the time, breathing heavy. Every now and then she'd have to stop; she'd call out, then catch up and lean on me while the labor passed. I practically keeled over then, with the weight of the blankets and the thermos and then JoAnn gripping my upper arm. And all the time I thought, Where? Where? We couldn't just go to the woods. The granary was too far, West House too close to the graded path. Then I spotted a low roof, way down a side path that went across a streambed. You couldn't see more than a corner of it, even through the bare trees. "This way," I said to JoAnn.

As we got close, I remembered this roof. It belonged to an old shed we used to hide out in, playing games with Gray's foster kids years back. It had been padlocked last time I'd checked. And sure enough, the lock was on, but not snapped shut, and JoAnn leaned against the wooden side while I wrenched the door open and scoped the place out. It was filled with sawdust and dry leaves; leaf-blowing equipment lay disassembled in the middle of the room. "They'll be back, then," said JoAnn. She'd slumped against the doorframe, her hands over her belly. "They'll catch us at it."

"Not on Saturday," I said. "State workers don't do overtime till it snows, I heard my dad say that once." I looked down at her; she'd taken her hands off her middle and was twisted sideways, clawing at the ground, her teeth clenched. "And you just had one of those three minutes ago," I said. "We don't have a lot of time to shop around, JoAnn."

She didn't answer. I stepped into the shed and cleared the leaf blower parts away, then took the broom hanging in the corner and brushed together the piles of leaves. Then I spread the blankets and sheet down on top of them. I had to move a couple of lawn mowers, too, to give myself room to maneuver. Any other time I wouldn't have been able to budge them. One had a sharp blade that cut into my jeans at the shin.

"GodfuckingholygoddamnittoJesus," I said, and then I told JoAnn she could lie down. I pulled off my sweatshirt and bunched it into a pillow for her.

She never did lie down much. She thrashed, she clutched at me, she bit into the washrag after I'd wet it from the thermos. The pain in her was like a Mexican jumping bean, it wouldn't let her stay still. For hours she walked around the shed, came in, sank down, grabbed at me till she'd left nail marks in my arm, and then rose up again. And then, when there stopped being pauses between the contractions, when all she had was just one long wave of pain after another, she started the yelling.

I can't describe how loud she yelled. I shut the door of the shed to try to hold it in, but I imagined the woods echoing with it. She yelled like she was ripping her body apart with sound—her fat body roiling in those blankets, making dust out of the dry leaves underneath. I just kept dipping the washrag and applying it to her belly and her face, letting her bite it to stop the screaming for a couple seconds.

And I was just sure, when she started in earnest, that somebody would come. I wanted somebody to come. If somebody didn't come JoAnn might kill herself and I couldn't do anything about it. By the time the sun was straight up over the shed, its light coming through a chink in the roof, I'd got suspended in disbelief that nobody was coming to help a person yelling like this. We were out of earshot from the hamlet, but people took walks in the woods all the time. Twice that fall I'd run into Gray's Benjy, and Miss Flanagan claimed she made the loop every day. Even if they thought it was an animal screeching they ought to come. I wanted to run away, get away from the sound JoAnn wouldn't stop making, but I was the only one there and every time I moved JoAnn screamed, "No! Shit! Don't leave me! I'm gonna die!" So I stayed.

There was a lot of blood. That was the first thing that came out of her, all over the pink, flowered sheet and soaking into the rust-colored blankets. She was screaming good by then. "Sit *up*," I kept telling her, "lemme hold up your legs," but it was like she didn't hear me. I didn't have enough arms to hold up all the parts of her the book said you were supposed to hold up. Then I saw it, right in there like horse dung when it's about to come out of a horse's rump, only this was between JoAnn's spread legs.

"It's him," I said to her. My mouth was so dry my tongue stuck to the roof. It felt like we'd been in that shed forever and would never leave. "I see his head, JoAnn. Push, JoAnn," I said.

She listened to me. She stopped screaming and there came an awful bottled-up silence. In slow motion the part behind her birth canal ripped—like wet paper, only bloody. Then I had the head in my hands.

I did just like the book said. I might have had it in front of my eyes, I remembered it all so well. How blue the head is, how you have to wipe it first, and clear the spit out of the mouth. Then you turn it a little at the shoulders, keeping hold of the head till the feet make it. How you shake it so it breathes, then it flushes all red and cries. The only thing that stopped me was the umbilical cord, trailing out from the middle of the baby, into JoAnn. How bright it was, how it beat just like a heart lifted out of the body—*WHOOSH whoosh WHOOSH whoosh.* I was going to have to cut it, somehow, but for a long minute I just watched it while I cradled the slick little head in my hand. What got me was the color, electric blue, not at all like the book but like something on fire with blue, something from another planet. Like a cord made by God, bright and pulsing, running from her into him.

Slowly, while the baby cried, it stopped beating. Then I did the one thing that wasn't in the book, because we had forgotten a knife and I knew enough not to trust any of the rusty blades I might have found in that shed. Bending my head down to where JoAnn couldn't see me do it, I shut my eyes and reached with my teeth. The cord was warm and rubbery, harder to gnaw off than I'd expected, but finally it was in two pieces and the queer taste of blood filling my mouth. I opened my eyes then, and with a string I'd found in my pocket I tied the end that hung from the baby. Then, only then, did I look at the baby's face. It had stopped howling and looked back at me, its eyes sleepy, Oriental almonds.

Then I remembered, you were supposed to put the baby on its mother's belly. That was what the book had said. But JoAnn had pulled her knees up and was just rocking side to side, moaning. I set the baby on a clean part of the sheet.

"One more push, JoAnn," I said.

"Unghh," she said.

"C'mon, we got to get the placenta out, it'll make you sick otherwise. This is the easy part, c'mon."

It came. I didn't look it over, hold it up to the light, the way you were supposed to. But it came in one piece, and I wiped her really well with the last clean washrag. I carried the placenta and the rags to the door, and for the first time since she'd started yelling I opened it. The sun blazed between the bare trees. I flung the mess into the thick undergrowth, far off the path. Then I went back inside the dark shed, and picked up the baby.

I picked him up for real, then. When he cried my heart came in two. "God," I said. Then he gurgled and cried some more. It wasn't like any other kind of animal you could think of. It was human, that was all. It was so gorgeous.

"We all done?" JoAnn said. I'd almost forgotten about her, way up there on the flowered sheet. She sounded caved in.

"Sure," I said. "Here he is." I took the used washrag from the thermos, squeezed it, and wiped off the blood and white cream sticking to him all over. I pulled off my T-shirt and wrapped him in it. Then I held him by the head and fanny and walked up on my knees to show him to her.

Her face was so fat I can't say it shriveled up when she saw him. But it did something to get all at once real old. Her cheeks rose up and squeezed against her eyes, and her mouth turned upside down. I knelt there, shirtless, holding the baby. She didn't move her arms.

"I hate it," she yelled. "Get it out of here!"

"It's your baby, JoAnn," I said. "It's a boy."

"Not my baby! That thing! Just kill it!"

"JoAnn, you got to hold it."

"I told you it wasn't gonna live!"

"That was a joke, JoAnn. This is your baby."

"I said *kill* it. It's not a baby, it's—it's gross! I'm gross! God, I wish I'd *died*."

And she turned her face away.

Just like I'd known what to do when she started to have the baby, I knew what to do now. I didn't need help from anyone, and I didn't need any book. I set him for a minute on a pile of leaves while I pulled JoAnn's cotton jacket over my nakedness. Then I lifted JoAnn's heavy body by parts—head, chest, hips—till I'd rolled down the sheet with its swamp of blood toward the bottom. She was still bleeding a lot, but that wasn't going to kill her. I tucked the blankets around her.

"You stay here and rest," I said. "Don't get up till you have to. You might get dizzy, with all that blood lost."

"You going to get rid of it?" she whispered at me. She turned her face to me again, her lips working the way they had in the church, light-years before, when they were pressed up against my ear, mouthing off about oral sex. This was what she'd been aiming for, even then. The fat on her face was dead, like a side of pork. "I won't tell!" she whispered again, desperate, like she was carrying something too heavy for her.

"I know, JoAnn," I said. "You stay here, now."

It was early yet. I picked the baby up. He wasn't crying now, just making sweet little gurgly sounds. His purple mouth was working and I stuck my pinky at it, and he sucked. His gums made a perfect clamp, like those round clippers my mom trimmed Trixie's nails with, tight and sure. All set to sling him under my arm if I had to, like a bundle of old clothes, I carried him out of the shed, along the broad dry trail. Before we got in sight of the hamlet, he'd fallen asleep.

When I got to my house I just nipped upstairs and got the big canvas bag, *NO NUKES* with the blue dove, the one my mom had given me in September for my fifteenth birthday. I stuffed a pillowcase and a beach towel into it and set him on top. Nobody in my house caught me till I was out the gate, and then it was my dad. Leaning out from the window to the barn, he waved and called out, "Hey! Hey Stick!"

"Yeah!" I said, slowing down but not stopping, not ready to stop for anything.

"Gonna fix me lunch today? Your mom's gone to her office."

"Sorry!" I called back. "Going shopping!"

And then before he could try a new angle I was past Miss Flanagan's house, past my bike leaning up against the hedge, past the post office, and then we were free.

chapter **18**

Practically nobody takes the bus to Castleton before noon on Saturday. I stood out on the shoulder of Route 9 with the bag cradled in my arms, the wind starting up and blowing dust into my sneakers, slipping through the weave of JoAnn's cotton jacket. The sky had returned to its usual pewter; I wished for dark glasses, like my dad. Soon I spotted the bus from two hills away, cresting and then diving into the valley. I leaned the bag into one elbow and dug in my pants pocket for change.

Behind me, there came a crunch of gravel. I turned, panicked.

"Christ," I said. "Lenny Dugliss. You scared me."

"I gotta get to the mall," he said, not looking at me or looking for the bus either, just focusing his eyes across the road.

"You okay?" I said. "I mean, the other day, you looked pretty wiped. When they took you. When you had that . . . that . . ."

"Fit," he said. His thin mouth curled up one side. "Sugar fit. The doc wants me to say *reaction*, but I like *fit* better."

"Fit's okay," I said.

"Not if you have too many of 'em, they're not."

"No, I meant . . . are you—"

"Yeah, I'm okay. They just stick me and talk at me. I guess I looked pretty weird, huh?" He kicked at the gravel, his mouth still drawn up, like a pencil curve. I looked down the road; no bus. I didn't know how to answer him. I held the bag close, the new, secret life inside. "My dad says I got to get new snow boots," Lenny said suddenly. "Timberland, he says. They're real expensive, he gave me his Visa card."

He held it up, like a cop showing his ID.

"He trusts you with that thing?" I said, relieved not to talk about fits, anymore. I kept the bag tucked into my elbow, the warmth of the baby coming through the canvas.

He shrugged. "I can't even use it, most places. Last time I tried, a guy took it away from me and called the cops. So my dad calls this store ahead of time. To let them know it's okay."

"Too bad," I said. "You could get some nice CDs or something."

"I need boots," he said.

For a second I wondered if he was really dumb, if that was all his weirdness amounted to. He actually thought throngs of night stars made the country too busy a place. He'd been friends with Benjy because they were on the same level, and his fits came because his brain wasn't all there. Then I saw he was tipping his head in a pretend shrug, one eyebrow cocked. "Well, yeah," I said. "Get what you can."

"What's in the bag?" he asked. His voice cracked a little. Just then the baby shifted. I tightened my armlock on it and sucked in my breath.

"Returning something," I said. "Leotard and tights. They were too big."

He shuffled around, leaned over and picked up a bottle cap. He looked smaller, out here waiting for the bus; his hair stuck up in a cowlick at the crown of his head. He ought to have had his brother with him at least, I thought. Plus he looked cold; he had on just a black T-shirt and slashed jeans; you wouldn't have picked him for having a rich family. JoAnn was probably cold too, back in the woods. The warm blood was still dripping out of her, soaking the blankets I'd left. And all she was thinking was how it was over and it hadn't killed her, and her mom would never find out. It was like she'd never had anything alive in her, just this cancer, festering under the layers of fat. On my lower arms I could feel a slight dampness; the baby must have peed, in there. Then the bus, out of nowhere, stopped in front of us, farting diesel fumes, and we climbed on, dropping two quarters into the meter, half-price on Saturdays. Lenny slipped down to the far back; I settled midway, in one of those single seats. There were three other people on the bus, two of them asleep.

As soon as I could, I peeked in the canvas bag, at the baby. He'd sunk into sleep too, his face tight as a button. I stuck my finger under his nose; he was breathing, all right, quick little whiffs like the air you can expel by pumping a medicine dropper. If you pinched his nose with one hand and covered his mouth with the other, he'd jerk once or twice and then lie still. That was what JoAnn wanted. With my index finger, I stroked the little bit of hair I could see; it felt damp and silky, like one of those trailing fins you see on tropical fish. The rest of his body was invisible, a lump of warm, barely moist towel.

The bus jerked when it stopped, and people got on. They mostly sat at the front. I heard them talking what a mess Halloween had been, and how fast the holidays were coming on us. They're putting Santa in the malls already, said one lady, it's disgusting. Another kept on about her sweet potato recipe. Aromatic bitters were the secret, she said, and people who used marshmallows ought to be shot. She looked around the bus, on the prowl for marshmallow types, but I ducked my eyes down, into the bag.

Halloween hadn't been a mess at Charlotte's house, where I'd managed to be invited to her party just because I took dance class with her. It had been perfectly choreographed, from the haunted maze you went through at the door to the showing of *Friday the 13th*. I wasn't going to go—those were the Outer Haven Motel days, still—but my mom had said she'd drive me and there wasn't a peep from JoAnn. So I'd worn my *One and Only* outfit, and when anyone asked who I was I said, "A gray bug." Charlotte's mom was dressed like the Blue Fairy in *Pinocchio*; it was enough to make you gag. But if she got her rocks off supplying the space—that was how one football player put it; he was dressed like Rocky in red silk boxers and stirring a Tom Collins—then he was for her. And no matter how much she flitted around the place with her wand, there were still a couple guest rooms in the basement with futons, and two plush bathrooms for cutting lines. I don't put things up my nose, I told the Rocky guy lounging on a futon. Though I licked my pinky and wiped the glass; the powder tasted sweet and medicinal, like Tums. Just then a clock upstairs bonged midnight and Charlotte's mom called out, "Movie time!" Out in the main room, the pitch-dark smelled of gin and smoke. Settled on the floor with everyone else just staring at the smoke-gray screen, waiting, caught in those few seconds of silence and expectation, I felt numbed by happiness, by the absolute absence of who I was and what I might have to do next.

JoAnn meantime had stayed home, handing out candy and suffering probably the worst PMS of her life. Now she was bleeding it out, in the shed. Women used to bleed to death sometimes, like that, before doctors. I looked out the scratched bus windows at the newly bare trees whipping by, and the houses you could see, now, through their branches. Then I looked in on the baby again, checked his breathing, and made my lips into a kiss for him.

The bus rolled past Windhaven, past JoAnn's church with its big gilded cross and ski jump roof and new paved parking lot.

JoAnn wasn't going to die. She'd done just what she said she was going to do, drop her kid like some Indian squaw. Now she could just make like a squaw and keep on going. That's what I thought as we rolled on, past the field with the Free Zone the other side of it, where Matt McPeck and his crowd were probably hanging right now, wasting a Saturday, filling a bong. JoAnn could do what she'd set herself to do, and what I did wasn't any of her concern.

Way back in the bus, Lenny Dugliss was huddled up like an Indian, his hands clamped over his knees; even from where I sat, I could make out his long fingernails. I could have sat next to him; I could have handed him this secret, like a giant ruby. We rolled on past the Windhaven mall, so that wasn't where he got off; then on past Hotung Digital. The bus was starting to take on Saturday workers, headed into Castleton; I couldn't move now. So I sat, one arm tucked into the canvas bag, palm down on the warm towel that covered the baby's body. And I realized, about the time we looped down the overpass into downtown Castleton, that I could just keep on going, if I wanted.

"Yes," I breathed.

"Huh?" said the lady across from me, a long-nosed snuffly type. She'd been waiting for someone to talk to her.

"Nothing," I said.

But I could. There were always places you could go, in New York City. There was Barbie, down in Florida. *A girl can always use a talent*, Philomena had said. All I needed was some kind of sequiny outfit and some false boobs. A granny type to watch the baby in the evenings. In the day we'd stay real quiet; I could get one of those baby packs and walk him around a park somewhere. I leaned into the canvas bag, shut my eyes, and smelled him; it was like pee, but the sweetest pee. Like some kind of drug.

"Whatcha got there, a bufday cake," I heard, and I looked up to see a tall black guy hanging onto the strap, snickering down at me. I folded over the top of the canvas bag and drew my hand out. *Talk to them*, my mom'd always told me, but I didn't have to right now. Someone got off at the first stop in the city, and he moved down to a seat. Then we were at the Main Mall in Castleton, and I knew something. In my stomach, in my heavy legs—I knew I wasn't going much farther; this was already too far, or almost, and I had every reason to think I'd get caught.

Still, while the bus changed drivers, I found myself stretching my neck to see out the window, to see onto the raggedy concourse of the Main Mall. There were more people milling around than you'd think; pumpkins ringed a giant haystack, while workers were already trimming the lampposts with fake greens. I scanned the thin crowd: not a troll among them. He'd left town months ago, the one I'd almost traded my virginity to. Or died, maybe, in his greasy hotel room. And if I had, if I'd done it . . . then JoAnn would have got what she was still asking me for, that very morning, in the woods: no kid. I pinched my thighs together, as the new driver boarded and the bus started up.

I stayed on till we hit the new mall south of Castleton, and it wasn't till I pulled the cord that I realized Lenny Dugliss was getting off with me. "Timberland store's here," he said as he stepped down behind me. "How come you're carrying that bag funny?"

"What? Oh," I said. Taking hold of the straps, I lowered the bag real gentle till it swung from my clenched fingers. I couldn't walk too fast, but I got the feeling Lenny was going to stick by me at any pace. Walking next to me and just a little behind, like we'd come to get a present together. Please, I prayed to the baby. Please hold on, just a little longer.

And then I don't know what got hold of me, because the baby did hold on. Held on and didn't budge, didn't squirm in the bag. A breathing statue, a miracle. But the doors swished open to let us onto the main concourse, and all I could see were faces hard with the look people get when they're determined to spend money, and something must have caught me scared. Because I stopped, right there by the green-lit store directory, and I spoke Lenny's name.

"You gonna tell me now?" he said. He'd turned my way, shoved his fists in his pockets.

"What?"

"What's in the bag. Not that I could care."

"Yeah, well—" I could have made something else up right then; asked him for bus fare, anything. But I couldn't stand having the baby so far away from me, dangling at the end of the canvas straps by my knees. It could squirm and I wouldn't feel it; die and I wouldn't know it. "C'mere," I said, and I sat down on one of the low walls bordering the plant clusters they always have in malls, thick and too green. I set the bag on my lap and spread the top open. "Look in here," I said.

He leaned across my lap. He was tall for a twelve-year-old, I realized. Maybe he was thirteen, by now. He was starting to smell like a guy: yeasty, bitter. His shoulder grazed my chest. "It's real, ain't it?" he said, when he'd lifted his head up.

"Course it's real," I said. "It's a boy. It's breathing."

"It ain't yours, is it?"

"You noticed me with a basketball in my belly lately?"

"I dunno." He looked back in at the baby, then he gave a weird giggle. "It must've just popped!" he said.

"Keep your voice down!" I whispered.

"Whatcha gonna do?" He'd pulled away from the bag, started cleaning his long fingernails with his dad's Visa card.

"You'll see," I said. "I need you to run interference."

"I gotta get my boots and be back on the noon bus," he said. "Or I get tanned."

"It won't take long, and it won't get you in trouble," I said. "I got a plan."

Which it has to be admitted I didn't. The whole thing had been just calling to me, showing me one thing to do after another. And whatever came next probably didn't require Lenny Dugliss. But you can only get so far on your own steam; you can smother the words that explain to your own self what you're doing only for so long, and then they have to breathe. So I looked up, and I saw down the concourse where they were setting up the Christmas display early, and I tucked my arms under the bottom of the canvas bag again. "Let's go," I said to Lenny.

It had been there in my head, what that lady on the bus had said about Santa. Sure enough, there was his throne, right at the end

of the mall, with a stage and a red rope for the line of kids and a
color photo for three bucks. It must have been his first day. SEE
YOU AT 1 P.M.! the sign read. Lenny and I walked along by the
shops; we passed the Timberland store, but he didn't even pause.
All the displays along the way were still aimed at Thanksgiving—
big plastic cornucopias, orange Mylar pumpkins, Pilgrim hats—
but they were sticking Santa into the scene, to get the buying
blood up.

"Hang here a minute," I said, when we'd got close to the setup.
We stood outside a video store window, pretending to look at the
fiftieth-anniversary *Snow White* display. Behind us, two guys were
just sweeping up piles of leftover straw. After what seemed like
forever, one of them said something to the other about a break,
and they stood their brooms in holders on their red cleanup dolly.

"Now if somebody notices, you know, what I'm doing, you
bump into them," I said. "You don't know me, okay? You just get
them to yell at you for a second, and by then I'll be gone. Don't
meet me anywhere."

His fists were back in his pockets; for a second I thought he was
going to turn me down. Then he stepped close, and pulling away
the top of the canvas bag, he reached inside. "Don't," I said.

"I ain't hurting him," he said. But my arms could feel the little
body, under all those layers, starting to squirm. Lenny pulled his
finger out, and it was damp—the kid had been sucking on him.
"You better know what you're doing," he said. And he laid his eyes
on mine so that all of a sudden I was tired, so very tired, like I'd
been awake the last nine months solid, and all I wanted was to lie
down with Lenny Dugliss and sleep.

"Just watch everybody else," I said. "Don't watch me."

I stepped toward the display; no one was there now, the cleanup
dolly and the crew had rolled away. A red carpet led between the
ropes up to a little stage covered with green carpet. On the top
step, right below where Santa's feet would go, there were all these
boxes wrapped up like presents. I didn't even look around me—I
had to count on Lenny, if I looked around I'd give the whole thing

dead away. I didn't hurry. I just lifted the towels and pillowcases and baby at once out of the canvas bag. I got a whiff of that pee perfume as I set the whole bundle down in the middle of those bright empty boxes, on the smooth green carpet. I didn't touch him or kiss him; I acted like he was a doll I'd got too old for. He blinked his almond-shaped eyes, I think, but he didn't even start to cry, for a bit.

Then I hid myself. What I mean is I didn't go back to where Lenny was looking out; I didn't stay near the display. I went shopping, real casual, in the first boutique I saw, which I think was something like Stuffed Shirt. Then I slipped out of that one and into the next, which was a narrow place selling nothing but hats. I tried on a bunch of them, and while I was looking in the mirror with this huge black Stetson on my head I saw Lenny, behind me and off to the side, pulling on a ski mask. I was about to turn to him, pretend like we'd just seen each other, when I saw the manager come up and tap him on the shoulder. So I took the Stetson off and went out onto the concourse again.

I junked the extra pillowcase and towel in a bin with some punctured inflatable ghosts and folded up my canvas bag, so no one would think I was shoplifting, the way they did Lenny. When a tall saleslady in the next place asked if she could help me I gave her my skinny-girl smile and said, "Just browsing for Christmas." She left me alone, with a look like she thought I was underfed so I wouldn't have spent much anyhow. Lenny came out of the hat shop, but he headed for the Timberland store, and even when I called his name—"Hey! Lenny! You, Lenny!"—he didn't stop. So then I looked in windows, up one side of the concourse and down the other, only never getting too far from the Santa stage. I wondered if Lenny was pissed at me; I wanted to find him. But Timberland was too far away.

It was twelve-fifteen. Just when I thought I'd have to keep myself hid till one when Santa came, the baby gave out a big cry. Bigger than anything he'd done in the woods, and so pretty he broke my heart again. I was back outside Stuffed Shirt, and it was all I

could do not to pull away from the window and run to him. I
thought I would, too, but this lady with a perm came tearing out
of a mattress store and beelined right for the baby.

"My God," she yelled, her voice bouncing off the walls of the
mall. "Help, somebody, help! It's a newborn child! Oh, thank
God! It's alive!"

Then the whole mall, practically, swarmed over there. I hadn't
figured there were so many people tucked away. You could hear
JoAnn's baby crying above the lot of them, though, this awesome
announcement in a language none of them spoke. I melted back
into another shop and then out the parking lot entrance before I
could even take another look. I couldn't have stood another look.
Outside, I turned toward the sun, weak but out of the haze now. I
shut my eyes, and for a second I flew into God's face like Christa
McAuliffe, and I knew it hurt, to dissolve like that.

"I missed the bus," I heard behind me. "My dad'll be pissed."

Lenny stood there grinning, holding a green plastic bag with a
mountain printed on it.

"Don't blame me," I said. "I told you not to meet me."

"Yeah, then you call my name," he said. "Like a goddamn girl."

He said *goddamn* like he'd learned it from his brother. "Look,"
I said, "tell your old man some guy tried to pick your pocket for
the Visa card. You had to chase him down."

"Yeah, right."

But he was still grinning—like the cat that ate the canary, my
dad would have said. People moved around us on the sidewalk,
heading for the mall entrance. They were ignorant, none of them
had heard the lady inside or the cry that came over the crowd.
They were just hurrying from their cars, with their purses and
bags dangling from their wrists and shoulders, frantic to get going
with holiday shopping.

"Next bus doesn't come till one," I said.

"So what d'you want to do?"

"I'm hungry," I said, and as soon as the words were out it was
true. I had to concentrate to remember the baby's face, or to fig-

ure JoAnn, lying bleeding on her leaf bed in the woods outside the hamlet. I had this big hollow place in me.

"Me, too," said Lenny. "But I only got bus fare, and this card." He held it up again, like a badge.

"You can't use plastic at those snack places," I said. We started walking toward the bus stop. When we got to the patch of grass we sat down. I tipped my head back till the sun blinded me. "No stars out, now," I said.

"Sure," said Lenny. "Plenty."

"Well, technically," I said, and I gave a little laugh that came out like a hiccup.

"You want me to ask any questions, or anything?" he said. He'd flopped on his stomach and was pulling out blades of grass, sucking on the white roots. His voice reminded me of the wind just before it rains—the way it wants to crack into some other dimension, but can't quite.

"No," I said. "I sure am hungry," I said again. But Lenny didn't answer; just left me to feel it, while we waited for the bus to take us away from that place and carry us home again.

book two

REENTRY

chapter **19**

For that one year, the year the Challenger went up, I held time in the palm of my hand, letting it trickle out as slowly as I dared, watching each grain go. A guy I met in New York a while back gave me a book by this poet Rilke, who wrote that sadness is nothing more than a moment when something new has entered into us. If that's true, then I had one long, drawn-out sad moment waiting for JoAnn's baby; but it was never sad so much as it was time carved out of time, and once it was done the minutes—no, the hours, the years—had to race by to make up the difference. They've only started to slow down now. I have only just now started to live my life around the new thing. And when I go down to the river, now, to watch the spring ice breaking up into floes, or when Matt McPeck comes home from law school for a weekend and we share a joint and talk about old times, I'm just starting to live with the easy exchange of talk, the cycle of seasons. Sometimes, when I look out my new window, in my old house in this same hamlet, to catch the sun rising the same old way it did that day, I just gasp in astonishment.

I never talked to JoAnn about her baby. Even that day, that very day of the birth, I didn't go back out to the woods but straight home, where I had this huge lunch and sat in the library with homework in front of me all afternoon. It must have been supper-time when I finally called over to JoAnn's house.

"She's sick as a dog," Mrs. Harlett said on the phone. "In bed. Worst menstrual cramps I ever saw in a girl."

"I was wondering would she want to come over and watch HBO with me," I said.

"I should say not. I got some Percocet left over from that time I went through the porch. I gave that to her and a hot water bottle, and she's snoring this instant. We going to see you at the Sanctuary tomorrow, Stick?"

"I can't. I've got stuff to do," I said. I hung up and went to fix myself a turkey sandwich. I could hardly wipe the grin off my face.

Next morning, when JoAnn called, she said she had my sweatshirt and I told her I'd bring her jacket back. "Any . . . any problems?" she asked.

"It's okay, JoAnn."

"I'm scared," she said. "My *tits* feel funny."

"Bind 'em," I said.

But she didn't come out and ask, even when the story ran in the paper that day and all through the next week about the newborn baby that had been found at the mall, and nobody to claim it. JoAnn was playing sick—flu, she claimed when the cramps had gone down. She spent time in the school bathroom, even, making plenty of vomit noises so no one'd be surprised when she lost a little weight. Who knows if she put two and two together? She'd always been slow on the uptake, and I didn't go to her—not ever. After that first time I wouldn't even take her phone calls, which my mom held out to me like the receiver was prescription medicine.

I stopped cold turkey, too, with the Reach Out for Christ people—Pastor Gwilliam called twice, and when I wouldn't take his calls he got some pimple-faced boy to try to talk to me in the school cafeteria—and you could tell, from the way she looked at me in the street, that Mrs. Harlett thought I'd run right back to whatever devil I started from. A couple of times I went up to our barn loft, but I didn't even take out my old cross and stuff. God was in what had happened that November day, in that broken-down shed, and God was sometimes in my feet when Philomena could still get me going on her polished wood floor; but suddenly, that winter, God wasn't someone who played hide-and-seek, or whose job was to do favors. So I didn't need the Sanctuary for a single thing.

My job was to blank things out, one by one, like an eraser moving across a white page. Like how warm he was—the temperature you are, inside—and how tired from all his work to get out. How the white cream oozed from the pockets and folds of him, and his legs just two little wormy things under the apricot of his tiny butt. That sweet pee smell. I got to where I didn't think about him except in a rare fierce moment or two, and then it was mostly the sound of his cry that came back at me.

Time races, catching up. By that summer, the newspapers were reporting that another shuttle was due to go into orbit. No civilian this time. *What did the bumper sticker say on the Challenger fuselage? If you can read this, thank a teacher.* That was one of the last jokes to go around. On the radio there was a rumor that they'd found the black box in the fall, but whatever it contained was classified. NASA wasn't going to let anyone know until the year 2005. They recovered a lot of stuff in the end. Even the bodies. You got the feeling they weren't in bits and pieces after all, just burned up some from falling through the atmosphere. But *Time* magazine still harped on the mystery, whether it was decompression that got them or slamming into the ocean. One of my roommates in New York, later, claimed that most people who commit suicide by jumping from tall buildings are dead of heart attacks before they hit the ground. And you want to believe that, at least about the Challenger crew—that they died from explosion, if not of their bodies then of their hearts and lungs, that they flew upward into the face of God rather than plunging to earth like meteorites.

At least you did, then. Now people have forgotten, and death is once again a matter of starvation in Africa, mass graves in eastern Europe. It's all about the earth, about darkness and dirt and silence, and nothing to do with the universe at all. JoAnn really thought I'd drowned her baby, she thought that was the thing that let her get away with it all, that she could count on me for the ultimate deed, for the toilet flush.

But as it happened, by that same summer JoAnn's little boy had landed—gently, unlike the Challenger people—in the lap of my mom's place, in Haven House. It seems to me I must have known as it was happening; I must have followed the papers through that spring. But all I remember is time racing by, while I let out breath and took it in fresh, until one late-July Sunday my mom was on the phone a long time and then got off and said she'd have to go down to the frame house. The frame house used to be the principal's, across from the elementary school; when it became vacant my mom had snatched it up for her mothers and infants. She was saying to my dad, "With all that uproar last November, you'd think someone would've taken him in. But they all want perfect babies."

"Can't blame 'em," said my dad. "Shoot, look at that moron Gray took in, that Benjy. Far as we know, *he's* the source of all Gray's trouble. They knew he was slow, they never guessed he was a pervert. It's all genes."

"That's exactly the trouble," my mother said. "People like you, making assumptions. We don't even know, that trial's not even finished—"

I was stretched out in the open bay window, trying to fix my leotard. Not looking up, I called to ask what genes were. "Your mother's stuck with a retarded baby," my dad said, moving into the library. "I knew this would happen, Wanda," he said in the other direction. "Soon as you opened up that frame house. You get too involved, you make yourself sick."

"Whose baby?" I asked. I tried to act like I was still stitching the shoulder back, but my needle lay caught in the knit.

"That one they found at the mall last fall," my dad said. I heard the clatter of dishes: my mom, filling the sink with soapy water before she took off for work. "It's got alcohol on the brain," my dad said. "If it doesn't die, it'll drag society down all its life. Look what it's done to your mother already."

"You mean he's at Haven House?" I said. "For good?"

"He'll land in an institution," my mother said. "We're just the holding pattern, between the hospital and whatever foster homes will take him while he's still little." She'd come into the doorway, her linen jacket on and her pocketbook over her shoulder. She'd gotten way too thin. My father was back working with Dugliss, nothing steady, three months to go on his unemployment—but he seemed light and easy about it, he ate well. Meantime my mom was smoking a pack a day, and her office clothes hung loose on her. She made me think of the reeds by the river, how they sway in the wind. "We're pushing for tests," she said. "There's a light in his eyes you don't usually see with these kids. Anne-Marie thinks so too."

"Can I come see him?" I said.

"Look," said my father, "now you're involving Stick."

"Just forget I brought it up," my mom said. "And no, Gwyneth, you cannot. These poor babies have too many grown-ups around them already, they don't want gawkers. Especially that one. When I think of the kind of woman who could do that to a child, I could just—"

I was glad she broke off. I didn't want to think what she could do to JoAnn or to me. After all, I'd been drinking too. I'd delivered the baby. I probably severed the cord too soon and screwed up his brain. I watched my mom hustle out, jam the car into reverse to go fix what she thought was society's mess. My dad asked did I want ice cream—I'd been eating better since that winter, he'd gotten used to me saying yes more than no—but I couldn't put anything in my mouth. I sat with him at the table, though, and listened to him bitch about how my mom was killing herself over people the rest of the world had given up on, while my hands clasped and unclasped under the wood, making some kind of prayer.

That whole night I couldn't sleep. I went crazy, wanting to tell someone about it. All those things rushed back at me—the smell, the wetness, the blood, that sound he made when his breath first came. Finally I opened my bedroom window and let a little of the cold night air in. "Baby," I said to nobody, but of course to him, "you know we didn't mean harm. You know I'll make it up to you." Then I heard him asking, *How? How?* and I said, "By my whole life. There ought to be something in there you can use."

I don't know what I'd figured on happening. That some lady wanting a kid would come claim him from the county, I guess. That once she held him, she'd be hooked. I'd pictured a rich person's home, a white crib, a couple dozen teddy bears. Love.

What I hadn't pictured was foster homes. I'd wanted to be in one myself once, of course, when *foster father* meant Gray and the fosters' playground was the street in front of the store. That September Gray and Benjy's case finally went to trial; and to whip up interest again, the paper ran a couple of articles about foster homes and how vicious they could be. The idea was you didn't want any kid in one, certainly not any kid you cared about. Each time I checked with my mom and learned the mall baby was still at Haven House I got a rush of relief.

"Maybe he can just stay there till he's adopted," I said.

"Not likely, honey. We're not funded or licensed for that."

"But he's happy, isn't he?"

"He's nine months old. The worst of his life was in his mother's womb. Sure, he's happy."

I was working at Camp Torture again, though Anne-Marie was full-time at the frame house now, and a cow of a woman named Tabitha ran the place. I tried to get my mom to let me quit and come work at Haven House. "I don't care about the money," I said.

"Well, I do," she said. "I don't have much left over for your pocket expenses, with your dad out of work."

"I haven't got pocket expenses. I'd rather be doing something useful."

My mom shut her eyes, the lids translucent; then she opened them again. "Maybe next year," she said. "When you're older."

"I'll be sixteen in a month. In Central America girls get married at sixteen."

"They do that in Castleton, too, in a manner of speaking." Her voice tightened. "I just don't want to deal with you emotionally, Gwyn, on top of everything else at work. That's the plain truth of it," she said.

I was mad, at that. I banged out of the house and skulked around the hamlet for a couple of hours. I thought of running away, stealing the baby back, heading for Florida. Then I came home and found my mom smoking a cigarette at the kitchen table, and I rubbed her shoulders and told her I understood, that I was just immature. At least he wasn't in a foster home, I told myself. At least he wasn't with people worse than Gray. At least he was where I could keep tabs.

chapter **20**

Gray actually got off within the first couple of weeks after the trial. It was something technical, some way the buck-toothed girl had fouled up her testimony; or maybe she'd tried the same story on another guy down in Castleton. I never got it straight. Anyhow Gray was off, and it had come out meantime in the papers that his wife had cancer, so the general hatred for him had started to soften a little. Benjy's end of it went on a while longer. I noticed because his name cropped up in the fights my mom had started to pick with my dad and me, on hot summer evenings. They were little fights, stupid fights. Sometimes they were over money, but more likely it was my bike in the driveway or my dad's clothes on the bathroom floor, or not enough food in the refrigerator.

My dad tried to pacify her. "If that fellow Gray'd open back up, we could jump out for things the way we used to," he said one night in September when she'd gone off the deep end wanting milk for her coffee.

"Now he's let off, you mean."

"Huh. They always do that, find some technicality. One of the young guys on Dugliss's crew says he knows one of the girls that retard went after. Says she has to see a shrink for what happened to her."

"His name's Benjy," said my mom. "And he's still on trial."

"He'll get off. They always do. Doesn't prove a thing. The proof is in those children, that's where the proof is. Hell, where'd that Benjy come from, anyway? Nobody to know, and nobody to watch Gray when he adopted him. Perverted from the start."

"But you'd shop at his store, now," said my mom. She was getting white around the lips. My stomach curled up.

"I just said I would," said my dad, clueless. "He's off the hook, now what's he doing with his time? That store ran a profit before all this trouble, and—"

"His wife is dying and his son's on trial, that's what he's doing with his time," said my mom.

"*Son*," my dad snorted, and winked at me.

"And it seems to me like the worst hypocrisy, just the absolute worst, that you wouldn't shop there before because you said he was a *pervert*—that's your word, Jasper—but you'll shop there now even though you still think he's a *pervert*"—she stopped for breath and to pace back and forth behind my dad where he sat at the kitchen table—"just because some court you don't believe in says he's innocent, so you've got some kind of excuse to get your eggs local again!"

"Hold on, Wanda," said my dad. "I mean, who is this guy, your wayward cousin? *You* didn't shop there, before. And everybody wants the place open now, it's not just me. The guy's paid his dues, whatever he did, and they've still got that Benjy at trial. *He's* the worst."

"You have always been this way, Jasper," my mom said. She went to stand by the back door; you could tell she wanted out of there, out of our house. "You go with the crowd, you have no mind of your own. That's why you never got that promotion at Hotung, that's why they finally let you go. You're a company man, and nobody needs company men anymore. Here you have a personal issue, a *moral* issue for God's sake, and—"

"I'm going for a walk," I said. "Can't get anything done around here with you guys going at it."

"Homework," said my mom.

"When I get back," I said.

"Sure, that's easy," she said. "You could get started around midnight the way you did last night, and wake up in time to miss the bus like you did last week—"

I stepped around her and out the door before she had a chance to get further. I didn't take it personally, the way my dad did; maybe because I knew what it was like to have something bugging you that you can't talk about, and how keeping that thing in makes you lousy to people close to you. My mom had something like that, inside her.

I sat on the stoop of the P.O. for a while, looking at the white dandelions dotting the tiny bit of grass they have there. I was going on sixteen by then, and Philomena had told me if I worked hard enough I could audition for work in New York by the next spring. I could quit school, move away. Already she was writing letters for me. My parents knew nothing about any of this, nothing about me at all. When Gray's car came around the corner, splashing through a mud puddle, I stood up and followed it down the street, toward the store.

I was going to ask the question that had set my parents off, whether he was planning to open the store or not. But when he'd shut off the motor he just sat there in the car, in the little gravel lot by the store, and I could tell this wasn't the time for that question. I knocked on the side window, and he rolled it down. "Hey, Stick," he said.

"My parents are having a fight," I said.

"Sorry to hear it. Want to go for a drive?"

"No thanks," I said, like this was something Gray asked me every day. "You just got back."

"From the hospital," he said. "We had to check my Emma in. She kind of, well, kind of collapsed down there at the courthouse this afternoon. So they want to hook her up to some respirator equipment for a while. Do some tests, you know."

"Gee, Mr. Gray," I said. "I'm sorry." I stepped back a little from the car. What he'd told me wasn't so bad, but I could see from his face that she was going to die, really die this time, and in the hospital, too. Cancer; I'd always thought it was slow, with remissions and a whole stage where you lost your hair and made jokes about it. I remembered how I'd thought of her, the fall before: *rich*, with her gold jewelry and those mouse-colored panty hose. You couldn't buy time with money. "Where's Benjy?" I finally said.

"Coming along, in the pickup. Said he was going to stop for pizza on the way. Benjy's about fifty percent pizza, you know," he said, and I smiled even though it was an old joke he used to tell, back when he joked around with the kids in the hamlet, and it didn't seem so funny now.

He opened the car door and hoisted himself out. I thought someone ought to be helping him, but I just stood there. He leaned back against the closed door, and I followed his eyes to the store, to the sign over the store and the big empty windows on either side of the front door, where his wife had stripped off the curtains. "My parents were wondering if you'd be opening up anytime soon," I asked.

"Were they now."

"That's what they were fighting about, actually," I said, and that seemed funny so we both kind of chuckled. Then he asked had they been fighting a lot. "Just these past weeks," I said. "My mom's kind of restless. All keyed up about . . . about something. Maybe work, I don't know."

"She works hard," he said. He started walking around toward the front of the store, and I followed. The dry smell of late summer was blowing in from the woods that lay just across the railroad tracks; the crickets were whining, one chorus coming in on another. "Final arguments on Benjy's case, tomorrow," he said, like that was what we'd been talking about.

"Oh, wow. Do you think—has he got a good chance?"

Gray shrugged, looked out toward the woods. "It's a jury trial," he said. "Human beings making human decisions."

Just then the pickup turned the corner and chugged down the small stretch of street to the store. Getting out with the pizza, Benjy looked like a junior executive who'd lost his way; he wore a navy suit and pinstripe shirt, with a tie almost too neatly knotted and still tight under his collar. "I got red peppers," he said. "It's a new item."

He lowered the tailgate of the pickup, lifted the box, and took out a slice very carefully. He nodded to me to have some, but I shook my head. Gray came to hook an arm over the side of the truck bed. "Careful with that tie, fella," he said. "You got to wear it tomorrow."

"I know, Dad, I know." Benjy took in the pizza in great bites, from the point to the crust, which he tossed in the bushes. He started to take another, then stopped. "Is Mom gonna be there?" he asked.

"Tomorrow?" Gray shook his head. "She's real sick, Benjy, we'll have to stop down and see her before we head downtown."

"I'm makin' her sick, aren't I?" Benjy asked. He picked up a second slice of pizza. "When it's over she'll get better. I can move out or something and she'll get better."

He said these things like he was talking about something in the newspaper. I wanted to sneak off, but he kept nodding over at me, as if I'd confirm what he was saying.

"That's not the right way to go thinking about it," Gray said.

"We *talked* about this, Benjy. It's a sickness been in her for a long time. Nothing to do with you."

"Well, I'm gonna show those sonsabitches," Benjy said. He reached for a third piece, but handed it over to me, and I took it. "Now look at that, Dad," Benjy said, watching me eat. "Pretty soon we can't call her Stick, no more."

They both looked me up and down, like they approved of me. It was hard to look in Benjy's face—it was too pale, for late summer, because he'd spent most of the time in courtrooms or lawyers' offices. The freckles that went across his nose stood out, like they'd been painted on, and his sandy hair was combed too carefully across his forehead. His eyes sort of flickered at me. "What're you gonna do," I said, "when it's all over?"

"Depends," he said, his mouth full of pizza.

"If you opened up"—I meant this for Gray, but said it to Benjy—"you'd get plenty of customers. People want to forget, you know, what happened."

"Well, I don't," said Benjy. He looked across the truck bed, at his father. "I want to give them back all those names they give me," he said. "Mom said I could do that, too. She said, 'Benj, you can hold your head high and call any sonofabitch a retarded sonofabitch, if that's what you want.' She said to do it for *her*, Dad." Gray was looking away, at the woods, disapproving. Benjy turned to me. "You retarded sonofabitch," he said. The words hung in the air between us for a second. Then he reached down and handed me another slice of pizza. His full, soft lips were wet with olive oil, and he was grinning.

"You perverted moron," I said.

"You sick weirdo."

"You rice brain."

And we were both laughing, the smell of pizza in the air, the laughter echoing in the street the way it used to when the other foster kids were there playing touch football. Gray waved a hand at us and headed upstairs. I stayed and laughed with Benjy, thinking up new insults, *worm breath* and *toad eater* and *booger bugger*, until the pizza was gone. Stuffing the empty box in the Dumpster, Benjy made me slap him five before he headed upstairs. I saw the light in the front room go on, and watched the curtain close.

And that was the last time I saw Benjy. The jury went out the next day, and returned six hours later with a guilty verdict. He went home in Gray's custody, but the next morning there was a note on the kitchen table and sixty dollars missing from Gray's wallet. Everyone figured he'd gone to the city. The sheriff issued a warrant, but I don't think they put a lot of energy into finding Benjy. He was over eighteen and not that much danger to anyone besides himself and girls who ought to know better, was what I heard. Anything he'd done had to have been at Gray's instigation, only Gray was wily enough to get himself off.

That was what they said, after Benjy disappeared. At the start they hauled Gray in, as the responsible party, and when they couldn't get anything out of him with questions, they took his bail money, let him go, and followed his scent. Maybe he'd scuttled Benjy away somewhere, paid him to vamoose. But after a week or two he was the only one pushing to find the guy, and I guess he pushed hard enough to be convincing. He moped for a while, then he set his jaw and opened the store. People shopped there. He put the stools back, and my dad and the rest started over for their decent coffee again. Wherever Benjy'd taken off to, we began to understand, he'd lifted a veil by leaving.

Then, just after Christmas, Emma Gray died. Gray closed the store that day—boarded it up, permanent. Sometime in the spring he put the place on the block for sale, and the Minimart people snatched it up. I found Gray in the back, the day the sign went up in the front window announcing a June 1 opening and the need for a manager.

"You still gonna live upstairs?" I asked.

He shook his head. "Florida," he said. "Got the old RV fixed up, and an acre just north of Sarasota that Emma and I put money down on, oh, five years back anyhow." He was hauling out boxes of old files, but he turned one on its side and sat on it. He lifted his baseball cap and scratched his head; he was sweating. "Emma wanted me to," he said. "Just before she went she said to me, 'Gray, cut bait.' "

"What about Benjy?" I said. "What if he comes home?"

"He won't." Gray reached for a plastic jug of water he had on the cement floor, and took a swig from it. "Benjy's a proud boy," he said, putting the cap back on the jug. "He didn't run from the judge or the sentence. He ran from the shame. And a boy doesn't come back, when he runs like that."

He stood up, hoisted the box he'd been sitting on by the handles, and started down the back steps with it. I stepped out of his way, then followed. He lifted the box into the rear of the RV and shut the back door. Standing by that big, sleek vehicle, he looked suddenly alone, like a big old ram cut loose from the herd. Florida, I thought, and tried to figure Benjy there, sent there by Gray six months ago. I tried to figure it that they'd won.

"When you taking off?" I said.

"Couple days." He came toward me, running his hand along the side of the RV. "She's a beaut, isn't she?" he said. "Emma and I, we were going to tour the country in her. Never got the chance. But she'll be home to me, till I can get something built down there."

"You gonna live alone?" I asked.

"Unless they find Benjy." He swallowed, his neck pulling at his jaw. "Unless they find him and we get him cleared."

"But you ain't sticking around for that."

He looked down at me, his eyes bloodshot. "He sent me a note," he said, "from the train station in Castleton. Said he was going off a long ways. Pointed out he'd reached his majority a ways back. But you wake up, you know, in the old place"—he waved his hand toward the apartment over the store—"and you expect the boy home. You go crazy."

"Like waiting for the prodigal son, you mean," I said.

"He ain't a prodigal!" Gray said quickly. "He's a good boy! And I am not one to welcome him back with a jail term, no sir." He turned away for a minute then, and I saw him draw a cloth from his pocket, to wipe at his eyes. He still could have been shamming; at least, I decided he was. It put a lid on things, locked a secret inside a secret. "I'll send you my address, hey?" Gray said when he turned back. "You tell your mother that."

"My mom," I said, and stopped. Gray did, too; waiting on me. Another secret. "You and my mom," I said.

Gray looked sideways at me, sizing me up. He wasn't slumped anymore, the way he had been during the trial. He'd lost weight, though, and his shoulders swung around broad and rangy. He wore a dark T-shirt, his arms white and flecked with reddish moles. "We go a ways back," he said, "your mom and me. She's a good friend." I'd come closer to him, into the shade cast by the RV. "You remind her for me," he said, when I'd got close enough and he could just graze my shoulder with his big hand, "that she never did a thing to hurt me, or Benjy. After I leave, I mean; she might need that reminding."

I got the feeling from the way he talked that he wasn't going to say good-bye to my mom. But I may have been wrong. She took Trixie for a long walk the next evening, and I remember when she came back, her face was blotchy from crying. She passed me in the hall and went straight for a shower, where if she kept up the tears you couldn't hear them, over the noise of the water. So my dad never knew a thing about it.

chapter **21**

If I'd never seen Daniel, I never would have had to go to New York. The sun would have risen from the same general direction every morning, but every other iota in the universe would have turned on its head, stopped in its tracks, gone another way.

That was his name, JoAnn's baby. Daniel. "Means brave," said Anne-Marie. "Like in the lion's den."

"If you've named him," I said, "it means you're keeping him awhile."

"Huh-uh. Means there's something to put on the form for the foster families. This one he just spent the spring with, they liked the name. When someone adopts him, if he's still little enough, they'll choose another name for him."

"*If*," chimed in Ben.

"Okay, I know it's not likely."

"Reality check," he said.

"I'd adopt him," I said, "if I could."

"Well, give him here, for now," said Anne-Marie. "He's poop city."

Anne-Marie was in charge of the babies at the frame house; there were five of them now, three with mothers, plus two girls expecting. I'd told my mom it was Anne-Marie I wanted to see, in fact; I'd been careful not to mention the mall baby for at least a week before I said I'd come by. Anne-Marie had been holding him when I walked in, and I'd known right away who it was.

He had this fabulous crop of hair, not dark the way he'd been when he came out but golden and silky on his round head. When she'd changed him and put him down on the rug he started right away to toddle—around the old sofa they'd put in the living room, crawling under the wooden chairs, picking up toys and tasting them, trying out his big set of teeth. He had a long, lithe body, not like JoAnn's at all, and he made a happy kind of crowing noise whenever he came on anything new. No words yet, though; and you had to admit, there was a look. Like someone had just given him a slap only he couldn't cry. When he stopped and sat down his mouth hung a little open; when I picked him up I noticed the bridge of his nose looked flat. Anne-Marie said they were doing studies. He was behind in his motor development but within the normal range for sensory response. "So he's not totally retarded," I said.

"We don't know that he's retarded at all," Anne-Marie said. She'd let me take Daniel and was giving a bottle to a stringy black baby who didn't seem to want it; the baby's eyes flitted from side to side. "We just know he's damaged."

I picked up a rattle and waved it at Daniel. He caught it from me and hit me on the chin with it. "I think he's cute," I said, my eyes tearing. His bottom fit into the inside curve of my elbow like a basketball. The wonder of him, the warmth of him soaked through my ribs into my bloodstream. I was singing with warmth.

"See what you think when he's five years old and can't pull up his own pants," Anne-Marie said.

Until I saw him, I had hung on. I'd gone from fourteen to fifteen while JoAnn piled on her camouflage pounds, and now I could drive a car. I'd put a blond streak in my hair; I'd done a tab of mescaline at a party. I'd stopped diagraming sentences and worked on the script for the junior class play. My periods came, now. Which hadn't been anything like what Dr. Stangel had said, because I hadn't put on much weight and I hadn't sprouted big breasts and I still hadn't had sex. They had just come, that spring, like an animal out of hibernation. So I was busy shaping myself, the way girls do, both slowly and swiftly, into a woman. And then I got to hold Daniel, and I knew I had to leave.

Philomena thought it was a fabulous idea, of course. "*Never* too young," she kept saying. "*Never.*" She could get me into Savion Glover's studio, she said, never mind that I was white. "Charlotte's going to my old friend Frankie at 890 Broadway," she said, "but just between you and me, that's all I could swing for her. *You*, now. You're another story."

What Charlotte and her mother had done was to squeak her through senior year at Windhaven High and take an apartment in Manhattan, somewhere in the West Fifties, so Charlotte could make her career as a dancer or a singer or an actress or whatever talent her beauty could take on. "I do *not* want her modeling," I heard Mrs. Petersen telling another parent after that spring's recital. "I know she could do it. I know there's enormous wealth, exposure. You should hear what the agencies say when they look at her! But they exploit those girls, in the end. Charlotte has talent. She shouldn't just be posing in front of cameras."

I went to work on Charlotte, first. "I bet you're excited," I said the next week at Philomena's. "The glamorous life. And you don't have to go to school anymore, either."

She cut me a look. Charlotte hadn't completely trusted me, I don't think, since that day I saw her in the parking lot. But she couldn't find my hidden agenda. "Glamor, sure," she said. "I have to share a bedroom with my mother. And she says no dates except Saturday. If I hadn't broke up with Garret I'd turn the whole deal down."

"You'll meet cooler guys in the city."

"Philomena says they're all gay." She looked up from buttoning her shoes. Her mouth was curled with sarcasm, but the edges of her eyes were damp. Now was the time to strike.

"Jeez," I said. "Sounds lonely, now I think about it."

"*Lonely!* You don't know, Stickley. Steph's pissed off at me, she thinks I'm proving something. Everybody's planning senior summer. I was gonna lifeguard. At the *club*." The tears had spilled onto her cheeks now, and she was whining.

"Wish I could go with you."

"You're a sweet kid. You really are. Jeez." Quickly she wiped her eyes with the back of her palm. The idea was cooking, I could tell.

And then a funny thing happened. If I hadn't seen Daniel, I wouldn't have felt I had to get away like a deer in the forest racing from a fire. But once the idea of tagging with Charlotte Petersen started cooking, I began to believe in New York for its own sake. I didn't know New York: all I ever saw in my mind was my mom at Grand Central—I'd seen Grand Central plenty, in movies—feeding soup to those homeless men, one of them being my handsome father. But Charlotte talked and talked about the city with Philomena, and I began to have a faith. When I dropped the mescaline at that party, for one thing, I danced so hard people said later they thought I was going to turn to butter, and I sang, too. I don't remember singing, but I do remember the music shuddering through me—it was that old song "Proud Mary," and whoever had the party kept putting the CD back, so it played and played—and my arms and legs working the air like they'd never quit.

I actually had a date to that party, Matt McPeck. Who it turned out was so shy that he didn't even put a move on me after, even though I was so turned on from the dancing that I was practically creaming my pants, wanting him to. It took until after I left the hamlet to realize that Matt McPeck had had a thing for me—he was clumsy with the signals, and I was running away so fast I couldn't stop to notice details. Now Matt's gay, I think, or else just buried in law books. Either way he doesn't give off vibes, anymore. Back then he had a wide, open face, the cheeks just barely rough with starting to shave, and he had a way of moving his hands when he talked, opening and closing them and dipping his forearm through the air, that made you want to lace your fingers with those fingers and do a kind of hand dance.

Maybe I do remember singing, at that party. My throat opening at "Proud Mary keeps on burnin'," and a ribbon of sound coming out. I was high, as I've said. And turning like a top in the middle of someone's basement party room—first my hips down, and then my legs kicking them back up and around, like a piston going at it. When I finally stopped I stood drenched in sweat, reeling.

"*You're* the one oughta be on Broadway, Stick," Stephanie said as the next song started up. Someone brought me a towel, for the sweat, and someone else brought me a beer. I channeled my way outside, to this person's backyard. Lenny Dugliss was lying there on his back on the grass, and he gave me a cigarette. I stood out there staring at the stars, the mescaline turning them bright blue, the syncopated four-four of the music still in charge of my heartbeat, and I thought maybe I ought to go, anyway. To New York. Maybe there was some other kind of promise there, and not just a frantic place so far from Windhaven that I could forget what had happened here.

The idea cooked. I told my mom how Charlotte Petersen's mom was taking her to New York to get her some serious coaching. I made a point of telling Charlotte how amazing her twists and brushes were—until, without considering why, she started to think of me as a person worth knowing, and she talked her mom into letting me spend the night at their brand-new A-frame house in Windhaven Hills Estates. I gave it a week, two weeks, three. I sat humbly in Charlotte's kitchen while Charlotte begged and pleaded with her mom to bring me along. I can't dance if I'm too *lonely*, she whined. I'll get *depressed*. Stick here'll cheer me up! Christ, Mom, you don't want me to turn into a *robot*, do you? Think what a pain in the ass I'll be if I don't have someone to *talk* to.

I began to think Charlotte wasn't so dumb, after all. I gave it another week. When Mrs. Petersen called once on the phone, I just gave my mom the general gist of the plan. When she stopped by our house, I made sure to be gone.

"I never thought I'd say this," my mom said, when I'd come back and Mrs. Petersen's fancy car wasn't in the driveway anymore, "but I wish you were friends with that JoAnn Harlett again, Gwyneth."

"I am. We're just too busy for each other these days, that's all."

"At least there was a human being there, in her mother. A bigoted, dull, brainwashed being, but *human*."

"Are you saying you don't want me to go?"

"Go?" my mom asked. She tipped her head to look at me, like she was trying to see the old woman in that optical-illusion drawing that keeps looking like a girl with a feather in her hat. "Have we talked about this?"

"I'm almost seventeen, I don't have to be in school anymore."

"No, no. Charlotte *Petersen* doesn't have to be in school anymore. She's *eighteen*, for one, and I can guess from her mother that she has rice for brains."

"Maybe I do too. I'm making C's, just the way you and dad said."

That got her where she lived. She opened her mouth, pinched it shut. She gestured with her palms splayed open. Her creamy complexion splotched red on her cheeks and forehead. Then she went to get a cigarette, and we talked.

Oh, not about Daniel. I explained about tap to her, all the things Philomena had promised me, how you had to start early and be serious about what you were doing, how I'd learned everything she had to teach. I even explained—and this part was the truth—how it made me feel to get on top of a tap routine. "Like everything's chinked into place," I said. "Like I'm a clock that'll always run on time. Like I've got music for muscles. It feels—well, it feels kind of religious."

"Whoah. Don't confuse your categories, honey." My mother crossed her legs, like a society lady. "I know you're Philomena's best little dancer, but I also know the difference between vaudeville and church."

"Religious," I insisted. "Like God's in there, pulling my strings."

"Not God. You."

I wasn't going to argue. It wasn't the tap driving me, anyhow. "If Mrs. Petersen'll let me live with them, you just have to worry about food," I said.

"And lessons."

"I can get a job after a little while, help pay for the lessons. Be real, Mom. What's going to happen to me in this high school in the next year? I'm going to learn how to guzzle beer without puking? I'll be able to reel off a list of the bombing campaigns in Vietnam, for history?"

"They're not totally unimportant, those bombings. They're a heritage we're all living with."

"*You* live with them. *I* live—" I threw an arm out, pursed my lips together to stop them from shaking. I couldn't fake this one. "I live where people I know *pinch* themselves all the time, and then they think they're dreaming because they don't feel the pinch. But their skin's gone numb, so their own pinches don't register. So whatever it is they do, what happens to them, they think it won't matter once they wake up. Only they're already *awake*, see."

My mom had her chin cupped in her hands. Her face was shaped like a pale heart, the blotchiness gone. "You think that'll change in New York?" she said. "It's a foolish idea."

"Please," I said. "Just let me go."

My dad took it harder than my mom. "Just when I'm getting started?" he said to her when she broke the news. "She can't take lessons here, help out a little at the franchise?"

What he was getting started at was the Minimart franchise, set up in Gray's old store, but with all new plastic shelving and a bright round Minimart sign on a fat pole in the parking lot. My dad had borrowed on his pension to get the franchise payment together—he'd sat up late with my mom, adding and readding the figures, how they were going to swing it. He'd had the place just a few weeks now, but already he ran it the way he had run the night shift at Hotung, like a company man. The company policies were posted behind the counter, with a smorgasbord of Minimart come-ons taped to the windows and hanging from the ceiling: 79¢ SPECIAL! FREE COFFEE REFILLS! DAILY LOTTERY! He wore his bright orange Minimart cap and apron, which he hung on a hook in the back of the store. When I took a soda out of the cooler he rang it up and put the seventy-five cents in the till himself. "Thanks, Dad," I'd say as he snapped the drawer closed.

"I need a routine," he said now. "I can't be running a business when I'm worried about my daughter getting mugged down in Central Park."

"She's going with a *family*," my mom repeated, patient. "The girls will have a *curfew*. It's just a few blocks from where she'll be taking lessons. I know it's not the safest place in the whole world, but neither is Route 9 on a Friday night with some boy driving his truck drunk."

"Stick doesn't go out with boys!" my dad shouted. I was sitting right there, but he gestured as if there was just empty space, my direction.

"She will," said my mom. "Especially if you keep up this attitude, she will. Look, we can wait a year and she'll go legally on her own, or we can let her live with the Petersens."

"With the Petersen *woman*," my dad said. "There's no father here. Don't think I don't notice that."

Then, just as we had my dad coming around to the idea—I had to promise to take the train up every other weekend, at least, and help him with the franchise when I was home—we almost lost Mrs. Petersen. I listened from the library when she came by to hedge her bets with my mom. "I want to make it crystal-clear," she said, "that Gwyneth's focus must be all on her lessons."

"Oh, I'm sure that's what she wants," my mom said. They were both on the couch; I could see their faces, bending toward one another like flowers. Mrs. Petersen wasn't pretty like her daughter—she carried a lot of extra weight in her thighs, and she'd messed up her hair with too much bleach and styling. She looked a lot older than my mom, though she was trying for the other way.

"Because I can't be in charge of two teenagers set loose in New York City."

"Well, surely *Charlotte's* not set loose. Gwyn tells me you've got her all booked up. Isn't that why you're going?"

I had to admire my mom. She thought this whole thing was stupid; she wished with her whole soul that I was crazy about history, or physics; if I could have cut through her surface, I bet I'd have found that she thought dancing was a teeny bit immoral, at bottom. But she could play Mrs. P. like a fish on a hook. The phone rang in the library, and I grabbed it up.

"I'm going *nuts* here," Charlotte said. "Are they going to nix this whole idea? Because if they do, Stickley, I am just going to flat out refuse. So what if I never get to model. I am not living in a tiny apartment with my mother by myself."

"I think we've still got a chance," I whispered. "Your mom's just afraid I'll cause trouble."

"You?" Charlotte's laugh tinkled, on the other end. "God, that's like saying the lamb's gonna eat the wolf."

"Wait a sec, I gotta listen," I said.

From the other room, I could hear Mrs. Petersen. "When my husband left, I tell you, Wanda, I just thought the world would end. And then he tried to cut me off, you know. Me *and* his daughter. And that's where I say thank God for lawyers. You just have to stick it to them sometimes. He doesn't like this plan for Charlotte's performance training, either, but it's all written down: he hasn't got a thing to say about it."

"They're talking about your dad," I whispered to Charlotte on the phone. "So I think maybe we're okay."

"Well, call me back, will you, Stickley? I am just in *agony*, over here."

It was on a trial basis, I managed to tell her later. If I made sure she got home by eleven any night she was allowed to go out, and if I could get her to her lessons on time, I was essentially hired. Mrs. Petersen wasn't thinking of me as trouble anymore; she was thinking of me as a free babysitter. "Which is just where we want her," I said.

"God, Stickley. Now I've got *two* mothers."

"Let's just get to New York," I said. "For all I know, *my* mom'll back out, next. So just focus on one thing, okay?"

My mom didn't back out, though—I'll give her that. She even spent a day with Mrs. Petersen, just the two of them driving down to Manhattan to scope out the apartment and the dance studios.

She came back sober and resigned, but with just this lurking excitement in her voice, like a patch of Mrs. Petersen's glitter world had rubbed off on her. Our last day at Hot to Trot, Philomena started to cry, wishing us luck; Charlotte jumped up and down and hugged me, like I'd been her best friend for years.

Once, before I left, I talked to JoAnn. She was sitting on the curb outside the P.O., drinking a cherry cola she'd bought at my dad's Minimart. The day was on the dry cusp of summer, premature leaves dotting the ground like dropped letters. A light wind lifted her thick buttery hair from her shoulders; you could see the daisy tattoo on her broad bare arm. She was eighteen that month, already past ripe, like the peaches you saw by then in my dad's tiny fruit section. "Where'd you get that, anyway?" I said, touching the daisy as I sat down next to her.

"Nate," she said. She took a swig of the cola, then set it between her legs, which were stretched out on the asphalt, bare up to her stretch shorts. She glanced over at her tattoo. She'd lost a little weight around her face, her neck; you could see how her chin knobbed downward, like her mother's. "When he found out he was my first guy, you know. He drove me down to Castleton, paid for it and everything. Said he wanted me to remember him always, no matter who else I was with. But he let me pick my own design out." She drank from the cola again, set it down, rubbed her hands over her bare shins. "He was a sweet guy," she said.

"Yeah," I said.

"So I hear you're busting outta this place."

"Just weekdays, mostly."

"You don't even have to finish school, you luck."

"I'm studying," I said. "My mom says I have to pass the GED by next fall or it's all off."

"You'll be back here with the losers, huh?"

"You ain't a loser, JoAnn."

"I didn't mean me. The rest of them. You never fucked me over, though."

"I haven't hung out with you," I said. "I couldn't, after—"

"Ssh," she said. Slowly she tipped the can of soda up and spilled it on the dusty asphalt. It beaded, then ran a thin brown stream, down to a weed-filled crack. "I lay out there," she said in a half-whisper, "sure you'd gone to get the troopers. And what my dad woulda done—you just don't know what my dad woulda done to me! I thought I'd kill myself if I heard sirens coming out my way. Thought maybe I'd swallow that bottle of peroxide, it could do the trick. *God*." She shivered, in the hot dry air. "Then you didn't come back." She turned to me, brushed her hair from her eyes. They were big now, blue and round, but I remembered how they'd squeezed up. "You never needed to do anything else more for me," she said.

I stood up. "I gotta run," I said. "Class." I felt unsteady on my feet, woozy as I slid behind the wheel of my dad's car and drove off from the P.O., leaving her there on the stoop. What I thought was I had to see Daniel, to know it had been a baby and not a knife I'd pulled out of JoAnn. I had to hold his bottom, watch his legs move, hear the sounds he made with his lips and tongue, his seven teeth.

But before I'd pulled all the way up to the frame house, I swung the car around. Daniel wasn't what I had to *see*, he was what I had to *leave*. Each eyeful of him nailed my feet to the ground, when the only sensible thing to do was run. I drove to Philomena's, to her tearful good-bye and Charlotte's hugs. That night, I packed.

chapter **22**

With me in New York, Charlotte didn't have to share a room with her mother. Mrs. Petersen did the square, high-ceilinged living room over in Marimekko, with twin beds covered by bold-colored spreads and scallop-edged curtains on the one window. "Just like a dorm," she said. At night she called "Lights out!" at eleven sharp and snapped off the overhead in the hall. The place settled into dusk, the courtyard light coming in swirled stripes through the curtain until morning.

I found out within a couple of weeks that Philomena had been either dead wrong about me or just out of touch. In spite of her promise, I didn't get into the Savion Glover school. Instead I ended up with Charlotte at Frankie's Fast Feet. Not that I cared. I'd begun to think there were reasons to be in New York besides running away from JoAnn's baby. I liked the catacomb of studios at 890 Broadway, the crackle of energy that hit you when the elevator doors opened. But then I started to learn how just having dance in your veins isn't enough.

"It's like this," Frankie said to me one day when I got there early and the little foyer behind his sliding door was quiet. "Your spark's just a little hot for Broadway. They want these robots, y'know, kids with pretty faces who put their feet down on the beat. So I don't want to train you for that. And the other—this stuff that's happening now, with these colored kids and the hip-hop, the wild kind of street stuff that Glover and them's doing—

you just aren't hungry enough for that. It's like you do the routines and you're satisfied, you got your rush."

"I am," I said. "I do."

"You got a dancer's body, you got a dancer's mind," he said.
"But your soul, it's somewhere else. Philomena, she's a Florida
gal, she don't see these things."

"'S okay," I said. "I'm doing okay in the classes, aren't I?"

"One of my best, I am sorry to say." Frankie was a round man—
round face, potbelly, round hands that clenched and unclenched
when he was trying to put a beat across. In the office he wore a
Yankees cap; in the studio his round baldness gleamed under the
lights. He'd been really good once, you could tell not just from his
feet but from the slight exact movements his arms made. He'd just
gone unhealthy and round, and now he gave himself to the young
hopefuls that piled through his door when their jazz class was over
or they were off from school or from waiting tables. They talked
choruses and lineups, auditions, injuries. They were all about my
age, maybe a little older, and he loved them—kind of like Gray, I
found myself thinking once, and his foster kids. But I shoved that
thought out of my mind.

"Your friend Charlotte now," Frankie said, "she is a case. She is
a mother-loved case."

"She'd rather be in community college," I said.

"Well, we will try," he said. "We will attempt to send her there.
And without killing her mother, too. But it may take some time.
Ah. Here come my darlings." And he rose to get the tapes ready,
while the rest streamed in.

For a year and a half I lived like that. I had the GED books,
which were easy enough, to go over in the morning, in the kitchen
of the little apartment, while Charlotte and her mother were at
voice lessons. Names of state capitals, ratio of radius to circle,
main character's goals in the selection just cited: I filled in blanks,
drew charts. Then after lunch I reported to the dog walking service three doors down. Doggie Do, it was called, and it was run by
this Quaker woman that Anne-Marie had gone to school with.

"Claire was always nuts for dogs," Anne-Marie said, when I reported back after my first week of working. "Kept them in her dorm room, got fined out the wazoo. Just promise you love Weimeraners, and she'll never fire you."

"I have to learn what a Weimeraner is, first," I said.

Which I did, and I gathered them up along with the poodles, spaniels, Russian wolfhounds, and other purebreds that Claire had trained, and took them with my pooper-scooper up the West Side as far as Seventy-ninth and back. We had keys to all the places where the dogs lived; I'd ring from the outside foyer, then let myself in, and Shortie or Cyrano or Bailey would be waiting just inside the apartment doors. At first Claire hadn't thought I'd be strong enough, but with Anne-Marie recommending me she said we'd give it a try, and she went around with me the first day to make sure I could hold all ten leashes and keep them controlled when I had to stop every ten yards to scoop poop.

"Winter or summer, rain or shine," she warned me. "Unless a dog's got blocked bowels, we're morally obligated to walk it."

"We've got three German shepherds at home," I lied. "I took total charge of them, no problem."

"What do they do with you gone?" she asked. She sounded genuinely concerned, like we might have to set up a branch outfit in Windhaven.

"My mom," I said. Then, recollecting that Claire might be talking again to Anne-Marie: "And two of them died last year, actually. So there's just one now. Trixie. My mom can handle one."

After I'd finished with the dogs and showered the smell off, I had a two-hour class with Frankie. Mrs. Petersen whisked Charlotte off to ballet from that, but I stayed, had a pizza, and took hip-hop with Frankie's studio partner, Sal. Hip-hop was one of the things that made me think about dancing for real. You had to take charge of every square inch of your body to do it right, because you had to move, always, just a fraction ahead of the beat. I would get dizzy, counting and getting the hip movements right, getting each ball and socket to work on its own. Plus Sal wanted everybody to look real cool and relaxed. "Wink an eye, here, at the end of the turn," he'd say, showing us with his long lashes. "Let's see a little grin there, Stickley. Cute."

Afterwards I stood out on the corner by Carnegie Hall and just breathed in the city—the rush of people, the heat from the buildings. My solution was working, I thought sometimes. I was forgetting. Once a week, because Frankie insisted, I even took voice lessons, way down in TriBeCa with this alto who looked like Morticia Addams. She insisted I was a soprano, though I've never believed it, and she made me spend ten minutes breathing and saying "Huh!" from my diaphragm before she'd let me sing whatever it was she'd assigned. Half the time it was Mozart or someone like that, with a bunch of trills around high F; half the time it was Broadway, and then she yelled at me to use my sinuses to get the volume out. "Sing with your face!" she'd say, holding her red-fingernailed hand over her own nose and cheekbones. "Here"—she'd punch herself in the belly—"and here"—she'd poke her hand at her face—"is where you made the sound happen. Not the throat, you poor creature. You'll kill that little throat of yours."

Back in the apartment, I slid between sheets just before Mrs. Petersen called "Lights out!" Then I lay awake in the dark, listening to Charlotte prattle about the boys in her ballet class and how many were actually going to make it into the corps. I reminded myself I was only there as a sop thrown to Charlotte. As soon as she didn't need a sleepover friend anymore, which meant as soon as she hooked up with a boy, I'd be on the train home. So I murmured whatever she needed murmured.

When Charlotte finally settled down to shallow, fluttery breaths, though, her boys and pliés flew from the room. Then—only then—the theme song from *Cats* dropped out of my head, and the catwalk combination shook away from my stretched legs. Only then did I let my thoughts go. And that was when I didn't forget, didn't ever forget, not for the whole year and a half.

· · ·

On the weekends I learned—between hearing about my dad's rough hours at the Minimart, my mom's newest push for funding—where Daniel was headed, what hope they were giving him. He never went far. "There's a family taking him for two years," my mom told me finally, in the spring, after he'd gone through two foster situations and landed back at the frame house in between. "He'll be almost school age by then. And if the state hasn't found an adoption, there's a residency program up in Oneonta. We got another like him in just last week, did I tell you, Jasper?"

"Nope," said my dad. He had spreadsheets covering the kitchen table, checking figures.

"Two years old. Came in on his mother's back. She'd walked all the way from Castleton, can you believe that? Six months pregnant, and the next'll probably be the same. She said she was getting hit—she had bruises, all over—and she was scared to call. Guess I'd drink too, if I could, under the circumstances."

"What do you mean, another like him?" I said. "Another what, what is the deal?"

"Well, they say Daniel's not so severe, but he's a definite FAS. And these others, you can tell just by looking."

"FAS?" I'd been clearing the table, around my dad. I slid the flatware into the blue plastic basket, in the dishwasher.

"Fetal alcohol syndrome."

I bent down; I lifted the lid, closing the dirty dishes in. Then I found my way out of the kitchen, into the library. I sank down on the couch. There in front of me, back on the coffee table, lay the glass dove. Neatly glued, it probably couldn't set fire to anything anymore. I touched it on its back, on the crack. I made my head stop spinning.

I'd pushed that from my mind—what I knew, deep down, about the booze on his brain. How much had JoAnn drunk, anyhow? A beer here, a beer there. No, bottles upon bottles, and I'd just stood there and watched. Helped her get them. I could smell the beer, in my nostrils, the stale putrid poison of it.

"We've had worse, since," my mom said, following me into the library. She perched on the edge of the couch. "The city hasn't got a monopoly on crack babies, that's one thing you'll find out if you stick around."

"I'm not sticking around," I said.

"I know, I know," my mom said, and from the defensive edge in her voice I could tell what I said had come out wrong. How could she ever have told I was running away from Daniel? I looked up at her, quickly. She was just leaning there, sipping her coffee. Tired—she always looked tired—but still beautiful. She didn't have a clue.

"You go to Meeting, still?" I asked.

"Christ, no. I'm too busy."

"Then why do you do this? What you do? With all these fucked-up people?"

"I don't know. Because I'm guilty, I guess. I mean, because I *feel* guilty. Because it's a job." She leaned down, took my hand and squeezed it. "Let's not talk about Haven House anymore," she said.

Then she stood up and went back into the kitchen, where my father was crunching numbers. Looking after her, I thought of Gray, how she'd squeezed Gray's hand that day in the truck. How he was gone to Florida. How easy it had been for me to run, how hard for her to stay.

A year and a half—and then Mrs. Petersen threw in the towel, packed it up, took Charlotte back. She didn't exactly put it that way, of course. She said she'd decided Charlotte should go to junior college. There wasn't enough for Charlotte's *mind*, she told my mother. All this stress on movement, on how you used your body, how far you could strain your voice, it was rough on a young sensitive person. Poor Charlotte worried about the most trivial things—the tilt of her nose, her leg extensions! And there was no intellectual stimulation. She had a nice place in mind, a private two-year school in the hills across the river. There were horses there too; Charlotte could learn to ride.

I thought how great she'd look on a horse. A bay mare, with Charlotte in black and tan riding gear, her hair peeking from underneath her cap, the strap supporting her fine chin. The shoulder pads, the long smooth black boots.

chapter 23

Me, I was four months shy of nineteen. The week before Mrs. Petersen made her little announcement, I'd have said I was ready to throw it all in. I was tired of what had started happening. As if by some force of gravity, after a year and a half, I'd started making these rounds—chorus calls, special-event shows, revues. There was a big bulletin board at 890 Broadway where they posted this stuff, and everyone went—including Charlotte, though she'd always go with her mother and I'd always take the subway down, and we'd never bump into each other at the place where the call was happening, and we'd never talk about it that night. It was weird. Of course I never made it any further in auditions than Charlotte did, but she and her mom were embarrassed that she hadn't turned out to be an instant star. They'd even gone to a cattle call at a big modeling agency—Charlotte confided this little tidbit, her mother wouldn't have admitted it—and got one callback, but that was the end of that. Her chin was too weak, they'd told her. Anyway, everything for me had gone to routine: classes, dog walking, waiting on line, waiting on line, waiting on line, getting dismissed, more classes. I wasn't just forgetting; I was going numb.

But then Frankie found out that an understudy chorus part had opened up in the revival of *Grand Hotel*. "It's a dumb show, not a good line in the whole script," he said, "but Tommy Tune's directing and it's into a long run. You gotta learn some ballroom stuff, quick. Come in every night this week, I won't charge you. We gotta get you up on tango, fox-trot, waltz. You got the tap cold, already."

"Charlotte's going back upstate, with her mom," I told him. "I won't have a place to live in a month. I thought I might just take a break, you know."

"Uh-uh. Not with this chance right in your face."

"You said I wasn't right for Broadway."

"Darling, this is Tommy *Tune*," Frankie said, sounding like Philomena. "I'm trying to hand you a job my other gypsies'd kill for. You want to make us both failures? Hunh?" He tipped his round face at me, his cheek in his palm. He looked as tired as I felt, only with years added on to the feeling. I felt a strange twist of excitement, just under my rib cage.

"I'll try it," I said. And for a week we worked, after classes, late into the night, until my feet blistered and my calves woke me with cramp at five in the morning and I knew the moves: I was a quick study.

The address he gave me wasn't posted on the board. I waited anyhow, on an endless line at the back of the Martin Beck theater—Frankie wasn't the only one who'd gotten a phone call—only this time my voice didn't crack on the song Frankie'd told me to use, and my feet were hot with the combination. When the guy asked me back Frankie made me go out and get a new outfit, this black thing with blue shimmers, and then Sal made me up just before the callback so that I looked like eighteen going on thirty. This time there were a couple of guys from the chorus there, and we had to do a tango with them. The one I got was wiry and quick; with everything Frankie'd drilled into me, there wasn't a way I could make a false step. From the dark at the back of the theater there came whispering—one of the girls trying out said she thought the tall shape back there was Tommy Tune, but I couldn't make him out—and then the casting guy said, "Stickley and McKnight can stay," into the mike, and the audition was over.

So by the time Mrs. Petersen gave her month's notice on the lease, I had something going that anyone in their right mind would have said was worth sticking around for. "Your life," as one guy at 890 Broadway said to me when he heard the news, "did not begin until this moment, Stick. Now your life has begun."

After my mom called—*It's not just the apartment, Gwyneth, it's not that simple*—I took the train north to the hamlet and spent a weekend letting my parents talk at me. College, they said. A social life. They'd pay for it, somehow—I'd passed the GED, I'd kept up my half of the bargain. If I didn't want to live at home, there were dorms. I could have a career that would last past my twenty-fifth birthday, when my body would start to break down, like everyone's.

They didn't mention Daniel, of course—why should they?—and I didn't ask. I clamped down on my tongue every time I started to ask. Having to clamp down so much told me that no matter where *he* was, *I* wasn't ready to come back to the hamlet. "Look, I *just* got into this chorus," I told them.

"In?" said my dad. "I thought you were the backup."

"That's considered in! You dance eight nights a month, average. You rehearse with the chorus. It's a big break."

"For the next two weeks, maybe," my mom said.

"It's supposed to be a long-running show! Okay, I know, long-running might not mean four years, but it pays okay. If I keep working for Claire I'll have plenty for rent even if it does close. Oh, not on a place by myself," I added quickly when their mouths opened. "With some other girls. You can meet them. You'd like them. It's not any different from a dorm, really. Just, I'll be doing what I'm good at."

It took a while. All weekend, in fact. And it was harder this time than it had been at first, oddly enough, because I'd started to believe I might be worth something, in that huge city. I was like someone infatuated; they're not truly in love but they still can't get control of the situation; they lean on Fate. Still, in the end I won: I could go back, a hundred miles away. I didn't see anyone else in the hamlet, that time. I didn't promise to keep taking the train up on weekends. I just packed up some of the stuff I kept leaving behind—my *Sentence Diagrams* book, my old Second Coming tapes, the Voyager photos—and went on my way.

And so I moved in with Coretta and Alice Jane, known as A.J., and for a while I kept trying to bend the thin pole of my ambition, thinking I could vault over a past that climbed higher even as I turned my eyes away from it. Not that I was really dancing. Mostly I hung around backstage with the eight other understudies—*ghosts*, people called us, because of the way we hovered—while the real cast ran off and on, wardrobe people at the ready with quick changes. We understudied three people each, three different sets of choreography and those little gestures that set one chorus member off from another. The show was about Germany between the wars, where it seemed like people wore a lot of black clothes and plastered their hair back against their heads. The chorus was all supposed to be bellboys and maids and dishwashers at this hotel, and they kept chanting this song "What We Have, We Have Not" while they trotted out and did intricate numbers and then parked themselves along the edges of the stage, by these gold ballroom chairs, to let the main action go on. I liked the show; I liked the ballroom dances, the complicated timing of them, the way the chorus made itself into shapes and then broke those shapes up. "It's all about illusion, this show," the dance coach had told us new ones while we warmed up, "about how disaster brews under the surface of the glitz. You got that?" I got it, I could have told him, I'd got it a long time ago back in Florida—but I was forgetting all the past, my life was beginning, like the guy had told me.

Once or twice I did see Tommy Tune, striding through the hubbub backstage looking about twelve feet tall and calm as water. My parents even came down once, when one of the three girls I understudied for was having arthroscopic surgery, so we knew I'd have to take her place for three nights minimum. It was only the second time I'd actually made it in front of the footlights. The one time I'd gone out, before, I'd been so scared that I'd swear no sound came out of my mouth when we had to sing, but the wiry guy who'd tangoed with me at the callbacks told me I'd got the footwork perfect, so I felt okay. Anyhow understudies got two comps each, total, no matter how long the show ran, so I called my parents and they came. They told me it was a terrific show, I was terrific in the finale, this bang-up number where you do these ballet spins and the gold chairs get all shuffled around the stage and the maids get to jump up onto the bellhops' shoulders. That was the only word my father seemed to know how to use, "Terrific!" Afterwards my parents came over to the apartment I shared, for tea and these great scones I'd bought to impress them.

"Ought to get these in the Minimart," my dad said. "Fat English muffins."

My mom didn't say anything; she just beamed. It took me a minute to put a name to the look she wore across her wide forehead, her hair done up with silver barrettes. *Pride*, I finally realized; she was proud of me. I'd never seen that look before.

We lived on Second Avenue, over a copy shop and an all-night deli, two flights up. A floor-through, they called it, a railroad flat—six rooms all in a row like train cars, all listing southward. Coretta had a boyfriend, so she got the room off the kitchen toward the back, which had a door that closed. A.J. claimed she was sensitive to noise, so she took the two middle rooms, each of them narrow as a train car and windowless, but she drew Indian curtains at either end and so managed to station herself like a roadblock in the middle of the apartment. My room in the front was like being back at Charlotte's, in that it doubled as a living room—only this one had big French windows looking out over Second Avenue, windows people probably used to lean out of, calling to their neighbors, welcoming the morning sun.

Now, though, the traffic drowned out every other possible sound, and the sun baked the room in the early hours of summer.

I'd wake and throw the windows open just to get a little air, then collapse back on my hot futon while the roar of traffic filled the room like yeast. Lying on my back, I'd shut my eyes against the yellow light, and cars roared by under my lids. Every other minute there came just the slightest pause, while the timed lights dammed up the last dregs of traffic before it could start streaming again. My dreams filled up with engine sounds. Even in the rehearsal hall down on Forty-third Street, the piano in the corner banging away on this number "Direct Your Call" while we all clackety-clicked, I could hear the roar of traffic in my ears, a roar with no rhythm and no letup.

I never knew who was going to be there when I came home to the railroad flat. A.J., who was a few years older than Coretta and me and had some steady money coming to her from somewhere, took to having a stream of visitors—not boyfriends so much as people needing a bed or a place to get straight. I'd get home late and they'd be in the kitchen or holed up in A.J.'s narrow rooms, smoking grass and listening to New Age tapes. Once or twice there were people in my bed, who moved back to the other side of A.J.'s curtain as soon as I tapped them on the shoulder, but their smell stayed in the sheets when I lay down—tobacco and that urine smell you pick up in the subway.

A.J. was the one who told me about suicides having heart attacks before they hit the pavement. I couldn't talk much to A.J. I could talk to Coretta, who had skin the color of doeskin and black hair neat and snug as a hooked rug around her head. Coretta was the one who'd gotten me in the apartment. She was McKnight, the other understudy who'd been hired with me, the first gig for both of us; we'd stood together in the final callback, got fitted for our maids' outfits and white lace caps together. But she was miles beyond me other ways. She earned great money modeling and spent it all on tap lessons, jazz lessons, voice—she was going places, out of gypsy life, on to the scene uptown, some repertory company or something. Gregory Hines was her hero, she said. We had to stop tapping and start hoofing. She got tapes of Savion doing TapTronics with a heavy metal band, and when she got excited she'd clear the chairs from the kitchen and haul me out there to work a combination with her, mixing long riffs and toe taps with those throaty vocals and electric guitar whines. I'd repeat all her steps back at her, the music pounding in my temples—stoked with it, my whole self in my fast feet, in the zone. Then we'd stop and she'd shake her head. "You are so freaking *precise*," she'd say. "Just like a white girl! Look at your hand on your hip there! You are talking Times Square, honey, and I am talking *Harlem*."

Coretta was pretty political about the hoofing thing too— showed me articles about how it came from African clog dancing, and got riled up when the *Black and Blue* cast took on a white dancer. Which would have scared me off from talking to her much except her boyfriend, Nicky, was white. Pale, in fact, a blond film major whose eyes taped her every movement; and she was different with him, soft and quick to laugh, to please. He was the one who gave me Rilke. It was Nicky's idea, too, to take me out to a singles bar in the Village for my nineteenth birthday.

"Let's face it," he said quietly to Coretta, eyeing me as I scooped up onion dip with saltines for supper, "she needs a man."

"She ain't even had a boy, yet," said Coretta.

"We dress her up," he said, "like the college sweetheart she really is, and we take her to one of those hot places near NYU, where she can get served. There's an engineering student there, with an enormous libido that just won't quit—"

"How 'bout a *wang* that won't quit."

"—and he keeps watching her. I come on to her a little, even though I'm with you, so he'll see how desirable she is. We check him out of course, make sure he's not a bully, or riddled with AIDS, or anything—"

"Oh, sure. We give him a blood test at the bar."

"—and when we're sure he's clean, and good in his heart, we ditch out."

"Do I get to help pick this pickup?" I asked, pouring myself a glass of Coretta's wine.

"No," said Nicky. "You never get to choose your first."

"Guys do."

"Guys, especially, do not. Mine was this ugly beast of a tennis coach. She wouldn't let me off the bed. Not my choice."

"I think Stick here," said Coretta, coming up behind me and twining her long arms around my waist, "oughta have her pick of all the healthy young men of this town. We oughta have a race. We oughta give her golden apples."

None of it happened, of course. I mean, we did go down to the singles place, where people of both sexes with great styled hair stood six deep at the bar, and we took a booth and ordered margaritas and nachos, and Nicky told Coretta and me the plot of this new film he was working on, a spoof of political activism that had dead people campaigning for their civil rights. "Zombie sit-ins," he explained. "Interviews with parents whose daughters have been dating dead guys." It was September, the students all back in droves, and Coretta spotted five or six young men who she was sure would move in on me as soon as she and Nicky quit the place. So we toasted my birthday, and Nicky paid, and then they slipped out arm in arm. When I'd finished my drink, avoiding eyes, I slipped out too.

It was a Monday night, the only night the theater was dark. I'd skipped my hip-hop lesson to come down to the Village. I wasn't used to being out in the evenings. Four nights a week, rotating, you hung backstage in makeup through the whole show, just in case somebody broke a leg or a vocal cord. By then, after four months, I'd been in the show exactly five times, counting the arthroscopic surgery. Still I was tired, even on the nights when I got to leave the theater before the show started. For one thing, even though I got paid for not dancing, Claire at Doggie Do had gone ballistic when I mentioned I might have to give up dog walking—so I'd switched to mornings, stuck with her, and banked the extra cash. Plus one condition of my being understudy was I'd spring for voice lessons with the music director's friend on the Upper West Side, three afternoons a week after rehearsal. This teacher wasn't big on Mozart; he was more into the Broadway approach, which meant lifting weights and doing sinus exercises so you could belt the words out. He told me to stop listening to Second Coming tapes and start gluing my ear to Streisand; I cheated, did my warm-ups in the shower with that O-rings song which was already old news.

But I have to admit, by then I was caught in the promise that this life held out to me, like a melting Popsicle. Frankie'd said that when the show went on the road I was sure to make chorus, and when we came back and it closed he wanted to be my agent. *Gigi*, he wanted me to name myself. "I mean, bury the nickname," he'd said. "And *Gwyn*, that's some romance book handle. You want people to know you got a Broadway soul, you give them a Broadway name."

"Couldn't we go with Jennifer?" I said. "Ashley?"

"Like every other gypsy bitch, you mean," he said. "I'm talking *soul*, Stick."

I was trying it on for size, falling asleep with it to the rush of the Second Avenue traffic. *Gigi Stickley*—or no, just *Gigi*, one word. I'd wait to ask my parents down again till I had that name on a program somewhere. There were a couple of new productions brewing, the girls in the chorus had told me, big-number productions; or else a repertory company, like Coretta was aiming at, something on the cutting edge. Bring my mom down and watch that look of pride mix it up with just a little shock value because I'd danced naked or shaved my head or gone out on the stage with no music, just my body moving like a bunch of pistons that people couldn't tear their eyes from.

So I hadn't missed getting out in the evenings. I was making good money, for a gypsy just hitting nineteen, and I had plans. Only now I was out of my element, on a nine o'clock street in a part of New York that hadn't a clue to what I did, and something was shifting in me.

I walked up from the bar to Washington Square, which had disappointed me big-time the one time I'd been there in daylight—the trees too spindly, trash all over the ground, people pushing drugs at you. Now it hummed with young people, and the air was soft. I leaned against a bench, ready to move as soon as someone hit on me. Things were working out, I kept telling myself. I worked for my living, I was an adult. Virgin or no virgin, I had a right to be here in this city. I had a right to it no matter what had brought me here or where I aimed to go.

Then I saw the thing that took what was shifting in me and pushed the needle off the seismograph. This won't sound like much—but across the street, under a flickering neon light, a tall black kid was tap-dancing for quarters. You could hear the taps across the square, backing up the low thump of music that drifted out of the bars, counterpointing the unending honk of cab horns. He was good. Fast but imaginative, he worked in his little space, his eyes fixed on the gutter of the street before him. I'd seen others like him on Broadway, just about the time I arrived for warm-ups, working the crowds. This one I had a clear view of, though, and I thought about my own feet, about rehearsal the next afternoon. I thought about where I'd be tomorrow night, watching from the wings, waiting for someone to twist an ankle though no one had so far. It seemed to me, as I stood across the soft-tarred street from the dancing kid, that no matter how close he came to the zone, what was happening with his legs and feet wasn't a whole lot different from what happened to the frogs in McGruder's biology class, back in Windhaven. It was like when you attached the electrodes to their dead bodies, and they kicked. It was nerves, that was all, and I had despised the frogs for it.

I looked up at the broad streetlamp that arched over the walkway, the empty fountain. It wasn't that my ambition was going to be short-lived, or that it was a shallow, narrow life that the people I knew uptown wanted to lead. I didn't care about any of that. It was that the dancing I'd done, once, was a kind of sex—I knew this, even though I still hadn't had any sex, not with a man—and it wasn't that any longer, or if it was, then sex was just something mechanical like electrodes. Or maybe it was the perverseness in me, that I would want for so long and try so hard to get control over everything, to hang on to the capsule that went spinning off from the rocket, only to find, once I'd got hold of it—and I did have hold of it, I could dance any style you handed me, as fast as you pleased, and register whatever degree of joy or smarts you required on my face—that what I still yearned after was the face of God, which you had to lose control in order to touch. That kid, for instance, the kid across the street—you could say he was in control, sure, but control came from the fact that for all his fast feet, his clever moves, those surly bonds had him tied right down.

The Popsicle melted, the infatuation popped. "I don't want to perform anymore," I said out loud.

I guess I said it pretty loud, too, or enough to hear. When I took my eyes off the streetlamp, the group of students that was sitting on the next bench over had turned to check me out. There were three girls and a guy—all real young, college kids, garbed in jeans and black leather and trying not to look so scrubbed. "Jesus," I said, when I'd sorted one out from the rest. I blushed red, embarrassed to be found like this, talking to myself in Washington Square. But my heart jumped, anyhow. "It's you, Barbie."

She stood up, pulled away from the others, came closer. "I don't quite remember . . ." she said.

"Stick," I reminded her. "From the hamlet. When we were kids."

chapter 24

"You ought to come to school here, is what you ought to do," Barbie kept saying. "I mean, I don't know if she could get in with a GED, but she was really smart, as a kid," she added to her friends. "You'd ace the SATs," she said. "And you could study dance *here*."

She turned to the others, for backup. It was well past midnight, now, and we were sitting in our second bar, a beery place with sawdust on the floor. They nodded and turned back to whatever they'd been talking about, I think it was their class schedules. This was a show they were only half watching, the Barbie and Stick show.

"I don't want to study dance," I said. "I'm all done dancing. That's the *point*."

"Well, then, you could study whatever you want. Interdisciplinary, even."

"I don't think I want to study anything," I said.

"Well, criminy. What do you want to *do*?"

"I'm earning some money," I said, "walking dogs. But I'll need more if I quit the chorus. So I guess I'll try for another job. Maybe a night job," I said. "The place where I live, it's pretty noisy at night anyhow."

"Wow, Stick." Barbie looked me up and down, like I'd just got out of prison and she was seeing the effects of the diet, the lack of sunshine. "You have changed."

I wanted to tell her she had, too, but she hadn't changed a bit—just gotten six years older, in a straight path. She was short, like her mom, with a sturdy-shouldered grace, her belly flat in tight jeans and her forehead framed by a perky widow's peak of light brown hair. Her voice had a little rasp in it, like there was something to clear out of her throat. She smiled at everything the people around her said, the way she always had—her eyes crinkled like you'd just cheered her up, she'd been waiting for you to think or say that very thing. She sat in the bar booths with her legs crossed or folded under her, or with an arm rounded over her flexed knee, her small foot in a black high-top tapping gently against her seat, by her thigh.

"What Barb means," said one of her companions—an older guy, thin and unhealthy, cigarette-smoking—"is what are you into. What is your bag. Your field. Your main squeeze, intellectually speaking."

I felt something hard in me, deep down. Not mean or cold, just solid and heavy, like a rock. "Look," I said to Barbie's friend, "I've been working for a living. That's what I just realized. And I like the working part more than all the—whatever you'd call it—the glamor part. I'm not sure working people take a lot of time to think about their bags."

"Well, that is pretty sad, if you ask me," said Barbie, but she still smiled at her friend like he'd made her day.

Her family still lived in Florida, she had told me already—her dad ran a chain of property rentals all around Orlando, and her mom had got licensed as an interior decorator. "Only they call it interior architecture now," she had explained. "All these architects are out of work, and they try to put interior decorators out of business. So they make it sound like they do something *fancier*. Like they don't just design closets, they *conceive* closets."

Her thin friend leaned in toward me, picking a thread of tobacco from his teeth. "The *real* question—is it Stick?" I nodded. "The real question, Stick, is what else are you good at. Besides tap dancing, if that's all done with."

I had to think for a minute. "Grammar," I said finally.

"So you can write."

"See?" said Barbie. "You could be an English major."

"I can't *write*," I said. "I can diagram. Sentences. I know their parts. The way they fit. I can't make them up myself or anything."

Barbie laughed at that, like I'd made a joke. "Shit, Stick!" she said, tipping her beer back. "Here you've been living in New York twice as long as I have—you've been performing on *Broadway*, for Chrissakes!—and you still sound to me like you just got off the bus."

"That," said her friend, "is because you haven't got off the bus *yet*, Miss Sophomore. You've been living at NYU. Stick here has been in the city. She knows the essential truth of the city: You lift your head up, it'll get mashed down."

He winked at me, but he wasn't talking straight, he was making fun.

"I gotta go," I said. "Less than five hours till I'm due at Doggie Do."

"Due at Doggie Do! Oh, that's great!" Barbie hugged her knee tighter, tossed her shiny hair back under the amber light.

She called me, just a few days later. "Are you really looking for a job?" she said.

"I quit the chorus last night," I said. "That's three hundred bucks a week I'm missing."

"Well, Christopher—you know, that beanpole I was with?—he says he might know of something. He's in law school, did I tell you?"

"No," I said. "Fast move, Barbie."

"Yeah, well, he doesn't have any money *yet*," she said. "He's broke and on loans, in fact. But he's been trying to write for the law review, you have to do that if you're going to get a job. He says this place that publishes it, they're always looking for people who can proofread. You know, check punctuation and spelling, that kind of stuff. You said you were good at grammar."

I was sitting at the kitchen table, on the phone. A.J. was asleep in the middle room, Coretta had spent the night at Nicky's. I'd done a double shift at Doggie Do, the day before, and my hands had some kind of hives on them—could be fleas, Claire had said, and she'd given me this fishy-smelling lotion to rub where the skin had broken out. It hadn't been easy, quitting the chorus. Coretta was already mad at me, for not bothering to pick anybody up after she and Nicky had set me up so well, and A.J.'d said she couldn't see why I messed with New York if I wasn't going to dance. The next day I'd gone to Frankie's Fast Feet—early, hours before classes started, because I knew Frankie got in there and worked up his combinations in the studio before anyone came in. *C'mon*, Frankie had said, even before I'd finished explaining why he couldn't ever be my agent. *We got to celebrate your freedom.* He'd shrugged on a dry shirt and pulled me down to the street, where we rode the subway down to Battery Park and took the Staten Island Ferry over to the island. We'd climbed the first hill, Frankie wheezing but ahead of me, wiping his head under his baseball cap, pulling me along. We'd sat on a broken-down park bench, facing the city, the waters of the Atlantic shifting from gray to teal as the sun broke through banks of clouds. *You can always just come on out here and look back at the place*, Frankie'd said. *You don't have to be anybody.*

Suddenly, I wanted to stay in New York. It wasn't for the promise it held out; I wasn't infatuated with anything. All that time, in fact— bunking in with Charlotte Petersen, talking about new moves and the value of hip-hop with Coretta, pushing for auditions—I'd fooled myself with excitement. As soon as the stage lights faded I'd hungered just to get back to the hamlet, to where I could check on Daniel, maybe even get to see him if he was between foster families. I'd known enough to fight against my heart; I told myself there was nothing for me up there where the woods crowded around the hamlet, and everywhere I'd look I'd remember how he'd slid out of JoAnn and into my hands. Wanting it so bad, I'd run from it. But as I sat there with this potbellied old tapper, the salt breeze on us and broken bottles strewn among the tall, seedy patches of grass on Staten Island, as I rode the noisy, oily ferry back across the turgid salt water, I came to know I was nineteen at last and it was time for me to stay in the city. Before he hustled upstairs to teach his darlings, Frankie kissed me on the forehead—a blessing, he said. He knew he'd never see me again.

"I'm real good at grammar," I said to Barbie, on the phone. "But I promised Claire four hours every afternoon from now on. She's taking clients on the East Side, too, now."

"This is nights," said Barbie.

"Nights, yeah. Well, okay, then. What do I do?"

"Well, you have no social life, for one. So just don't ever blame me for getting you into this. College is a lot more fun, Stick. I mean, it's *college.*"

"Barbie," I said, "you are perfect." I was sipping coffee, in the dark kitchen of the apartment, but I felt a little drunk. "You will always be my Perfect Friend."

• • •

Ten P.M., my job started. We punched in at the desk, the twenty-second floor of this chrome-and-glass building on East Twenty-third. The secretary was a middle-aged Italian woman, dark and pinched; she sat behind a Plexiglas partition and handed us our time cards when we showed ID. The offices we passed by, on our way to the proofing room, were all quiet, oval-shaped, with warm gray carpeting. Inside, there were a few lawyers—they edited the review, I think, but everyone called them lawyers—just wrapping up: making phone calls, pulling on their coats, hauling briefcases through the lobby, checking their watches. "Night, Nadie," they called to the secretary; but none of us called her Nadie—to us she was Mrs. Spizzifello, just the way it read on her nameplate.

You had to be in before ten-thirty or the doors were locked against you; if you missed work too often—no one would tell me what too often was—you'd be replaced. Mrs. Spizzifello left at eleven. After that it was just the proofreaders and the radio and the coffee machine, and the cleaning crew that came in at four A.M.

There were nights when I loved the work. No one else did, as far as I could tell. They were artists, most of them, painters who wanted to work in their Brooklyn studios in the daylight. They didn't wonder why I'd quit a chorus understudy gig to do this kind of work; they didn't connect to all that. They talked galleries, showings, new brands of pastel that went on like butter but crumbled in your hands. They wore lots of earrings; a couple of them smelled like oil paint, acrid and gamey. The radio blared, usually old rock, sometimes rap toward the early hours. We sat at gray metal desks, all facing the same way, each with a fresh load of galleys on it and the copymarked manuscript beside. Our job was to check the galleys, make sure they hadn't missed anything in the manuscript. The type had to be the size it was marked for, the spaces and indents and columns had to match up; only when you'd checked those things could you go to the punctuation, the spelling, the passages that had been taken out of the manuscript or added in, to make sure the typesetter had got all that right.

"Most of it flows in electronically, now," said the guy who

trained me, the first night. "If it's straight text, you don't have to check for much besides stacked hyphens and making sure they didn't key three paragraphs' worth of B-head type. But the stuff they take out and stick in, that's stroked at the type house. There's where the little things go wrong."

At first, it was hard not to read the sentences. "Listen here," I said to my training guy. " 'When Counsel refers to Sec. Eight Part Three, the same injunctions should apply when Counsel uses for a motion to forestall.' It oughta be 'that'—'*that* Counsel uses for a motion to forestall.' You've already got a 'when,' here. The 'that' could go up on a little platform, like this." And I showed him the diagram I'd already done, of the sentence.

"Fuck it," he said. "One of the things you'll learn here, Stickley, is that lawyers don't know an adverb from an asshole. Just assume, if it's in the manuscript, it's right."

"I'm going to flag it, anyhow," I said, pulling one of the sticky yellow papers off the pad glued to a corner of my desk.

My trainer rolled his chair over from the desk next to mine, where he was working. He had orange hair, a tiny gold ring through the skin at the corner of his thick black eyebrow. He put his paint-stained hand over mine, and gently removed the yellow tab from my fingers. "Easy way to get fired," he said.

But even though I couldn't fix the sentences that wouldn't diagram, I did find bulleted lists where there should have been dingbats, triple columns where there should have been double, stacks of hyphens five and six deep. Every two hours there was a coffee break—the review stocked up on doughnuts, chocolate chip cookies, miniature pizzas you could pop in the microwave—where I learned that we were expected to get through eight galleys an hour. You could punch out after you'd done forty galleys, which was five hours. Or if you were slow, you could punch out as late as eight A.M., which was when the morning secretary came in, and so long as you'd done forty galleys you wouldn't get canned, and you'd get the extra pay, though you might see a warning on your desk after a few weeks. Most of the proofers had learned to play this game: they'd finish their forty, then stretch out in the

carpeted hallway and sleep until seven or so. On the night their
first warning appeared, they'd pick up the pace for a few weeks
and clock out at three. Me, I was fast. I could usually finish the
forty galleys by two, if I skipped the first coffee break; and by
four-thirty I was done with the stack on my desk, which meant I
wouldn't get paid for any more. Then I'd find the quietest part of
the offices, which was the corner at the back end of the hall, by the
copying machine, and I'd curl up against the wall. Sometimes the
morning secretary had to wake me up; but I knew they weren't
going to can me. I got through an average of seventy galleys a
night.

"You aren't sleeping enough," said Anne-Marie. Married to
Ben now, she'd come down to visit Claire. They'd attended this
special Quaker protest against buildup in the Persian Gulf, and
now they both wore that placid alertness that I used to see in my
mom, after Meeting. "You get home at what, eight-thirty? And
you have to be here by three."

"I sleep at the review office," I said. "I'm done four hours early,
every time."

"Crunched into a corner against a Sheetrock wall. That's not
sleeping. That's like a homeless person."

"I told her," said Claire, "I could give her the morning shift
back. Okay, it's six an hour and not fifteen, but it's daylight, at
least."

"You could have a social life," said Anne-Marie.

"My hands would break out worse than they are," I said. "And
I don't want a social life."

The dogs knew me, now; they rubbed their sides against me
when I first leashed them up, and nuzzled my hand when we
stopped at street corners. People thought we were poetic, a real
New York sight like horse-drawn carriages in Central Park.
"Amazing how they get along!" they'd say when they took our
picture. "All sizes!" And at first I'd explained what Claire had told
me. That it didn't take long to get a pack mentality going, and so

long as they saw me as their leader and none of them had any go-
nads left—which they didn't, Claire wouldn't take dogs that
weren't fixed—there wasn't anything left to fight over.

But I couldn't take another hour of poop-scooping, and my
hands kept bothering me—"I think it's the leashes," I'd told
Claire, and she'd bought me cotton work gloves to wear, though
they didn't help.

"Maybe not a *social* life," said Anne-Marie. "But you could get
out. Meet a guy. Ben still knows a couple of people in New York,
they wouldn't be that much older than you. He might even know
someone at the review. Don't you get any nights off?"

"Weekends," I said. "And I can take one other night a week,
without penalty. They worked that out so people could go to
gallery openings."

"I'll talk to Ben," Anne-Marie said. She turned her wedding
band around on her finger. You could tell she liked being married;
even the bad part of her face had smoothed out and had some ex-
pression in it. The good part, meanwhile, was aging in tiny incre-
ments—just the whisper of lines around her eyes, the skin just a
fraction drier. By the time she was old, I thought, the two halves
would finally have come together again—all laugh lines and the
pull of gravity.

But I didn't want her talking to Ben. "It's the way they say it—
social life," I complained to one of the proofreaders at the coffee
break that night. "When you know they mean sex."

"Safe sex," she pointed out. Her name was Iris, I think—the
women were less regular than the guys, often pinch-hitting for
each other, so you could get them mixed up. Iris was tall, black-
haired; by day she was a welder, I think she'd said. "You don't run
risks, if it's a social life."

"I dunno," I said. "I guess I ought to do something about it."

"So go to the Met, Thursday nights. It's free, lots of guys come
through there, it's a pickup spot."

"Uh-uh," said another woman, biting into a chocolate dough-
nut. "Not the Met. I got herpes from a guy I met at the Met!"

"Well, they can't *all* have herpes."

"No, but they're losers. They don't know squat about art, they're just cruising. Go for MOMA, I say."

"Everybody's gay, at MOMA," said Iris. She was picking flecks of metal out of her hand; all along the back of the palm, little silver flecks like hairs.

"Not everyone. And you can have a conversation with them about art. You do want to *talk* to these guys, don't you, honey?" she asked me, opening her hands like she was measuring a frame. She was plump, olive-skinned; her ears and neck were weighted with jewelry that looked like it was made from rock candy.

"That's a good starting place," I said.

"All right, all right," said Iris. She put her coffee down and clasped her hands in front of her. "Tomorrow is Thursday. I will meet you at the entrance to MOMA and we will go cruising. Either of us meets someone, it's sayonara. All this jabber's not worth diddly unless you make a move."

"Hey-y-y, Iris," said the other one. "What about Dwayne?"

"Fuck Dwayne," said Iris, unclasping her hands and picking off more metal. "This girl needs a booster."

Next night I let an hour go by, outside the museum, but Iris never showed. It was warm, for October, a hot wind blowing down Fifty-third Street, blowing up papers and dust. My bare legs felt covered in dust. If I went home I could take another shower— Coretta and A.J. were both at performance, Nicky hadn't been staying over—and make it down to Twenty-third before the doors locked.

I thought of the gray desks all lined up, the long fluorescent tubes overhead, the slick stacks of galleys, the chalky smell of doughnuts. With a last glance up and down the street—no Iris— I swung inside the museum.

chapter **25**

RUSSIAN NEO-REALISM, the exhibit read. The two guys I picked up said they were Rumanian. They came over while I was pretending to stare at a painting of a naked woman on a horse, and it wasn't until they were on either side of me that I realized that between the legs of the person on the horse was a large penis. *Herm-Aphrodite*, the label read. All the art at the exhibit had looked like that so far—men and women mixed up, humans and animals, a kinky turn-on in thick oils, with high-sounding labels pasted on the walls. I wished Iris was there.

"Tell me," said the shorter of the two guys, "you women—are you really built that way?"

"Not the ones I know," I said. "But then, I don't know anybody with hair as red as that either." I motioned toward the painting.

"Ah, red," he said. "Red is in fashion. Yes, Tomas?"

"If you say so, Ivan," said the taller one. He was glancing around the room; Ivan kept his eyes on me.

"Tomas and I know," he said. "We are fashion photographers. We study women all day long."

I looked from one to the other of them. Tomas was all fine bones and angles. His mouth turned up at one corner, and his eyes narrowed as he looked at the painting. Ivan had dark, heavy features, long earlobes, a short neck; he wore tailored clothes that made him look like a gambler. He reminded me of someone, though I couldn't say who, at first.

Tomas turned away from the crowd and leaned down toward me. "Don't believe a thing we say," he said. His voice was dark velvet. "Not a thing. We're here passing the evening, just like you." He said *evening* in three syllables, with a kind of lilt: *e-ve-nink*. When I got him alone, I thought, he'd tell me what a jerk his little friend Ivan was. Meantime I felt a rush; I'd come there and picked up a couple of guys, easy as that. Social life.

A half-hour later we left the museum. Ivan had said he thought we ought to go for a drink. Tomas hadn't said very much. A couple of times he'd run his eyes up and down my body, though. I had on new clothes—leggings, which Coretta had said I should dress in exclusively, plus a big purple T-shirt with shoulder pads and a cartoon on the back. *Legs, honey*, Coretta had said. *Got 'em, flaunt 'em*. I thought for sure he was attracted to me. And for a minute, while we tried to hail a cab, I missed what they were saying, because I'd suddenly panicked about not having any birth control. I'd never thought about birth control, it was embarrassing. I could just hear A.J., calling me a little country idiot. *Nineteen*, she'd have said, *and you can't even get the word* condom *out in the drugstore*. Then the cab was there, and Ivan was motioning me inside. Tomas stayed on the curb.

"Isn't he coming with us?" I said.

"He'll join us," said Ivan, "in a short while. He has to meet someone. Tomas is always meeting someone." And he laughed and waved to his friend, while the cab took off.

Which was all wrong, of course—and when I turned to look at Ivan in the dark cab, I realized what he'd been reminding me of. The troll. The troll on the Main Mall in Castleton, wheezing and offering me a hundred dollars. Every time the cab stopped at a light, I told myself to open the door and just step out. Get away from the troll. But I didn't, and Ivan kept talking about fashion photography and all the Rumanians in New York, until we pulled over to the curb. We were in the West Seventies, a block full of brownstones, not a bar in sight.

"I told Tomas," said Ivan when he saw me looking kind of wildly around on the sidewalk, "to meet us at my place. I have every kind of cocktail. Pretzels, too. You like pretzels?"

I could say I went with him—into the marbled foyer, up the elevator, through the carpeted hall to his silent studio—because I was simply stupid, too young to know my way around. I could say I was doing what I thought Coretta wanted me to do—or Barbie, Iris, even Anne-Marie. But I think the truth is I wanted, finally, to beat the troll at his own game. To see what his next move was and then bail out. Or maybe I still hoped that Tomas would come, after all, and prove that he'd looked at me that way for a reason.

I recognized the foyer. Of course—it had to happen, all the apartment buildings I had keys to, all the apartments. "I walk a dog that lives in this building," I said. "Every afternoon at three. Russian wolfhound. Her name's Marietta. You ever see that dog?"

"Ah, yes," said Ivan. His mouth opened in a squarish smile, like a nutcracker mouth. He kept it that way all the way up the elevator, to where we turned left down the corridor—of course!—and into the flat I had a key to, a metal key that always stuck in the lock. His, however, didn't stick. "Mah-*reet*ta," he said as the dog rubbed joyfully up against me, licked my hand.

"I'll be damned," I said.

"Doggie Do," said Ivan, the smile slowly fading from his face. "A very good organization. But you should not have to be doing this sort of work. There should be other work, a beautiful woman like yourself."

I'd never really gone into the apartment—that was one of Claire's rules, you meet the dog at the entranceway, the owner keeps the leash by the door, you don't step in. If the dog doesn't come when you call it, you go find a pay phone and call the office. Claire didn't want my footprints, my fingerprints anywhere. Now, I stepped inside, the dog at my heels, nudging my hip. Past the entrance hall, the studio was all black and white—white leather couches, black rug—with a bunch of equipment set up in the far half, and a bar in the corner. Ivan fixed me a sloe gin fizz and set a bowl of pretzels on the coffee table. "You have a boyfriend?" he asked.

"Sure," I said.

"But he is not around."

"He's around," I said—feeling like I was back at Camp Torture, lying my head off. "I just like to go to the museum more than he does."

"Ah yes, the museum." He'd pulled off his jacket; in the dim track lighting, I could see sweat stains under his arms. "It's a fine museum. We have nothing like it, where we come from."

"You and Tomas."

"Yes, Tomas and I."

"Rumania."

"Yes," he said. He was drinking something clear; we both took sips from our glasses. I crossed my legs and took a pretzel. Suddenly Ivan heaved himself up from the other couch and came toward me. Marietta moved out of the way, like she was used to this. "I want to photograph you," he said. He nodded to his right, where the equipment was set up. Against the wall there hung a bunch of proof sheets, and a couple of stools were set up. A bunch of cameras and lenses lay on a shelf.

"Why?" I said. I took a big drink of my sloe gin. This was the time to go, but I didn't go. I thought, for what seemed like no reason, of Charlotte Petersen. Then I remembered that afternoon in high school, when she'd gone to meet the modeling guy.

"You can hang your clothes here," said Ivan. He took my drink and set it back down on the glass coffee table. Then he reached a stubby hand and pulled me up from the couch. My heart was banging in my chest. This was what Charlotte had done, this was the scam she'd fallen for. Taking my other hand as well, Ivan led me backward, over toward the stools. He was smiling in what he probably thought was a reassuring way, his thick lips curled upward and his eyes glimmering. "Here," he said again, and nodded at some coatracks on the wall. Then he dropped my hands and sort of scurried back to the coffee table, to get my glass as if I'd asked for it.

"Hey!" I called over to him. It seemed like I'd found my voice when he let go my hands. "I didn't say you could photograph me! I didn't say I would . . . you know."

He was already back with the sloe gin fizz, refilled and glowing red in the spotlight he'd switched on. "Please," he said. He marched up to me, close to me. He was maybe three inches shorter than me, but thick in the chest, like a wrestler; stronger than the troll had been, I thought quickly. Pulling my chin downward, he kind of pecked me, lightly, on the lips. "I won't publish them," he said.

I don't know, maybe he put something into the sloe gin. Something to take away my willpower. Or maybe I'd been running away too much, and I'd decided, at the worst possible moment, to stop running away and just face whatever music I had to face. Anyhow, I took off my clothes; I hung them on the hooks. It hadn't occurred to me that he *would* publish the photos—that was the least of my fears. He was the troll, come back, uglier than ever. He was the phony who said he was looking for models and banged high school girls in motel rooms. The metal stool Ivan told me to sit on stung my rear end with cold; I shivered all over, in fact, and the one time I glanced down I saw my nipples were pinched and erect with the cold. From the couch, Marietta watched me—sympathetic, dumb.

Meantime Ivan picked up one camera after another. He told me to tip my face up, to bend my neck, to turn my shoulder, to lift one arm. And I did it; I'd practically asked for this, by now. I could have gotten out of the cab; could have walked away from them both, at the museum.

"Relax," he said, finally, when the cold had stiffened me up and my blood all seemed to have gone into my stomach. I watched as he set the camera down. He was really sweating now; his front was all damp. I'd stopped wondering about Tomas. I'd never see Tomas again; Tomas hadn't been laughing at his pal Ivan, but at me. Ivan was going to kill me.

Then Ivan walked up to me, with a strange kind of professional look on his walnutty face, and he knelt down. He knelt and put his hands on my cold thighs, and then he bent forward, and he put his tongue there, in between my legs. I didn't move. I was made of stone. In a second he got up, backed away, and took up the camera. He clicked the shutter—photographing me like that, wet with his spit. Then he put the camera down and came forward again; and this time when he knelt, he began to suck.

"I'm leaving," I said. The words came out of me like a key turning in a lock. Before he could grab me I'd swung one leg over the high stool and was down on the floor. I pulled on the leggings and the T-shirt; I slipped into my sandals. Ivan stood there, looking at me. He wasn't trying to please anymore, but had the same stamp on his face that Tomas had had, laughing inside at a secret joke.

"You're being stupid, you know," he said, when I'd grabbed my pocketbook. "You can finish your drink. I will not touch you." Only he said *tooch yew*, and I was already at the door. The dog trotted after me, like she was going to get to join her friends for a late-night stroll, all wagging tail and open mouth; I shoved her away. Then I took the stairs down, six flights, and then I was out and on the sidewalk, and running to Columbus Avenue and south to the crosstown bus. I had money for a cab but I didn't want to take one. I didn't want another close, dark space.

I'd caught my breath, finally, by the time I got off the bus. Later, I would feel stupid and ashamed. Right then I was glad just to be walking, just to be alone. A.J. would be back from performance by now, with whoever was crashing in her room tonight; Coretta might be home, with Nicky. They would ask why I wasn't working; I'd say I had quit the review. I *would* quit. Along the sidewalk I noticed everything—all the lights of the late-night fruit stands and bars, all the harsh voices of people going in and coming out of doorways. There was trash all over Second Avenue. Not just paper and plastic but food, half-eaten hot dogs and crushed pizza, and dog crap like an irregular growth on the curb.

I got to the doorway of our building and breathed in urine while I dug for my keys—someone'd got into the foyer again, and pissed a great puddle in the middle of the black and white tile. Then I heard a sound behind me: my name. I whipped around, with the sudden, crazy idea that this guy Ivan had followed me here. Now it was my turn, to kill *him*.

But it wasn't Ivan. It was Lenny Dugliss, from the hamlet, tall and bony, in a white T-shirt and torn jeans, his head tipped to one side and his dark eyes crinkled at the corners, his hands shoved into his pockets.

"Christ," I said. "How'd *you* find me?"

"I been meaning to come see you," he said. "I had your address wrote down a long time back."

"Why?" I said. I pulled out my key ring and let it dangle. "You didn't run away again, did you?"

"I turned seventeen last month," he said. "You don't call it running away."

"Okay." I put the key into the lock; I didn't know if I was inviting him in. I couldn't really piece it together, what I'd done with Ivan and now Lenny Dugliss here, in this other world. "But you're not living in New York, are you? You can't be."

"I get down here," he said. "I got my own car. And there's an old friend of Nate's lets me stay with him. Just a few days at a time, you know."

He'd moved closer. I hadn't seen Lenny Dugliss since I'd left, more than two years before. He stood a head taller than me, with thick shoulders and ropy arms that looked like he'd turned into a high school wrestler. His thin mouth was grinning, like I'd cracked a joke too good to be spoiled by laughing out loud. I turned the key in the lock, and he followed me inside.

chapter **26**

It was about his brother Seth, Lenny told me. Seth and JoAnn Harlett. "You ain't heard?" he said. I'd gotten him a beer and a box of crackers from the kitchen, and we were sitting on the rug in the living room, my room. From the other side of the curtain flowed A.J.'s music, but if anyone was in there they weren't coming out. When I'd gone to get the beer I'd seen a light on in Coretta's room; her voice, low and sleepy, confiding in Nicky, came through the closed door. It was one A.M.

"What?" I said. "That they had a knife fight in front of the P.O.? Or did he finally admit it, what he did to her?" I'd taken a beer for myself, too—it cooled my head down.

"No, not that." Lenny leaned forward and traced a pattern on the rug. "When was it you were up there, last time?"

I had to think. "Fourth of July," I said. "My dad's tried to take over the fireworks—you know, since his Minimart's in Gray's old store, he thinks he has to do it. He does such a lousy job." I heard myself laughing, that soft embarrassed sound people make when they talk about things that used to be familiar.

"Yeah, the fireworks," Lenny said, and as he lifted his face to mine I remembered his brother Nate, and that day of the fireworks so long back. My cheeks got warm, and I stuttered something. He waved his hand, like he was brushing away gnats. "I don't think they were an item, last summer, him and JoAnn," he said. "No, lemme think. She moved into the house the day I started working for my dad, that was the middle of July. So they must've been, already."

"She moved *in*? With *you* guys?" I shook my head clear of the

Fourth of July, and blinked. Whenever I tried to picture JoAnn, the only thing I got was her pale face twisted in pain and hate on that bloody pallet in the shed. Who would want a monster like that in their house? "Her mom must've kicked her out," I said.

"Yeah, she found out she was . . . you know." Lenny took a swig of his beer. He didn't mean pregnant; he meant sleeping around. He was seventeen, shy. "And Seth and her, they said they were gonna get married."

"You've got to be kidding!" I couldn't stand it anymore; I got up and went to the window, unlatched the wooden shutters, looked out onto the teeming street. "After all that—that *mess*. I didn't think your brother gave any more of a shit about JoAnn than anyone else, which is no shit at all. And JoAnn was gonna be pissed at him for the rest of her life!" But it occurred to me, even as I said the words, the sound of traffic blowing back with them into the dim room, that I didn't have any idea what JoAnn and Seth felt about each other. I knew about a baby, that was all.

"That's not what I came to tell you about." Lenny stretched back, rested his head on the cushion of our one armchair. His beer sat loosely in his right hand. As I turned back to the room, to him, I sort of felt his presence, *registered* him, for the first time. Not Lenny the weird younger brother, but this lank young man, within touching distance, a stranger to me. "They were into the drinking scene," he was saying. "I mean, Seth was working for Dad, but at night him and her would take the truck and go see their friends down at Cassidy's or somewhere. He turned twenty-one last spring, you know, so he could do that. Then there was that bad thunderstorm last week, and they were out in it. They had Woody with them, too."

"I don't know Woody," I said.

"Yeah, you do. Her brother."

"Bobby."

"No, the little guy. Your mom saved him, or something, I don't know."

"Oh, God," I said. "The train."

He looked up, surprised. "You know, then?"

"Know what?"

"About the train."

"No." I picked up my beer, but didn't drink. A chill threaded through my arms. "I don't know anything about the train."

"Well, Woody was with them," he went on. "Maybe they were supposed to be babysitting him, who knows. I think they'd been to Cassidy's, and they were in a hurry to get Woody home by his bedtime. So, you know that crossing where the bar doesn't come down? Just lights and noise?" I nodded. "I guess they thought they'd try to beat the train there. Then maybe Seth changed his mind, at the last minute—he always does that, gets chicken and slams the brakes. So they tried to stop, but they fishtailed. Anyhow, the train slammed into them. Carried the truck five hundred yards before the engine could stop, on the tracks." He looked over at me, making sure I had the plot of the thing. "Killed them both, my brother and JoAnn. Woody just lost his arm. I thought, I don't know, you'd want to hear about it."

I found my way past the ratty sofa and the coffee table, over to the rug. My head pounded. "Say that again," I demanded.

"They're both dead," he said, soft but without any quaver in his voice. "The coroner said they didn't feel a thing, either of them. It was instant, he said. Woody, I guess he was in a lot of pain, but he's healing up."

I curled down to where I was sitting cross-legged, my knee against Lenny's outstretched calf. My hand went over his jeans, the ragged edges where he'd slashed them, the smooth length up to his hip. "God," I said. Then I bent down farther. As I laid my head on his thigh, I could see with my eyes still open the thing I'd kept out of my field of vision, all this time—JoAnn and Seth, with all their crimes, their early wasted lives, wrapping themselves around each other and feeling good for once. *Instant*, Lenny'd said. I hadn't understood anything. "God," I said again.

Putting his hand on my head, Lenny stroked it gingerly, and I let the tears come.

• • •

That night we both slept with our clothes on, on the futon, our breath rich with beer and the roar of Second Avenue filling our ears. Only I didn't sleep, at least not below the level where I replayed the scene with Ivan over and over and then shifted without warning to JoAnn in Seth's truck, her pale yellow hair bouncing forward as they whipped around and the brakes screamed, her round face opening as the train hurtled at them. Ivan and JoAnn, JoAnn and Ivan, and me the gaping witness. Shame and remorse crawled over me in the hot night.

Then, as the windows grew pale and a morning breeze kicked in, I got up and tiptoed outside the apartment to avoid A.J.'s rooms; I passed through the long common hall and back in through the kitchen door to the bathroom. I peed, then drank two glasses of cool water; I took an aspirin. When I got back to the living room Lenny was sleeping lightly, his arm thrown back over his head. Peering closely, I thought I could see the scattering of points on his upper left arm, where the needles had gone in with his insulin. You switch off between the hip and the arm, one guy in the chorus had told me, getting his own injection ready. You never get needle tracks like an addict. Lenny's cheek was stubbly, over his long chin and down onto his sunburnt neck.

I was tired of thinking, of seeing things in my mind. I knelt by his hips. I touched his jeans, the stiff seams near the waist, the double stitching. I was concentrating on those lines of orange thread, on the geometric shapes they made, a triangle for the coin pocket, a long rectangle at the zipper, tiny solid squares of orange securing the belt loops. The cloth was soft but the seams were still stiff. My fingers were touching the brass brad at the corner of the front pocket when his hand reached down to mine. It lifted my hand and placed it—gently, the way you might place a bird that's fallen from its nest—on the lower part of the zipper, the gradual stiffening underneath there. When his hand left mine it made a quick gesture, unbuckling his belt, then left me with my new territory.

Scared, yeah. But I liked the motion of it, of my hand setting the button and zipper free, like unlocking a secret. Cautiously I replaced my hand where he had put it, only white knit between us now, between my magic hand and his cock, and I shifted my gaze upward. It was then his eyes opened. They looked surprised, as if his hand, before, had been up to something on its own hook, preparing this for him unawares. His face was very pale, his hair falling over his eyebrows. After a long minute, he took hold of my upper arm and pulled me up to him, to his rough face, and kissed my mouth. He slipped the rest of his pants off by himself, though part of me would have liked to do it, and then he worked on mine. By the time he put his mouth to my breast I was so scared I was shaking; he had to stroke my back, long steady strokes down to my hip, to get me to stop. But I did stop, finally, and then we were easy with each other—the way people are, I guess, in grief or other times when you can't quite lay hold of your heart. Plus I'm not sure either of us knew much about what we were doing. But I took him deep inside me, and I didn't break. Even the pain wasn't as bad as I'd imagined; it loomed like a sharp peak, and then we'd crested over it. The sound of the traffic washed through us, the music of the city.

Even so, when I first came back, it wasn't for Lenny Dugliss. My dad needed me. "I'll tell you first, before you get mad, that this is your mother's idea," he said over the phone. "She says she heard about it from Anne-Marie, that you're not doing the dancing, anymore."

"I gave it a little break," I said. "I'm working, now. It's okay."

"Well, look—I said this was your mother's idea, right?—but if it's just work you're doing, not, you know, a *hobby* or anything like that, well, just so you know, anyhow, I'm going to have to hire someone on." His voice faded in and out, like he wasn't keeping his lips near the mouthpiece.

"What do you mean, hire? At the store?"

"Yeah. You know"—he gave a nervous laugh, quick breaths jerking up from his belly—"you'd think I must be doing well with it, hey, to hire someone! But that's the irony of the situation here. There's this new Grand Union, opened up on 9G. And you know how it is, competition . . ."

His voice faded out. "Dad, talk into the phone," I said. "Are you losing money? With the Minimart?"

"No, no. Just, I gotta buy into some more of their promotional material. Keep my competitive edge. And the capital—well, it's not so much there, at the moment. And Gus Dugliss, meantime, has this major contract, over at the mansion. So I thought I'd grab my twenty-five an hour with him, and get a girl in this place."

I could hear my mother in the background, trying to tell him what to say. I was peeling my hands, peeling off the little blisters I got walking the dogs. Underneath, the skin was raw, wrinkled. I'd already cut back my hours with Claire—I didn't want to do the West Side anymore, I'd told her—I was convinced it was those dogs, giving me the rash. My father had never asked me for anything before. I could hear his breathing, over the wire.

"How much you paying?" I said. Knowing it would be five, when I could pick up fifteen at the law review and sleep half the time. Knowing my place was still in the city. I told him I'd think it over. But his voice kept getting tighter, pulling on me—until, before we hung up, I'd told him I would try it for a couple of weeks. "After that, you should probably get somebody else," I said. "They won't hold my job, here, past that."

This was a family emergency. That's what I told Mrs. Spizzifello, a few days later. I had actually read, in the contract I'd signed, about how they'd hold your place for a family emergency. She told me to send documentation within the week; she showed me where it was specified, in the contract, and she gave me the envelope to send it in. I didn't ask what documentation she was talking about. "Hey," said Iris, if that was her name, when I passed her on my way out. "The Met, when you get back to town. We'll meet at the lobby. I promise, this time." She never said where she'd been, before.

I walked with my bag up to Grand Central, and took the train north.

I'd done this enough, now, that the landscape had printed itself on my brain, a line of cluttered railroad-yard debris and quick vistas. It was near Thanksgiving; the leaves were all down from the trees, so you could see the river from most points once you'd got past the Bronx. This was Amtrak, the expensive train. The people on board were students heading out for the weekend, business-men who kept an apartment in the city and joined their families on weekends. A few long-distance travelers, aimed at Chicago; there was a sleeping car toward the rear. Ordinary people took the commuter train, with all its stops at Yonkers, Tarrytown, Cold Spring, Beacon; they sat on pale blue cushioned benches and nod-ded with the jolts. But this one had mahogany seats, deep, com-forting. Little trays popped up if you wanted to go to the snack bar and bring something back to your seat. Going faster and faster, you passed the commuter stations and looked back on the wives parked in the little lots. The Hudson flashed by like gray silk. A middle-aged man sat across from me and circled things in the financial pages of the *Wall Street Journal*. I shut my eyes and let the train rock me.

My mom had called, after my dad. To make sure I was going to do it. "He could hire someone up here," she said. "But it's his pride. This way, it seems like he's working for that man because he likes carpentry, or something."

"It's okay, Mom," I said. "I can use a break from the city, it's okay."

Then she said little Daniel, that baby I'd been so fond of, was back at Haven House for a short while. I could see him, if I wanted. He was four years old, he'd done eight different foster families. The county needed to think about a school for him. About a live-in place.

"An institution," I'd corrected her—standing in the kitchen of the Second Avenue railroad flat, Lenny back in my bed, A.J. sit-ting at the square wooden table drinking coffee and smoking a foreign cigarette.

"We don't call them institutions anymore," my mom had said. "Anyhow, just thought I'd let you know. Since you're coming up."

"You want to tell me why the fuck they *don't* call them institutions?" I'd said to Lenny when I went to wake him up. It was his third time, staying with me in the city. He'd pulled me under the cover, where I could inhale the scent of him.

"Maybe"—his lips played over my forehead—"it's not a nice word."

"That's just it. Things that aren't nice don't deserve nice words. You don't solve a problem by renaming it."

"Look, your mom was great to me," he said. He was naked. Turning me around, he held my back to his torso and spoke into my hair. "That time I ran off," he said. "The old guy had let me have it, said he'd let me have it again. I'd asked him about my mom, how she died, and he laid into me with a two-by-four."

"How *did* she die?"

"Pills," he said into my hair. "Your mom, she let me talk it out. Said I didn't have to go back. I ought to stay at least a couple days at the shelter, she said, to let him know I meant business. Said I could press charges, if I wanted. But she allowed as how it'd be better if I *could* go back after a while, work it out. She gave me numbers to call. It was the right thing to do."

"That's just what annoys me," I said. "How she always does the right thing. She's so damn *good* with other people. Christ, it's even cool to be a Quaker, now. And she uses all those fucked-up words."

"What words?"

"*Homeless person. Needs-based funding. Physically challenged. Urban renewal.* And *syndrome*, all these *syndromes*." I felt him bite my shoulder—gently, tasting. "I'm not saying she's a bad person. You just don't want to scratch her surface, that's all."

But maybe something had scratched it, anyway. Ever since Benjy'd disappeared and Gray sold the store and moved away, there had been just a little edge of something real about my mom. Like when silver plate's been rubbed too hard, and you start to see the metal underneath. She'd come down to the city a couple times since that first evening when she'd seen the show with my dad. Once for a Quaker conference, once without an excuse. I'd taken her to a couple of night spots Coretta knew about, places where dancers hung out and drank mineral water. Her eyes had roamed the dark room, almost like she was cruising. Looking for something she'd left behind in the city, a couple decades back.

Now she wanted me home—she'd set my dad to it, but she wanted me too. She'd called about Daniel, mentioned him on purpose.

It had taken me a few days to find another girl, a tapper from the chorus, to buy the futon and sign onto the lease—it was better, I kept telling her, to have all dancers in the place. I'd even fixed her up with Claire, to walk the East Side dogs till I came back to town. I'd taken her around myself, taking the West Side keys as well, at the last minute—"You might need a sub over there," I'd said, "better get her introduced to the pooches." At Ivan's apartment, Marietta practically knocked me down, she was so happy I'd come back. "Hold on a sec," I told the new girl. I broke the rules and stepped in—my fingerprints were still on stuff, I figured, even from a month ago, and my shoes were clean. Everything was just the way it had been, that night, except two new eight-by-ten photographs were clipped on the wall. The pretty girl in them looked hollow, spaced-out, her eyes perfect circles and her shoulders hunched; her bare skin was grainy. I pulled them down and crumpled them into my jacket pocket. "C'mon," I said to the new girl. She'd started out scared of the bigger dogs, like Marietta, but already she had the hang of leashing them up and handling the scooper.

Leaving the railroad flat for the last time, I hugged Coretta, who cried pretty real tears; Nicky kissed me on the forehead, like a priest. I wrote A.J. a note; I almost left her my tap shoes—hers were gone at the heel—but took them with me at the last minute. You never knew.

I hadn't ever told Lenny why my mom had called, the other morning. Back where he was now, in the hamlet, he had no clue I was on this train. I wasn't coming home for Lenny. Though I got a rush when I thought of him, and a hollow pit of terror when I thought how different it could be, with him and me, out of the city. But I opened my eyes and looked out at the bridge spanning the river just below Castleton. At the bare gray trunks and the deep evergreen on the other bank. If it got bad, I could just walk out into the woods. Just walk and walk, I thought, until I wore my legs out.

chapter 27

Looking back, it's hard to remember that I did not come home in order to nurse my father. The accident came so soon after I stepped off that train that the two things blur in my mind, and I seem to be stepping off the train just in time to miss catching him as he falls from Meyenhold's tower. Or else it's me who causes it— I step off the train, I loop the Möbius strip and bring catastrophe with me.

Though Dugliss was really the cause. That's what people kept telling me: my dad fell because Dugliss rushed the work. They were working on the north tower at the Meyenhold mansion, the tower that had burned almost to the ground the year before the Meyenholds left, the one JoAnn and I had used for a hangout. "It's all for the movie," my dad explained while he helped me get the store going, the morning after I got back. "These people want to make a movie about that tower, so they come up here and they hire Dugliss. He's got to have the place back to its original look in three months. Well, it's a tough time for old Gus."

"I heard," I said, "about Seth. And JoAnn."

"Tragic, huh? Sure, tragic." My dad was getting the coffee going, arranging the thin Styrofoam cups with their orange streak down the side. He'd opened a box of doughnuts and set them in a pink plastic wicker basket. "But life goes on, and Dugliss hasn't seen this kind of money in a long while. None of us have. So he's hired me, you know, to set up the scaffolding, oversee the morning crew. It's work I like. Outdoor work. Rain or shine. Hey," he said. "We've got a half-hour before you have to open this place. How about you come help me get the ladders up. Hey? It takes two, really, and my back don't like the work. Just take ten minutes. That okay? Look at my daughter," he said, "I've got her moonlighting, already."

On the way over he explained how the upper half of the tower had to be rebuilt, and how it had been raining, now, for two weeks straight. One of the jokes on the crew was that if it had just rained like this the day the Meyenhold girl set fire to the place, the whole trouble would have ended before it began. Of course there wouldn't be a movie then, either. "She was a nutcase," my dad said.

"I know," I said. "The ladies at the P.O. told me about her. How her dad built this place for her, and she jumped."

"They won't burn it down in the movie, you know," my dad said. "They burn a model. So the state'll profit from the whole deal, if the movie takes off."

"I liked it the way it was," I said, thinking about the beanbags, my first tap dance tape, JoAnn. "Kinda like a ruined temple."

"Yes, well, the way it was didn't bring in a lot of tourist dollars."

We parked just outside the wrought-iron fence. "We'll put in a bid on this, too," he said as we toted the ladders around.

"What, to cart it off?" I said.

"Hell no! Blast the rust, replace broken spikes, repaint. This is an heirloom, here."

"Looks like something they used to decorate with chopped-off heads."

"That wasn't this country," he said. "This country never did no atrocities like that."

"Joke, Dad."

The ladders were slippery, a mica-thin coating of ice under the night's rain. "Wish I'd worn gloves," I said, and that was when my dad gave me his—beige cotton work gloves, blue plaid at the cuffs. We set four ladders up, three against the ruined tower itself, one against the half-built scaffolding. "Great," said my dad, chunking the ends of the last one into the spongy ground. "That'll do her. You can take the van back, Stick. I'll get a ride with one of the men. Have to come get a decent cup of coffee, hey?"

I crossed my arms, nodded. "I'll just watch, for a sec," I said.

As he went up the ladder, the one against the scaffolding, I leaned back against the rusty iron fence and imagined myself a daughter. Like that one in the play we'd read, the year before I left Windhaven High. The one who cares for her old king of a father, when the rest have betrayed him. Cordelia, that was her name.

"Hey, Dad," I said a few minutes later. "I've still got your gloves on! Dad! Aren't your hands gonna freeze? Here!"

I waved them, in the marrow-chilling air. My dad was at the top of the ladder by then. Nails in his teeth, he was hammering into the scaffolding boards. He may have been leaning back, right at that instant, to drive the nail home. He'd turned to look my way, his feet on the icy slick of the rung, when the ladder shifted in the soft ground below. Just a little shift, but my dad dropped the hammer, and then he lost his balance and went down. Nails spat from his mouth. Flailing, falling through the air, he ought to have managed to right himself. But he went down, face forward, his body splayed out like a flying squirrel. I saw the spikes and him aiming for them, I knew which three he'd hit. *Dad!* I think I yelled. And then he landed. Caught on the fence, the fence I'd been leaning against, the iron fence that ran around the whole mansion, the one we used to joke about. His body fell onto that fence, his stomach punctured by one of the spikes at the top, a rib cracked by another, a third spike in his side. And I ran and I ran and I ran, but I couldn't catch him. I could only push him off, my knees and elbows like coiled wire springing up, releasing the catch that was my dad's body.

The tarp came from the van. I covered him and cried out for help—maybe ten, twelve times, I lost track. It was Saturday, the park guys had gone home. Still I thought somebody would hear— just like I'd thought they'd hear, years back, JoAnn giving birth. By the time I found the keys and spun the truck around and drove down to the emergency phone at the bottom of the hill I'd yelled myself hoarse. But no one came till the rescue squad pulled up, running the siren like wacko.

By then I'd driven back up the hill, starting what I'd never known was in my bones, was my death chant, was my kneeling-song by my father's body. *We will never forget them as they waved good-bye. They slipped the surly bonds.* The blood seeped out from him; my knees were deep in it. *We will never forget them.*

"Where'd you go?" He interrupted me. I don't know why, but it really freaked me out to hear my father talk, like it was his ghost talking. I guess I'd stopped thinking of him as my dad, just this body, the one I'd seen in the air and unscrewed from the fence. "Where'd you go?" he asked.

"Ssh," I said, mostly so I wouldn't have to hear his voice. "Ambulance is coming."

"What happened to me, Stick?"

"Lemme see." I could hear the siren, down on Old Post Road. I lifted the tarp. Blood was pouring out of my father's stomach like there was a pump in there, and you could see the red wormy entrails trying to push themselves out of the spike holes. "Can't put a tourniquet on this," I said.

"Bleeding bad, huh?"

"Yep." I pulled off my shirt. Reaching under the tarp I said, "I'm gonna stanch it now, Dad. There'll be some pressure." Then I spread the shirt over his belly and pressed down. Blood spurted from behind his back, and his eyes rolled up again. "Oh my God," I said. Even when he didn't answer, I had to tell him. "Dad," I said, "they went *through* you."

But he didn't answer, and the chant rose in my throat.

• • •

Down at the hospital, impossibly alive, my dad ended up hooked like a fuse box to all these tubes. Some going in, others going out, some with blood and others with food and water and others with his wastes. As soon as he got over one operation to stitch up his insides, they seemed to cart him off for another. Seventeen in all, I kept track. Six organs got hit—stomach, liver, spleen, kidney, intestine, appendix. They took out the appendix, I guess it gave them a little more room there to get their hands in and sew things up. For the first three or four days he was either knocked out on drugs or just asleep naturally. I'd come from the store and find my mom perched by his hospital bed, staring at his face while the noise of soap operas floated over from the other side of the curtain.

When my dad started having spells awake he was woozy. I never got over how messed up his insides were and still he could talk. His face looked just the same, only waxy pale, the lips like thin slices of liver; his arms and hands worked fine. He'd train his eyes on me, though I wasn't sure how clear he was seeing, and he'd ask real simple questions like had I remembered to run vinegar through the coffee machine. If I bore guilt, he didn't know it—he'd forgotten what had happened while he was up on the ladder, what he had seen. All he remembered was climbing the ladder and then the iron spikes flying at him, and no idea how he'd got from one to the other. And me, I found myself shaking whenever I left the hospital and saw the low roofs below the parking lot coated in ice.

We kept the Minimart closed, the first few days. So when I went home there wasn't much for me to do except rack up long-distance charges to New York or call Lenny Dugliss or go clean out the barn. I cleaned out the barn. When I got to my old cross and the candles, I have to admit I came close to praying. If it hadn't been for seeing Pastor Gwilliam around the hospital, making his smarmy rounds of patients in his leisure suit—he'd thickened a fair amount around the middle, I guess he didn't figure he looked so good in pressed jeans anymore—I would have prayed. For my dad's life, you know. But seeing Pastor Gwilliam, I just hated all that. So I hushed up my mind and didn't let it speak to God, not on any subject at all.

Three times, back there in the hospital, I went to the white room where they had you lie down and hold out your arm. They swabbed at the inside of my elbow and jammed the needle in. I counted, each time: four thousand three hundred seconds, a pint of blood. When it was done I felt lighter, better. Colors seemed brighter, noises sharp. They put the blood in a refrigerator, marked for my father. *Subcutaneous*, I thought when I lifted up the cotton ball and peeked at the tiny red mark left there. *Intravenous. Plasma.*

chapter **28**

So now I was stuck. Now I was in for it. The envelope Mrs. Spizzifello had given me for the documentation sat on the top of my dresser, but even if I sent her down, what?—the hospital admittance chart, a note from my dad's doctor?—I couldn't be back there in two weeks. I called Claire to give her the news. "My hands couldn't take it anymore, anyhow," I said. "It wasn't just the West Side."

"It's okay. That girl didn't work out, though," she said. "She stepped inside the apartments. One lady said she got dog shit on the carpet, can you believe it? Anyhow, I figured you wouldn't be back—I put an ad up at Hunter College, I'm covered. Find peace," she said before we hung up.

We opened the Minimart back up. I ran it and made my mom eat supper when she got back from the hospital; I walked Trixie, who seemed old and slow and crotchety compared to the sleek beasts I'd had in the city. For two weeks after the accident, the doctor from the hospital made me wear braces on both my knees—I'd sprung the tendons, he said. An acute, sudden attack of housemaid's knee. His eyes had crinkled up, being kind. The braces were made of spongy stuff, bright blue. When I peeled them off at night, the skin underneath was ridged; I could feel the heat of the inflamed tendons spreading out from the knee joints.

So I'd cleaned out the barn and called New York, and now there was a franchise to run—orders to take in, papers to sort. Still, back of my mind, once we could tell my dad was going to live, there was always Lenny Dugliss. I'd thought, returning, that I'd be avoiding him. I'd thought I would have to play a game, the kind of game I'd seen Coretta and other girls in New York playing, but I just hadn't got around to, before. At no time did I admit that my pulse beat fast in my wrists when I heard his name, or that the sight of his truck going by on Old Post Road —another new truck, his sixteenth-birthday present, just like Seth's before him—turned my injured knees to jelly. I'd been living away from home two and a half years, on my own since spring. I was a woman, and Lenny Dugliss was a high-school boy.

But then he didn't come around. A couple of times he actually walked into the store while I was behind the counter in my orange Minimart cap, but I was always ringing up another customer, and he'd just be picking up a Coke or a can of Dinty Moore stew. He'd lay the bills on the counter and flash me a sweet, sideways smile before he rushed out. People in the hamlet said he pretty much lived his own life. His dad was so depressed, what with Seth gone and now my dad busted up, that he was about to subcontract the project at the Meyenhold mansion—that was what the workers said, when they came in for their decent coffee and to ask about my dad. Old Dugliss couldn't be expected, they said, to keep track of whether Lenny was going to school or working or what. Though you'd think, with two out of three boys gone, he'd pour his energy into the third. *Numbah One Son*, I remembered Lenny saying to me once, late at night on my futon in the city, *I'm so sadly not.*

Anyhow, sooner than I'd ever care to admit, I found myself staying up—long after we'd been to visit my dad and my mom had taken a new pile of state reports to bed—to drink wine and feel sorry for myself that Lenny Dugliss hadn't picked up a phone and called me.

This is why, I told myself. *This is why I never wanted to get into it. Into the stupid sex thing. It makes an idiot out of you. Now I'm an idiot.* I talked that way to myself, late at night.

But Lenny wasn't playing a game. He was older than I was, older than anyone I knew. His heart circled around and found its place. When he finally opened his mouth to really speak to me, it was at the Sunoco station on 9G, where I'd taken the van for gas on my way to the hospital. We were both filling our own tanks, only he was done first and he came straight over.

"We got to find a way," he said. "To be together." I started to answer, *You could've called,* but as soon as the words formed in my head I saw how ludicrous that would have been—for Lenny to call me like he was asking for a date, for us to fit ourselves into some slimy social scene. Social life—that was what all those people had tried to find for me.

"Well, we can't go back to New York," I said.

"No." I'd let the nozzle rest in the gas tank; he reached out a hand and took hold of one of the buttons on my jacket. At first he rubbed his thumb over it, feeling the rough leathery grain of the button. Then he slipped his hand inside and found my breast—a quick feel, a sort of hello. I stood slack, my hands at my sides.

"It's thawed, a little," I said when he pulled away. "We could go for a walk through the woods."

He leaned back against the car while I returned the gas hose and paid at the window. "Y'know what I was gonna do?" he asked when I got back. Grinning, he looked lighter, handsomer. His black hair blew back in the wind, and you could see how narrow the bones of his face were, how the forehead and temples cupped the deep sockets of his eyes. "I was gonna pack a bag and show up at your place in the city," he said. "Man, you'd of hated me for that."

"No, I couldn't!" I said—and then, when he shifted to face me: "Well, maybe. Not hate. But maybe it wouldn't of been a good idea."

"I didn't ever think you'd be back here, that's for sure," he said.

"I wasn't going to stay," I said.

"But you'll have to, now."

"I want to now," I said.

"It isn't anyplace, really," he said. "Just your family, if you've got one."

"I didn't want to call you," I said. "Is that stupid, or what?"

He didn't answer for a minute; another car had driven up to the gas island. He opened the door to his truck and climbed in. "I'll take you into the north woods," he said, leaning out. "When the snow's off the ground. North of the mansion, you know, where no one but the deer goes."

"There aren't any paths."

"Yeah, there are. Only me and Benjy knew about them."

"Benjy," I sort of breathed, and shook my head. "*That's* the one I kept expecting to see."

"Hey, he's long gone."

"I mean in the city. Around every corner, some homeless bum looking for a handout. But I never did."

Lenny shrugged, his long arm trailing out the open window. "Maybe his dad got him away," he said. His fingers drummed against the metal of the door. "With that note, and everything. Hey, Mr. Gray was a sly guy."

"He used to say *you* were sly."

"Takes one to know one."

"Okay," I said. Though I didn't know exactly what I was saying okay to. And he didn't touch me again, just started up his truck and drove away, while I went on down to the hospital.

• • •

It wasn't until my dad got to come home, after almost two months in the hospital, that the puncture wounds on his midriff each got their own dressing. He could stand up then, with help, and he stood in front of the full-length mirror in the upstairs hall and lifted his sweatshirt. He wanted to show me, he said. How the three places in the back echoed the three places in the front. "They're my stigmata, I have been told," he said. "And all I can figure from it is the good Lord meant me to live."

"The good *what*?" I said. I looked at him, curious.

"Yeah," he said. "Him."

That was when I found out my dad had got religion. I grilled him, though I don't suppose I had any right to. I should have noticed it from the beginning, in the hospital, with my dad's TV suddenly turned on and not to soap operas either. Now, at home, he started keeping it up. When the Reach Out for Christ Sunday show didn't come in clear, we had to bring the cable guys out to fiddle with the wires. When Pastor Gwilliam came around on Wednesday we were supposed to have coffee ready.

"You know what he wants from you," I said. "He wants a tenth of your income for his church, and he'll draw himself a fat salary out of his coffers."

"I read the news," said my dad, patient with me. "I know it's fashionable to curse the preachers. I also know that everything which happens to us happens for a reason. Gwilliam says the reason is God, and I got no cause to disbelieve him. Maybe this is just something you got to feel inside you, Stick."

A white streak of anger ran through me, that my dad the company man would lecture me about holy feelings. I let it run through and out and then I said, "It ain't your feelings we're talking about. It's your bank account."

"It is," he said. "It is my bank account."

We didn't talk about Pastor Gwilliam after that. I didn't remark how the newly polished cross, on the wall, reminded me of the Sanctuary with those embroidered hangings—REPENTANCE, OBE-DIENCE, BLESSING—or how, looking at it, I'd almost catch a whiff of the place in my nostrils, fresh pine and chlorine from the baptismal pool, and the baby powder JoAnn Harlett used to dust her skin with. I held my lower lip in my teeth sometimes, just to keep a lid on myself.

By early spring the day nurse had stopped coming around and I was changing the bandages for him, disinfecting the puncture wounds and fixing fresh dressings. The holes themselves were puckered closed, like three drawstring bags, each with a crusty discharge and a rainbow spreading outward in mustard yellow, snot green, purple. Other, neater slices, where they'd gone in to patch him up, were stitched closed, and the whole thing smelled a little like day-old beef. On the back there were just the smaller, tighter exit holes.

"Pierced through," he said one day while I was cleaning. "Like a butterfly on a pin, hey, Stick?"

"Does it still hurt you?" I asked, swabbing. Sometimes, when I shut my eyes, I could see him again— falling, spread-eagled. The points on the fence a magnet, his body metal. I straightened my knees—no braces now, a little flame in the tendons.

"No, no. But you know what it's like?" He was lying on his back on the hospital bed, looking up at the ceiling. "It's like you thought you were solid, and suddenly you're just empty space. Like Superman—you know that old Superman series, on TV? No, you wouldn't." I shrugged, kept swabbing. "Well, he went through walls," he said. "Superman was supposed to be able to walk through walls, and I always used to wonder what happened to his body between one room and the next. Now I've been thinking it's more like the wall went through *him*. Like he turned into space."

"There," I said, laying fresh gauze over the punctures, "you're clean."

"Gwilliam says God's sort of like that," he said, pushing himself up and pressing the button to raise the head of the bed. "Like a space that opens up inside you, and he passes in."

"Better God than a fence baluster," I said. By then I'd trained myself not to take the bait, about Gwilliam and God. Hell, he'd never talked to me, all that long summer and fall when I tailed JoAnn over to the Sanctuary. My mother just glanced at the titles he ordered from the library—*When Bad Things Happen to Good People*, *A Stairway to Heaven*—and frowned. It seemed like we were a family that went looking for God on our own, each in his time and without help from the other two, like whatever news each of us had brought back was written in a language neither of the others spoke.

Once, Pastor Gwilliam caught me when he was on his way out from reading Luke with my dad. He sneaked up behind me in his Vibram soles where I was leafing through a pile of college catalogs my mom had brought home from the library. Noiseless, smelling of Altoids, he crouched on the rug by my chair. "I was sorry," he said in his soft, chapel voice, "that you weren't up here in time for the memorial service."

"What memorial service?" I kept a catalog open, a ready distraction. He cleared his throat. "Oh," I said. "You mean for JoAnn Harlett."

"And for Seth Dugliss." He pronounced it *Doogless*. "He'd joined our church, you know. They were both very strong young members. It was a terrible loss to the community."

"Yeah," I heard myself saying. "JoAnn could be a good person, once you got to know her. She wasn't always so . . ."

"So angry," he said. And I looked at him in surprise, that he'd know that. Surprise, too, that some part of me had been grieving for JoAnn, the same part that had forgiven her long, long ago for her outburst in the woods. For her actually wanting to kill her own child. She was a good person, I could say, and mean it.

Pastor Gwilliam stood there a minute, and I started to tense up, thinking he'd try to hook me back into the church, now that he had my dad on a line. But he didn't. He put his hand on my shoulder and just said, in a voice that sounded a little bit less plastic than usual, "She thought the world of you. She told us all the time what you were doing, how well you were doing in New York. You were a good friend to her."

I could have been flip, could have denied it. Instead I smiled and drew myself up, a little. "I tried to be," I said. And he squeezed my shoulder and went out.

chapter 29

I went to see Philomena. Her studio had grown. She'd hired someone from out of the city to teach jazz, and had two levels of classes going. But all she could do was fume at me for quitting. "I heard," she said. "From that Frankie, that rat, who should've kept you chained to a bar."

"I was sick of it," I said. "I wasn't good, really. It was just—" I looked around her studio; everywhere, mirrors gave us back ourselves. "An outlet," I said.

"Outlet! Tommy Tune's show an *outlet*? Don't you realize what a break you were getting? Oh, just to see his *face*."

"He didn't come around a lot, actually," I said. "I mean, the show'd been running almost a year."

"You're a little country idiot," she said. "I oughta move to New Jersey, where the girls know what they're missing."

But there was the teeniest fraction of her that was glad to have me around again. She opened the forbidden cupboard and poured us each a shot of vodka, cool and sharp. "So what's your outlet, now?" she asked. "Start eating, get fat, get married, make babies?"

"There's my father," I said.

"Yeah, your father's got the world to watch after him. And then?"

"I was thinking maybe I'll take the SAT," I said. "Maybe start college in the fall."

"What does a talent like you need with *college*?" Philomena had taken to wearing heavy makeup, and her eyelashes seemed to sweep toward me. "I tell you, darling, you stay here in the boonies another six months and you'll wake up one morning ready to *shoot* yourself."

"*You* don't," I said.

"I'm older. I had my day. Your day was just dawning. Oh, why did I waste my time on a ninny like you!" And she frowned and shook her head over me.

My dad needed new dressings every five hours. Even when he made it onto solid foods it was a careful diet: poached eggs, broth, fruit juices, Jell-O. Arrowroot biscuits, with the picture of the teething baby on the box. He needed help getting up, help hobbling to the bathroom. He got mail order audiotapes that Pastor Gwilliam had recommended, all about putting your life straight and your trust in the Lord. Gradually I got used to the idea of having a brainwashed father. "He used to be a HotDig. Now he's a Gwilliam groupie," I said to my mom. "What difference does it make? He's happy."

She shook her head. "Those people are dangerous."

"That's what you told me five years ago."

"Your father's more susceptible than you were."

"So fight back. Get him some Quaker tapes."

"Quakers don't make tapes," she said.

You could tell it really bothered her, though. One Sunday and then the next, she went back down to her Quaker Meeting like it was an ammunition depot. As spring wore on she took the plunge; she started sitting in his room with him, her hands on the bedspread, talking faith. Me, I made a run out to the barn. I had to check, again, on my old cross and candles. I laced the cross in my hands and spent an odd moment gazing out the tiny window up there, toward where the woods were starting to thicken up again, obscuring the mansion and the bend in the river.

• • •

I wrote a letter to Barbie, asked her to send me the catalog for NYU. It came along with a little note: *Took Christopher home with me over spring break. My folks think he is AWESOME. Burned my back at the beach. I'm taking anthropology this semester, all they talk about is puberty rituals. When are you coming back to the city? Love ya, kid.* It was written in this loopy scrawl, on aqua-green paper that matched the front of the catalog. Inside there were pictures of serious young people hunched over textbooks in what looked like Washington Square, but all cleaned up and lush with foliage. I tossed it onto my dresser, on top of the envelope I was supposed to send to Mrs. Spizzifello.

Then I went to see Daniel. I'd known I was going to do it, but I'd held off, held off, held off. He'd be gone, I told myself. I'd get there too late, and he'd be gone to his institution, somewhere upstate where I'd have no excuse for visiting. End of story. Until one snow-melted Monday my mom called needing a thick file she'd left by her home computer—*right now*, she said; she was heading into a meeting. I could visit with Anne-Marie, she said, my dad would be fine for a couple of hours.

So I went to see him. He was four and a half, no baby—but I knew the shape of him, the way he moved. As soon as I got inside my mom's office I spotted him through the window. He was playing by himself, in a yard they'd fenced by the frame house. "Stop," I spoke aloud to myself, as I crossed the gravel lot. "Stop, turn around. No one's seen you, no one knows you. Stop."

But he turned, and he saw; and though he did not know me, he came my way, and then it was too late.

Still blond, and tall—he was clumsy on his feet, true, but clamoring always to get outside and play. It got to be, as soon as I opened the door of the frame house, he'd spot me and run for his jacket. "Play monster!" he'd demand, and we'd head for the big school playground, behind the main facility, where I'd growl and chase him over the climbing structure and through the mud. The last foster family he'd been with had kept him a full year—Anne-

Marie told me this—and had thought several times of signing adoption papers. But then the woman got pregnant. *We've realized,* she wrote in the note Anne-Marie showed me, *how caring for little Daniel would lay stress on our new, biological family. We want him to have a clean start with school, so this looks like a good time to part ways.* Anne-Marie didn't think it was fair to define a kid as a liability just because another piece of joy has floated into your life. But I couldn't say I was sorry they'd done it.

The frame house had got fixed up nicely. Ben had laid a new coat of paint on the outside, and a new roof. Inside, people had donated enough stuff so the living room looked like anyone's home, with a tattered rug and a comfy couch and old standing brass lamps in the corners. I tried reading Daniel books on the couch. Tried each time I came by, but he wouldn't sit still or be held close. He wanted to run across the front hall, into the den where they had a TV and a donated Nintendo set up.

"This is Super Mario," he explained to me. "I can get him into King Koopa's castle. Only there's the flying turtles—see there? In the third world. I can shoot them, though. I can climb the ladder. Watch. Watch." He didn't ever seem to remember my name. The two or three other kids near his age gathered around as he worked the controller buttons, jumping and shooting and exploding things on the screen. His own world, but not completely. The more of us that were there, the faster he made the game go, playing to the crowd.

"He's very good at it, actually," my mom said when she came by. "Most of his language centers around it."

"So he can't be retarded," I said. "Not if he figures all this action stuff out."

She shook her head. "The specialists don't give it a lot of weight," she said.

I went to the Castleton library and read up on FAS. She was right. There were boundaries those kids never crossed. And when I battled myself over how much JoAnn had really had—*beer, six-packs maybe, but never gin, never bourbon, never blind drunk*—there were articles to set me straight. It didn't take a lot, they said. Stuff went straight to the placenta. Sometimes it didn't do great damage. Sometimes it did. You had to accept, accept, accept, the articles said. You couldn't change the picture.

Still, I sat with Daniel and learned the ins and outs of his Nintendo, how many worlds there were and what turned Mario into a superhero. Sometimes he'd pause the game to turn and explain it to me. His pale eyes looked right through me, like there was a remote crowd out there he was explaining this to, a crowd that knew how important it all was. Still I figured I got a foothold, just by listening. Then, at home, I'd repeat the whole business to my mother. She claimed she had no interest, she was busy; she countered with what was being done, down in Castleton, to place Daniel. *They* weren't an agency, she said. The county had to make its decision.

But I could tell she was getting hooked. Slow and steady, that was the best way to work on her. We got a girl to help in the Minimart—this girl who'd had to marry JoAnn's brother Bobby, in fact, they needed money to move out from under his parents' roof—so I left her and her baby in charge in the afternoon while my dad napped, and I drove my dad's pickup down to the frame house. I made up a tap dance, to Super Mario's theme music. Every day, when Daniel beat the monster, I performed for him, his reward.

It took a very long time for Lenny Dugliss and me to get around to a walk in the woods. It's hard for me to explain why, even now, except to say we were still real shy with each other. Not nervous, just careful around a thing that wasn't going to come our way more than once, and that still explained itself in a strange language we hardly knew how to speak. Unlikely things—*unfortunate* things, I made myself think, once—had happened in New York. Here, there was nothing between us—nothing but his brother and my albatross of a friend, and a secret that didn't bear talking

about. He came around the Minimart; he came by to see me tend-
ing my dad, and report to him on the work up at the mansion. His
dad hadn't subcontracted it, after all; just brought workers up
from Castleton, guys laid off from Hotung and willing to learn a
new trade. Snow finally came driving in, all through March, and
when I closed the store and went walking it was alone, along the
white tunnels shoveled out by the park workers. But by April the
snow had melted; the trees wore that iridescent green you get just
for a few days in spring, before the leaves have burst forth for
good; and I turned the store over to Bobby's wife and headed with
Lenny and a blanket for the north woods.

To get there we parked in the lot below the mansion and then
hiked around by the tower my dad had been working on, when he
fell. The fence had been taken out; wells of deep mud filled the
holes where the posts had been. The scaffolding was all in place,
the tower finished up to its conical roof. Already film crews had
been coming up, scouting the scene, for two and three days at a
stretch. They were supposed to start shooting the movie that
summer.

"C'mon," I said to Lenny. I started pulling one of the aluminum
ladders from its resting place over by the stone wall.

"Where the hell you taking that?" He stood by the pile of cut
granite that was left over now, ready to haul away.

"To the tower. I want to get up on this scaffolding."

Lenny didn't move. "My dad'll be pissed," he said.

"So when's he not pissed at you? I want to go up," I said.

"You can't get those bitchin' marks your old man's got."

"I'm not after stigmata," I said.

Reluctantly Lenny came over and helped me drag the ladder.
He'd done some of the work for his dad, over the winter, and built
up his muscles. The skin on his hands was thick, callused: workers' hands. "They ripped the fence out, anyhow," he said.

"I just want to feel what it felt like. Before he went down."

"Crazy woman. Why don't you just climb to the roof of your
house?"

We'd dragged the ladder over, set it square into the firmer mud. "Because the view's not the same," I said. Going first, I scaled the ladder quickly and then swung myself around onto the first platform.

"Hey," I said. It was a great view northward, up to where the water bent eastward, flashing blue; as I looked, the Albany train came out of the woods and began crawling along the river again, a silver centipede. Clouds scudded across the low hills on the other side of the river, and from far off you could hear the drone of the thruway.

Shaking his head, Lenny followed me up. I liked watching the sharp angles of his face change, as he drew closer. His nose had a little hook in it, his chin a small cleft that hadn't been there in the fall. He crouched on the plank: bird-man, ready to fly. Pointing down to the woods on the north side, he said, "I'll take you through there."

"Look at it. There's a hill, sort of. I never knew there was a hill."

"That's one of the places I hid from the troopers. You remember? I could look down and see 'em coming, and make it to the river before they even cut into the brush." Lenny giggled, like a kid, his elbows resting on his knees. Then he followed my eyes straight down, to the dotted line left by the iron fence.

"D'you think she was crazy?" I asked. The wind seemed to take my words away. The platform we'd crouched on was swaying, a little. "To jump, I mean. The Meyenhold girl." He shrugged his shoulders, looking down. "I remember Miss Flanagan said once she was in love," I said. "But that doesn't seem enough, unless you're crazy. I mean, to set fire, and all."

Lenny stood up. He walked toward the edge, his soft tread making the wood creak. "Look," he said, "maybe she just couldn't live like . . . like this." Holding on to a metal strut, he waved one arm back toward the rest of the mansion. "With all this fake stuff."

"My roommate in New York says most people who jump get heart attacks before they hit the ground," I said. "But I wouldn't think that'd hold, for her."

"Nah," he said. "Look at your dad. He didn't get a heart attack."

"No," I said. "He didn't." But as I let my eyes carry me downward, somersaulting through the air, it seemed like something
would have to burst, before you landed on the iron spikes. If not
your heart, then your bones, or your mind. I remembered my dad,
talking—*Like a space that opens up inside you*. Not from getting
speared by the fence, but from entering the air.

"Hey." Lenny caught my shoulder, held me steady. "We don't
want to make you Numbah Two Fallen Daughter."

So we climbed down, put the ladder back, and let the front lawn
take us down to the river.

The path to the north woods—the woods that the Meyenholds
had never tamed—started way around, beyond the old dock and
the skimpy beach, right where an old stone wall was starting to
crumble and the weedy outgrowth of the woods was reaching toward the muddy shore. We almost crawled under a canopy of bri-
ars, then the ground was tamped down and we could stand, and
make our hidden way in.

Lenny'd brought a blanket, but we didn't make love until we
had reached a place where the ground wasn't so muddy, past
where anyone had the remotest chance of seeing us. We hadn't
done this since New York, hadn't talked about doing it. Once, after he'd checked up on my dad, looked politely at a couple of the
Jesus pamphlets, we'd sat by the fire in the library and shared a
joint—my mom was out working late and anything was possible—
but like I said, we were shy. Another time, I'd touched him—just
let my hand go to his hair, the thick black waves of it—but he'd
pulled away. When he said goodnight it was from halfway past the
door, and then he was gone into the night.

Now he spread the blanket out, under the coaxing sun, and we
pulled each other down. We kept at it a long time, time snatched
out of time. It was as if everything that had happened in New
York, those odd nights in my room slanting southward, the roar of
traffic always with us in our touchings, our fumblings, had just

been some kind of preparation. Lenny's skin—the sweet odor of it, the rough and smooth parts of it—was like this huge private terrain I had to explore with my mouth, my hands, my nose. He smelled like apricots, like bread rising, like moss. He lay there and let me love him. His eyes traveled with me as I followed the curves and hills of his muscles, his hand stroking my hair, urging me along. I hadn't known I wanted so much, wanted to make so much happen. Then he began moving in me, in all parts of me. He slipped in and out, thrust and circled. Once or twice we paused and he lay on his back and I touched him—that skin like the skin of eyelids, pulsing—then he found a new rhythm, or a new place. "Oh, God," he was finally saying, and I kept saying, "Oh sweet, sweet, sweet"—because it was, like candy only given through a different mouth, too sweet to describe and then melting as soon as I'd tasted it.

Even when we were done, even when the cool air passing over our bodies made us slowly fetch clothes and put them on, we kept having to touch. I ached, letting go of him. When I stood I felt dizzy, and leaned on Lenny for support, and then his arms were around me and his mouth on my mouth, and if he hadn't been so worn out we'd have been down on the ground again. But we gathered the blanket and walked on, with my head light, that sweet orgasm still seeping its way through my veins like a drug.

Lenny'd brought a machete, to hack away at the brambles starting to grow over the path. "There's a view at the top of this hill," he said, once we were walking again. "There was, anyhow, last time I went in here."

"When was that?"

"I dunno." He shrugged, then stopped to consider. "That night my old man beat me up, years back," he said. "Before I found my brother, and he took me to your mom's place. I guess I had this crazy idea of trying to camp out here. Benjy and I used to talk about it, about setting ourselves up in a tree house here and living off the deer and the squirrels. We knew nobody'd find us, anyhow. That crazy man, that Benjy." He chuckled a little, at the thought.

But some cold bit of knowledge, a premonition as surely true as what we'd just done, there, on that blanket, had come into my mind. And so, when we stumbled across what we stumbled across, after Lenny had taken me up to the top of his secret knoll and shown me the south view of the river down to the marina and the glimpse you could get of the whole Meyenhold mansion, I wasn't totally thrown.

We'd been starting back downhill, the other side of the little hill. I'd spotted deer, two tawny does trotting under the canopy of new green. "This path'll come out by the old stables, the north end of the property, if we go on," Lenny had said, and I wanted to. Only he went in front, with his machete, so he was the one who spotted the rough shed, first, and the torn, mud-caked blanket.

"This wasn't ever here, before," he said.

"It looks old," I said, nervous with the cold knowledge in me. "It looks abandoned." He'd put the machete on the ground and stepped off the path to get a closer look. "Watch out for snakes," I said, not moving from the path myself. "My dad says they come out in spring."

"There's a couple things in here." He stooped toward the opening at the front of the shed. It wasn't more than a lean-to, anchored by two large trees at the corners of it, old boards and branches nailed and tied together. He bent down, picked something up, then stood again. "I recognize this blanket," he said.

"C'mon out of there, Len," I said. "You're scaring me." The light was fading behind us, on the other side of the hill. Slowly he stepped away and brought what he'd picked up out to the path. "Flashlight," he said. "And a gun."

It was a big, black model; he shook out the chamber. "Loaded," he said. "You could kill a deer with this, I bet."

"Anything else in there?"

He shook his head. "Maybe the leavings of a fire. A couple old cans, opened with a pocketknife. But I recognize that blanket." He stood close to me, taller than me; I could smell our sex on him, in the warmth of his chest in the cooling air.

"It isn't . . . it isn't Benjy's blanket, is it?" I finally asked.

He didn't answer, but picked up the machete and started hacking away undergrowth, first around the makeshift shed and then down the other side of the path. The ground was deep with last year's pine needles, ferns springing up everywhere like small violin shafts. I stood still awhile, then followed Lenny. When I caught up to him he was standing down a ways from the left side of the path, where the ground sloped sharply and ended in what looked like an old streambed, just boggy now. With Lenny chopping away at the tangled bushes blocking him, the birds overhead had started to chatter, to spread the news of destruction. A startled chipmunk raced across my path. Carefully I started down the incline, gripping small branches and balancing myself on tree roots. The air got even cooler as I went down, a late-afternoon breeze blowing down the stream.

Lenny had been bent over, moving in no fixed direction, maybe following signs he saw of broken branches or old paths to the stream. But by the time I got close he was standing by a big old beech, where its huge root lurched out of the incline and twisted into the boggy stream bottom. I stepped down from a rock and trapped my foot in a sudden depression, and almost pitched forward. Lenny put out a hand for me to catch onto, but he barely turned his head my way. And once I had my balance again, I looked to see what he'd finally stopped at.

From where we were standing—almost in the mud of the streambed by then, our sneakers soaked and brown—I could see we were actually between two huge roots of the beech, the other shooting off at an angle but also diving down into the stream, so the two roots were like the two giant arms of a muddy, sinking armchair. And there, curled up between them, was something between a human body and a skeleton.

As soon as he could tell I'd seen it, Lenny turned away. I could hear him, behind me, throwing up into the streambed.

I didn't throw up. I crouched down. The thing looked like he was sleeping, like he'd curled up for a nap, with his shreds of clothes still on and the leaves for a blanket. He looked very small, like a small child hugging its knees, with the innocent, sort of amused look skeletons get. He didn't look like he'd frozen to death, or had anything violent happen to him. He looked as together as any other dead person would have looked.

"Benjy," I said. Not as if to identify him—because even though you couldn't have told from looking, I'd known who it would be if we found him—but as if to greet him. "Benjy—Benjy," I said. Then I pulled away to get Lenny, and to hold him while he cried.

And still I didn't know, really, what it was we'd found.

chapter **30**

We didn't think to go to her first. Why should we have? My mother had had no more to do with Benjy than anyone else in the hamlet. Even what I'd seen with her and Gray—what I thought I'd seen, at least, the whole thing fading with time and becoming part of a secret footnote, *My mother once loved someone else*—had nothing to do with *Benjy*.

So we'd gone, like good responsible young people, to the troopers up on Route 9, and we'd filled out a report of what we'd seen and what reasons we had to identify the remains. We hadn't had to go back to the north woods; Lenny's directions were excellent, the sergeant said, and sure enough, while we sat in the station still filling out forms, the searchers radioed back that they had located the body and would be bringing it in, in a sealed bag.

They would be contacting Gray, they said, as soon as they got hold of his address in Florida—on his acre north of Sarasota, where I'd imagined him meeting up with Benjy, stashing him awhile, then taking him fishing, finding him a job he could handle. It was enough for the moment, the troopers said, that I could name the type of flannel shirt Benjy used to wear, and the black sneakers he'd had on. They had our names, our phone numbers, our story down on paper. They thanked us and let us go out into the night.

I called my father. "I'll be there in an hour," I told him. "Something's come up. A kind of emergency."

"It's all right," he said. "Pastor Gwilliam came by. Even helped me with the toilet. Poor fellow's in some legal trouble."

"I'll make some bouillon, when I get there."

"I said it's all *right*. I'll just sleep awhile. Your mother'll be home later too. That girl's at the store?"

"She'll lock up," I said.

"Then have some *fun*, Stick. Lord never said we couldn't have fun."

I climbed into Lenny's truck, leaned back against the seat, and shut my eyes. He started the motor and drove, I didn't ask where. But when he stopped we'd crossed the river, below Castleton, and parked at a brightly lit diner, blinking EAT and BURGERS off and on.

"We gotta feed ourselves," he said.

And so we went into the ordinary, electric light of the diner, where Lenny ordered pot roast and I asked for a Reuben and fries. We hadn't driven far to get there, but I felt as though I'd been traveling; I stretched my legs under the booth table, rubbed my knees. I kept passing my hands from my forehead across my eyes, like I'd been watching the road and had to clear my vision. Lenny didn't say much, or look at me. The afternoon seemed very far away. Finally, when the food came, he cut and chewed several bites of the pot roast and swallowed them down with water; then, like he'd needed the energy to do it, he looked me full in the face.

"It's not your fault," I said when I saw how he was looking. "It's not any way your fault." And I remembered with a jolt that I'd said much the same thing to Gray, long ago, about Lenny.

"What he told me, that time I run off," Lenny said slowly, "was he'd gone looking for me in the north woods. He'd gone looking down the path he'd shown me when the troopers were doing their exercises. He told me he was just sure I'd of been there. Said if I ever wanted to set up camp, there where the forest got thick, he figured he could slip me enough equipment and food and things so I could last a winter. He wanted me to know that. In case things got so rough at home, again, that I just couldn't stand it." He took another drink of his water, and started in on the mashed potatoes. His mouth worked quickly, eating, as if the simple food and the simple action were a way to keep from exploding out of his skin. He'd shucked off his jacket; and from his dark T-shirt, the one I'd helped take off in the woods, his neck rose long and pale and a little nervous, the Adam's apple bobbing.

"He didn't expect you to go looking for him," I said.

"Yes, he did."

"Well, if he did, it was a stupid game, and—"

"And Benjy was a stupid person. He had the brain of a kindergartner, that's why I liked him when I was a kid."

"And anyway," I plowed right on, "you didn't go. You had a life to lead."

"I could of led my crappy little life and still gone to find him."

"So why didn't you?"

"Why didn't I?"

"Yeah." I bit into my Reuben; it was salty and oily, the cheese like glue, but my stomach was an empty pit.

"I don't know. I don't know." He set his fork down and looked suddenly as though he couldn't touch a bite. "I guess I wanted to believe he took that money and went somewhere safe, away from everything here. I didn't want to be some part of bringing him back, if it came to that. I mean, he never did any of that stuff, to those kids. That had to of been his old man."

"What makes you say that?" I set down the Reuben. Now it was my turn to lose my appetite.

" 'Cause he tried me once. Well, okay, not really tried me. Not the way you'd think, what they were after him for. He just kissed me."

"He *kissed* you?"

"Yeah." Lenny took another drink of water; his Adam's apple jumped. His face had gone pink. "You know, in the back of the store. I'd gone to get a Coke or something. He came up behind me and put his arms across my chest, and he leaned his face around. He kissed me."

I reached my hands across the table, and he took my fingers in his own. The lighting in the diner made our eyes into hollows, the eyes of tired people who can't think straight. I thought of my mom, kissing Gray; of Gray putting his hand on my shoulder— *You think I'm guilty, don't you, Stick?* "Well, I forgive him," I said. "And I forgive you. And I forgive Benjy anything that needs forgiving."

"Yeah," he said. "I can do two out of three of those."

"Then"—and I laced my fingers tighter with his, not willing to lose him—"I forgive you twice."

But we hadn't told her, my mother, because there hadn't been reason to. When I came home late that night she'd taken her mystery novel to bed, and my father was up watching a videotape that Pastor Gwilliam had brought him, a reenactment of the Last Supper with bad American actors. "I do realize," he said while the video droned in the background and I set up to change the dressings, "that the guy is mostly after my money. He says the IRS is after *him*, and they probably oughta be. I'm not such a sheep as I can't see that, Stick. But he's made me see—I don't know why, maybe I needed a little bit of dramatics to make it come through—that all things that happen happen for a reason. That there's a bigger picture. I don't know what I'll do with myself once I get on my feet, but it won't involve wearing some corporation's little orange cap, hey?"

"I don't know the reason," I said, "why Benjy Gray had to die in the woods. I don't know what good that did him or anybody."

"Benjy?" said my father. He lifted his chin up from the pillow.

So I told him how we'd found the remains, and reported it to the troopers. I couldn't explain how Benjy had died; it wasn't something we'd ever know for sure. Some forensics expert, weeks later, would come to suggest he might have been bit by a rabid squirrel—but even then, there really wouldn't be enough of him left to say anything definite except that he hadn't starved and he hadn't taken his own life. "He looked like he'd fallen asleep in the roots of that tree," was what I told my dad.

My dad took it in stride. He'd never hated Benjy, he kept re-peating—one time too many, for my ears—but he was just certain the event was part of God's plan. I got his dressings fixed up and brought in the bedpan. When we were done, I went to my room. It was dark, late, suddenly cold; I fell into a brief, dreamless sleep.

I woke up to the sound of the radio or my mom sobbing, I wasn't sure which had gotten through to me first. I got up and took a stinging-hot shower, then wrapped a robe around me and found her in the kitchen. Her arms were folded on the table, her head facedown on them, and the sobs were breaking from her like waves. She wasn't even making a pretense of hiding them. Next to her a cigarette was burning itself out in an ashtray I'd made in fourth grade.

"Mom," I said.

She looked up, saw it was me, and turned back to sobbing. Her face was splotchy red, her eyes swollen. You wouldn't have guessed she was a beautiful women, right then, or that she'd gone through her life as a Quaker, finding the center and controlling the extremes. Slowly, while I stood there, she lifted her head off the table, but only to cradle her forehead in the palm of her right hand, while the sobs kept shuddering out, leaving no room for speech.

I walked around her and snapped off the radio; it was *All Things Considered*, and they were talking about the Kurdish refugees. From the other room I could hear my father—"*Stick? Wanda? What's going on out there!*"—and I shouted back, "In a minute, Dad!"

Then I sat down next to her and put my arm around her shoul-der, and held her close. I'd never done that before; never felt how slight she was, my mother. I was much stronger, really, and I held her until she'd let her hand drop and leaned her head into my chest, to let the sobs land there.

And it was only after a long, long while—after the cigarette had burned itself down and the coffee cooled to where the cream stood like a comma in the center—that the sobs changed even a little, and then it was just to two words. "Oh, no," she kept mouthing, first against my chest and then flinging herself back to the table, and then to me again. "Oh, no, oh, no, oh, no!"

I was going to let her go on as long as she liked, whatever it was, so long as it didn't have anything to do with Daniel—and when I'd asked, "Something at Haven House?" she'd shaken her head violently and shouted, "Oh, no!" But then I saw my dad had managed to pull himself out of bed and into his chair, and wheeled to the door of the kitchen. He sat there, pale as milk, staring at us— or at me, more, like I'd done something to his wife. So I finally took hold of her hands, and sort of enclosed them within my own, and started saying, "You've got to tell us what's wrong, Mom. Whatever it is, there's got to be words for it."

And she did, though she stuttered as she brought it out. "B-B-B-B-*Benjy*," she managed at last, and then the sobs came for a long time while she said the name over and over. But I still didn't get it, though I figured the local radio must have announced what we'd found, in the woods; I sat there with my heart splintering at my mother's sobs, with my father wheeling himself into the kitchen, frowning, and I couldn't dredge up a clue. "Benjy," she said. "Oh, Benjy, Benjy." And then she said, "Benjy, my boy, my boy, Benjamin"—*Benjamin*—for the first time, and then I got it, or at least the rough outlines of it, my grandfather's name, and I felt more than I heard the cry that came out of my throat.

"My God," said my father.

"I thought my mom was having an *affair* with him," I told Lenny. "I thought she was just cheating on my dad, lying. I didn't know how to tell the past from the present."

"Even if she had been," he said, "there are worse things."

"But I don't think she was, ever. Not since I'd been born, any- how. There had just been that time, sometime after Gray came back to the hamlet with Emma. And you didn't have abortions, back then, and she was all Quakered out by that point, anyhow.

They made this plan that she'd move across the river for a while, have the baby, then give the baby up. They thought just the same way I thought, with JoAnn. That it'd be white, and people would fall all over themselves to give it a great life. They never counted on it drooling too much or not learning to sit up till it was two. By the time they had a clear diagnosis, at the hospital where she'd left Benjy, she'd met my dad, and she must've gone into denial bigtime. Then Gray started taking in the foster kids, him and Emma. So it became obvious, what they had to do. He took Benjy in. Made Emma love Benjy. And not too long after, they filed adoption papers. It was all perfect, until the court case got rolling."

We were lying naked on Lenny's bed, the windows thrown open to a warm night breeze. His father was out at a bar somewhere; Lenny said he'd taken to spending most evenings at Luigi's or the Beer Barrel. Gray had been found, had flown north for the burial. I'd seen him sitting, one long afternoon, with both my parents on the new deck outside our house, his face nodding from my mother to my father, getting the story out.

But I hadn't heard it along with Gray; I hadn't had to. My mother had told me herself, that morning after I'd wheeled my dad out and taken care of his morning needs, all the while promising, *I'll get it figured out, Dad, right now she just needs to cry*. We'd called Haven House to say she'd be late, and filled the sherry glasses, and she'd told me while her eyes were still swollen almost shut and she had to keep lighting cigarettes to steady her fingers. So, when Gray flew up and sat out on our deck, I'd left the three of them alone there. And when Gray left to fly back to Florida, there were my mother and father, with each other again— strangers, in a way, but better with each other than they had been in all my memory.

"You're making it sound," Lenny said, his voice just a little tight, "like you're getting ready to leave town. Like you've wrapped things up here. With your dad on his feet, and all."

"Oh, no," I said. "It's just—well, it's a miracle, really. Even with all the sadness of it. I mean the way everything's ready, now. For me to do what I came to do."

"But I thought—your dad—"

"Yeah, that. But all the time there was someone else." He'd propped himself on one elbow—curious, maybe ready to be jealous. "Daniel," I said. "The mall baby. You remember him."

And I thought, as he leaned over me, that the question wasn't whether I loved Lenny Dugliss. He *knew* me. I had been waiting, for years and years, to be known. Though it was frightening, because I could look up, then, into Lenny's dark, hard eyes and see there what I was going to do, the ropes I was going to tie onto my life.

chapter **31**

But it wasn't until my dad got well enough to think about chucking his Minimart cap that my mom really got the idea in her head of taking Daniel. Maybe if I'd told her the truth—told her whose kid it was, what part I'd played—she might have gone for it sooner. It's hard to say. *She* hadn't ever told anyone, not even my dad, about Benjy, and she lost Benjy. If she wanted to stop this—the losing, the *fft-fft-fft* of lives gone forever—she should have been made to know the value of claiming what's yours.

But what kind of position am I in, to scold? I've never felt anything move in me, out of me, the way she did. Maybe, given what my dad was back then, a company man, she'd have lost *him* if she'd come out with the truth. Maybe I'd have just pissed her off. Daniel wasn't mine, she'd have pointed out, he was JoAnn's, which meant he was the world's. And she was already doing what she could for the world.

What I wanted was to finesse the deal—no confession, just ownership. Long ago, people had stopped asking what sky he dropped out of. The point was to catch him before the sea swallowed him up.

For a long while my mom couldn't seem to do much more than get out of bed in the morning and see to my dad's breakfast—he could eat most solids by that spring, and move his own bowels. She had taken over changing his dressings, she administered the medications he hated. I'd leave them both a note before it was light in the morning and take the car, straight to Haven House. There I'd do whatever begged to be done—answer yesterday's mail, jot down numbers from the answering machine, leave notes for Anne-Marie and Ben. Before I tore back up Route 9 to open the store I'd drift over to the frame house to check on Daniel— see if he'd woken up, if he wanted to play monster so early.

"You really love that kid, don't you?" was the first thing my mom said when she got her head straight enough to come back to Haven House herself. She said it wistfully, like she'd been noticing a long time and couldn't see much more than pain coming my way. "You always have, ever since he got in here. Before the foster homes."

"He needs me," I said. "Look here, what he did yesterday." And I showed her a drawing Daniel had made of the Underground World in Mario Brothers Nintendo—all slimy green pipes and flying objects, with a stick figure in a red cap jumping past the traps. "Anne-Marie says he's never drawn anything before," I announced.

"Well, I think the county's found a place that might take him," she said, looking at the drawing. "Out on Long Island, a residential school with state funding. He'll be able to draw there."

"But who'll look at it?" I said.

"I don't know, Gwyn." Sitting at her desk, she leaned her head against her hand. Like my dad, she'd aged years in a few weeks. Deep lines seemed to cut her cheeks back from her small, neatly carved mouth. Her hair started away from her temples in new streaks of gray.

"No one will," I said. Then, when she seemed to draw a quick breath and hold it, I pressed my advantage. "*I* would take care of him, Mom. You wouldn't have to do anything, not even shop for his clothes. He'd cheer Dad up, get him off this God thing. I don't *want* to go back to New York. I could help Dad build up the store, a real store; he could hang there with us."

"I thought you were thinking of college." She bit the words off.

"Well, all right, I am. All right. But he'll have to go to school too, right? I mean, there's that special-ed place, down in Castleton. I could take him there, go to my classes, pick him up on the way home."

"Why this one?" She sat up, leaned forward on her elbows. She was frowning. Thinking back. Inside, I froze. "We get fifteen, twenty of them through here in a month. You're so"—she put her hand to her small mouth, tapped her lips—"so *fixed*. What does he *solve* for you? Because I'm telling you Gwyn, if you think you can avoid your life with a—" She stopped. She pinched her eyes closed, held up a hand. Her breath shuddered a little as she took it in and let it out. Eyes still shut, she lifted her brows and finished, slow and clear: "With a *baby*, you're making the same mistake these Castleton girls make, when they land in here."

I unfroze and thought fast. Whoever thought faster would win this. "I didn't say *I* wanted to adopt him, Mom," I said. "I thought *we* should. As a family. It wouldn't be such a big deal, if we all helped each other. Just one more mouth to feed."

"Oh, Stick, Stick." She shook her head. A bubble of triumph floated into my throat; she'd never called me Stick before, it had to be a good sign. "We've all been through so much, as a *family*. Why put yourself—why put *us*—through anything more?"

"Because in giving you receive," I said.

"Oh Christ, babe, don't quote Bible to me. People quote stuff at me every time I turn around, it feels like." She looked away from me, out the window toward the little playground. True, there was a race on at our house as to who could bring the most casseroles and little inspirational books, the Quakers or the Reach Out for Christ people. The Reach Out for Christ people were winning in terms of sheer quantity—pasta shells with ham and American cheese as opposed to tabbouleh, Hamburger Helper casserole versus a book on meditation. Otherwise it was a draw.

My parents didn't argue God anymore, just heated up the food and sat together at the kitchen table, knees touching, pretending to eat. Religion wasn't a thorn in their side anymore, just a sort of thin blanket of comfort. It kept them from just looking at each other maybe.

"How about we try it?" I kept on. "For a month, or something? Sign foster papers, or something? He won't even be five till fall, he doesn't have to be in school. We could see how Dad takes to him."

"He won't." The smile vanished from her face.

"You don't know that," I said. "Surprising things happen."

Which was ninety percent b.s., on my part. I kept pushing, though. Bought Daniel a couple of new Nintendo games, helped him color in a Mario Brothers book, got him to help me fix the rotting climbing structure, in the small play yard by the frame house. He passed nails to me, took a wooden meat pounder and hammered the ones that were already in. I made sure all this happened while my mom was looking. When she finally agreed to two weeks, I thought the happiness of it would tear me apart. I went and spent my savings on a Super Nintendo set for my room, with five games and a joystick. I set up an easel in the corner, with a wide paint bin so he wouldn't spill and a big vinyl cloth underneath.

My dad came into the scene cautiously. He'd only seen Daniel once, before the accident, and at first he said all he could remember was how listless the boy seemed. But he didn't call a halt to my preparations, and when we got home, that first day, he stood in the door of my bedroom while I unpacked Daniel's things and made up the spare cot in the corner. "Hey boy," he said to Daniel, who was going through the box of games I'd bought.

"His name's Daniel," I said.

"Hey Daniel." Daniel looked up. His lower lip was drooping; his head seemed tipped at an odd angle. He didn't look his best. "You gonna play baseball with me, kid?" my dad asked.

Daniel didn't answer. "Christ, Dad, you just got out of a wheel-chair a week ago," I said. "You shouldn't be talking sports."

"Okay, then. Checkers. You play checkers, son?" My heart began to sink. What my dad wanted— But then I saw Daniel's face light up.

"Yeah!" he said. "I'm good at that! I'll king you dead!"

"You got yourself a game, then, boy," my dad said. And he left the room.

"Jeez, kiddo," I said. "I didn't know you played checkers."

"I play lotsa things," he said, and he wrinkled his nose at me. "Anne-Marie taught me. Not you."

There wasn't anything remarkable that happened those first two weeks. Most of it was just plain tough. I was up in the night, for Daniel's nightmares—he thrashed and chewed on the covers, and couldn't seem to wake up but just moaned and cried. At night he wouldn't let me put a diaper on him. I tried to wait until he was asleep, then slip it around his hips—but I got tired, with the store and Haven House. When I forgot, he wet the bed, and the whole room smelled of sour urine, like the hallway of the building where I'd lived, in New York. During the day, it took every variety of coaxing to get him away from Super Mario, and then he wouldn't use a fork to eat, or pick up the food he dropped on the floor. The couple times he got mad at the Nintendo set he went wild, kicking at the TV and throwing the toys I'd bought him around the room. But we did get out in the yard to play monster, and he liked coming to the store, to help my dad restock the shelves.

"No more Minimart," my dad had said. "We do this on our own. A country store plus the lottery. We put the chairs back in front of the picture window, we give out pickles. We make it back into a place where people'll talk to each other. And if we still need to draw customers, the manager'll put on a freak show." And he lifted his T-shirt and turned, slowly, for a full view of the stigmata.

"But you don't have the money," I said, "to buy them out."

"Let 'em stick it to me. Pay on time. We'll get the greedy bastards off our back one day, won't we, boy?" he said to Daniel.

"Kapowee," said Daniel. "We *got* 'em."

And then, at the end of a week, when I'd read Daniel a story he didn't seem to listen to, and tucked the blankets around his thin form, he clutched unexpectedly at my hand before I could stand up. "I don't wanna go," he said. "I don't wanna go from here."

"Okay."

"And I don't—I don't want y-*you* to go from here."

"I'm not," I said. "And you're not. I'm just heading downstairs for a little while. I'll be back up to sleep."

"*Don't* head downstairs!" There was a little wail in his voice; his hand clutched tighter. Bending down, I could see his lower lip tremble, the bright tears in his eyes.

"Hey. Hey," I said. I sat back down on the rug. "I'm doing my best, Daniel honey," I said. "I'm trying to get us all together. You got to help me, though."

"I'm bad," he said—looking away, at the dark window.

"No. You're good. You're brave. Daniel means brave," I said. And he blinked the tears away, and no more came. But still he wouldn't let go my hand, so I just stayed there, while he clutched onto it like a drowning person hanging on to a block of wood, until he fell asleep.

My dad, meantime, was playing checkers with him, and softening each time he let Daniel win and saw him jump up and race around the living room in victory. "He's a boy," he said once. "I think I'm partial to boys. Got kinda ticked when you popped out and there was just no little dinkie, there. No offense, Stick."

Whoopee, I thought. A boy. Advantage, Daniel. I blessed JoAnn, wherever she was, for having a boy.

For my mom, nothing was easy. I could feel her watching me, sometimes, while I bathed Daniel and got him into his pajamas at night; could feel her question aimed at my back: *Why now? Why him?* But I'd cast my lot with silence on that score, praying the spell would work on her regardless. And it did, but like the undertow of a wave—pulling at her, bringing her down faster the more she struggled against it.

It got, in fact, to a bad point—to a point where my dad said, two days before Daniel's official time with us was up, in the store, "I'm not sure all this is going to be good for your mother, Stick."

"But she'll go for it, won't she?" I said eagerly. "If we both tell her we want to keep him?"

"Oh, she'll go for it." He slit open a box of cigarette cartons he was stacking into the display case. Except for a softness around his middle and the pale slackness of his face, you couldn't see signs of the accident, anymore. He could walk, he could eat— Miracle Man, the doctors had called him. "But she'll be angry, for a long while. She opened up too wide, there, when she learned about Benjy being dead. Now this is keeping her open. She don't want that. She wants to close right back up, to live without feeling all this pain. It's easier for her. She gets her work done better."

There was a long quiet, with the sound of the razor on cardboard, the slick *tock* of the plastic-coated cigarette packs sliding into their slots. I watched my dad's hands, clumsy well-meaning hands. "Did you know," I asked at last, "about Benjy? About him being hers?"

"I think I must of," he said, not stopping his work. "What else made me hate him, all those years? That sandy hair, I always hated looking at it. I just never let myself ask why."

"Seems like you and mom," I said, "you don't let yourselves do very much."

"It's called being an adult."

"Well, then, I don't want much part of it."

"Oh, you're already in the thick of it," he said. "You've already got stuff buried, Stick. I don't know what—I don't want to know!— but I can see where you've smoothed over the ground. It shows, right here." Tucking the last pack in, he reached across the counter and traced a line on my forehead, with his long white finger.

Still, he talked to her, that night. And by morning they'd decided, however deep down it drove her. We were taking him, for now anyhow. One step at a time, just like drug rehab.

That summer, Lenny and I went riding ice, the way his brother Nate taught both of us, years back. He was spending his days at the college south of Castleton; they let him take classes there, physics and computer, labs all afternoon. "You never told me you were a genius," I said when he signed up.

"I ain't," he said. "I just can't work for my old man. I'll kill him, if I have to work for him. And this stuff is programmed in my head, and they let me go there for free."

I hadn't done much about the college thing. Now and then I leafed through the catalogs, but they were all about ivy and cable-knit sweaters and green chalkboards; when I tried to read the columns of print below the pictures, my throat tightened up and I couldn't breathe. I'd started teaching for Philomena instead, late afternoons when Daniel could hang at the store with my dad. She'd scattered posters and fliers with my name on them like it was a big deal, and when I got more than eight in a class she handed me a fat bonus. "If you're gonna waste your life out here you might as well line your nest, hon," she said.

With Philomena I could get nostalgic about New York—about Frankie and Charlotte, about the couplings backstage at *Grand Hotel*, even about A.J. and Coretta, how I'd danced challenges in the sloping kitchen. I never did tell her about the night proofing job, the stacks of printed galleys, the garbled dreams I had sleeping in the back of the hall by the copy machine. My hands had healed up, so all I told her about the dogs was how one of them had turned out to be Ivan's wolfhound. That was part of the story I told her about Tomas and Ivan—only Tomas got a slightly different role, the one she would have wanted him to have. Her eyes lit up; it made her happy to have a new story, something besides Miami and the gangster.

It was after dark, then—after I'd taught class and helped my dad close the store, with Daniel too hyper to sleep and the air still thick with heat—that Lenny came to get us. He'd have been to Angie's Bait 'n' Tackle and loaded up the back of the truck with a couple blocks of ice and a bunch of towels. We'd drive to the top of the golf course, Daniel sitting between us, squirming. Looking south from the first tee, we could see the lights at the marina, boats settling into their slips. Northward there was dark mass of the mansion, a single yellow light marking the rebuilt tower. Plans for the movie had stalled out just as Dugliss finished his work; the whole thing sat on hold while the producers scrambled for funds.

Then we'd make a train of ourselves, mostly me in back with Daniel between my legs, my ankles hooked around Lenny's waist. We folded the towels on top of the ice, so our butts wouldn't freeze, and starting at the first putting green, we'd push off. Sometimes Lenny and I'd be a little high. My breasts like teardrops in a white tank top, I'd push my block back to the top of the hill while he gave Daniel a ride up. The ice was so cold it stuck to our shorts right through the towels, and as we went down again, the hot air rushed at our faces, lifting my hair off my neck. When one of us would take Daniel alone, the other could try for stunts—standing on the block of ice, or riding belly down. A couple times I used Lenny's lighter to melt hand-holds in the sides of my block, and I'd coax Daniel to sit by himself, holding on, while I rode next to him and we both shrieked. By then the block would have started to melt, and be going fast.

Once I fell off, holding Daniel, and cut my shoulder open on a rock. I didn't care. I sat at the top of the hill by the fourth hole while Lenny and Daniel went down again and again until the blocks were almost melted away and the green was pretty well torn up. Then we peeled off the towels and shared a joint in the truck before heading down to the hamlet. My shoulder was sticky with blood, pulsing with pain. Daniel sat on my lap, probably getting a little high by osmosis, but sleepy at last, a gentle heaviness on my damp thighs. I would put him down later in my old room. I'd moved my stuff, or mostly, to the attic my dad had finished before his accident, a sweet little triangle I could tuck myself into and look out the hexagonal window onto the train tracks.

"Look," said Lenny, pointing through the windshield. Above the river that ran below us on the other side of the dark trees, the night was thick with stars; no moon. One had just shot downward, and in a couple minutes another followed. "*Fft-fft*," I said. "Another shuttle crew."

"Vacationing all over Florida," Lenny said; and we laughed, but it was the dope.

"Touching the face of God," I said, still laughing. But then we quieted down, and watched a few more fire off. Even Daniel pointed to one or two, and Lenny told him how they were zillions of miles away. How if he could travel there fast enough, and come back, everyone on Earth would have gotten old while he stayed the same age. Daniel giggled sleepily; he didn't get any of it. He was just crazy about Lenny.

Who left, finally. Out to California, where they've got some young-genius program he's hot on. He calls; he comes back, holidays. If I think about him too much I get on fire, I burn. I try to have faith in time; I try not to think in terms of days.

I tell Daniel about the Challenger, sometimes. We walk, on fall evenings, up the access road to the top of the golf course, and sometimes we'll race from there to the first tee, high over the hamlet, where we rode ice with Lenny, two years ago. We'll throw ourselves on the ground and drink in the sky.

"You wonder what we're doing up there," I say to him. "Look at all those worlds. Who needs us, up there, fucking everything up?"

"There's my house," he says. "Right down there. I see the lights. I see my room! Right there." He's sitting up, not even looking at the sky. Space shuttle, teacher, explosion, he doesn't get any of it. "Tell about the boom," he says when I get to that part.

It wasn't until Anne-Marie and Ben took off last year for Central America, and the state agency put pressure on about remedial school for Daniel, that my mom would talk adoption papers. For all the goodness in Anne-Marie, she was working against it. "I want your mom free," she said to me before she went. There was a fierceness in her face, even in the immobile, damaged part. "She's given up too much of herself already."

"Maybe," I said, an old throbbing working its way into my temples. "And I think you're cool, Anne-Marie, I've always thought you were great. But on this one, with all respect, just please fuck off."

There were a lot of late nights with my dad, a lot of talk about the store and his health. He'd had some bleeding inside, there was more surgery scheduled. He tried talking God with her again, which didn't exactly smooth her out. I'd hear her voice, thin and rising, and then my dad's coming in slow and careful, and then I'd hear Daniel's name, and then mine. I prayed, I don't know to what.

Finally I put it to him, early morning in the store while he was sorting the newspapers and bringing in the muffins he bought himself, now, since he'd cut the Minimart connection. Tell her, I said, that if she doesn't take the baby you'll go looking for a new job, a company job, and not this store that doesn't make any money. You guys'll have to relocate, and I'll move out. Maybe she cares, about this place. Or me.

He set down the newspapers—he wasn't as good with them as Gray, the stack sort of sprawled—and put his hand on the back of my neck. I'm not pushing anybody, he said.

But something got into motion. Anne-Marie and Ben left, my resourceful mom got a grant to hire new staff, and Daniel's here with me, above the hamlet, coming out for stars.

Christa McAuliffe's family still goes around dedicating high school gyms, astronomy labs. With Star Wars out of the picture, a lot of the NASA guys are working for private corporations, and people talk about downscaling, about the benefits of unmanned spacecraft. Once in a rare moment you hear something about the cause Christa died for, which is I guess that we kids would have stood on those bleachers and cheered, and gone home to flush the marijuana down the toilet and studied our geography books instead of letting the Japanese get ahead.

"I think," I say to Daniel, high up on the golf course, "we'd have turned on her. She'd be a name to memorize instead of forget. Betsy Ross, Jacqueline Kennedy, Christa McAuliffe."

"King Koopa's castle," he says, like he's adding to the list.

Over at the mansion, they're finally shooting the movie—all lit up, day-for-night. Daniel likes to watch the floodlights swing over the trees. He's started looking more like JoAnn, the way his eyebrows peak in the center and the cowlick in his hair. She'd cut hers off; Lenny showed me a picture of her with Seth, a week or so before they died, with her in funky old clothes and cropped hair, a heavy metal cross around her neck. She's looking up at Seth and beaming, a big healthy plain country girl in love.

Most days are pretty awful. We didn't want to hire a tutor, and the schools won't mainstream till next year. So my mom tries, early in the morning, to teach Daniel colors and numbers, how to stack cubes by size. He throws the cubes, rips the paper; he kicks his way under the coffee table. When she comes to me, white-lipped, I just nod and haul myself out of bed. Then she leaves for work, letting the door slam just a little bit loud behind her. After that, I lie down on the floor with him. He's so surprised to see me there it usually stops his tantrum in its tracks for a minute. We still play monster; he's taught me Super Mario. Lately he likes to put his fingers in my mouth and pull my cheeks apart, and make me say, "Higglety pigglety pop, the dog has eaten the mop," which makes him laugh so hard he gets short of breath. We learn numbers by counting the levels of Nintendo and the red kings in checkers. On good days, he'll charge through the woods with me, past the old shed to the granary, where I can make him see triangles, squares, diamonds in the hewed blocks of old stone. If it's raining I'll put on some Second Coming and try what Savion Glover does with TapTronics, fitting the riffs and spanks and toe taps into the heavy beat. Daniel swings his arms and does lopsided somersaults.

But at the end of the day it's true what my mom says: we're treading water. There was a chance, at the beginning, to give him back to the county agency. Maybe we would have, except my mom likes to finish what she starts, and me . . . well, I gave him life. My dad is the mystery. I hand Daniel over to him at the store when I leave to teach at the studio. He spends hours chasing cans that Daniel's rolled down the aisles. Sometimes he has to close the store for a couple of hours just to take the kid to the house and manage him till I can get home. It would be easier if he still had a Minimart license and wasn't on his own, but he's set up a table for coffee drinkers in the morning, and he'd have to give that up if he joined the franchise again. Anyhow, by the end of the day he's pretty wrung out.

So it astonishes me when I catch my dad, sometimes, in the middle of the night, sunk low in the living room couch. He's holding Daniel—he hears them first, now, the nightmare cries—like a big, long-legged doll. His soft arms are around Daniel's back, where the PJ top hikes up; and they're pressing cheek to cheek, just waiting it out together, while those low, hard groans quiet down.

About the Author

Lucy Ferriss is the author of two previous novels, *Philip's Girl* and *The Gated River*, as well as essays in *The New York Times*, *Washington Post Book World*, and *Boston* magazine. Her fiction has won national awards from the Faulkner Society and the National Endowment for the Arts, among others. She lives with her husband and two sons in Clinton, New York, where she heads the creative writing program at Hamilton College.

52 "dumb and sexy" 53 sentence diagrams
195 challenger 235 gravity 264 father's
accident
284 find Benjy's skeleton 289 Benjy was
Shick's ~~se~~ mother's illegitimate son, her half-brother
300 challenger reference